10/11/01

Solitude and Its Ambiguities in Modernist Fiction ∾

Solitude and Its Ambiguities
in Modernist Fiction ~

Edward Engelberg

First published 2001 by
PALGRAVE™
175 Fifth Avenue, New York, NY 10010 and
Houndmills, Basingstoke, Hampshire, England RG21 6XS.
Companies and representatives throughout the world.

Palgrave is the new global publishing imprint of St Martin's Press LLC
Scholarly and Reference Division and Palgrave Publishers Ltd (formerly
Macmillan Press Ltd).

ISBN 0–312–23947–5 cloth

Library of Congress Cataloging-in-Publication Data
Engelberg, Edward, 1929-
Solitude and its ambiguities in modernist fiction/Edward Engelberg.
        p.   cm.
    Includes bibliographical references and index.
    ISBN 0–312–23947–5
    1. Fiction—20th century—History and criticism.   2. Solitude in
literature.   3. Modernism
(Literature)   I. Title.
PN56.S665 E54   2001
809.3'009'04—ds21

                                                              2001021295

Design by Letra Libre, Inc.

First Edition: July 2001
10 9 8 7 6 5 4 3 2 1

Printed in the United States of America.

Permissions

As ever,
for Elaine,

and for our six splendid granddaughters, in birth order:
Ilana Suzanne, Alexandra Frances,
Anya Sophia, Isabelle Amber,
Moriah Cecelia, Sarah Julianna:
May their solitude always be in company.

Contents

Preface		1
Introduction		7
Chapter I	Self Against Self: Toward Ambiguous Solitude in Modernist Fiction	21
Chapter II	Discourse With Oneself and The Solitude of Place: *Robinson Crusoe*	49
Chapter III	"Soliloquy in Solitude": *To the Lighthouse*	75
Chapter IV	O Altitudo! O Solitudo! Exilic Solitude and Ambiguous Ethics on *The Magic Mountain*	97
Chapter V	Solitude of Questionable Freedom in Cartesisan Antagonists: Sartre and Camus	117
Chapter VI	As They Lay Dying "Rotting with Solitude": Endgame in Beckett's Trilogy	141
Conclusion		163
Notes		175
Bibliography		207
Index		217

. . . there is a solitude which each and every one of us has always carried with him, more inaccessible than the ice-cold mountains, more profound, than the midnight sea; the solitude of self.

—Elizabeth Cady Stanton, "The Solitude of Self"

In solitude for company.

—W. H. Auden, untitled poem

The other side of the mind is now exposed—the dark side that comes uppermost in solitude, not the light side that shows in company.

—Virginia Woolf, "How Should One Read a Book?" in The Common Reader, *Second Series.*

I shall not be alone . . . I shall have company.

—Beckett, The Unnamable

There are always ways to fail in solitude as well as in company.

—Montaigne, "On Solitude"

Preface ～

Oh, who could tell us the story of this subtle
feeling, which is called solitude.

—Nietzsche, *Dawn of Day*

The "word [solitude]," Maurice Blanchot wrote with some impatience, "has been much abused."[1] This study does not intend to contribute further to such abuse: its aim is to facilitate our understanding of a deceptively contentious and ambiguous issue. It cannot tell the whole "story" of solitude, but it highlights one of the most critical points in the arc of its long history, the period after the Great War (WWI) to Samuel Beckett's *Trilogy*, published in the early 1950s.

1

With the exception of that indispensable tale of human isolation, *Robinson Crusoe* (1719), I have chosen works from the critical years of High Modernism.[2] Although poetry and drama have both confronted the subject of solitude, only the novel offers the writer the opportunity for an in-depth development of the intricate subtleties of the solitary state. Fiction alone provides the generosity of space that permits the luxury of development, contradiction, and sometimes synthesis.

Although the presence of solitude in literature has often been noted, how solitude functions thematically to shape meaning in literary works has been slighted. And what solitude *as a condition* has contributed to the making of a trope in certain classic modern novels has been neglected. No sustained analysis of the functional purpose of solitude exists for any of the works here examined—not even for Beckett's.

The key to the argument of this study is solitude's *ambiguity*,[3] and in particular (from, say, mid-eighteenth century onward) how such ambiguity was sharpened to shape major doctrinal positions of the argument in modernist fictions: how to achieve solitude and then cope with its newly emerging contradictions. In one sense, the story of solitude as we move into the twentieth century relates how the solitary state moves from the Self's removal from Society to, say, Nature to the Self's opposition with itself. What had once functioned as a retreat from the tumult of the worldly eventually develops into a tense face-off where the Self confronts itself and its inevitable aloneness.

2

My interest in the subject of solitude has evolved both from teaching and research over many years. In the Conclusion to *Elegiac Fictions: The Motif of the Unlived Life* (1989), I offered some brief observations about solitude and alienation, since this seemed an appropriate exit to a discussion of the unlived life and the consequences of separation and isolation that were markedly associated with it. Then in the summer of 1995 I accepted an invitation to deliver a paper ("Faces of Solitude") at the annual conference of the British Comparative Literature Association hosted in Edinburgh. Yet these small contributions left me with a feeling of incompleteness, as I began to realize that the state of solitude was an imposing subject and needed a study of its own. This volume is an attempt, at least in part, to fulfill that need.

When, some years ago, I asked a group of undergraduates what connotations the word "solitude" evoked in their minds, they were nearly unanimous in their response: solitude conjured up negative associations. Most of them connected solitude to adjectives such as antisocial, uncommunicative, selfish, snobbish, and most of all neurotic, even psychotic. Some leapt to solitary confinement as their only locus, which reminds one of Kierkegaard's sarcastic observation in *The Sickness Unto Death* (1849):

> In antiquity as well as in the Middle Ages there was an awareness of this longing for solitude and a respect for what it means; whereas in the constant sociality of our day we shrink from solitude to the point . . . that no use for it is known other than a punishment for criminals. But since it is a crime in our day to have spirit, it is indeed quite in order to classify . . . lovers of solitude, with criminals.[4]

Living in an age of networking, virtual reality, E-mail, voice mail, CD-ROMs, interactive TV, the World Wide Web replete with chat room sites, confessional TV and radio talk shows, and endless memoirs baring all, my students were convinced that solitude grants no benefits. Actually, they believed solitude posed a threat to those who indulged in it, turning them into the loners depicted by the media—violent outcasts or serial killers. There is no denying that such a view in the 1990s also embodied inherent self-contradictions, for these very same students had long been sustained on such notions as their inner and outer "space," craving privacy in the midst of their communal longings. They had also jealously guarded and internalized the "child within," pursuing a special aloneness, an individuality and freedom from authority that became so common it lost all semblance of the unique and assumed the characteristics of a substitute authority. So when I pressed my students to defend their position, most of them admitted that, on reflection, solitude was not always such a bad idea, that sometimes it was also good to be alone. Their negative tilt toward solitude was an initial response, prompted by cultural bias: better to be grouped than solitary.

Their evolving ambiguous position, however, was not surprising: these students merely confirmed an historical constant. For in fact it has always been true that ambiguity and resulting controversy have dominated discussions of solitude over the centuries. The introduction that follows raises some general questions about these issues that have attached themselves to solitude as concept.

≈ ≈ ≈

Chapter IV appeared as "Ambiguous Solitude: Hans Castorp's Sturm und Drang nach Osten" in *A Companion to Thomas Mann's The Magic Mountain,* ed Stephen D. Dowden (Columbia, S. C.: Camden House, 1999). The essay has been expanded for the present study. I express my thanks to Camden House and the editor for permission to include the essay here.

A Note on Texts and Translations

For non-English fictional texts I have chosen the latest, most reliable translations. In a few instances I have made some alterations to be more true to the original, and these have been noted. For some brief excerpts from untranslated French and German critical texts I have made my own translations or paraphrases.

Acknowledgments

There are many to whom I am indebted, for a variety of reasons.

First, as always, I want to thank my wife, Elaine, for her support, for reading the manuscript, some of it in several versions, and for giving me her insightful reactions.

Special gratitude is due my friend and colleague Robert Szulkin who encouraged me from start to finish—or more accurately, *to* finish. He read the manuscript in its entirety (some chapters at different stages) and made several crucial suggestions that improved my own understanding of what I was attempting to say and, in turn, made for a better work. It is no exaggeration to say that he lived with the writing of this book almost the same way I did.

I am grateful to Philip Winsor, senior editor emeritus, Penn State University Press, for encouraging me all the way and for reading the entire manuscript and providing me with many useful corrections and suggestions.

Stephen Dowden also read parts of the manuscript and he, too, offered some sharp and helpful ways to improve the first chapters. Haskell M. Block, Monroe Hafter, and Max Day supplied useful titles of books or essays (they are all acknowledged in the Notes). Several colleagues loaned me books and expressed a sympathetic interest in this project: Rudy Binion, Stephen J. Gendzier, Jane Hale, Patricia A. Johnston, Edward K. Kaplan, Denah Lida, Jessie Ann Owens, Michael Randall, Esther Ratner, Murray Sachs, Nancy Scott. Robin Feuer Miller was, as always, graciously on my side.

To my students over the years, graduate and undergraduate, who sat through classes and seminars on "Solitude"—in various incarnations—my deepest thanks. Their searching questions and often sparkling responses taught me much and kept my interest alive.

Anne Hermann (Department of English, University of Michigan) read the manuscript, and some of her queries about the opening sections helped me to reorganize and sharpen my argument. I am indebted.

Since I am computer-skill challenged, I offer my appreciation to Andrew Swenson, my neighbor to my right or left—depending on what direction you walk the hallway—who, on countless occasions, bailed me out of desperate situations. And my special gratitude to Richard Lansing, who spent hours helping me with his unmatchable computer know-how, while at the same time offering me names and titles about Renaissance solitude. Karen Grundler-Whitacre, academic administrator to the Department of Germanic and Slavic Languages, was also ready to help in moments of computer-stress. Anna Huang, academic administrator to the Department of Romance and Comparative Literature, gave aid and comfort in a variety of ways.

Gregory Shesko, assistant provost for Academic Finance and Administration, remained an interested friend who also supported this project with timely funds.

My thanks to all the help graciously extended to me by various people in the Brandeis library, from Interlibrary Loan to Reference and Acquisition.

I am grateful that Brandeis University, and especially the department of Romance and Comparative Literature, and its chairs, have continued to permit me the use of office space and bestowed other privileges, without which this project would have had a far more difficult road to travel.

Elisabeth Ellington was a splendid research assistant, who generated both the bibliography and the index. I appreciated her patience and professionalism. I wish to express my thanks to all the persons at Palgrave, Global Publishing at St. Martin's Press who have helped to bring this book to life. Especially, I want to single out its editor, Kristi Long, who was both encouraging and helpful with substantive issues; Sarah B. Schur, her assistant, who extended many kindnesses; and Meg Weaver, assistant production editor, who patiently oversaw the final stages.

Introduction ∾

The capacity to be alone was adumbrated as a valuable resource, which facilitated learning, thinking, innovation, coming to terms with change, and the maintenance of contact with the inner world of the imagination.

—Anthony Storr, *Solitude: A Return to the Self*

All our forces strive to abolish our solitude.

—Octavio Paz, *The Labyrinth of Solitude*

I live . . . alone, entirely alone. . . . But I remained close to people, on the surface of solitude, quite determined, in case of emergency, to take refuge in their midst. . . .

—Jean-Paul Sartre, *Nausea*

1

Derived from the Latin *solitudo,* the English "solitude" has always conveyed a state of "deprivation"; but according to the *Oxford English Dictionary,* it was a word not commonly used until the seventeenth century. Its current meaning as "living alone, loneliness, seclusion" assumed general coinage in the eighteenth century. The celebratory connotation of solitude belongs to those who have sought solitude in the higher, nonworldly venues of the spiritual realm, or to those who see solitude as personal space for pleasure and creative self-indulgence. The former reigns in the Middle Ages; the latter takes root in the Renaissance. However, Petrarch writes a secular celebration of solitude, and solitude as a spiritual experience never really loses its relevance. In any case, for most solitude is a hard choice: even Thomas Merton writes in *No Man is an Island* that "One has to be very strong and very solid to live in solitude."

Solitude has increasingly become a magnet word attracting a lexicon of nearly synonymous but also discrete terms: aloneness, loneliness, isolation, estrangement, exile, and alienation, to cite some obvious examples, and to extricate one from another is an intricate, if not impossible task. What differentiates solitude from any similar state is its predominant associative connotation with gratifying peace, a rewarding sense of well being. Such a reputation is not entirely misplaced; but as this study demonstrates, solitude is far more complicated, its internal tensions generating not only ambiguous but countervailing arguments. Throughout its history as a concept, solitude has been presented as an appealing path of escape from the anxieties of the world; at the same time, the caveat that solitude and the isolation that defines it can also be hazardous has been equally recognized. Although familiarity with one's solitary Self once seemed a logical step toward self-knowledge and self-improvement, beginning with the Romantics and culminating in a state of crisis with the Modernists, such familiarity begins to breed self-contempt, a step beyond the misanthropy we find from Shakespeare through some of the Romantics.

Solitude is also associated with several important themes, among them the elegiac and pastoral motifs of retirement, and withdrawal into Nature, which marked a strong literary tradition, especially in England, where it generated spirited debates over the merits of country versus city life. But in addition to literature, as an expansive and variegated experience, solitude encompasses several converging areas—psychology, cultural history, philosophy, and theology. Here is the title of a recent study: *Solitude versus Solidarity in the Novels of Joseph Conrad: Political and Epistemological Implications of Narrative Innovation.* This weighty title signals the author's attempt to be all-inclusive, to deal with literary issues but also to enlist sociological heavyweights—Darwin, Marx, Durkheim, Weber—in an effort to balance those "epistemological implications" found in these writers with aesthetic outcomes of narrative strategy executed in Conrad's fiction. The Conrad of *Heart of Darkness, Lord Jim,* and *Nostromo,* sees "the tension between solitude and solidarity" as it is manifested in Kurtz, Jim, and Nostromo as "a soul divided against itself; an individual torn between engagement and detachment, . . . between radical individualism and social cohesion. . . ."[1] Considered generically this is an accurate description of modernist solitude: but it is only a starting point requiring further refinements.

2

Perhaps because the theme of solitude has so dominated modernist literature, it has also generated some problematic misconceptions. For example, one of the more prominent conclusions about Modernism emerging over the past six or seven decades is that the twentieth century invented the alienated, lonely, isolated, abandoned, exiled solitary. Acknowledgment to a kinship between the modern and the nineteenth-century solitary is inescapable, but rarely is the modern solitary referenced to earlier centuries. The inference is clear: Modernism is exclusive host to the "loneliness of the long-distance runner," to quote the title of Alan Sillitoe's engaging novella (1960). Most often, the modern isolate is portrayed as cherishing solitude, welcoming its severance from all human relationships, and fixating on the Self so narcissistically that solitude is aggressively sought and eagerly embraced. Such a representation of modern solitude is partially accurate but also misleading.

Many causes for the ubiquitous presence of the modern isolate have been suggested, all of them familiar: modern technology has dehumanized us; the value system of modern morality has been more than disingenuous; God's death has left us forlorn; isolation breeds anxiety and "social emptiness"[2]; the diminishing status of scapegoated artists has made them the chief victims who, in self-defense, create plaintive, autobiographical works that lay bare their solitary and exilic condition. By and large the modern solitary is characterized as a voluntary outcast, the outsider, Camus's "stranger": virtually all canonical modernists have contributed to this formulaic portrait.

Yet while Chekhov and Conrad, Joyce and Kafka, Gide, Rilke, and Woolf, Hesse, Mann, Beckett, Camus, Sartre, and scores of others have all contributed to and enriched the portrait of the modern isolate, each has provided a distinctive emphasis. These differences have often been neglected in the eagerness to portray a hegemonic image of modern isolation. But modernists do not speak with a single voice. And in time the endless repetition of the motif of the alienated dramatis personae of Modernism has turned the motif itself into a cliché. While clichés are not necessarily untrue, they tend to trivialize, and they blur accuracy and individuality. This particular cliché took on a life of its own and, by oversimplifying, ignored both individuality and history, in the process minimizing complexity. Modernist approaches to solitude, while sharing much, also yield highly individual perspectives of fictional solitaries and the problematic of solitude they encounter. The initial embrace and subsequent repudiation (sometimes by the same critics) of Colin Wilson's *The Outsider* (1956) is a good example of the dilemma. Wilson's book, which remains valuable, had a tendency to use a broad brush. Its all-inclusive perspective of the "outsider," though refreshingly bold when first published, with time appeared to be too indiscriminate and lacking in historical perspective. A uniform, monolithic modernist portrait of solitude is untenable; equally unrewarding is to ignore solitude's provenance and long history.

Problematic aspects of solitude are already apparent in the Greeks and in the Old Testament, in the mythic and dramatic figures of Western canonical literature. Odysseus, Oedipus, Prometheus, Cain, Job, Hamlet, Lear,

Faust, Don Quixote, Robinson Crusoe, Gulliver, Frankenstein's "creature," Ahab, Zarathustra—each embodies a certain solitary modality, and all (often tragically) rise to that state of frightening solitude where they stand defined and marked as separated from everyone and everything around them. All of these figures weep—literally or figuratively—as they contemplate the aloneness they seek, while nostalgically engaging their memories of what they have abandoned (family, home, society), tallying the price paid. Even Zarathustra is not entirely exempt, though Nietzsche said with typical outrageousness, "for a pious man there is no solitude,—we, the godless, have been the first to devise this invention."[3]

Significant changes in attitude about solitude occurred over the centuries, and each change has its special signature. The ancient, biblical, and medieval concepts of solitude differed substantially from those of the Renaissance, just as the seventeenth, eighteenth, and nineteenth centuries introduced identifying features of their particular cultural moment. As for the twentieth century, it markedly displays dramatic changes in the way solitude is viewed: an almost cultist preoccupation develops, and the concept of the "alienated outsider" announces itself with a sense of urgency that is without parallel.

3

In *Solitude: A Return to the Self* (1988), Anthony Storr urges us to rethink solitude and to reconsider the more positive associations it had once evoked. Solitude, he reminds us, has in the past often been regarded as an opportunity for reflection, for self-awareness, for taking stock; and the "capacity to be alone," far from indicating neurosis, suggests that the modern preoccupation with forming "attachments" has made the "absence of this . . . capacity pathological." Storr, himself a psychiatrist, implicates post-Freudian psychoanalysis for fostering this notion and laments that other criteria, such as "emotional maturity," which permits aloneness, have been virtually eliminated from consideration. Freud himself was uncertain: he does not quite equate fear of crowds with desire for solitude, but an unreasonable fear of many phenomena, among them crowds, he declares a phobia. Yet "[s]olitude, too, has its dangers and in certain circumstances we avoid it; but there is no question of our being able to tolerate it under any condition for a moment." The implication is that solitude can be as phobic as society, that at least it, too, harbors "dangers."[4] Storr is also even-handed: he does not deny the need for interpersonal relationships, even asserting that we need more—"a sense of being part of a larger community. . . ." Essentially he argues for balance: "*The capacity to be alone . . . [should be] linked with self-discovery and self-realization; with becoming aware of one's deepest needs, feelings, and impulses.*"[5]

The trajectory of this study supports Storr's observation that the shift in attitude toward solitude as pathological is "a recent phenomenon,"[6] except we need to insist that "recent" is a generous measure, that the conflict about solitude, as welcome or dreaded, has deep roots. Nietzsche lamented our seeming inability to experience solitude: "I have . . . come to see . . . [the] most general defect in our education and training: nobody learns, nobody teaches, nobody wishes, to endure solitude."[7] Indeed solitude has never enjoyed—for very long—a consistent judgment, whether positive or negative. Even within shifting attitudes, the abiding tension between praising the virtues of solitude and fearing its dangers has always been essential to the debate.

Storr's assertion that solitude has been frequently identified as a time for self-evaluation and contemplative creativity, as Petrarch and Montaigne argued, is of course paramount. But Modernism's engagement with solitude tends to center on what Virginia Woolf called its "dark side."[8] These encounters also unveil the increasingly conflicted nature of that dark solitude—the urgent desire to move more to the light of human connection or, as is the case in Beckett, at least to light. Such conflict, although certainly present before the twentieth century, differs considerably from certain nineteenth-century attitudes toward solitude—those, say, of Romantics like E. T. A. Hoffmann or Byron, or, in mid-century, Poe or Dostoyevsky—in which solitude is expressed both as a marked fate and a chosen way of existence in which protagonists thrive and suffer, sometimes to the point of insanity. Not that some of the personae in the texts here examined avoid a similar fate, but it is how these modern solitaries take the measure of solitude that makes for a changing and more complex relationship between its darkness and the search to accommodate or conquer it. Dostoyevsky's underground man not only seeks out solitude, he flaunts it: it is part of the strategic games he plays with himself and the reader. Yet he, too, has moments when he deeply yearns for human companionship, yearnings that are his undoing. But in, say, Virginia Woolf's *To the Lighthouse,* no one really flaunts solitude: clearly imprisoned as several characters are in solitude's enclosures, the constraint of such captivity is a fate from which most of the major characters in the novel desperately attempt to escape—at least at times—for the sake of grasping at human relationships. They are, it is true, not wholly victims, for their own inability to reach out, for different reasons, encourages their remaining apart, but they are not entirely willful. Whereas Dostoyevsky's Underground Man covets companionship only to destroy it, Woolf's characters genuinely search for but cannot achieve it.

Aspects of this difference have been insightfully analyzed in Frederick Garber's *The Autonomy of the Self from Richardson to Huysmans,* which examines the "willingness of . . . separateness" within a context of the "dialectic of aloofness and association. . . ." Garber's book focuses on the issue of separation and the opposing tug of social relations dealt with here within the context of solitude; it ends with Huysmans. Garber emphasizes "autonomy" rather than solitude, although the distinction is sometimes necessarily blurred. Autonomy is the desire of the individual to achieve freedom to facilitate the act of what Garber calls "self-making . . . modes of the self that were as difficult to sustain as they were to put together."[9] Solitude may be one of the outcomes of achieving autonomy (and it may not always be welcomed), but it has its own etiology and indeed its own consequences.

Both Petrarch and Montaigne suggested that youth is the best time for solitary reflections. They were, of course, addressing a well-to-do audience that could afford financially, and by virtue of the education that the privileged class provided, to "retire" for an unspecified period to read, think, and reflect before reentering the world. Although conditions changed, some part of the youth and solitude equation survives, if in a very different shape than that envisioned by these early patricians. In the course of the last three centuries youthful solitude has changed its objective. Rather than highlighting that time in the lives of young men (but seldom women) of means when they enjoy unfettered access to reflection and bookish education, the youths of picaresque fiction, the Bildungsroman, and its close cousin, the Künstlerroman, seek respite from society for identity-making or are involuntarily banished waifs who survive by native wit. Inhabiting the works of novelists from Defoe to the present are young adults whose solitary periods are interludes seized by the author as moments of crisis that shape and define Self and its choice of action. In this group, then, we count the picaros and the legions of solitaries in European fiction who experience every form of solitude: fear and anguish, regret and madness, doubt and rage, hate and guilt, abdication and willfulness, and suffering and annihilation.

4

The preoccupation with solitude is already apparent in the literature of the 1600s, and its initially incremental progress explodes exponentially in the nineteenth and twentieth centuries, when the loner emerges as a cult figure. For a time every self-respecting poet composed an obligatory "Ode to Solitude" that became an integral part of a cultural bias, whether it extolled solitude or cast doubt on its benefits. In fiction, however, the solitary found the space to debate how the Self came to awareness of its own consciousness, what power and terror such awareness made manifest, and how the Self viewed its relation to Other, from the microscopic venue of the immediate family to the macroscopic arena of Society. It has long been recognized that the rise of self-consciousness paralleled the emergence of the novel so that fiction and solitude became inevitably, and inseparably, linked.

In addition to philosophical and psychological elements of the state of solitude, the circle is completed by cultural history, which often shapes the shifting views about the solitary state. Robert Sayre's *Solitude in Society: A Sociological Study in French Literature* (1978) views the subject of solitude from a Marxist position, with mixed results. In the present study some of the cultural and historical aspects related to altering positions about solitude are alluded to in the first chapter; the variations as well as the common elements in twentieth-century treatments of solitude emerge from the reading of the texts presented in each separate chapter.

5

Aside from solitude, three subtexts bridge the works here examined: the function of the "I" diary-narration, even in the two novels written in the third person; the presence of the "island," literally or metaphorically; and the import of solitude and the contingencies of sexuality.

Seven of the nine novels (counting the three of Beckett's trilogy) discussed here are first person narratives, what Mikhail Bakhtin called the "Ich Erzählung" and what has recently been examined as the "diary novel."[10] Thomas Mann and Woolf are the exceptions, but it may be argued that both *The Magic Mountain* and *To the Lighthouse,* though not first-person narratives, are rendered as diaries, of an evolving consciousness in Mann's novel and of several evolving consciousnesses in Woolf's. The ubiquitous "I" dominates, even when plural as it is by implication in, say, Woolf and Mann, or explicitly in the interchangeable "I"s that face the reader in Beckett's trilogy. The classic modern novel, even when it is not literally a first person "diary," makes every attempt to capture the reader in its confessional net. This objective is motivated not so much by the desire to excite the reader's empathies (like the contemporary memoir) as to make the object-reader and the subject-I interchangeable. And surely the experience of solitude is the more powerful when we are enabled to respond to the stated or implied "I" with no, or very little, authorial interference. That is why Camus's *The Fall* is so stunningly successful in making the reader *absorb* the narrator's guilt.

The island-venue of *Robinson Crusoe* is continued, either literally or figuratively, in all the novels analyzed in these chapters. In *Robinson Crusoe,* the island served its purpose as a physical Eden and Hell from which the individual, after periods of alternating joy and anguish, must be extricated. The modern island offers little joy, mostly anguish; and the need to be rescued from the island (that is from the Self) is quashed by the grim possibilities of a newly gained freedom. If the island-self leaves itself there is nothing left; we arrive at that place which Yeats, in a Nietzschean-inspired play, called *Where There is Nothing.*

With the exception of the brief middle section, Woolf's novel is set on an island, pointedly emphasizing the novel's company (the Ramsay family of ten and guests) in isolation. After all, the lighthouse, too, is on an island, and even the final achievement—if that is what it is—of the journey to it is only, on one level, a journey from one island to another. Snowy tundras that resemble sand dunes, a sanatorium in the Alps, a room within that sanatorium, the dark chamber of the psychoanalyst Krokowski, the mysterious X-ray chamber with its thunder and lightning mechanism, the enclave where the gramophone is stored, the spooky room where ghosts are brought back—all of these are Hans Castorp's islands each and together separated by a sea of space and time from the flatland world.

For Sartre's scholar Roquentin, the town of Bouville becomes an entombed island with ever constricting circles (the library, the brothel, the museum, the café, the park) and, of course, his own room with its mirror reflecting his progressively dissociative state. Meursault, too, inhabits islands: the restrictive world of his life before the murder is encircled by the sea on one side and the desert on the other; the killing on the sand that stands between these two worlds lands him in the prison-island through whose bars he seeks out the island from which he has been banished. And in the final pages Meursault envisions himself as an island surrounded by a mob whose defilement he seeks for self-definition. Beckett's islands (Ireland, to be sure) are also sometimes real and sometimes figurative. Surely all three narrators of the trilogy inhabit islands: beds in empty rooms in isolated houses, forests travelled by night in hiding from threatening dangers—"the island, I'm on the island . . . ," is the cry of the Unnamable.

Solitude raises obvious questions about sexuality. Whether celibate by choice, based on religious doctrine, or simply because partners are unavailable, the isolate's sex life is, at best, confined to self-pleasuring and fantasy. Critics long wondered about Robinson Crusoe: did his over quarter of a century of abstinence not damage his sexual nature permanently? According to Defoe, apparently not. After his return home Crusoe marries, fathers three children, and when his wife dies he leaves them in the care of his nephew and sets out for further adventures; we are not told whether they are celibate.

Our modern solitaries engage the sexual vicissitudes of solitude somewhat differently. From all the evidence in the text, Hans Castorp has sexual relations once in seven years: his erotic fantasy is fed more by absence than presence, and his isolated imagination appears to be activated and strengthened by abstinence. Meanwhile he views disapprovingly as bad manners the sexual adventures of his fellow-patients, like the "bad" Russian couple next to his room whose nightly roughhouse lovemaking keeps him awake.

The sexual identity of Woolf's characters is not easily categorized: Mr. and Mrs. Ramsay have eight children, some still young, but the sex that brought them to life is not easily imagined as spontaneous, passionate, or erotic; Mrs. Ramsay perhaps longs for sexual tenderness, but her husband is unable to offer it. Lily Briscoe may be one of those hermaphrodites that Woolf pondered about elsewhere, but her longings for Mrs. Ramsay can at least in part be explained as sexual. All marriages in the novel flounder or are torn apart by death. Sex in the novel is nearly as silent as in *Robinson Crusoe*.

Sartre's Roquentin's sexual relationships with his landlady are relieving sessions, as with a prostitute; whatever happier sex he might have had with a former lover is clearly no longer available. The Autodictat is a homosexual of whom Roquentin disapproves (though he defends his rights). In no entry of his journal does he admit to missing sex: solitude has once again accomplished its depriving mission. As for Camus's Meursault, sex is accomplished to satisfy physical needs, absent of any personalized awareness (whether such ignorance is willed or not). And when in prison, Meursault at first can think only of Marie, the sex he had with her, of other women he has slept with; this proxy sex tortures more than pleasures. He is released to contemplate other issues that his confinement enforces only when the sexual fantasies disappear.

And Beckett's "I" in the trilogy is reduced to absurd sex (e.g., Molloy and Lousse) or masturbation, and in *The Unnamable* even these activities disappear when his penis falls off as part of a process of advancing decay during which he loses all extremities. Still sex (as other physical necessities) preoccupies each narrator in the trilogy; the very inability to attain it becomes an integral issue of the "I"'s solitude.

On the most fundamental biological level, sex is the most direct route toward the Other; the deprivation of that most elemental means of human connecting is clearly felt in modern novels: it is not glossed over as in *Robinson Crusoe* but made to function, in one direction or another, as a signal symptom and consequence of solitude. In Beckett's *The Lost Ones* (see the Conclusion), it is made explicitly clear that the lost couples of this hell attempt, but cannot succeed, at coupling—the distance is always *just* enough to make consummation impossible. That portends the postmodern solitude, in which sexual severance is a kind of punishment.

In many ways Beckett's "I" of the trilogy crystallizes the three motifs: he is the indefatigable narrator who on his island slowly declines into a state of impotence, not only sexual. He is the most modern of Crusoes, however different his journeys and sojourn. Indeed it is his difference from Crusoe that both encircles and closes the arc of this study.

The process of unfolding the modernist texts reveals the nature of their depiction of solitude as paralysis, silence, unmaking. Obviously the stakes of solitude have increasingly become higher. Hobbes included "solitary" in his infamous adjectival description of the human condition; Conrad made it much darker: "We live as we dream—alone." And Sartre offered an ever harsher vision: "we are alone, abandoned on earth . . . without help. . . ." Milton suggested that solitude's ambiguity is part of the post-lapsarian human dilemma: "For solitude sometimes is best society, / And short retirement urges sweet return." The burden of modernity is that "sweet return," even when desired, is too often out of reach. In modernist fiction, the conciliatory return that Toynbee and Octavio Paz describe becomes increasingly elusive, both literally and in the geography of the mind itself. Leopold Bloom returns home, but not exactly to harmony; Joyce's admiring pupil, Samuel Beckett, made the disharmony of "return" one of his principal motifs. What often characterizes the "withdrawal" in much of modernist fiction is the absence of "return" altogether. The outcome is pain, anxiety, and despair, for "[a]bsolute solitude," writes Nicholas Berdyaev, "is inconceivable; it must . . . be relative to the existence of others and of the Other Self."[11] In *The Enchafèd Flood,* W. H. Auden assigns to the sea, the desert, and the mountains the freedom from restraint. But "precisely because they are free places, they are also lonely places of alienation, and the individual who finds himself there, whether by choice or fate, must from time to time, rightly or wrongly, be visited by desperate longings for home and company."[12] As Octavio Paz insists, the human creature alone is "aware of his lack of another . . . of his solitude."[13] Such self-consciousness about solitude and increasingly intricate strategies devised to resolve intractable contradictions between aloneness and communality remain principal problems.

6

The organizational principle of this study is roughly chronological. Choice of texts is always a challenge, but solitude presented an unusual task, since it is a major component in so many Classic Modern novels.[14] Obviously this dictated a selective approach to modernist novels, and those works chosen are illustrative of different issues. This introduction has raised some of the issues that suggest the problematic of solitude, specifically its ambiguities:

the lure of isolation and freedom from social constraints and the ache to salvage some human relationship. That dilemma forms the argument of the first chapter which, surveying the English and some continental attitudes toward solitude, offers a synoptic narrative of solitude in the West, with emphasis on the late Renaissance to the twentieth century. Its chief objective is not to exhaust the subject but to reveal the solitary's double bind at various historical moments, and to call attention to those junctures where significant shifts of attitude occur. In particular, it ends by putting forth the outlines of how solitude functions in modernist fiction.

Chapter II offers an account of *Robinson Crusoe,* the defining text in the post-Renaissance trajectory of solitude. It is a tale of survival but also a parable of psychological isolation and overcoming, of the sweet rewards of power and freedom of solitude along with the punitive and painful yearnings for human response. Crusoe, by turns, revels in his solitude and abhors it, triumphantly flaunts it and ruefully dreads it. In many ways Crusoe sets the tone for the contradictions that will plague the states of solitude as these are debated in the pastoral and elegiac poetry of the eighteenth century and in the Romantics, both in fiction and poetry, of the nineteenth. On many fronts Crusoe is an ancestor of Dostoyevsky's heroes, who so arrogantly embrace their isolation by day and suffer its frightful terrors by night. And Crusoe prepares us for Joyce and Woolf (both of whom had their say about Defoe's novel) and for all those moderns who struggled with the freedom of selfhood and its often horrific implications.

The remaining chapters engage a selection of twentieth-century fictions in which the state of solitude is explored in five major directions: 1) the solitude of spatial emptiness resulting in a form of psychological and physical aphasia (*To the Lighthouse*); 2) the hermetic solitude of self-promoting illness and the pursuit of Eastern lassitude that isolate the self to the point of physical and moral paralysis (*The Magic Mountain*); 3) the solitude of dissociation from self (*Nausea*) and 4) the solitude of emotional agoraphobia (*The Stranger*); and, finally, 5) the solitude beyond redemption of "company" (Beckett's trilogy), in which, as Adorno said of *Endgame,* "[c]onsciousness gets ready to look its own end in the eye. . . ."[15]

Virginia Woolf's *To the Lighthouse* occupies the third chapter. That novel's tenuous world, in which individuals strain to communicate across chasms of language, offers us an opportunity to observe the painful consequences of a different kind of hermetic experience. However, everyone still attempts communication and feels deeply its severance from human interaction. My reading of the novel also suggests that its conclusion may be less optimistic than many critics have said, indeed that it may be self-canceling, with everyone of importance being in some sense marooned on the same island replicated in personal islands of their own making.

Whereas *To the Lighthouse* maps out islands of verbal solitude forever unable to connect with another, the hermetic life of *The Magic Mountain* is encapsulated in torrents of verbiage that, when one considers the novel's totality, conspicuously fail to establish bridges between human relationships. Chapter IV, then, explores the vagaries of the solitary in Thomas Mann's hero on his magic mountain, where the solitude of various types of illness is manifest in a variety of conflicts, personal and cultural. Illness and health, virtually inseparable, drive Hans Castorp into physical passion and highly intellectual speculation, but self-examination, whether of lungs or psyche, leaves unresolved the critical question of how to negotiate the worlds of the hermetic solitary and the freely engaged.

Chapter V links Sartre and Camus, for each takes solitude to a new level of complexity and sophistication within a common framework. Roquentin, the protagonist of Sartre's *Nausea,* overcome with the symptom of the novel's title, finally discovers the relationship between freedom and solitude: "Is this what freedom is? . . . I am free: I haven't a single reason for living left. . . . Alone and free. But this freedom is rather like death."[16] Camus's Meursault attempts to salvage his equally questionable freedom by accepting its foredoomed consequence of death as a moment of self-definition. As a condemned man he has no choice, but almost to the end he searches for the "loophole."

Beckett refines these sentiments in the decades following *Nausea,* especially in the trilogy of novels that concludes with *The Unnamable.* These three novels are the subject of the sixth and final chapter, and in them Beckett offers the most difficult challenge, standing as he does somewhere on the boundary of modernism and whatever follows it. In recent years one critic has published *Samuel Beckett and the End of Modernity,* and Beckett's latest biographer entitled his volume *Samuel Beckett: The Last Modernist.* At the same time, postmodern interpretations of Beckett have flourished in the nineties. Since there are no rigid dividing lines, it seems proper to consider the Beckett of the 1950s as representing the end of Modernism, but poised to enter postmodern territory. The Beckett of the trilogy is a contemporary of Sartre and Camus, and like them (however different his import and means), he is defiant in his unrelentingly severe perception of life (mitigated only by his honesty and wit). Also like Sartre and Camus, Beckett echoes one matter on which the two agreed, best said in a philosopher's recent remark: "We discover truth alone, we err in groups."[17] But for Beckett, "alone" is not to be equated with being lonely, for—especially in the trilogy—the former is the condition, the latter is the subject's affect that Beckett dissociates from the condition (aloneness, solitude). Beckett's "I" appropriately concludes the study proper, for solitude has been taken as far as any subjective perception can tolerate. Once again Beckett stands on the brink. The Concordance to the trilogy lists 127 references to "alone," but only 3 to "lonely."

In the conclusion, Beckett's *The Lost Ones,* a work of the 1970s, serves to reveal some telling aspects of the fate of solitude in the postmodern era: It seems the best, if not the earliest, manifestation of a time we are still struggling to define and delimit.

Chapter I ∼

Self Against Self: Toward Ambiguous Solitude in Modernist Fiction

Solitude is the profoundest fact of the human condition. Man is the only being who knows he is alone, and the only one who seeks out another.

—Octavio Paz, *The Labyrinth of Solitude*

I am *solitude* become man—That no word ever reached me, forced me to reach myself.

—Nietzsche, Appendix, *Ecce Homo*

And one again I am, I will not say alone . . . but, how shall I say . . . restored to myself, no, I never left myself, free, yes, I don't know what that means but it's the word I mean to use, free to do what . . .

—Beckett, *Molloy*

The Issues

Much has been said about the "existential crisis" so dominant in the isolates of modernist fiction, but far less has been said about the ambiguities that attend the solitary's choice, from the start. *"In solitude, for company,"* wrote W. H. Auden, and this paradoxical counterpoint best expresses the double bind that encumbers the solitary throughout western history. Solitaries have often created a variety of strategies in the hope of maintaining a balancing act on a precarious tightrope between psychic exile and its gift of freedom and the recognition, often wistful and sometimes bitter, of the ultimate price that solitude exacts. Some have experienced the joy of solitude and others its miseries, but the possibility that both exist has escaped no one.

Why has solitude, for the most part, elicited such complex responses? Why have such strong ambiguities attached themselves to the issue? Why, in spite of being potentially destructive, has solitude continued to hold such a powerful attraction, especially for modernists? Perhaps the entanglement of psychological and ethical issues holds a key. In addition to the state of mind inherent in any condition of isolation, solitude often poses an ethical dilemma. Among religious communities (at least in the West) that problem has always been obvious: serve God in isolation from humanity or serve humanity with a diminished commitment (necessarily) of Self to God. Later, when more secularized, the issue revolves around *amour propre* and *amour de soi*. In any setting, is the withdrawal and subsequent isolation of Self a form of narcissistic indulgence? Is the abandonment of Society also a betrayal of humanity? However much isolation may be fertile ground for self-knowledge and inner growth, where is the line that, when crossed, brings one into the realm of ego-gratification at the expense of Other? In short, how can one navigate solitude while still maintaining that link to social order that ensures some measure of balance?

The perception of solitude has always swung uneasily between signifying pleasure or destructive isolation. Solitaries appear afflicted with double vision, like Swift's Laputans: one eye "turned inward, and the other directly up to the Zenith" (religious solitaries), or one eye turned inward, the second positioned horizontally toward social companionship. This binary posture—in different directions—constitutes a conflicted, divided Self that defines the problematic of the solitary's issues. It is a commonplace that solitude has suggested either the opportunistic exclusivity and ecstasy of aloneness (Petrarch, Montaigne, Thoreau), or evoked the cursed state of alienation, the latter becoming increasingly articulated beginning in the eighteenth century. In the existentially tormented protagonists of the modernists, the vertical vision no longer functions, and both eyes are horizontally fixed: inward and outward between extremes of self-contempt and a longing, however grudgingly and ironically expressed, to reconnect with Society.

Solitude and Society

The most commonly invoked antithesis to solitude has always been Society, however interpreted, although Society has not always necessarily been viewed as preferable. Nietzsche, as usual, offered up icy candor: "In solitude the lonely man is eaten up by himself, among crowds by the many. Choose which you prefer." Or, at more length and with greater ambiguity:

> Solitude has seven skins which nothing can penetrate. . . . At the best one en-counters a sort of revolt. This feeling of revolt, I suffered . . . at the hands of almost every one who came near me; it would seem that nothing inflicts a deeper wound than suddenly to make one's distance felt.[1]

The nineteenth century featured a chorus of discordant voices challenging the authenticity and authority of Society, Nietzsche's being perhaps the loudest and the most biting. However, in *Either/Or*, Kierkegaard writes with re-proachful irony, "There is so much talk about man's being a social animal, but basically he is a beast of prey . . . all this chatter about sociality and commu-nity is . . . hypocrisy and . . . perfidy."[2] But we have been most often defined as creatures who need both the seclusive environs of being alone as well as a relationship with some form of social unit. *Ecclesiastes* 2:18 reports God's mes-sage that Adam requires a companion, for it is not proper for "the man to be himself alone." In a study of the motif of solitude in the Old Testament a critic concludes that solitude in biblical times was an "intensive and overarching ex-perience," unlike that in prior religions where access to deities was common and easier, since the gods were available in animal forms, whereas the monotheistic God was invisible, forbidden to be represented. This profoundly affected the Old Testament experience of being solitary. Nor, of course, did the shape and intensity of solitude cease with Christianity and its medieval mani-festations, though Christ's intercessory role with God is transitional from the Old Testament's unflinching depiction of solitary desolation.[3]

Debates between the relative merits of solitude versus Society are not, of course, solely Western. Ancient Eastern philosophy was split on the issue: Confucius counseled that wisdom and "serenity" were attainable only by "discharging social obligations"; Taoism, led by Lao Tse, advised the oppo-site route, "withdrawing" from Society and focusing on self-enlightenment in solitude—"Solitude is healthy, according to the Taoist. . . ."[4] After the Desert Fathers and the medieval tendencies of monastic withdrawal, the issue of the individual's preeminence in relation to both Self and Other ad-vanced the debate about solitude: Conflict and blurred boundaries were an inevitable and common outcome.

Francis Bacon, Daniel Defoe, David Thoreau, and Octavio Paz, among many, have each, in their respective centuries pronounced what they con-ceived as the essential relationship between solitude and Society and how they conceived of solitude as a condition of life.

Bacon, in his essay "Of Friendship" (1625), after mentioning Aristotle's famous pronouncement on solitude that only a beast or a god can live wholly as a solitary agrees that there is truth to part of the stricture that "a natural and secret hatred or aversion towards society . . . hath somewhat of the savage beast." At the same time, he rejects the "divine nature" (Aristotle's "God") except, of course, for religious hermits who seek solitude not for pleasure but for proximity to the divine. Bacon complains that solitude is little understood: "a crowd is not company," and he quotes the Latin " . . . 'Magna civitas, magna solitudo'" (a great state, a great solitude). It is, he says, "a miserable solitude to want true friends, without which the world is but a wilderness. . . ."[5] For Bacon human society remains the essential component of being human. On the heels of *Robinson Crusoe* (1719), Defoe publishes two volumes (ostensibly sequels), the first of which, *Serious Reflections of Robinson Crusoe,* opens with a chapter titled "Of Solitude." How Defoe's opening discussion of solitude tends to compromise his view of solitude as developed in *Robinson Crusoe* is discussed in the next chapter. Suffice it to say here that in the "sequel," solitude is quite sternly presented, with Defoe insisting that Crusoe's involuntary solitude is really not solitude at all. Further, he rejects all "hermit-like" solitude as an "escape from human society" moving counter to man's natural inclination to be social.[6]

A little over a century later, in the summer of 1846, across the Atlantic, a young man began his journal entries that were later published as *Walden, or Life in the Woods* (1854). Writing in the section he called "Solitude," Thoreau manifests a confident resolution to his own reflections. On the whole he finds it "wholesome" to be alone, and company is "soon wearisome and dissipating"; the most "companionable" companion is solitude. Only once, shortly after settling into his cabin, did he doubt himself, wondering whether the "neighborhood of man was not essential." But he quickly discovers this to be an aberration, "a slight insanity in my mood," and recovers the beneficent sense of commonality with Nature, which he so lovingly and accurately begins to observe and describe.[7] As is common knowledge, Thoreau was never a total hermit, visiting his friend Emerson and others whenever it suited him, but this should not detract from his experiment with solitude nor from his deeply felt appreciation of its opportunities.

Emerson, on the other hand, was less clear, more mainstream. In "Society and Solitude" he recognized the same dilemma as had Bacon and Defoe. The "necessity of solitude," he wrote, "is organic." But at the same time, "man must be clothed with society. . . ." There are the exceptions, those "exquisitely made" who can be alone, but most of us are "undone" by isolation. Neither state is satisfactory: "If solitude is proud, so is society vulgar." Emerson contends that this dialectic is one that Nature delights in—he calls it one of the "extreme antagonisms" that we are obliged to navigate with the greatest skill. Though "Solitude is impracticable, and society fatal," we are of necessity forced to be in both states. To engage Society without the vulgarity it threatens, we must interpret the social impulse as "the readiness of sympathy . . . the natural element" rather than a mere tussling with the crowd.[8] Thus, Emerson hopes, we may negotiate our existence between isolation and frivolous engagement. "Heidegger," a recent critic asserts, "would tell us that 'solitary' does not signify 'alone,' or at least not in the sense of a negative isolation."[9] Yet few solitaries escape at least in part the pain of isolation, however keen they may be to attain their aloneness.

Speaking as a modern, Octavio Paz, in *The Labyrinth of Solitude,* weaves a more complex dialectic of solitude than those of Bacon and Defoe or Thoreau and Emerson. He suggests that life is a transitional period—between "what we were" and "what we are going to be in the mysterious future." So in Paz's scheme we are nostalgic for the safe past (before birth) and in search for communion—though such communion may be attained in this life, not the next. The initial sense of communion we experience, severed from the womb, dissolves into a state of solitude that, in time, is transformed into a form of "self-awareness":

> Hence the feeling that we are alone has a double significance: on the one hand it is self-awareness, and on the other it is a longing to escape from ourselves. Solitude—the very condition of our lives—appears to us a test and a purgation, at the conclusion of which our anguish and instability will vanish. At the exit of the labyrinth of solitude [i.e., life itself] we will find reunion (which is repose and happiness), and plenitude, and harmony with the world.

The first part of this description—"self-awareness, and . . . a longing to escape from ourselves"—is an experience common in the works of the past two centuries; but the opposite coda, "reconciliation" within "harmony," belongs more to the wishful thinking of a mythic paradigm. It is true, as Paz maintains, that solitude is "a punishment but it is also a promise that our exile will end": This accents our first text, *Robinson Crusoe.* To support his dialectic, Paz refers to Toynbee's concept for his paradigm of "'the twofold notion of withdrawal-and-return. . . . '"[10] Toynbee had in mind the mythic and historical accounts of withdrawal for the sake of self-realization and return to make available this wisdom to community.[11] Whether Paz also had Nietzsche's "eternal recurrence" in mind is not clear, but Zarathustra's withdrawal and his problematic "return" certainly form part of the same dilemma. Freud transforms withdrawal and return into a continuous psychological phenomenon—from infancy to adulthood—centered on our anxiety of withdrawal (that of others as well as our own) and the terror that often accompanies our awaiting the return. Among others, T. S. Eliot expressed the temporal and spatial implications of such ambivalence in "The Dry Salvages":

'Fare forward, you who think that you are voyaging;
You are not those who saw the harbour
Receding, or those who will disembark.'

Transitions

In mapping the changes in attitude toward solitude in England, Janette Dillon has focused on the transitional period between the late sixteenth and early seventeenth centuries where she observes a "shifting balance between individual and social concerns" which, she notes, produced "violent controversy" and "blatant self-contradiction." As the sixteenth century moved away from the "medieval idealisation" of social bonding toward an "increased reverence" for the cultivation of the isolated individual, "[t]he pleasures of solitude and introspection began to usurp the sense of community. . . ." Social engagement began to be viewed as a "duty" at odds with the "desire for privacy." Nevertheless, the conflict persisted: "moral duty" took a dim view of the pleasure of solitude, which was condemned at the same time a "cult of solitude" began to emerge. Only when solitude became accepted and "morally respectable" after the first quarter of the seventeenth century did the cultist feature of solitude disappear.[12]

These dialectical oppositions provoked by solitude were framed by Aristotle and Plato, each concerned that too much isolation from the state was a form of self-indulgence. Despite the admonition to know ourselves and examine our lives, the Greeks discouraged excesses of self-reflection or inwardness. Dillon refers us to Aristotle's famous statement that "'man is by nature a social being'" (Dillon 4). (In *Thus Spake Zarathustra*, Nietzsche responded to Aristotle: "To live alone one must be a beast or a god, says Aristotle. Leaving out the third case: one must be both—a philosopher"). From Anglo-Saxon literature through Malory, Dillon observes that the solitary was a creature of "pity": the exile, the wanderer, was not considered free but incomplete and lacking any meaning (Dillon 7). In the early Christian era, solitude conjures up devotion to God, retreat from worldly matters, perfection of the soul. But aloneness outside the presumed comforts of religion remained a sometimes contentious issue: "What is this world?" asks Chaucer, "what asketh man to have? / Now with his love, now with his cold grave / Allone, withouten any compaigne." Even when medieval theology dominated, debates rooted in psychological and moral issues made their presence felt. Always there was the reminder that withdrawal from the world was threatened by temptation. The anchorites addressed in the *Ancrene Wisse* (1230?) are confronted with the transparent glass of the window image, cautioned that the world within and without—and the temptations of the latter—are fragile protection indeed.[13] In addition, the good Christian has always faced a moral dilemma: whether to indulge in a kind of holy solitude betrothed to God or whether to serve, and help, one's fellow-beings (a dilemma not resolved, as witness the worker priest movement in modern France and in Latin-American countries).

Petrarch's *De Vita Solitaria (The Solitary Life)* [1346] is a prose Ode to Solitude, extolling that condition unequivocally for allowing the poet both the time and environment to engage his beloved books. Once considered religious and spiritual, the Treatise is now seen as a secular defense of solitude, drawing examples from the Ancients, the Old and New Testament, the lives of saints, popes, poets. Withdraw from the tumult of the cities, Petrarch advises, and submit yourself to solitude, which is, he says, "holy, innocent, incorruptible . . . the purest of all human possessions." Petrarch's perspective may be historically on the threshold of the Italian Renaissance but, as Salavatore Quasimodo notes, "From the stone of Arquà, the man still medieval . . . and the European poet speak to us even today with the voice of solitude. . . ."[14]

In early sixteenth-century England, the fate of the monasteries makes it clear that all "[w]ithdrawal from the community was condemned whatever the motivations . . ." (Dillon 10). But this objection was not universally accepted; the conflict between an ongoing desire for "religious enclosure" versus engagement in "civil life" is evident in the works of Thomas More and others. While initially rejecting "inwardness," the English gradually came to accept its potential, especially the pleasures of "secular solitude" that Petrarch had so praised. Eventually the "growing fashion for solitude is indicative not simply of changing preferences but of a changing morality, which valued the private good above the public good" (Dillon 11, 23). In addition the exodus from the countryside to the city was a further move toward the decline of the close-knit social order of the countryside; later on, the reverse trend—a migration back to the countryside—tended to support a turn toward privacy, leisurely pleasure, and a diminishment of social duties. The pendulum never ceases its motion. Intellectual solitude became equated with superiority, being "special," and an alternative to spiritual superiority (as it would again, of course, in modernist fiction—in Joyce, Gide, Mann, Proust, Lawrence and others), but the issue was never clear-cut:

> On the contrary, the same individuals can be found praising solitude at one point, who condemn it in another. This apparent self-contradiction arose partly out of the conflict between personal preference and moral conviction, since the attractions of solitude were clearly felt long before it acquired moral respectability. (Dillon 32)

For the Elizabethans (and to some extent the Jacobeans who followed them), solitude became a richly textured state adaptable to many conditions:

"the country life, the contemplative life, the melancholy humour, the refusal of public office, the studious disposition." Such variety made ample room for conflict and contradiction, and permitted one to conceive of solitude on a spectrum from "self-love, love of the community, or love of God." It would never again enjoy such inclusive flexibility. Views of solitude had come a long way from the early Elizabethans, who distrusted it, to the mid-seventeenth century when solitude was given the highest perch—it was "natural." Now the solitary hero was seen as a person of moral "autonomy" and "individual freedom," and increasingly the "inward world" was accorded more trust than the "world outside" (Dillon 34–44).

Douglas Bush is right to draw attention to the Renaissance hero's independence, not the much later "alienated" victim, but as the solitary who faces the world with conscious freedom. Hence the Renaissance poets are "distinguished . . . in that their heroes are not seen as helpless, unresisting victims of either fate or society; they make their choices and are responsible for their acts. . . ."[15]

Montaigne's essay "On Solitude" (1572) epitomizes solitude's secularization in the Renaissance, providing one with the fruits of retirement to the country, cultivation of the mind in solitary repose, and perfection, not so much of the soul as of the intellect. One commentator characterizes this change as "the disintegration of the synthesis of action and contemplation," though someone like Erasmus, more than 60 years earlier, was already seeking a "more sympathetic view of the secular, humanistic community" and tended to remain "ambivalent," cautioning "against the manifold abuse of the monastic ideal."[16] Montaigne begins by impatiently dismissing "the usual long comparison between the solitary and the active life. . . ." It is indeed "ambition" itself, with its "evil means," that pushes us to abandon that course and to seek contentment elsewhere. Solitude, says Montaigne, "shun[s] society"; "the aim of solitude is to live more at leisure and at one's ease"; "let us cut loose from all the ties that bind us to others . . . live really alone . . ."; "We have lived long enough for others; let us live at least this remaining bit of life for ourselves." While Montaigne admires spiritual solitude, he believes that the true retiree should "build himself in solitude a life that is voluptuous beyond any other kind of life." Clearly such an attitude toward solitude is absent any guilt or misanthropy: Montaigne celebrates solitude as a normal and healthy withdrawal, without any hint of selfishness or any pathology of loneliness. Almost a century later, Andrew Marvell was still celebrating in "The Garden" (1681): "Society is all but rude / To this delicious solitude."[17]

However, neither Montaigne's nor Marvell's sanguine approach to solitude was shared by all. In England, during the 50 or so years following Montaigne's death, the question of solitude was hotly debated. Shakespeare seemed ambivalent, creating both misanthropic malcontents, whose selfishness and egotism sever them from Society and make them contemptuous characters to be mocked or scorned (e.g., Malvolio, Jacques) and the inward-looking reflective Hamlet, whose calling to know himself clashes with duties of righting the social order. Donne said, "No man is an island entire of itself," which encourages intervention; and Prospero ends *The Tempest* when departing from his island with a declaration of release: "As you from crimes would pardon'd be / Let your indulgence set me free," his solitude in exile now perceived as an imprisonment.

Pascal sides with the interventionist trend in the seventeenth century, when he insists that we are driven by "motion," and that "complete rest is death." We feel our "nothingness" and "emptiness" when we are unoccupied, and this steers us into unimaginable "gloom, sadness, fretfulness, vexation, despair." That is why prison is so "horrible": "hence it comes that the pleasure of solitude is a thing incomprehensible,"[18] what has been called Pascal's empathetic understanding of "cosmic homelessness."[19] (Victor Brombert demonstrates how this becomes reversed in the nineteenth century. Referring specifically to this shift from Pascal's version, he develops a convincing argument for the later view of Stendhal's "happy prison."[20])

"The theme of solitude," according to Renato Poggioli, was "almost totally absent" from classical pastoral. Not until the seventeenth century does pastoral become related strongly to solitude, when there emerges a new kind of "pastoral of melancholy," a "variant of the pastoral of solitude." This change occurs "when both the idyll and the elegy of love are over," when the concern is "less with the heart and more with the soul." In the mid-1600s Thomas Traherne begins his "Solitude": "How desolate! / Ah! how forlorn!, how sadly did I stand / When in the field of woeful State / I felt . . . Comfort [could not] yield in any Field / To me / Nor could Contentment find or see." And for Gongora in the *Soledades* (the first of which dates to 1613), that "pastoral solitude ceases to be a retreat from and becomes a triumph over the world."[21] The distinction is important, for when solitude itself passes from the state of passive "retreat" to active "triumph" it also carries with that change a very different perception by the solitary—from disengagement to engagement, even if at first such engagement is with Nature rather than human nature. In France, Saint-Amant twice goes to his Belle-Isle-en-Mer to write first his *La Solitude* (1617), an apostrophe to the pleasures of nature as he walks the island grounds: "Oh, how much I love solitude! / These places, sacred to noise, / Removed from the world and noise, / Pleasure my inquietude!" Ten years later he writes *Le Contempleur,* a more sophisticated reprise of *La Solitude.*[22]

By the eighteenth century, many solitaries elect solitude as an antidote to Society, a condition from which to challenge and engage the outside world with the intention of assuming a superior status to it. Or, conversely, they may also feel the beginnings of alienation, buttressed by a fragile sense of superiority. With such changes, of course, some of the doubts and anxieties of the solitary begin slowly to reappear in the form of the self-righteousness and defensiveness that characterize those who oppose a collective majority with a mission not always clearly conceived. At the start of the century, the youthful Pope still strikes a conventionally optimistic and cheerful note in "On Solitude" (1717): "Happy the man whose wish and care / A few paternal acres bound / Content to breathe his native air / In his own ground." But such simplicity would not long attend a still argumentative issue. The eighteenth-century dilemma of seclusion and inclusion is detailed in W. B. Carnochan's *Confinement and Flight: An Essay on English Literature of the Eighteenth Century.* Selecting Defoe, Swift, and Uncle Toby from Sterne's *Tristram Shandy,* Carnochan comments on their affinities for islands and concludes:

> Crusoe calls his island "a scene of silent life" . . . Gulliver moves to a position of speechlessness; words put Toby's life in danger. . . . And all of them with varying awareness, are of two minds: on the one hand, they want to be rescued from insularity because, like Pascal, they find it full of terrors; on the other, they do not want to be rescued because, like Rousseau, they live comfortable lives and resent intrusion.

So he argues that, in Crusoe's case, the "forbidding silence of the footstep superimposes itself on the comfortable silence of isolation. . . ."[23] Another study accentuates how such fears surfaced in increasing volume: "By the mid-century, retirement has hardened into retreat. The poet . . . longs to be not only far from the madding crowd . . . but far from everybody." The "futility of 'industry'" and the accompanying reverence of "reverie and retreat"[24] dehistoricize most of the attendant issues and prepare the way for the melancholy self-disputations that mark the latter half of the eighteenth century and point toward the Romantics.

The Eighteenth Century: A Quest for Balance

The eighteenth century—in England and on the continent—was richly fertile ground for poems, cautionary books, and general debates about solitude's seductive and sometimes fatal invitation, with the emphasis often equally divided. Philosophers weighed in, and striking changes of taste assumed a revolutionary fervor at the close of the century as the sensibilities of the Romantics began to shift the premises of the argument. Overall, the conception of solitude in the eighteenth century continues to attract both positive and negative responses, and the issue remains clouded.

Abraham Cowley bemoans our post-lapsarian state in his ode "Of Soli-tude": "Oh Solitude, first state of Human-kind!," which was blessed until "two (alas!) together joyn'd, / [And] the serpent made up Three." But in his introduction to the poem Cowley complains: "It is very fantastical and con-tradictory in humane Nature, that Men should love themselves above all the rest of the world, and yet never endure to be with themselves." The only so-lution to "set right" and "fit" solitude properly is to meet a set of prerequi-sites: [O]ne must have sufficient recognition of the world to see its vanity; one must have enough "virtue" to dismiss such vanity; and the mind must be purged of "Lust or Passions."[25] James Thomson begins his "Hymn on Solitude" (1729–1750) almost defiantly: "Hail, mildly pleasing solitude, / Companion of the wise, and good; / But, from whose holy, piercing eye, / The herd of fools, and villains fly."

Afflicted with melancholy all his life, Dr. Johnson warned, borrowing from Robert Burton's *Anatomy of Melancholy:* "If you are idle, be not soli-tary; if you are solitary, be not idle." In his *Dictionary,* he defined solitude tersely: "Lonely life; state of being alone." A confirmed Londoner, Johnson was unimpressed by Cowley's desire for country solitude and by the whole affectation—as he saw it—of escaping into solitude by removing oneself from city to country. Cowley's notion (and that of others) that one can leave behind one's care and escape into some sanctifying solitude struck him as "chimerical." Cowley appeared not to realize that solitude cannot exist without all the woes it is purported to relieve one from: "He forgot . . . that solitude and quiet owe their pleasures to those miseries which he was so studious to obviate"; and he "never suspected that the cause of his un-happiness was within . . . ," that changing venue does not remove one's un-happiness (*Rambler,* no. 8). In *Rambler* no. 135 Johnson is even more caustic about retirees to the country, who merely "quit one scene of idleness for another. . . ." Only in *The Adventurer,* no. 126, does he take solitude se-riously, though he is no more sympathetic. He believes that many enter into solitude self-indulgently, and others are "seduced into solitude merely by the authority of great names. . . ." While conceding that "learning may be conferred by solitude," he insists that its "applications must be attained by its general converse." In addition he warns that solitude may encourage ig-norance and hence narrow one's perceptions. Seemingly respectful at least of those who seek solitude for the sake of piety, he sees no benefit in their isolation for others. These "guardians of mankind," once they "withdraw to solitude" may be said to "desert the very station which Providence assigned for them." Even conceding his bias, clearly Johnson keenly understood the bifurcated nature of solitude, and he obviously believed that solitariness was often a screen for self-indulgence that prevented giving anything back to share with Society.

At the end of the eighteenth century, William Cowper wrote his unambiguous verses "supposed to be written" by Alexander Selkirk, long assumed to have been a possible model for Robinson Crusoe: "O Solitude! where are the charms / That sages have seen in thy face? / Better dwell in the midst of alarms, / Than reign in this horrible place."[26] Or, as Cowper wrote in his long poem, "Retirement": "For solitude, however some may rave, / Seeming a sanctuary, proves a grave . . ."

Johann Georg Zimmermann, a Swiss physician, published the first edition of his subsequent tome, *Solitude* (eventually titled *Über die Einsamkeit* 1784–85), in 1755–56, a book so popular at least 90 English editions and a number of French translations appeared between 1791 and 1900. At the request of Catherine the Great of Russia—one of Zimmermann's most ardent admirers—Zimmermann sent the book to the Russian court; Catherine rewarded him with a casket containing a diamond ring and a gold medal bearing a portrait of herself. The volume's impression is on subsequent Russian literary motifs of the nineteenth century—that is, "Oblomovism" or the "superfluous man"—have yet to be measured.[27]

Zimmermann's study is in two parts: the first instructs us on the advantages of solitude; the second outlines its dangers, to which Zimmermann himself succumbed. *Solitude* is a primer of caution, illustrating the ever growing ambivalence toward and suspicion of the rewards and dangers of solitude. In praise of solitude Zimmermann states a classic Enlightenment view: it "elevates the mind," "diminishes the troublesome passions," and calms the nerves, acting as a balm in illness and misfortune. On the negative side, solitude "is . . . unfriendly to the happiness and foreign to the nature of mankind": it may encourage misanthropy; its indolence can lead to the dreaded afflictions of hypochondria and melancholy, adversely affecting the imagination. In the last analysis, "Life is intolerable without society," and the "idleness" that solitude may encourage is "the root of all evil."[28] Even Schopenhauer—an advocate of solitude—cautioned in his "Psychological Observations" in the following century that "[m]isanthropy and love of solitude are convertible ideas." In short, solitude creates pathologies of various kinds, a view consistent with that held by the philosophes in the *Encyclopédie* who find little redeemable in solitude, "a state opposed to that of society," which generates only misery and, even more pointedly, a condition at war with Society: "destructive, barbaric and directly contrary to [its] well-being."[29] Zimmermann, of course, is less one-sided, attempting to find and define balance. Aware of solitude's delicate antinomy, he quotes an unidentified German author who finds solitude "'holds in the one hand a cup of bliss . . . and in the other grasps an envenomed dagger.'"[30]

Roland Barthes may have been partly right when he called Voltaire "a happy writer," the "last," who "suspended time" and "[forgot] history" to fashion a philosophy of "immobility." Rousseau, on the other hand, "set history moving again" when he blamed human corruption on Society: he established "the principle of a permanent transcendence of history." From then on, Barthes laments, "the intellectual will be defined by his bad conscience": inner turmoil and self-contradiction become inescapable.[31] "Retired" to the Hermitage, on the l'Isle Saint Pierre, Rousseau composes his *Reveries of the Solitary Walker* in 1772 (published posthumously in 1782). Paranoia made Rousseau a good candidate for solitariness, as he positions himself to become, historically speaking, a bridge between the philosophes whom he in part rejected and the coming Romantics who will embrace him posthumously—whether or not he would have welcomed it. His subsequent importance for Modernism (Sartre in particular) is now more generously acknowledged.[32]

The "central theme" in the *Reveries,* writes Peter France in his introduction to the Penguin English translation, "is the tug-of-war between solitude and society." Robert Sayre proposes, quite convincingly, that Rousseau invented modern solitude. However, though Sayre believes that Rousseau's "thematics of solitude" is "highly original," he also recognizes the residual influences of the eighteenth century: "that man's natural state and greatest happiness are in society rather than in solitary retreat,"[33] though one would hardly perceive this from the tortured and often self-contradictory arguments of the "Walks" that constitute the text. *Reveries,* Rousseau's last work, begins somberly enough: "So now I am alone in the world."

Yet in spite of the occasional theatrical posturing, for Rousseau solitude is a philosophically autonomous state that initiates significant changes in attitude. In prior centuries solitude was not a trivial subject, as we have seen; yet it did sometimes function as a sentimental literary parlor game, occasioning either obligatory celebration or rejection. Rousseau is in earnest. When he travels to his island, unlike Saint-Amant, he is entering more than a physical place of nature: he penetrates the islands of cognition and affect. Rousseau claims he has modeled himself after Montaigne, but (perhaps exaggerating the difference) cites a different "motive"—to discover himself, to find out "What am I?" Like Thoreau's, Rousseau's desire to exile himself was curiously ambivalent: he quickly sent for his "housekeeper, his books, and his small set of possessions"; some of his possessions he left packed, no doubt feeling pleasure in seeing them in a suspended state. He seemed to have a need for these accoutrements as a prop: he wanted it both ways.[34] The Fifth Walk is unequivocal: "Complete silence induces melancholy; it is an image of death." And in the Seventh Walk he admits that his solitariness has made him an "unsociable misanthropist because I prefer the harshest solitude to the society of malicious men. . . ."[35] With its multilayered and seesawing patterns, the *Reveries* become a palimpsest for the subsequent decipherers of solitude. Rousseau establishes the modern paradigm of Self: the "I" assumes a largesse of freedom, thereby becoming vulnerable to an open-ended risk of failure: henceforth conflict about solitude is inherent in the Self's having to account for itself.

The Nineteenth Century:
Romanticism and the Beginnings of Alienation

If the eighteenth century observed solitude somewhat ritualistically as a temptation for good and ill but confident that—except for aberrations—we could strike a balance between the positive and negative, a large number of voices in the nineteenth, the Romantics signaling the way, embraced solitude as they did opiates: as a cure for all ills, the ultimate conveyance to tainted happiness. In time, however, solitude turned into an illness often without cure. Whereas the eighteenth century had by and large equated beauty and solitude with sublimity, the nineteenth began to conceive of beauty and solitude in darker terms.

Schopenhauer warned that those incapable of "pure contemplation" (willlessness) are condemned to ennui: our "ability to endure solitude" and "our love of it" serve as a litmus test to measure our ability to avoid boredom. Most of us, he was certain, lacking "genius," or what he called "objectivity," do not "like to be alone with nature; [we] need company. . . ." As a consequence, "in solitude even the most beautiful surroundings have [for such a majority] . . . a desolate, dark, strange, and hostile appearance."[36] But such was the reality, unfortunately, not as he thought it should be; Schopenhauer, especially in the second chapter of *Parega and Paralipomena* (Counsels and Maxims), extols solitude as the only sensible choice for any human being—solitude or "vulgarity." Learning to be alone, he counsels, should be a required subject in any young person's curriculum of life. We become sociable because we tire of ourselves, and thus betray our "inability to endure solitude." Socialization becomes an excuse for abandoning one's Self: "It is the monotony of his own nature that makes a man find solitude intolerable." Although "solitude is the original and natural state of man," it does have its "evils"; but Society is "*insidious,*" and our pursuit of it is suspect:

> the social impulse does not rest directly upon the love of society, but upon the fear of solitude; it is not alone the charm of being in others' company that people seek, it is the dreary oppression of being alone . . . that they would

avoid. They will do anything to escape it . . . and put up with the . . . constraint which all society involves. . . .

As humans we make mere excuses to be sociable; if only we were to overcome our fear of solitude, especially as we age, we would realize that only in a state of solitude are we in the *natural* habitat, "as water to a fish."[37] Although published in 1851, these remarks on solitude and society were already seedlings in *The World as Will and Representation* (1818), where Schopenhauer elaborately outlined his essential philosophical posture. Thomas Mann described it in his introduction to the slim "Living Thoughts" volume: "As so often, the situation respecting freedom was just contrary to that conceived by ordinary common sense. It lay not in doing but in being, not in *operari* but in *esse*."[38] This became a dangerous premise by the mid-nineteenth century, and Mann in fact would undertake to show us the innermost parts of such dangers in his own *Magic Mountain*. Dangers of solitude, already perceived by the Romantics in Germany, France, and England in the early decades of the century, would be gradually recognized in their full measure as the potential consequences of solitude became increasingly more disastrous.

Rousseau's elegiac, even sad, solitude also embodies many of the elements that suggest why the Romantics were drawn to his work. Much of their conceptualization of solitude, however dubious at times, is rooted in the Rousseauian idiom, especially in the Romantic recognition that the alignment of solitude with Nature is often insufficiently reassuring and brings one back upon oneself. It has even been suggested that we can date and identify the break between the Enlightenment and the succeeding Romantics with the personal break between Diderot and Rousseau, for (among other reasons) it was a dispute about solitude that precipitated the rupture of that friendship. Diderot, Ernst Cassirer argues, had led the way in proposing that solitude was cherished only by "evil" men, which, of course, was an affront to Rousseau.[39] Although the identification of this locus as *the* dividing line between the Enlightenment and what followed may seem arbitrary or whimsical, it is neither. Despite the many issues that evolved to divide the philosophes from the young Romantics, their profound differences about solitude were paramount: they defined the critical debate over the self-conscious creation of individuality versus the individual's service to social needs.

Romanticism encodes solitude into the poetic consciousness and, as Nicholas Berdyaev remarks, "throws a great deal of light on the problem of solitude" because it becomes synonymous with it. Berdyaev locates Romanticism "from the time when the Ego became abstracted from the objective hierarchical order. . . . The romantic Ego postulates a divorce between the subject and the object . . . made inevitable by the Ego's repudiation of the objective order of things."[40] To a point this is true, but Berdyaev underestimates

the strong tensions that develop when many Romantics recognize the annihilating dangers of such a divorce, especially with respect to their overzealous
sense of transcendence into Nature. Kant had already warned in *The Critique
of Judgment* that the sublime "is not to be sought in the things of nature, but
only in our ideas . . . ,"[41] that is, in our minds, what later was codified as
"imagination." A partial solution to this tension between the outer and inner
worlds was to strive for clearer individuation: "Solitude comes to be cultivated as a space for consciousness," in which the individual is free; "and the
waste landscape becomes the site of value" since it is "a peopled solitude," a
process of "anthropomorphizing" Nature without having to confront "the
pressures of a competing consciousness."[42]

Country retirement, the genteel option of the eighteenth century, metamorphoses in the nineteenth into a sublime, and sometimes threatening, confrontation with the natural world. Ludwig Tieck, in *Der Blonde Eckbert*
(1796), can still sing of the solitude of the woods *("Waldeinsamkeit"),* "which
gives me joy / Tomorrow and today, / For eternity. . . ." Yet while comforting
and rewarding to the senses, solitude in Nature also becomes capable of in-
stilling the sublime terror that Kant and Burke defined in the previous century. Although a whole life of solitude "contradicts our being," Burke writes:
"Absolute and entire *solitude* . . . perpetual exclusion from all society, is as
great a positive pain as can almost be conceived."[43] In Mary Shelley's
Frankenstein, the attraction and terror of solitude as loneliness, played out
against the backdrop of alpine peaks and ice deserts, makes for a powerful ac-
companiment to the tale of isolation of the novel's major actors: Frankenstein, his creation, and Walton, the failed explorer. This form of solitude
continues to reappear in mid-century solitary misanthropists such as
Rochester in *Jane Eyre* or in the inconsolable Heathcliff of *Wuthering Heights.*

Romantic poets generally viewed solitude with suspicion and ambivalence. Shelley's *Alastor; or the Spirit of Solitude* casts a shadow over the virtues
of solitude. If the visionary poet's search for solitary perfection costs him his
humanity then, Shelley suggests, his death is earned punishment for forfeit-
ing that humanity. Shelley himself attempts to explain his poem in a preface. Inviting us to conceive of it as "allegorical," Shelley describes his poet as
being initially a Faust-like figure who, after drinking "deep of the fountain
of knowledge," remains unfulfilled, "insatiate." Once the objective world no
longer satisfies, the Poet seeks a synthesis of imagination, beauty, and intellectual faculties in "a single image." But the quest, conducted in the solitary
state of a Narcissus-like search for his own counterpart, is "in vain": "Blasted
by his disappointment, he descends to an untimely grave." It is the poet's
"self-centered seclusion," then, that serves as the cautionary part of this tale:
"Those who love not their fellow-beings live unfruitful lives," for they have
embraced the "loneliness of the world" that will doom them.

Some Romantics choose a retreat from Society. In *La Vita Solitaria* (1821) Leopardi proclaims, in wistful and uncertain tones, his discouragement with the "black city walls where pain and hatred follow," choosing Nature, the "lonely place," where he might recapture peace. In England (and on the continent), solitude as alienation begins to take shape. In his apostrophe "O Solitude!" Keats also pleads that he *not* dwell "among the jumbled heap / Of murky buildings," but within Nature; yet, two years later, in the "Nightingale" Ode (1819), one senses a premonition that transcendence into Nature carries with it annihilation of Self. The chilling "to toll me back . . . to my sole self!" accentuates the ambivalence of "sole": his aloneness is cause to be "forlorn" but is also salvation from annihilating Nature. (Yeats, of course, was to learn a similar lesson from "Sailing to Byzantium.") Coleridge's Ancient Mariner's lament, "Alone, alone, all, all alone" is a gloss on much of his life and work, both weaving patterns of alienation. The Mariner's compulsive need to share his tale is fully parallel to his compelling need to be alone; but the eternal promptings to share his misery serve in large measure to insure that he suffers not alone but in company. His tale will change the listener's happy or carefree mood, a case of transference and transcendence of the Self: "at an uncertain hour, / That agony returns; / And till my ghastly tale is told, / This heart within me burns."

In that, the Mariner resembles the wanderer in Wilhelm Müller's *Winterreise* (put to song by Schubert) when, in the twelfth song, "Solitude," the bereft lover wanders through the desolate landscape alone, surrounded by the vibrancy of life. Only this wanderer has no one to share with: Alas, he complains, when it was stormy and the natural elements were more in tune with his sorrowful aloneness, he felt less pain than now, alone but surrounded by a world that goes on in its "happy" course, indifferent to his suffering.[44] The Mariner's Ego requires closure by fulfilling his aloneness with an Other's sharing; Müller's Wanderer has a bruised Ego, for the world is indifferent to his sorrow, as he sees himself as the unnoticed Icarus (as in Brueghel's painting). That, for Berdyaev, is the essential "contradiction" of Romantic solitude: Each Ego is "seeking communion with another Ego. . . . longs to find another Ego . . . who would identify himself with it and thus confirm it . . . in a word, reflect it."[45] Both figures are emblematic of Romanticism: the Mariner expresses the desperate need to relate; the Wanderer the inability to effect a response. The first is the not so secret sharer who anticipates Dostoyevsky's Raskolnikov and Kafka's Josef K. in *The Trial;* the second is frustrated and bitter, anticipating the men and women of Chekhov's plays and the early isolates of Thomas Mann.

A dark road map of solitude emerges in De Quincey's opium dreams; in *The Confessions of an English Opium Eater* and in the *Suspiria de Profundis,* he underlines that "all men come into this world *alone;* all leave it *alone.*" So the solitude we experience in the interval between birth and death (especially keenly felt as children) is on a continuum of a "deeper" solitude in the past and an even deeper one in the future, "reflex" and "prefiguration." Though solitude is a "burden" it is nevertheless "essential to man," for in the end it connects him to God:

> O burden of solitude . . . O mighty and essential solitude that wast, and art, and art to be, thou kindling under the torch of Christian revelations, art now trans-figured forever and hast passed from a blank negation into a secret hieroglyphic from God, shadowing in the hearts of infancy the very dimmest of his truths![46]

Confounded by the city in *The Prelude* and elsewhere, Wordsworth appears to make his peace with solitude, but again Nature is not merely a quieting but a *dis*quieting experience. Seeking pastoral peace, Wordsworth's need for Other is debated in poems like "Tintern Abbey," where his sister's presence as memory countervails the solitude of revisiting. In most of his dealings with solitude, one finds the "two-fold discovery of wonder and of solitary fear."[47] Still, Wordsworth was in search of what one critic calls "*solitude of identity,*" and despite ambiguities, that search led him to Nature: "It was to counter the city's threat of melting and reducing by restoring the identity of the individual that solitude became an ideal." "*Solitude of alienation,*" on the other hand, "looks into the abyss," and here the reference is no longer to the English Romantics but to *The Brothers Karamazov.*[48] In any case the Solitary's tale of woe in *The Excursion,* though sympathetic, is melancholy and unnurturing.

But it is Byron whose portrait of solitude as alienation will last for generations, although in some instances he still pays homage to the pain of solitude: "The worst of woes," he writes in *Childe Harold's Pilgrimage,*" is to see all our own dead "[a]nd be alone on earth, as I am now." Again, in the same poem, "'Tis solitude should teach us how to die." However, the Byron of *Manfred* and the Turkish Tales creates the Cain-like solitary who exemplifies the misanthropic prototype, severed from Society, either by voluntary or involuntary exile, "Cursed from the earth . . . / A fugitive and vagabond on earth" *(Cain).* Brooding, mysterious, disaffected, this unhappy hero, the son of Goethe's Werther, Chateaubriand's René, and Constant's Adolphe becomes the father of Pushkin's Eugene Onegin, Lermontov's Pechorin, Turgenev's Bazarov and, by mid-nineteenth century, Dostoyevsky's Underground Man, who in turn inaugurates a second phase in the parentage of the classic moderns. For a time there are two strands to this type: the self-exiled wanderer who takes on the risks of the forest, and the banished prowler of cities (Byron's Cain), whose acute isolation in the crowd surpasses anything Bacon or Defoe could imagine. The nineteenth century's gradual shift of the solitary experience from Nature to City also accelerates in Poe (whose "Man of the

Crowd" was perhaps a defining piece), Dostoyevsky, Dickens, and in the perambulations of Baudelaire's *flâneur,* whose most extreme caricature is part of the portrayal of Proust's Marcel in the latter sections of *Swann's Way.* As the solitary urban prowler becomes ubiquitous, the *event* of solitude enters a new and harrowing phase.

"Alienation"—a new form of often self-imposed exilic exclusion—first becomes codified in the misanthropic figures beyond Byron through the whole of the nineteenth century. However, Byron manages to create parallel states of solitude and alienation: the solitary was still capable of silent, sympathetic melancholy; the alienated side of the same persona was a defiant rebel. Byron's misanthropes were adventurers, specially marked for aloneness by some secret past, some enormous transgression. As we move into mid-century the characterization of this state changes. One still finds disaffection, rebelliousness, or indifference—narcissistic misanthropy. Society emerges not merely as a way of life from which one retires, but as an object of hostility, something to oppose. Alienation is identified with the Hegelian "self-consciousness" that effects an almost unbreachable division between persona and Society. And, of course, Marx's impact on the perception of an alienated humanity becomes perceptibly visible, as will Freud's command to plumb our inner, most hidden sanctuaries. From the defiance of Byron's Manfred to the indifferent criminality of Wilde's Dorian Gray, from the sulking self-lacerating isolation of Goethe's Werther, through the bizarre characters in Poe, Baudelaire, Huysmans, Conrad and the early Thomas Mann ever shifting patterns emerge. Solitude serves increasingly as a base camp to ascending deeds (and some are criminal), striking out *against* an enemy: solitude has now lost some of the tension between isolation and the need to connect. Rather, the problem of solitude reinvents itself to become a self-imposed retreat from whose relative safety the solitary feels compelled to carry out a guerilla warfare fueled by rage and disillusionment. "When I have succeeded in inspiring universal horror and disgust," wrote Baudelaire, "I shall have conquered solitude"[49]—surely anticipating Meursault's image of his beheading in the final paragraphs of *The Stranger.* But the Underground Man, certainly an equal in disgust to Baudelaire, writes, "In the end I could not put up with it [isolation]: with the years a craving for society, for friends, developed in me."

High Modernism and the Self: Face to Face

As we cross over into the twentieth century, solitude becomes increasingly synonymous with what will evolve as modernist alienation. In the process it loses some of its aggressive character and turns into the obsessive, self-absorbing loneliness of Proust's Marcel, Joyce's Dedalus and Bloom, Mann's Aschenbach and the characters that inhabit so many of the classic modern novels of the twentieth century. In a mode of reverie, partly reminiscent of Rousseau, solitude now often ends in sheer suffering; and while at times still self-imposed, one observes a return of the tension between the suffering to be endured by the solitary and his or her desire for its resolution in some return to the world. Whereas Romantic solitude often accented a sentimentalizing *Weltschmerz,* suicidal, and seemingly indifferent to the world,[50] the modern strives to rid solitude of any sentimentality. That does not mean minimizing the solitary's pain; on the contrary, suffering becomes so intense it can often no longer be felt.

Sartre and Camus may be the most obvious examples: In *Nausea, The Stranger,* and *The Fall,* the solitude and isolation of their neo-Cartesian protagonists make them at times cry out for release, if not reconciliation, and their alienation is more a state of self-definition than abnegation, more ablution than rebellion. As much as postmodernism has stamped its mark on our perceptions with its insistence on indeterminacy, Modernism offered visions with resolute certainty, even when, perhaps paradoxically, such visions were of a fragmented, lost, and *unattainable* world. Romantic landscapes, often absent of humans, or humans dwarfed by mountainous terrain (Caspar David Friedrich is a good example[51]), contrasts sharply with, say, the paintings of Francis Bacon, Thomas Eakins, or Edward Hopper where people dominate—alone or in company—but fail to connect.

An avowed opponent of Wittgenstein's *Tractatus Logico-Philosophicus* (1922)—"a poem to solitude"—Ernest Gellner identifies two opposing visions inherited from the Cartesian heritage: the atomistic and the organic. In the atomistic vision, the "solitary individual [is] a foreigner in his own world, separating him from it, requiring him to assert his independence. . . ." On the other hand, in the organic vision, "[m]an cannot act on his own, but only when sustained by and interacting with other participants. . . . The ideas of a culture . . . of an ongoing community, work through him." For Gellner, modern "[a]tomistic individualism" is "culture-corrosive," for it "makes the world less habitable, more cold and alien." The British empiricists, culminating in Hume, brought the "atomistic vision" to its flowering before a countervision—the organic—emerged in the Romantics. Yet there remained a conflict between atomistic "individualism" within the larger construct of society and "communalism" (English does not possess the subtle distinction between the German *Gesellschaft* [society] and *Gemeinschaft* [community].) And Gellner claims that "tension . . . pervades and torments" modernized societies—the "great confrontation of rationalistic individualism and romantic communalism. . . ." Romanticism, Gellner proposes, replaced the *"universal"*

with the *"specific"* and the *"calculating"* with the *"passionate."* But the "patho-genic" nature of "rootlessness" led eventually to xenophobic racism.

Such a view is provocative, for it challenges our way of viewing modern solitude: if the solitary adheres to an unrelenting vision of self-sufficiency, he becomes, however unwittingly, himself a member of an "icy, individualistic Society." In this sense "Solitude may well be overdetermined" and "[c]osmic exile" leads to "cultural exile," directing us into Wittgenstein's "dreary world—his *"Entfremdung-effekt."* For what Wittgenstein omits is the "ambi-guity" (not to be confused with relativism) that allows for intellectual/emo-tional (if not moral) flexibility. Solitude is less rigid than a mere withdrawal into intellectual autism. Gellner finds both the atomistic and the organic views unacceptable: the first leads to arrogant and illusory self-sufficiency; the second, considering the isolated individual as a "pathological abstraction," views life a "team game." Therefore, the challenge to us is to recognize the tension between the two views and work toward some form of "co-existence," for we have moved into a new, transitional "single society" that cannot ac-commodate either self-sufficiency (which Gellner throughout his study calls the "Crusoe model") or communality in their pure form. Since Gellner never completed this volume (it was assembled and posthumously published by his son), the conclusions are vague. Still, the analysis is clear and confirms once more that the tension between isolation from and interaction with some form of humanness remains the essential dilemma of solitude itself.[52]

Quoting from Balzac's *The Inventor's Suffering,* Erich Fromm cites a pas-sage to which several other commentators on the solitary condition have re-ferred: "'man has a horror for aloneness. And of all kinds of aloneness, moral aloneness is the most terrible.'"[53] The passage attracts because it has a pointed meaning for modernists. Although Dostoyevsky virtually adopted the dilemma of "moral aloneness" as his obsession, and Kierkegaard, Niet-zsche, and others of the nineteenth century continued to explore it, it is in the twentieth century that "moral aloneness" becomes, in its most generous definition, the critical pivot in the debate about solitude, whether such aloneness was that of the solitary or of a whole culture, as in Gabriel Garcia Marquez's *One Hundred Years of Solitude.* Zarathustra begins his ascent of the mountain by abandoning Society for solitude, the "good" solitude:

> Flee . . . into your solitude! . . . Where solitude ceases the market place begins; and where the market place begins the noise of the great actors and the buzzing of the poisonous flies begins too. . . . Flee . . . into your solitude! You have lived too close to the small and the miserable. Flee their invisible revenge![54]

In a similar vein, he had railed against the "vengeance" of the small-minded—"these petty vengeful people": "Do we not occasionally deny the existence of the sun and sky merely because we have not seen them for so long?" For this Nietzsche offers a single response: "—Well then, solitude! because of this, solitude!"[55]

When solitude as theme virtually overpowers modernist literature in all genres, the ambiguities of the modern solitary state assume a new dimension. For the paradox of seeking and regretting solitude in modernist works is no mere continuation of what preceded. In earlier articulations, the double bind—however much its characteristics might differ—was clearly marked out; Modernists, adding irony and paradox to all things, add it also to their experience of solitude. These ironies and paradoxes clarify the special aspects of the solitude-problematic that marks High Modernism, a culminating, unique time in which solitude becomes the premise for an often autobiographical debate between author and work and author and reader.

What defines modernist solitude? The solitary no longer merely refuses Society to embrace, say, Nature, but rejects Society *and* Nature, an act that forces an inevitable confrontation with the Self, whose consequences are devastating. The nineteenth-century *Doppelgänger*—who informs so much of the literature of European Romanticism to the end of the century—represents the first extended attempt to deal fictionally with the phenomenon of the Self's multiplicity. For modernists, the doubling device to create alter egos would eventually seem simplistic, artificial, naive, but for E. T. A. Hoffmann, Kleist, Poe, Gogol, Dostoyevsky, Stevenson, and Wilde (to name a few), the creation of two opposing selves was a breakthrough solution, permitting them to pit two personas against each other, each expressing a challenging moral vision. When these two selves squared off in the ultimate confrontation, the moral issue would be joined with an emerging victor, either the "good" or the "bad" Self. If evil triumphed, the reader could still pity the 'good': the better William Wilson in Poe's story, the victimized Goldyakin in Dostoyevsky's *The Double,* and Dr. Jekyll, but not Mr. Hyde. With two selves in play, one is the object of dread, the other is the beneficiary of our compassion. Also, two selves provided a kind of comfort for each, however perverse, as one Self of the double was always reassured by the presence of the other: it provided "company."

In modernist fictions, however, when Self confronts Self, what emerges is a reductive, self-reflexive image that reinforces solitude, leaving a Self burdened with fear, with a sense of vulnerable mortality, or with disgust. Certainly Defoe's Crusoe confronts his Self, and he undergoes numerous moments of gloomy doubt, self-reproach, and even guilt. But in the end, Crusoe survives, not merely because of his ingenious and inventive mind, but because he really likes himself. Such indulgence of Self continues into the following century, even in tales of severe crisis when the Self is sternly tested. At the end of Poe's story, as the two William Wilsons are about to annihilate each other, the "good" Wilson sees his double as a "large mirror" that turns out to be no mirror at all, but his "own image" bloodied and wasted in its death throes. But when Sartre's Roquentin looks into his real mirror, he is overcome with nausea: There is no second Roquentin; Camus's Meursault, once in prison, is eventually abandoned and left to call forth the image of facing his death against the imagined picture of a hostile crowd, his mirror. Mann's Hans Castorp, looks into the fluoroscope machine, which mirrors his double in the truncated image of his hand, revealing not only the bones of death, but all the potential of disease; Lily Briscoe gazes at the empty canvas before her second attempt to paint Mrs. Ramsay, only to be forced first to confront herself, a Self toward which she feels little affection. The empty canvas prompts self-reflection. And Beckett's "I" in the trilogy is always trapped by reflections and refractions of the Self: There are no "Others," except those "puppets," whose creation is part of an ironic displacement game. This unrelenting experience of severance, where Self meets Self with no intermediary, replaces the *Doppelgänger*, intensifies the solitary existence of modernist personae, and empowers their sense of abandonment and exclusion that so characterizes modernist works. This constitutes their crisis. Pirandello's "Henry IV" only *acts* at being the old medieval king: what he lives throughout the play is his present, wasted and empty life.[56]

Consequences

So modern solitude evolves its shape from a paradox about the Self: The more the "I" is isolated, the more it searches out itself; and the more the "I" searches for itself, the more it needs isolation. Erich Fromm emphasizes that an acute sense of aloneness is exacerbated by a special form of self-consciousness, not unlike what Paz has identified as "awareness." With increasing independence gained from all "external authorities" (Fromm, of course, had in mind democratic societies), we have also inherited the consequences: "growing isolation" and with it increasing feelings of "insignificance and powerlessness."[57] As we fulfill Schopenhauer's *principium individuationis*, we may well be fulfilling his pessimistic vision as well, where we are free to be bound, where choice is all we have, and yet that choice is something we would rather not have at all. For all of Nietzsche's staring down Schopenhauer's fatalistic vision, in the end Sartre's "inauthenticity" and "bad conscience"—inevitable outcomes—are desperate prices to pay for the rootless freedom that leaves us so often with tragic choices. "Moral aloneness," then, becomes the equivalent of both choices made and not made: Camus's unnamed monologist in *The Fall* has an opportunity to save a life or to ignore the splash of the woman who plunges into the Seine. Having chosen the latter, he experiences the rest of his life unraveling, revealing other instances of "bad conscience." In *Doctor Faustus* (see Chapter IV), Thomas Mann's Adrian Leverkühn compacts with the devil for a life of musical genius; the price he concedes is that he shall forever forego the experience of love. But that choice is bitterly regretted when love, like a disease, attacks Leverkühn's sterile heart. Isaac Bashevis Singer was once asked whether he believed in free will, and his response, though witty, is a perfect expression of the modernist dilemma: Of course, he said, I have no choice. "Alienation," for modernists, becomes synonymous with solitude; alienation from God and Society is now trumped by a severance of Self from Self. But a stronger, more individual Self fails to materialize: the Self is unmoored, weakened into a state of immobility. The process was gradual. From Burton's *Anatomy of Melancholy* through the eighteenth century, melancholy and despair were no strangers; by the middle of the nineteenth century, however, the stakes were gradually raised. Baudelaire and the *symbolistes,* many of the major Russian writers, countless figures from the English 1880s and 90s, the early Thomas Mann—all of them prepared the way through their visions of the "dark night of the soul" for the ultimately paralytic state, the somnambulism, the condition of Self at war with itself or of Self subtracting from Self in a zero-sum game.

Perhaps no clearer example comes to mind than Beckett's disembodied voices, and in variously differing ways one finds earlier signs of such developments in Lawrence, Joyce, Mann, and Virginia Woolf. In some nascent Romantic expressions of the problematic Self in the nineteenth century, its travails were serious enough; but mostly the Self manages to hold together to attain recovery at dawn as in, say, the silence ("I cannot speak anymore") of "Morning," the penultimate section of Rimbaud's *Season in Hell* (1873). True, these recoveries may place the Self as survivor from night terrors back into a reality no less appealing, but they *do* manage to get back. Perhaps that is why R.M. Adams titled his book *Nil: Episodes in the Literary Conquest of Void During the Nineteenth Century.* "Conquest" at least implies some overcoming; eventually, even that will cease to be an option. In the nineteenth century, selves were still in the process of *remaking* themselves (Dostoyevsky refined the redemptive metamorphosis); in the twentieth, from the frozen tundra of what Hegel meant by *Geist,* they begin the process of *unmaking.* That unmaking is accompanied by a sense of helplessness exceeding desperation; "Things fall apart" not only cosmically but internally as the Self's center implodes like Poe's House of Usher. Confrontation is displaced by retreat, and solitude is transformed into an annihilating force. What was once melancholy and mournful advances into the realm of indifference, the expression of numbness that Hemingway excelled at, as in the conclusion of *A Farewell to Arms,* another instance where the hero forces himself to resist any feeling of loss.

Baudelaire's prose poem "Solitude" (1861) and an excerpt on the solitary from Rilke's *Notebooks of Malte Laurids Brigge* (1903–1910), provide a clear contrast. Baudelaire's caustic tone has all the *l'épater le bourgeoisie* that we have come to expect: he is defiant and challenging. On the other hand, Rilke's observations—though not without irony—while bitter are sad; defiance has given way to fated, inevitable acceptance. Both Baudelaire and Rilke ridicule the popular attitude that solitude is somehow aberrant, and both, of course, uphold the solitary's superior status. But whereas Baudelaire is dismissive of those who fear and reject the solitary—"I despise [them],"— Rilke is more focused on the hatred of the those engaged in despising. Baudelaire concludes with the triumph of solitude, Rilke more with the triumph of those who stand on its other side:

> 'Almost all our woes come from not being capable of remaining in our rooms' said . . . Pascal, I believe, by way of summoning to their meditative cells all the panic-stricken who seek happiness in movement and in a prostitution I could call *fraternitary* . . .
>
> (Baudelaire)
>
> They tracked [the solitary] to his hiding place, like a beast to be hunted. . . . And when [the solitary] would not listen, they . . . ate away his food and breathed out his air and spat into his poverty . . . [and] . . . cast stones at him to make him go away. . . . [H]e was indeed their foe. . . . They suspected . . . that they had fortified him in his solitude and helped him to separate himself from them for ever.
>
> (Rilke)[58]

While Rilke ends his passage with the suggestion that the lure of fame "distracted" both the solitary and those who hunted him, the major thrust of his commentary on the solitary prefigures Camus's Meursault of *The Stranger,* while Baudelaire, through his very combativeness, remains in touch with the revilers. Active hatred energizes and mobilizes attachment to the enemy hated; passive suffering, as Arnold and, after him, Yeats proposed is not a subject for poetry, by which they meant that inaction leads, quite literally, nowhere. It is a state that will come to define one central modernist condition, wherein, as Arnold said, "suffering finds no vent in action; in which a continual state of mental distress is prolonged, unrelieved by . . . resistance; in which there is everything to be endured, nothing to be done" (*Preface to Poems,* 1853)— those last four words echoing through Beckett, whose passive figures assume a new and different kind of rage. What Arnold could not yet anticipate is the modernist form of resistance beyond hopelessness and helplessness: "I can't go on, I will go on," are the final words of Beckett's *The Unnamable*. But the "will" in that sentence bears no resemblance to willpower or to Nietzschean will: it remains a passive will, a will with no choice, perhaps more like the cosmic will of Schopenhauer, except that it is now internalized. Eliot's line about the "patient etherised upon a table" was more prophetic than he realized, for so many modern protagonists tend to be numbed, as they become patients, at times—as in Mann—literally.

The man in Kafka's "Parable of the Law" (in *The Trial*) cannot get beyond waiting (for his own Godot); all his life is spent in a state of paralytic solitude standing in front of a gate until, when it is too late, he is told that the gate was open for him all the time, awaiting merely his choice to enter. Proust's Marcel cannot move beyond the past: When the future is before him he has ceased to write for us, and what lies ahead are the immobile states of remembering—like those of Beckett—that create the novel preceding the intent to write one. In describing *Dubliners,* Joyce himself aimed at a portrayal of stasis in what he called his "moral history," for he saw Dublin "as the centre of paralysis." In the major novels, D. H. Lawrence's characters are unable to "come through," and the personae in the fictions of Conrad and James are often ambushed by encounters with wishful alter egos. Thomas Mann's Castorp (*The Magic Mountain*) and his Leverkühn (*Doctor Faustus*) are lured and entrapped, respectively, into strangely immobile lives. Modernist solitude goes far beyond anxiety and nightmare: it not only annihilates motion, it retards and destroys emotion. When affect is arrested, when there is no road back to Society (Sartre's *No Exit*), when the ego is self-devouring, then we have reached a state of solitude beyond alienation—the state of silence.

In Hemingway's "Soldier's Home," when the returned soldier son is transfixed by the bacon fat "hardening on his plate," it is the prelude to his simple statement to his devastated mother, "'I don't love anybody.'" Of Septimus Warren Smith, the shell-shocked veteran in *Mrs. Dalloway,* Woolf writes, "he could not feel." This extinction of the affective source from within is in part the result of a new form of Cartesian division: "the Cartesian turn towards a reflexive model of consciousness, wherein the ego . . . is able to 'curl back' on itself by thinking upon itself as an object to itself."[59]

Differentiation between subject and object becomes increasingly difficult as the object becomes the subject (or vice versa). Such a neo-Cartesian state is, of course, a consequence not an aim, and we can see its outcomes—and the struggles against them—at the heart of Modernism in, for example, Conrad and Lawrence, Camus and Kafka, and, most notably, in Beckett. "The fear of loneliness," writes one commentator, "is a sickness that promotes dehumanization. . . . In the extreme, the person stops feeling altogether and tries to live solely by rational means and cognitive directions."[60]

Not all modernists create an immobilized protagonist, but even when there may be an attempt at defiant rebellion, reminiscent of the Romantics, the heavy price paid is always noted. Take Stephen Dedalus's famous last conversation with his friend Cranly, as Stephen explains his decision to exile himself, to sever himself from family, religion, and country in *A Portrait of the Artist as a Young Man* (begun about the same time as Rilke's *Notebooks*):

> — . . . I do not fear to be alone or to be spurned . . . Cranly . . . said:—Alone, quite alone. You have no fear of that. And you know what that word means? Not only to be separate from all others but to have not even one friend.
> —I will take the risk, said Stephen.

And risk it is. For we know from *Ulysses* that Stephen Dedalus's rupture has cost him pain and guilt: "Agenbite of inwit. Inwit's agenbite. Misery! Misery!" Stephen is incomplete and his search for a father is, in the end, a search for reintegration.

≈ ≈ ≈

Philosophers, theologians, sociologists, and psychologists continue their attempts to deal with solitude (or aloneness, alienation, isolation, estrangement) and, at times, to make distinctions that seek out ameliorating resolutions. While many have found it impossible to separate, say, loneliness from solitude, Paul Tillich searches for a way to differentiate them: "our language has sensed . . . two sides of man being alone. It has created the word 'loneliness' in order to emphasize the pain of being alone. And it has created the word 'solitude' in order to emphasize the glory of being alone." Yet even Tillich does not underrate the difficulties of solitude, for he sees the state where "[w]e meet ourselves, not as ourselves, but as the battlefield of creation and destruction"; "Solitude," he concludes, "is not easy" (not even Jesus was exempt from struggling with it). Only "love" and the spiritual permit us to overcome the terror of aloneness, "to face the eternal, to find others, to see ourselves."[61] Another student of solitude remarks epigrammatically that "[t]he only individuals who crave solitude are those who are not condemned to it," adding that there is a distinction between "loneliness anxiety," which is pathological and "existential loneliness," which is not. The "self-conscious awareness of isolation" yields the existential terrors found in modernists, from Dostoyevsky through Hesse.[62]

Embedded in the concept of solitude is an antinomy that defines modernist texts: In all those examined here, an internal struggle emerges, often between the obsessive urge to attain solitude being undone by the equally obsessive urge to break out of solitude and connect with some version of

Other, singly or collectively. Characters are whiplashed from longing for solitude to longing to escape its finality: they want to be alone; they need to be with others. As cases of animal-raised human children have shown, they appear to be unique among species, unable to grow into human adults without human company. Arnold, echoing Milton, wrote, "Ah! two desires toss about / The poet's feverish blood; / One desires him to the world without, / And one to Solitude." Or as Yeats teasingly wrote, "I have found nothing half so good / As my long-planned half solitude."

This account of solitude falls far short of revealing all the complexities of change that underlie the multiple perspectives from which solitude has been viewed and the significant moments when shifting attitudes brought momentous changes to the argument. Obviously the problematic of solitude continues to be interrogatory. Despite what appears to be a certain common approach to solitude from the eighteenth century to modernist fiction, questions remain. What becomes of the connotation of solitude? Is the condition a negative experience with its own psychological economics of rewards? Can those rewards ever be affirming to mind and spirit or, quite the contrary, does modern solitude at last sever us from Society, alienating us from the human, causing us any number of ill effects, ranging from melancholia to near-suicidal misanthropy? Questions beget still more questions, until solitude, initially perhaps a simple word to describe a well-known condition, emerges as a complicated designation describing a multitude of conditions, some coexisting in what seem contradictory postures.

In *Robinson Crusoe,* Defoe is the first to respond, in a coherent sequence, to nearly all these questions by creating an eighteenth-century *débat.* In this extraordinary novel, Defoe endows his protagonist with all the cunning and self-doubt necessary for a rich depiction of ambiguity of attitude toward solitude. Crusoe's isolation is involuntary, since he does not will his own shipwreck (though, it has been argued, his irresponsible actions invite it, and Crusoe himself suggests this); but once on the island he makes choices that eventually generate a debate with himself. How that debate plays itself out is a benchmark—whether in similitude or contrast—for all subsequent novels of solitude, especially those of the modernists.

Chapter II ~

Discourse With Oneself
and The Solitude of Place:
Robinson Crusoe

I argu'd with my self . . .

—*Robinson Crusoe*

The feeling of solitude . . . is a longing for place.

—Octavio Paz, *The Labyrinth of Solitude*

. . . it was possible I might have been more happy in this Solitary Condition, than I should have been in a Liberty of Society . . .

—*Robinson Crusoe*

Virginia Woolf's essays and reviews on English fiction are particularly astute, and most of her observations hit the mark with exceptional accuracy. However, on Defoe's *Robinson Crusoe* she appears to have misfired, and what is of interest is not that she did but how and why. One reason clearly was her relentless, almost irrational, fear of realism as embodying the destructive power that ruined fiction and threatened its future. Her dismissive comments on the Edwardians are well known, but with Defoe she was taking on a classic, and somehow she meant her essay to celebrate rather than condemn the novel's realism. That proved not so easily achieved; she devised an elaborate rear-guard maneuver, with such hesitations and rationalizations that it is clear Woolf was almost fearful of her own strategy. Whether one reads the first version in *Essays* or the somewhat more toned-down version in *The Common Reader,* Second Series, an uncomfortable feeling emerges that—because she is self-consciously dealing with a "classic"—Woolf is coercing herself into praise of a method she may have admired in Defoe but toward which she felt an innate antipathy.

Woolf concedes that *Crusoe* is a "masterpiece" because Defoe consistently adhered to his "perspective"—describing physical objects with a sense of intimacy. But the tale of a single man on an island in "peril and solitude . . . is enough to arouse in us the expectation" of sublime visions of nature, of metaphysical ponderings about the nature of humankind and God. Yet as we read we are rudely "contradicted"; Defoe offers no sunrises or sunsets of grandeur: "there is no solitude, no soul. There is nothing . . . but a large earthenware pot . . . reality, fact, substance. . . ." For Woolf, Defoe had no choice; he assumes a role "opposite" that of the psychologist by describing the "effects of emotions on the body, not on the mind." To be sure, the unerring focus on that earthenware pot forces us to "see remote islands and the solitudes of the human souls," but this is not the 'universal' of the 'concrete universal,' the generalized souls, not the soul of Robinson Crusoe. In the final sentence of her essay Woolf asks rhetorically: should not Defoe's perceptive rendering of reality arouse us as much as some figure standing in "all his sublimity" against some grandeur-filled landscape?[1]

However, this is not an altogether convincing defense of the very kind of realism she had roundly condemned not only in "Mr. Bennett and Mrs. Brown" (1924) but in countless utterances throughout her life and in the writing of her own novels. What Woolf *does* admire in *Crusoe* is its singleness of goal and its consistency of method. Surely she fails to see the solitude of soul so often in evidence in Robinson Crusoe's various crises, although just as clearly these are not (and there she is right) displayed in sublime expressions. For Defoe, Romantic Weltschmerz or modernist existential crises are not yet an appropriate postures for fiction. Michael Seidel, in perhaps the happiest combination of words, calls Defoe's style "subjective realism" and develops a strong case for its psychological subtlety.[2]

This chapter addresses Woolf's assertion that in *Robinson Crusoe* "there is no solitude, no soul. There is nothing but . . . [r]eality, fact, substance." Professional critics have sometimes responded in similar fashion, or they have offered up a variety of readings of *Crusoe* in which solitude is explained—or explained away—by means of various arguments ranging from theological to allegorical. Crusoe's solitude was both real, if totally *un*realistic, and full of psychological implications of ambivalence and ambiguity.

1

Few works have proven to be both so popular and problematic as Defoe's *Robinson Crusoe* (1719). Ian Watt believes that the novel "falls most naturally into place . . . with the great myths of Western civilization . . . a single-minded pursuit by the protagonist. . . ."[3] Because of its eventual popularity as a children's adventure story, it has commanded (like *Gulliver's Travels,* published in near proximity [1726]) serious attention as an adult work relatively late. Recently a critic writes that *Crusoe* "has remained one of Europe's central texts for nearly four [*sic*] centuries."[4] As an adventure and travel book, *Crusoe* has been the source for many imitations and spin-offs, especially in German (*Robinsonaden*) and French and English ("Robinsonades").[5] Defoe's novel has also often been regarded, even by serious readers, as a fine instance of individual ingenuity and as a primer for survival skills. But the embracing question, still asked as late as 1971 by the British biographer and critic of Defoe, James Sutherland, turns on this issue: "Is *Robinson Crusoe* a simple story of adventure, or has it a deeper significance?" though Sutherland recognizes as essential to the novel Crusoe's "loneliness and anguish,"[6] clearly pointing to "deeper significance." (Sutherland's view of "significance" tends to center on the theological issues). The reply to Sutherland's question begins to be implicitly answered in the nineteenth century when *Crusoe* was paid some serious attention, though it is true that not until mid-twentieth century has Defoe's novel invited the kind of scrutiny reserved for adult canonical works. As recently as 1990 Martin Green, in *The Robinson Crusoe Story,* still believes that taking *Crusoe* too seriously as a novel has hindered our appreciation of it as adventure story: "*Robinson Crusoe* tells the story of how a solitary castaway makes a desert island into a happy home."[7] But a year later, Michael Seidel, in *Robinson Crusoe: Island Myths and the Novel,* insists (and correctly so, certainly for the English novel) that "[n]o matter what talk there is of the forbears of the novel, very little reads like a novel until Defoe develops the form beginning with *Crusoe*. . . ." Seidel, following the first reading Ian Watt renders in *The Rise of the Novel,* places *Crusoe* into the Western mythic pattern, its literary trope of the island invoking a familiar theme.[8] A provocative suggestion is offered by a critic who has written extensively on the social and psychiatric aspects of loneliness: "I should like to suggest . . . that it would be . . . illuminating to consider *Robinson Crusoe* as exemplifying the powerful existentialist theme of human solitude . . . ," a position that to some degree is accepted in this chapter.[9] So both with respect to placement and interpretation, *Robinson Crusoe* has spawned a variety of problematic issues, and they have surrounded the novel for nearly three centuries.

Is *Crusoe* the first English novel? Is it a novel at all? Is it a credible story? And there are also some specific points of contention: Crusoe as representation of practical, or natural, man; as allegorical figure of the Prodigal Son; as mythic figure of exile; as redeemed sinner—there are many more. Some of these general and specific problems raised by the novel will be addressed, but the emphasis remains on Crusoe's ambiguous (and ambivalent) state of solitude. What apparently has attracted recent critics is what one has called the novel's "contradictions": "the contradictions in *Crusoe* are basic to the human predicament—the hunger for solitude and the fear of isolation; the worship of individual striving and the desire for social order. . . ."[10] In the twentieth century this duality of *Crusoe* has continued to fuel a variety of approaches to the novel, creating a number of fine-tuned themes in a variety of directions. It is not easy, therefore, to divide neatly the modern responses to *Crusoe* into those that celebrate Crusoe's individual entrepreneurship and those that focus on his rupture from the social fabric—his solitude and his religious conversion as a "solution" to it—or those who read it as spiritual allegory. The following section attempts to identify some of the principal responses to *Robinson Crusoe* in the twentieth century that recognize the importance of Crusoe's prolonged solitude as a measure of the novel's meaning. Such preparation clears the page for an analysis of Crusoe's solitude as it figures in the design of the present study.

2

Contemporaries, of course, were quick to comment on *Crusoe,* the book being immensely popular and a work about which most writers of the age felt compelled to speak out, whether in praise or criticism. Pope admired *Crusoe,* Rousseau deemed it the only worthy novel for the education of his Emile, and Dr. Johnson bracketed it with *Don Quixote* and *Pilgrim's Progress.* In the next century, Coleridge, Wordsworth, Poe, De Quincey, and Hazlitt were struck by the novel's universality. Some noteworthy detractors spoke out, among them Dickens, Macaulay, and Virginia Woolf's father, the humorless Leslie Stephen, who was among the first to call *Crusoe* "singularly wanting as a psychological study," "a book for boys rather than men," though he grudgingly concedes that it had some value "to have pleased all the boys in Europe for near a hundred and fifty years. . . ."[11]

Controversy has causes, and in this instance one cause for such mixed reactions is surely that *Crusoe* is unique as a work of fiction. For virtually the entire novel, Defoe is limited to *one* voice, one persona without the help of any other voices. In most first person narratives such other voices are at least reported—and recorded—if not always in direct speech. (Camus's *The Fall* reads like a monologue, but the narrator answers questions put to him by an interlocutor, so there is an inferred presence of a second person.) *Crusoe* is restricted to one narrative voice because for most of the novel he is alone, and this solitariness created a substantive strategic problem (and perhaps an underrated challenge) for Defoe the novelist. There are a few early references in the novel to Crusoe's conversations with his father (later these simply become memories), but once Crusoe is shipwrecked as sole survivor some 30 odd pages into the novel, other humans literally disappear until more than two decades have passed and Friday emerges. It is only by creating a *débat,* by erecting a Bakhtinian "dialogic" structure for the novel, that Defoe rescues it from stasis.

In fact, Defoe creates a Crusoe who debates himself in what Bakhtin called an "Ich-Erzählung"; and from this debate arise several voices— Bakhtin's "polyphonic" orchestration. Crusoe is by turns pessimistic and optimistic, apprehensive and content, arrogant and contrite, practical and grandiose, secular and religiously repentant, free and guilt-ridden. And, of course, above all he wavers between being a happy solitary and a despondent castaway pining for human society. All these opposing pairings form the structural connections that both advance the narrative and keep it cohesive. One should not underestimate Defoe's novelistic problem, nor should we minimize how he compounded it by having his protagonist remain a solitary for nearly a quarter of a century. Obviously the longer the event of solitude without any opportunity of interaction, the more urgent the problem of sustaining its interest. Just to take a measure, Crusoe is alone more than ten times longer than Thoreau is in Walden—and after all, we know Thoreau was not really always a solitary.

Walter de la Mare identified the critical conundrum of *Crusoe* earlier than most professional critics. If, he wrote bluntly in 1930, " . . . Defoe had really faced . . . the problem set in *Crusoe* his solution could not have been in that book's precise terms." Admiring as he is, he wonders what a more "creative imagination" might have made of the Crusoe story "if the attempt had been made to reveal what a prolonged unbroken solitude, an absolute exile from his fellow-creatures, and an incessant commerce with silence and the unknown, would mean at last to the spirit of man." After all, he argues, Defoe opens the terrain: "What *is* this being alone, this condition we call solitude . . . affecting both mind and spirit . . . [?]" De la Mare subjects the problem to his own musings. For example, he wonders about the "the demon of the ego-centric" that can overtake the self in solitude; and indeed, he asks, can one really be totally alone, totally a "nought"? Well, a "sort of nought," he responds, "but one which . . . could not but still be pining for some strange inscrutable presence to slip in before that cipher, and make of its nothing all."[12] In short, nothing is something. De la Mare has certainly proposed the questions that Defoe's work invites. Whether his seeming disappointment with the lack of what might be called in shorthand Defoe's "inner self" is justified quite in the terms presented (a lack of "creative imagination") is open to debate.

Ian Watt complains that Defoe has "disregarded two important facts: the social nature of all human economics, and the actual psychological effects of solitude."[13] As for the first of these "facts," one might insist that Crusoe had little choice; as for the second, Watt misses the essential tension between solitude and Society that forms the connective tissue of the novel and supplies it with ample "psychological effect." Seidel makes the case for *Crusoe's* psychological insights: he emphasizes Defoe's deliberate effort to create a human who will need to decipher the problems of "the psychology of everyday island life": "island space is . . . the map of Crusoe's mind. . . ."[14] Certainly, Defoe did not lack "creative imagination"; insofar as was possible for him at the time, he was fully aware of what he was *not* doing with Crusoe's inner mind. Nor did such probing suit his purpose, and it was certainly not characteristic of eighteenth-century prose fiction to tunnel one's way (Virginia Woolf's metaphor) into the consciousness of the character and to plumb the depths of that person's inner Self. Crusoe's nature is singularly private, so that he reveals as much to us as to himself. Baudelaire played with the issue of solitude in his prose poem, "Solitude": "No question that a chatterbox, whose supreme pleasure consists in speaking from the heights of a pulpit or a forum, would certainly risk going raving mad on Robinson's island." "Perhaps," he concludes, "solitude is dangerous only for idle and wandering souls who populate it with their passions and chimeras"—more true of Crusoe than many have been willing to acknowledge. So it can be argued that Defoe succeeded in meeting some of De la Mare's objections if we take careful note of other ways in which Crusoe's mind is laid bare, namely to pursue further how Crusoe's attitude toward his state of solitude shifts throughout his "island time" to give us ample evidence of his ambiguous and ambivalent, and ever-changing evaluation both of himself and his island "captivity." Once we understand Crusoe's variable sense of place on this patch of land he often calls his "home," we can better understand the novel's remarkably dialogic shape. For Crusoe's island exile, prohibiting conversation for nearly three decades leads to an enforced dialogue with himself and the reader—and, of course, at one point, with God.

Place becomes a physical and psychological habitat: At first Crusoe moves from one to the other with ease, until he realizes how his physical surroundings—the island itself—radically alter and shape his moods. After that, his movements from inner place to exploring outer place are wary, as suspicion and fear prompt caution, disturbing and eventually destroying his feelings of peace. Not until the end of the novel is Crusoe able to reconnect that sense of objectivity where outer and inner place coexist in a state of mutual accommodation; but there is also a recognition that subjective mind is master of the objective world only when it respects that world's indifference and potential for destroying, not only the mind, but the whole being.

Allegorical readings of the novel are encouraged by Defoe's invocation of "allegory" in *Serious Reflections* to describe one level of his work. J. Paul Hunter reads *Crusoe* as "spiritual biography," as a "pilgrim allegory, the tale of the Prodigal who "sails away" from home, is "isolated from God," and then delivered. For such a reading the island serves as "both punishment and potential salvation." Alienation from the world equals alienation from God, and Hunter cites Puritan religious works "full of metaphors of loneliness and isolation" that elucidate the "disruption of communication between God and man in a post-lapsarian world." Hunter's reading casts Crusoe's plight as a paradigm of the Protestant Ethic—the severance of humanity from God as "a result of his sin." Still Hunter rejects those interpretations that deprive Crusoe of introspection, and he makes a case for "Crusoe's search for understanding" as "both introspective and self-analytical" when viewed in its historical context. Crusoe's introspection is necessarily retrospective since the whole experience (except perhaps the Journal) is told by one who has survived 36 years of exile, nearly two and a half decades of these in solitude, severed from any human (he rescues Friday in his 25th year on the island).[15]

A number of Hunter's successors, with some refinement, have read *Crusoe* as a novel of imprisonment and spiritual deliverance. For example, Daniel Blewett sees Crusoe's island exile as both punishment and preparation for ablution. So solitude, this deliberate break with Society, is brought on by Crusoe's "obstinacy and blindness": "the island expresses the central paradox of the novel . . . [it is] . . . 'imprisonment' and 'deliverance'. . . ." Also the footprint in the sand acts as a dividing boundary between Crusoe's solitude and his "return to the world," which occupies the latter half of the novel.[16] Whether such a return occurs (notwithstanding the two volumes of sequels) is debatable, but redemptive readings are not scarce. G. A. Starr's title—*Defoe's Spiritual Autobiography*—signals his reading of *Crusoe* as a parable of sin and redemption. In fact he interprets solitude as a deliberate reflection of the religious teachings of the time: "[S]olitude has special compensations for those who realize that they are never out of the presence of God"[17]—a state hardly applicable to Crusoe.

Although Crusoe experiences a conversion episode on the island, rigidly allegorical readings limit the novel's dimensions and inhibit a more generous perspective of Crusoe's continual conflicts. Michael McKeon's history of the

English novel offers a more sophisticated reading of Crusoe's "spiritual autobiography" with "dynamic" tensions between "journal and narrative, Character and Narrator." Crusoe's conversion is considered an enabling spiritualization of his plight to keep his balance and compensatory to his severance from Society. Moreover, Crusoe's success in his various labors confirms his "sense of election" because the "neutralization of its social volatility has been ensured by his utter solitude." McKeon also conceives Crusoe's journey as leading him from conversion to God and back to human society, a "hard-won lesson" that demonstrates that the "metaphysical realm of the spirit may be accommodated and rendered accessible as the psychological realm of the Mind."[18] That, it seems, is for McKeon the major achievement of *Crusoe*—the capaciousness of the story that permits its protagonist to wander uninhibited and virtually unimpeded from realm to realm through the thickets of the human experience. Solitude is as liberating on one level as it is restrictive on another.

Such an approach is common to several other critics, especially Pat Rogers, who believes that we "admire Crusoe for what he achieves *in spite* of loneliness." Rogers traces the theme of loneliness in the eighteenth century, its inheritance of the medieval and Renaissance obsession as to the merits of the "[c]ontemplative ways of life" and the Horatian ideal of exiling oneself from the corrupt influences of the city. This, in turn, leads to what Rogers considers "the heart of the novel"—the "desire to conceal the self, to erase traces of one's being."[19] Once he sees the footprint, Crusoe's desire to conceal himself has perhaps been overly psychologized: the event of coming upon the footprint occurs about halfway through the novel and halfway through Crusoe's stay on the island. Crusoe seems able to adjust himself to the prudent and preemptive self-concealment just as he was eager to seek out the adventures on the high seas, both before and after the shipwreck. On the practical level Crusoe becomes a farmer and hunter to survive, and his curtailment of exploration is less concealment and more precaution. E. M. W. Tillyard places *Crusoe* more in the arena of epic than novel. Sympathetic to the Prodigal Son theme, Tillyard also emphasizes the spiritual travail of Crusoe, his movement toward "spiritual rehabilitation." For Tillyard, Crusoe is "Everyman, abounding in Original Sin . . . yet one of the Elect . . . to be saved through chastisement."[20] These spiritual-allegorical readings are, one suspects, a direct response to Ian Watt's early reading of *Crusoe* as a manifest document of capitalist triumph and ingenuity over both Nature and Fortune:

> *Robinson Crusoe* falls most naturally into place . . . with the great myths of Western civilization. . . . a single-minded pursuit by the protagonist of one of the characteristic desires of Western man . . . a *hubris,* an exceptional prowess . . . he can manage quite on his own . . . [with his] inordinate egocentricity [which] condemns him to isolation. . . . [21]

Perhaps this in part explains Joyce's attentiveness to *Crusoe,* having in mind *The Odyssey* and the Homeric hero with whom Crusoe has some qualities in common: courage, wiliness, cunning—and a streak of *hubris.* Seidel identifies Joyce's fascination with *Crusoe* as the way Joyce saw the novel— "a radical experiment in narrative-mythic form: myth located in the bedrock of physical space and local artifact."[22] In his more recent appraisal of *Crusoe,* Ian Watt, while expanding on his reading of *Crusoe* as "myth," still clings to Crusoe's "economic individualism," which he had stressed in *The Rise of the Novel.* Now, however, he enriches his reading by adding two new elements. First he pays more attention to the spiritual motifs of the story, particularly the conversion episode—though he is unconvinced that it is lasting. Second, he credits the popularity of the novel neither to its economic nor its spiritual themes, but to the "mythic power" of the Crusoe saga, "the universal appeal of solitude . . . to the imagination" and to the process of how Crusoe becomes a "model . . . in how he learns to manage his desolated state." Watt never fully develops this appeal of solitude, and the "desolated state" leads him back to his original view of Crusoe as an exploitative master imbued with "rational [and material] self-interest" who owns two slaves, Xury and Friday. Such a position, Watt writes somewhat wryly, is not "uncritically egocentric, and . . . flourishes exceptionally well on a desert island."[23]

In two critical studies, 20 years apart, Maximillian Novak offers more balanced views. In the first he stresses not Crusoe's self-interested individualism but his natural and perpetual fear in the throes of his solitude. The "freedom and purity" of the island are "minor advantages compared to the comfort and security of civilization." Moreover, Crusoe's fear is activated not merely by the normal terrors consistent with being abandoned by all fellow-creatures but by the realization of the potential of "bestiality" in humanity. Novak rejects the portrait of the "'economic superman'" and reminds us how much the eighteenth century emphasized "man . . . [as] a social animal," drawing (perhaps too eagerly) on Defoe's negative remarks about solitude in *Serious Reflections.* Crusoe, he asserts, is only "occasionally content with his isolation," aware of the deficits of "the state of nature" and the urgency of "social intercourse" with all the security such relationship with Society bestows.[24] Intent on countering the image of the happy Rousseauean savage, Novak may overemphasize Crusoe's fear of solitude and underplay the long periods when Crusoe is genuinely content with his island isolation. Though difficult to quantify, the tension between contentment with solitary life and the yearning for human society is sufficient to balance the central structural foundation of the novel. Twenty years later Novak has refined his views. Conceding that Crusoe's triumph of nearly subduing the island is "mostly an economic conquest," he now also sees it as an "imaginative conquest" of a "mythic figure," a "visionary realist." Crusoe emerges as one who "*half* believes" (italics mine) that his island "provides him with a greater contentment than he ever met in his former life." Novak acknowledges that Crusoe is "occasionally content" with his isolation, but that the state of nature remains an anxiety-ridden existence and that without "social intercourse" life is neither happy nor secure.[25]

In any case, the tendency to choose sides in interpreting *Crusoe* has remained a constant. One critic identifies the "The Crusoe Theory" as an assertion that *Crusoe* encourages the misconception that we are isolated, not bound to others. In this "theory" Crusoe turns from being an economic egotist to being a spiritual egotist, and stands accused as a devout believer in self-sufficiency—"Crusoe as an island of existence." This view is countered by this critic when he defines *Crusoe* as a "phenomenological description of religious faith" or, bluntly put, a rejection of the seventeenth-century Hobbesian view that "[t]he natural state of man is one of isolation, not community."[26] Yet the image of Crusoe as an ego-centered and self-imposing loner has held on with surprising stubbornness. In a recent study of the English novel, Homer Obed Brown writes, "Robinson's thirty years of solitude . . . is the metaphor of [his] selfishness"; indeed, in this reading Crusoe is never really alone, since aspects of his very fears are his company, his specters: "the footprint of a man, the Hand of God, the constant presence of the older Robinson. . . ."[27]

Nevertheless there are signs that the *ambiguous* nature of Crusoe's solitude, its unresolved tension, is gaining more attention and acceptance. In *God's Plot and Man's Stories,* Leopold Damrosch conceives of Defoe's novel as an attempt to show Crusoe's attempt at survival, first to "dramatize the conversion of the Puritan self and then end[ing] by celebrating autonomy instead of submission." Resembling a debtor's prison the island, Damrosch argues, "allegorizes the solitude of soul needed for repentance and conversion." Yet such conversion does not imply socialization: "Nearly all of the essential issues cluster around the crucial theme of solitude," and Defoe "clearly gives it a positive valuation, suggesting several times that Crusoe "could have lived happily by himself forever if no other human beings had intruded." Damrosch identifies *Crusoe* as a work in which "the idea of solitude [undergoes] a drastic revaluation"; in place of the idea of descending into one's Self for repentance, self-scrutiny becomes the norm for all who wish to survive. So "[a]t the very moment when the Puritan's continuous self-analysis begins, Crusoe's ends."[28] In an *Antioch Review* essay (1958), Harvey Swados ("Robinson Crusoe—the Man Alone") has kidnapped Crusoe into the twentieth century as an alienated outsider who nevertheless overcomes modern *Angst,* loneliness, and "agony of doubt."[29]

This review of some of the opposing interpretations of Crusoe's solitude prepares the ground for a textual analysis whose major aim is to lay bare the see-saw tensions that attend Crusoe's own feelings about his solitary state. While almost all critics have conceded that Crusoe's solitude is the pervasive motif of the novel, many—as we have seen—have offered readings at variance with one another as to what that solitude means, both for Crusoe the man and *Crusoe* the novel.

3

We have it only second-hand, but Frank Budgen has been a reliable source. According to Budgen, Joyce—"a great admirer of Defoe" who had "read every line" of his works—remarked that *Robinson Crusoe* was "the English *Ulysses.*" Indeed, in *Ulysses* the wandering Bloom remarks that "Every Friday buries a Thursday, if you come to look at it." And Friday no doubt makes him think of Defoe's novel, for he immediately parodies Crusoe's account of his parrot with his own version:

> O, poor Robinson Crusoe,
> How could you possibly do so? (109)

In the original the lines read *"Robin, Robin, Robin Crusoe, poor Robin Crusoe, where are you Robin Crusoe?"*[30] But Joyce asks not of Crusoe's whereabouts but how he could "possibly do so," leaving ample room for speculation what it is the parrot sees as so curious—how could he possibly do *what?* To say that for Joyce the parrot asks after the condition of Crusoe's aloneness is as good as any other inference.

That Joyce was taken with Defoe early in his life comes to us first-hand by way of his Trieste lectures delivered, in Italian, in 1912–1913: "Realism and Idealism in English Literature: Daniel De Foe—William Blake." The translator and editor of these lectures suggests that it is indeed not difficult to see Robinson Crusoe and Leopold Bloom as "comparable variations on the theme of Ulysses. . . ." In Defoe Joyce saw, as John Warner recently put it, one of his "grandfathers"—and the great precursor of realism; he called *Robinson Crusoe* Defoe's "masterpiece." We have, says Warner, like Joyce, "become accustomed to reading Defoe as more than a realist; indeed allegorical and symbolic readings are now perhaps the norm rather than the exception."[31] And while Joyce, in his lectures, recognized Defoe as the quintessential "prototype of the British Colonist," he was also sensitive to Defoe's "mythic" side: "He who immortalized the strange solitary, Crusoe, and so many other solitaries lost in the great sea of social misery like Crusoe's in the watery sea, felt perhaps, as the end grew near, nostalgic for solitude." Joyce treasured Defoe's realism with something close to awe, as worthy beyond itself, for is not "the print of a naked foot," he asks, "more significant" than the "sparkling beryl and emerald" that St. John beheld on the walls at Patmos?[32] When Joyce delivered these lectures he was fresh from *Portrait* and *Dubliners* and plans for *Ulysses* were in the early stages. Still it is intriguing to consider *Crusoe* in light of Joyce's comparison with *Ulysses,* and to ask which among many reasons may be foremost in causing Joyce to compliment Defoe's novel as being the "English *Ulysses*"? For in asking the question one confronts one of the puzzles of *Crusoe,* namely the ambiguity with which Defoe treats the condition of endless solitude endured by his protagonist, almost all of it devoid of any human contact. To ask how such ambiguity—and ambivalence—emerges throughout Defoe's text yields insights not merely into Joyce's affinities but into the nature of solitude's complexity. In his study of the exilic experience, Seidel includes both novels and comments that Defoe "plays on the paradigm of the prodigal son as Joyce plays on it in *Ulysses*—leaving the father's land or motherland 'to seek misfortune'—and [this] becomes the essence of exilic alienation."[33]

4

No man may be an island entire unto himself, but Robinson Crusoe spends 28 years and some months (or 27, depending on what math we accept)[34] *on* one, most of that time as a solitary, and as scores of readers have skeptically remarked he seems none the worse at the end of his stay. In fact, as Crusoe makes clear on several occasions, he is not at all sure that he *wants* to be rescued from a life to which he eventually becomes contentedly habituated, one that he wholly controls without human interference. That is not to say that Crusoe is instantly or always happy to be a shipwrecked solitary, far from it; his psychological profile undergoes continual adjustment in both directions—despair with his isolation and contentment with its benefits. Such shifts seem at first to follow a natural trajectory, moving from fear and terror of solitude to fear and terror of Society, of human intrusion into his paradise. But a great deal else is at play, much of it centered on what is, after all, the main focus of the novel: Crusoe's solitude and how he attempts to cope with its problematic challenges. A close reading of Crusoe's feelings about himself and his condition on what eventually becomes in his eyes *his* island allows complexities to emerge that signify a constant shifting of affect toward what throughout the novel he refers to as his "captivity."

The "quiet, retired Life" that Crusoe's father so urged upon his son instead of following his "inclination of wandring"—from the beginning "to seek out for the *Islands*"—(38,29) ironically becomes a quiet life of another sort, more quiet, more retired than any he might have found in an inhabited venue. All available records, actual and anecdotal, in Defoe's day and since, show that survivors of total solitude deprived of human contact for an extended time tend to become mentally unstable after several years. (It happened to Alexander Selkirk, long assumed to be Crusoe's model, after only close to four years of isolation.) Hence the incredibly balanced, sane mind of Crusoe, after close to two and a half decades of solitude (until he meets up with Friday), can only be understood within the framework of the parabolic: it is not "realism." Those who have complained about this seemingly unaffected-by-solitude experience by calling it out of tune with real evidence (hence unrealistic) have perhaps missed the point of the novel. Defoe as a (realist) novelist was too clever, too calculating by far to have overlooked such a faux pas; it is clear that he created Crusoe's extended solitary life not unawares but precisely for a purpose, namely to better depict his anatomy of solitude for which he needed the ample space of (novelistic) time. In addition, it is clear that the other complaint, that Defoe was insufficiently interested in giving Crusoe that modern type of self-reflection we call introspection, is equally off the mark. Crusoe's self-debates are full of introspection, though they do not, of course, feature either the language or the culture of twentieth-century modernity.

Now Friday's appearance is, of course, not the first intrusive event in Crusoe's solitary life; that distinction goes to the uncanny (surely it fits Freud's definition of *unheimlich*) *single* footprint in the sand, discovered in Crusoe's sixteenth year on the island. After this bizarre sighting, Crusoe never again feels alone. This interruption of what had become a stable and satisfying life occurs precisely in the *middle* of the novel, the apogee of the narrative; everything from now on may be read as a descent that leads to Crusoe's eventual, and inevitable, departure. Yet what may have seemed captivity evolving into freedom now reverses course: From the sighting of the footprint onward, Crusoe truly becomes enslaved in the captivity of fear and anxiety. Henceforth his peace is shattered, and many of his assumptions about the benefits of solitude, hard-earned as they have been, are deconstructed, undermined, reflected in what is at best a dubiously accurate mirror. For to the rational Crusoe, the single footprint, mysterious as it may be, only suggests completion: There is yet another shoe to drop, so to speak, another footprint. In short, the island is inhabited, not by one-legged aliens, but by two-legged humans like himself. Does this, then, signal a renewed rush of desire for human company? Hardly. Again the response is ambiguous. From the moment of his awakening to his shipwrecked exile, Crusoe, as is his habit, creates a dialectical argument. He sees every reason to believe it a "Determination of Heaven, that in this desolate Place, and in this Manner I should end my Life. . . ." But his gloomy prospect is immediately interrupted by survivor guilt and a sense of destiny: "Well, you are in a desolate Condition 'tis true, but pray remember, Where are the rest of you? . . . Why were not they sav'd and you lost? Why were you singled out? Is it better to be here or there? and then I pointed to the Sea" (62–63). A cynical reading only reaffirms the portrait of an all too-reasoning Crusoe, coldly calculating his good fortune to be the one rescued; yet this kind of self-doubting dialogue becomes a coping mechanism of survival and reveals far less certainty than the mere words might indicate. Only moments later, he laments "the Scene of silent Life" he has involuntarily embarked on: "I ran about the Shore, wringing my Hands and beating my Head and Face, exclaiming at my Misery, and crying out, I was undone, undone, till tyr'd and faint I was forc'd to lye down on the Ground to repose, but durst not sleep for fear of being devour'd" (69). Again, he freely admits some pages later that when he first discovered he had survived, he had "[f]light of Joy . . . *being glad I was alive,* without the least Reflection upon the distinguishing Goodness of the Hand which had preserv'd me and had singled me out . . ."(89), followed a few moments later with *"Why has God done this to me? What have I done to be thus us'd"* (92). So while Crusoe does much to cheer himself up, he consistently appears to challenge his own reassurance with yet more complaint and cries for pity. This contrapuntal exchange-structure forms one of the most obvious bases of Crusoe's ambiguous attitude toward solitude, beginning at the start of his exile. After one year he marks with "Humiliation" his "unhappy Anniversary . . ." (103). It is in his second year Crusoe muses that " . . . it was possible I might be more happy in this Solitary Condition, than I should have been in a Liberty of Society, and in all the Pleasures of the World" (112). But it awaits the sixth year "of [his] Reign, or [his] Captivity" that he finally builds a reasonably sized boat, not to escape the Island but to explore it (137).

5

The vagaries of Crusoe's affective responses both to his (solitary) confinement and the potential of freedom from it clearly invite us to probe their implications. First it was clear that Defoe (long before Dostoyevsky or Nietzsche made the issue *the* modern problematic) raised the problem of freedom as a double-edged state, and suggested that its meaning depends on through what aperture one takes freedom's measure. Crusoe has enormous freedom in his captivity, that is obvious; yet equally obvious are the very constraints of that freedom that engender what Erich Fromm would call the "escape from freedom." Free to be free is one thing; free without choice is quite another.

If "captivity" is the most commonly used word Crusoe chooses to describe his stay on the island, then a chronological ordering of just how Crusoe views the island "prison" itself reveals both the ambiguity of his feeling as well as the significance of changes as they occur. One critic comments:

... the island is interpreted in incompatible ways: it is "my Reign, or my Captivity, which you please." For Crusoe, the island is a way for defining moods. . . . The *"Island of Despair"* is the wilderness where Crusoe must undergo the suffering that will take him through repentance to the promised land. But he transforms the wilderness to the garden; the island itself becomes his deliverance. The contradictions in his own thoughts are clear to Crusoe: he must subdue his anguish at being cast away, but he *should* also hope for his deliverance.[35]

While one may not accept all the premises of a "providential" reading, this observation about Crusoe's anguish of exile and hope of deliverance—feelings that sometimes arise simultaneously—points accurately to the novel's essential tension. What remains to be seen is how constant the trajectory between captivity and salvation turns out to be if one follows it faithfully from the beginning to the end of Crusoe's stay.

Having in mind his subsequent castaway state, Crusoe remarks that his life at one point before his actual shipwreck had been isolated, "like a Man cast away upon some desolate Island" (35), observing immediately that one should not sin by calling a state something which it is not. Soon enough he would really be a castaway stranded, in his first descriptions, on a "horrid Island" (63), a *"horrible desolate Island, void of all hope of Recovery"* (66), "this dismal unfortunate Island, which I call'd *the Island of Despair* . . ." (70). For some time it remains an "unhappy Island" (98), one that is "certainly a Prison to [him]" (96), where he anticipated his "Bondage" (101). Gradually, however, Crusoe begins to accept his fate, begins indeed to be content with it. Having explored east of his abode, and finding it in fact "much pleasanter than mine" (110), he nevertheless has developed a sense of *home,* and is grateful to return to his "old Hutch" and "Hamock-Bed," his "own House . . . a perfect Settlement" (111).[36] He resolves that he "would never go a great Way from it again," while it should "be his Lot to stay on the Island" (111). Still it remains an "Island of Hardness" (122), and in the sixth year of his "captivity" he ventures out again for further eastern exploration, but this time inclement weather and inhospitable terrain isolate him in a new wilderness, where he is lost, hungry and homesick, "driven from [his] belov'd Island":

And now I saw how easy it was for the Providence of God to make the most miserable Condition Mankind could be in *worse.* Now I look'd back upon my desolate solitary Island, as the most pleasant Place in the World, and all the Happiness my Heart could wish for, was to be but there again. . . . O happy Desart, said I, I shall never see thee more. O miserable Creature, said I, whether am I going: Then I reproach'd my self with my unthankful Temper, and how I had repin'd at my solitary Condition. . . . (139)

This sense of place, or home, becomes extraordinarily reinforced (and yet ambiguous as well) after Crusoe discovers the solitary footprint in the sand. Crusoe now feels his privacy violated, his space, so carefully nurtured, invaded; his composure and contentment for the first time tested—he is under siege. In contemporary terminology, he experiences a momentary panic or anxiety attack, and he retreats (literally and figuratively) into his "Castle." There is even denial, as he thinks briefly that perhaps the footprint is a chimerical delusion, that it possibly is his own print remaining from when he first came ashore. But Crusoe is too level-headed to remain either in a state of panic or delusion. Once again, he will come to terms: "To Day we love what to Morrow we hate; to Day we seek what to Morrow we shun; to Day we desire what to Morrow we fear . . ."(156).

Henceforth Crusoe must adjust to what, as he points out, ought by all rights to have made him ecstatic but instead instills dread: that his island, "so exceedingly pleasant," was inhabited. With such knowledge he decides that his best line of defense is concealment. The savages are, of course, for Crusoe not "humane"; so that despite this knowledge of other human presence on the island, it remains, in the twentieth year, an "Island of Solitariness." Crusoe continues mentally to distance the "savages" from himself, to remain in his own mind-set, a solitary whose sole fear is being captured and devoured by his unwanted co-inhabitants.

In a Lacanian reading of the novel, Thomas M. Kavanaugh posits several important points. Defoe, he argues, wrote *Robinson Crusoe* as "the story of a man alone; a story of how, within that solitude, [Crusoe] achieves an awareness of self denied him during his time among men." Such a view he sees in concert with the eighteenth century's "new sense of the individual" and in that context makes a useful comparison to Rousseau. After all, one of Rousseau's major arguments was that our severance from Nature had in turn substituted the concerns of society for those of the "essential self. . . ." Hence Crusoe (far from being depicted as losing his mind) was for Defoe what the Noble Savage was for Rousseau: "two versions of the healthy—each defined by their common opposition to a state of sickness: one before the poison [the Noble Savage], the other [Crusoe] after the cure." To reinforce this point, Kavanaugh cites the passage already quoted, namely that Crusoe argues he might be better off in solitude than in society. And from this, Kavanaugh argues that Crusoe's solitude is "fundamentally split, irreparably divided." Indeed it is this that makes *Crusoe* a part, perhaps the progenitor, of "the modern novel of society"—the "depiction of a solitude in which individual consciousness confronts its epistemological dependence as a constant projection of the self as Other. . . ." Literally, Crusoe remains two selves (or a Self and an Other) just as he postulates the pros and cons of his shipwreck. As the "societal Other" pressures Crusoe and he seeks to escape it, he finds himself in a more "complete isolation only to find that the Other is within himself . . . ,"[37] and that this dialogue between the two selves will sustain his lengthy confinement.

Such a reading opposes the notion that Crusoe is not self-reflective and also the oft-stated emphasis only on his isolation or the overemphasis on Crusoe's self-satisfaction as a materialistic, self-aggrandizing colonizer. In fact, Crusoe remains torn between the genuine pleasure he takes in his solitary state, and the fear of encroachment by anyone, on the one hand, and the inherent longing for companionship, on the other. He can and does argue this issue both ways, and Defoe resolves it finally, but not simply, when he permits Crusoe to "negotiate" the terms of his rescue in such a way that he is left with supreme independence short of solitariness.

6

Crusoe's reputation as a pragmatist is certainly amply merited—it is what keeps him level and it sustains him. Yet it is also part of that pragmatism that prompts him to offer us his famous list of the debits and credits of his status, his dialogic paradigm:

I am divided from Mankind, a Solitaire, one banish'd from humane Society.	But I am not starv'd and perishing on a barren place. . . .

(66)

It will be a long time, however, before the credit of food and shelter will even remotely balance the debit of being a "solitaire." And, of course, even when that balance is achieved it is at best temporary.

Not much time passes before Crusoe plans his own rescue, but one may wonder whether his first attempt to build a boat to leave the island is not unconsciously governed by a desire to remain. What he builds is so huge and so heavy, so far from the sea itself, that once he surveys it, he remarks it would have taken him "ten or twelve Years" to push the boat close enough for launching (128). For someone as clever as Crusoe, such an exaggerated miscalculation seems odd. In any case, it is then that he justifies his stay by seeing his situation from a more optimistic perspective: "I was remov'd from all the Wickedness of the World here. I had neither the *Lust of the Flesh, the Lust of the Eye, or the Pride of Life.* I had nothing to covet. . . . I was Lord of the whole Manor . . ." (128).

Crusoe recognizes the dialectic tension between resenting or appreciating his aloneness as the inevitable swing motion of life. In his sixth year on the

island, when he ventures forth by means of that small boat to explore the island and eventually is lost, he remarks: "Then I reproached my self with my
unthankful Temper, and how I had repin'd at my solitary Condition; and
now what would I give to be on Shore there again. Thus we never see the
true State of our Condition, till it is illustrated to us by its Contraries . . ."
(139). His view of the island suddenly becomes altered; it is a "desolate, solitary island" still, but that part he calls "home" is "the most pleasant Place in
the World, and all the Happiness my Heart could wish for. . . . O happy Desart, said I. . . ." (139). When he safely reaches the shore of his familiar
place, the sense of which has been strongly established, he falls on his knees
in thanks to God and his grace. Much later, in his fifteenth year, Crusoe
again postulates the homily, "[t]o Day we love what to Morrow we hate" and
explains the reaction to the sight of the footprint in the sand in light of this,
indeed rationalizes it. His only "Affliction" had been his aloneness, his ban-
ishment from Society, his "silent Life," and in this state of isolation to have
"seen one of my own Species, would have seem'd to me a Raising me from
Death to Life. . . ." And yet it seems not to be so simple. The disquieting in-
dent of a human footprint has quite the opposite effect: "I *say* that I should
now tremble at the very Apprehensions of seeing a Man, and was ready to
sink into the Ground at but the Shadow . . . of a Man's having set his Foot
in the Island" (156). Indeed, as he now labors to build himself a fortress
against the dreaded savages, he recognizes the ironic nature of that fear:

> All this Labour I was at the expense of, purely from my Apprehensions on the
> Account of the Print of a Man's Foot . . . for as yet I never saw any human
> Creature come near the Island, and I had now liv'd two Years under these Un-
> easinesses, which indeed made my Life much less comfortable . . . [living] in
> the constant Snare of *the Fear of Man*. . . . (163)

When Crusoe first beholds other human beings on the island it is
through the ghastly spectacle mirrored forth by a cannibal killing field: "the
Shore spread with Skulls, Hands, Feet, and other Bones of humane Bodies"
surrounded by a circle and charred earth where he presumed the devouring
feast has taken place. His response is a "Horror of the Degeneracy of Humane Nature" he finds inexpressible [foreshadowing *Heart of Darkness*]
(164–65). That this synecdochic tapestry of devoured fragments further
panics Crusoe is reasonable, but it also signals a symbolic structural device
Defoe implements to great effect. Defoe's method of reintroducing Crusoe
to humanity is incremental and deliberately fragmented: the *single* footprint,
the scattered body parts, the incoherent savages, the corpses of Spanish
sailors from the first shipwreck, and finally Friday, who is reclaimed gradually to communicate and become, in Crusoe's eyes, a fellow human, still par-

tial, never equal. Even the evil mutineers precede those "good men" who finally resemble the normal world Crusoe had left behind decades before. Such a gradual reacquaintance with human society is surely deliberately planned, as if Defoe is intent on guiding Crusoe through an allegorical, almost Dantesque journey—a carefully calibrated schedule of reentry into the human world. After debating with himself what course to take, including the option of killing all the savages so that no witness would be left, he rejects this and concludes that he ought simply to leave them to their business and to make certain only that they would not believe that "there were any living Creatures upon the Island; I mean of humane Shape" (173). Thus (as some have noted) follows a long and deliberate period of concealment, a freeze on future plans of departure, and a sense of acceptance and contentment. It is 23 years into his island exile that he sees the first live savages.

When at last the second ship arrives, which he eventually discovers was caught up in mutiny, Crusoe—now nearly two and half decades into his exile—finally shows the first signs of a genuine social hunger: "a strange longing or hankering of Desires . . . in my Soul . . ." (187). A longing for social intercourse has been building and now it explodes on the page in language more passionate and insistent than at any time before:

> O that there had been but one or two; nay, or but one Soul sav'd out of this Ship, to have escap'd to me, that I might but have had one Companion, one Fellow-Creature to have spoken to me, and to have convers'd with! In all the Time of my solitary Life, I never felt so earnest, so strong a Desire after the Society of my Fellow-Creatures, or so deep a Regret at the want of it. . . . Such were these earnest Wishings, That but one Man had been sav'd! *O that it had been but One!* I believe I repeated [these] Words . . . [a] thousand Times; and the Desires were so mov'd . . . that when I spoke the Words, my Hands would clinch together, and my Fingers press the Palms of my Hands, that if I had any soft Thing in my Hand, it would have crush't it. . . . (188)

Never before or after does Crusoe bare his anguish with such fervor or admit to such desperate loneliness in his solitary state. Here there remains no ambiguity, no ambivalence: he is desperate to reenter human society. After discovering the two dead men, however, it is two more years before he realizes that the "savages" have kept four men from the ship prisoner. Before that discovery, he continues to compare the "happy Posture of my Affairs, in the first Years of my Habitation here" to "the Life of Anxiety, Fear and Care . . . ever since I had seen the Print of a Foot in the Sand . . ." (196). It is now at last that he will rescue Friday and begin the next step toward full embrace with the world from which he had been torn. It would have been improbable that Crusoe would make Friday his equal, but some of the current accusations that Crusoe, the arch-imperialist, creates a master-slave relationship with Friday ignore at least the contextual setting. In fact, Crusoe at once recognizes his responsibility toward Friday (to be sure, with the benign colonizer's sense of duty) and, having two mouths to feed, immediately plants more corn, teaches Friday English, and concludes that "[t]his was the pleasantest Year of all the Life I led in this Place . . ." (213). It is a time of preparation for that moment when he actually sees the first white men and, having learned to be cautious, he approaches that situation not with hasty embraces but with suspicion. Not until he can be certain of loyalty and feel free of harm does he effect a relationship, and the metamorphosis from solitary to social creature is at last achieved.

7

Although the third volume of *Robinson Crusoe, Serious Reflections* (1719), is really more a series of essays on sundry matters by Defoe (who keeps up the pretense by insisting that they are penned by Crusoe) than a sequel, its first chapter, "Of Solitude," is of critical relevance to the novel proper. If there is any doubt about Defoe's ambiguity toward solitude it is resolved in this opening discourse on the solitary state. Defoe's purpose seems less to justify Crusoe than to distinguish what he believes to be the two kinds of solitude: genuine solitude of the soul, achievable anywhere, and the religious solitude ("monkish"), which is deliberately chosen. The latter involves self-isolation in hermitage-locales such as deserts, forests, or islands. Crusoe clearly belongs to the former: on any conscious level, his solitude is an accidental consequence of his shipwreck and in no way a free choice of retreat into retirement.

Crusoe has, he says, frequently looked back to the "long tedious life of solitude" he had endured. At times he has wondered why the state of solitude is considered a "grievance or affliction," since "it seems to me that life in general is, or ought to be, but one universal act of solitude. . . ." Since in the end all of our existence points inward "man may be properly said to be alone in the midst of the crowds" (3–4)—an idea that gains high profile currency in the nineteenth century in such major figures as Hoffmann, Poe, and Baudelaire. "Multitude, solitude: equal and interchangeable terms for the active and fertile poet," says Baudelaire in his poem, "Crowds": "He who does not know how to populate his solitude, does not know either how to be alone in a busy crowd." In the proper sense that Crusoe defines, solitude is "contemplation" in internal retirement; echoing Montaigne, Defoe writes that "he that cannot converse properly with himself is not fit for any conversation at all." Yet there is a caveat, "many good reasons why a life of solitude, *as solitude is now understood by the age,* is not at all suited to the life of a Christian or of a wise man" [italics mine] (4–5). For Defoe insists that his own notions of solitude differ from those of his age, namely those concepts of solitude that insist a deliberate separation from Society and a retreat to "deserts . . . cells, monasteries, and the like" are the requisites for solitude. And as for being on the island—"that was no solitude; indeed no part of it was so, except that which . . . I applied to the contemplation of sublime things, and that was very little . . ." (5). London, he insists, affords him greater solitude than the island ever did, partly—one assumes—because he was, after all, preoccupied with survival, beset with anxieties, and in constant stages of strategizing either how to enhance the future or ensure his safety, especially after first sighting the footprint in the sand. Defoe's insistence (through the voice of Crusoe) is that the soul's purity of life, its "solitude," is as easily managed, if not better, in the "midst of a throng" as it is in some actual place of physical isolation. So long as the soul "is truly master of itself," it achieves the contemplative state of solitude; indeed, the isolation of an island, he insists, inhibited such solitude by confining him to the "anxiety of [his] circumstances." Solitude on "a religious or philosophical account, is a mere cheat." Retreat for its own sake is a waste. "Let the man . . . that understands the meaning of the word [solitude], learn to retire into himself." And "[s]erious meditation is the essence of solitude" (8, 12), and all the retreats into empty spaces deprive and inhibit rather than further contemplation. Logical as these observations may appear, they run counter to the various cultist and fashionable views of solitude that preceded and followed Defoe.

While the notion of solitude in the midst of Society became an especially cultivated motif among the Romantics and beyond, the idea of solitude as physical retreat has been a steady fixture in most discussions of aloneness. Putting aside Defoe's religious agenda, one must conclude that his adamant objections to religious and philosophical solitude based on physical isolation stems from his own ambiguous view of solitude itself. In the end, he marginalizes the solitude Crusoe experienced on the island, quite contrary to the textual evidence, perhaps in order to be able to convince us of his ulterior point:

> Man is a creature so formed for society, that it may not only be said that it is not good for him to be alone, but 't is really impossible he should be alone. We are so continually in need of one another, nay, in absolute necessity of assistance from one another, that those who have pretended to give us the lives and manner of the *solitaires* . . . are frequently put to the trouble of bringing the angels . . . to do one drudgery or another for them . . . to make the life of a true *solitaire* possible. (14)

Humor aside, Defoe insists on making us think of Crusoe as far too preoccupied to be a true *solitaire,* never needing any angels to help him in his survival strategies. But Crusoe's lamentations for human company are rather conveniently sidestepped, if not forgotten. In the end, "[l]et no man plead that . . . he loves solitude . . . 't is all a delusion" (15); and certainly "complete solitude," Defoe/Crusoe concludes, is as available in the "most populous cities" as in "an uninhabited island."[38] *Serious Reflections* shows nothing of what has sometimes been diagnosed as a "desire-fear ambivalence: desire for freedom, fear of being destroyed." Indeed, for one critic the tension is reduced to an oversimplified formula: "The problem of man's isolation is stated in the crudest possible terms: to get enough to eat and to avoid being eaten."[39]

The kind of quasi-apologetic argumentation in *Serious Reflections* sets the tone of Defoe's conflicting views about the state of solitude; and his insistence that the island is either as good or less as a place to experience true solitude comes close to a palinode: Crusoe may *seem* like a *solitaire*, but he is not, whatever he may at times say or think. It remains a matter of speculation as to why, on reflection, Defoe is so eager to distance Crusoe from that part of himself in the novel that was clearly aligned to the *solitaire*. What is clear is that the text of the first volume and these reflective comments in the sequel are evidence of the tension that informs what the world knows as *Robinson Crusoe*.

8

Michel Tournier's *Friday, or the Other Island* (in English, 1969)[40] is a most compelling modern version of the Crusoe story. Tournier keeps half of Robinson Crusoe's name intact (it has become traditional in French Crusoe versions to call Crusoe by his first name, Robinson); some of the main facts are also parallel, at least for most of the book: the shipwreck, the retrieval of provisions from the sunken hull, the building of a boat too heavy to launch, the suffering and the intervention of religion, the Journal, the cultivation of the land, the accidental rescue of Friday from cannibals (he intends to shoot him but misses), the creation of the island as a private domain, even the number of years on the island until the arrival of a rescue ship. But Tournier is a modern and so is his Robinson, who reflects what was neither available nor empathetic to Defoe.[41]

After only a short time, Tournier turns his Robinson into a philosopher, a self-reflecting solitary who has both a sensitivity and a penchant for anger beyond those of Defoe's hero.[42] Instead of a preoccupation with a father, Tournier's Robinson is overcome with memories of his mother and Proustian reminiscences of his childhood; solitude first becomes this solitary's "implacable bride" (40), and the island is originally christened "the Island of Desperation." In time Robinson sanctifies it as "The Island of Hope"—

"Speranza" (48); but there also lurks the marsh-pit, slimy and degrading, the temptation during the early periods of near-insanity and despair. This cast-away is more prone to lose his mind, at least initially, and solitude almost immediately becomes a philosophical dilemma: "Solitude is not a changeless state imposed on me by the wreck of the *Virginia*. It is a corrosive impulse which acts on me slowly but ceaselessly, and in one sense purely destruc-tively" (50). Solitude "destroys" whatever "meaning" he once had, and like Defoe's Crusoe he is desperate, at first, for salvation—"God save us, *some-one!*" (51). Like Crusoe, Robinson has nightmares, but he is also visited by erotic visions. One of the first deviations from the original is the solitary footstep; whereas the original Crusoe conjectures it might be his own, Tournier's makes it a fact, not to mock Defoe's version (as some have thought) but to emphasize Robinson's self-reflective existence. With passing time he, too, begins to guard and value his solitude against "invaders, valu-ing his solitariness," recalling long walks of his childhood, when "We got to know each other, solitude and I . . ." (76).

Then one day Robinson sees what he perceives to be "another island," one that will be elusive forever but takes on the shape of a mythic connection with otherness, "a place more living, warmer and more fraternal"—a utopian par-adise that lifts his sagging spirits.[43] It is then that Tournier's Robinson begins to cultivate philosophy, contemplating epistemology, and concluding that there are two kinds of knowledge, the "knowledge *through others* and the knowledge *through oneself* . . .": "the *self* unrelated to others" is a rarity (87–88). At this point Tournier's hero turns radically from Defoe's: Physically he will become a savage of Nature and in his mind he develops a more mod-ern self-reflective and self-conscious view of his plight than Defoe's Crusoe would have thought wise or possible. He feminizes the island, thinking of it as shaped like a woman: " . . . Speranza became wholly maternal . . . haunted by the memory of his mother" (97). And he pays a price: "The strength I drew from the womb of Speranza was the perilous price of a regression into the sources of myself" (103). Unlike Defoe's bachelor Crusoe, Robinson has left a wife and children; sex is not avoided in Robinson's account, but discussed and practiced. Robinson finds a large log shaped like thighs, filled with moss and quillai, and "for several happy months" he has intercourse with this extension of Nature (109). One day a spider bites his penis and he feels rebuked, but Robinson's sexual needs find new comforts. After the spider puts an end to the episodes with the log, he finds a soft spot of earth and literally makes love to it feeling delight when mandrakes grow as if children of his semen.[44] But the absence of real human company makes him doubt his own existence, until he accidentally rescues Friday, who in time, however, "was playing havoc with Speranza, he was poisoning his master's soul" (156). Friday imitates Robinson's love-making with the earth and produces striped mandrakes.

The relationship with Friday is sometimes less happy and more ambiguous than Defoe's, and Robinson has moments of high anger when he actually thinks of killing Friday for minor transgressions coupled with moments of deep awe for the purity of this essential "Adam." At the beginning of their relationship, Tournier's Robinson is far more harsh in his treatment of Friday than Defoe's Crusoe; the change comes only when an explosion of the cave that is accidentally caused by Friday shows Robinson the folly of his so-called civilized world. Finally the rescue ship arrives, but there are no mutinous sailors, no battles. Robinson visits the ship but, dining at captain's table, well received, he reacts with no happy relief: "What principally repelled him was not so much the coarse brutality, the greeds and animosities that emerged with a naive unawareness from these two civilized and perfectly honourable men." It was, rather, a deeper "evil": it was their "incurable pettiness in relation to life . . . which all men so feverishly pursued" (213).

In Defoe's tale it is Crusoe who eventually (in the sequel) abandons Friday; in Tournier's it is—ironically—Friday who is attracted by Western magic and betrays his own freedom, departing with the rescue ship. Robinson chooses to remain on his Speranza and is joined by a young cook's boy (who had been mistreated on the rescue ship), and although he calls him Thursday he associates him with Sunday: "It is the day of our resurrection, of the youth of all things and the day of our master, the Sun" (224).

What Tournier made of Defoe's hero we know because we have his revision; what Defoe would have made of Tournier's revision we can only conjecture. But it is fairly safe to assume he would have ridiculed this Crusoe as an unmanly and self-absorbed creature who foolishly forgoes life with fellow human beings and worships a solitude that can only destroy and deprive. And to some extent it is precisely these qualities of Defoe's Crusoe that prompts Tournier's revision. In his autobiography Tournier provides some amplifications in his chapter "Friday," where he reveals his ambivalent view of Defoe: he admired Crusoe but, influenced by the Algerian civil war and relativist anthropology, considered *Crusoe* an imperialist and racist book. Yet recognizing the powerful mythic hold of the Defoe hero, he pronounces Crusoe's "myth . . . surely of the most topical and vital that we possess. Perhaps it . . . possesses us." It is like a "mould into which we pour our modern sensibilities." For Tournier, "freedom, wealth, and solitude are the three faces of the modern condition." On the island Crusoe faces all three in their modern nascence, and as for solitude, Crusoe "is not only the victim of . . . [it] but also its hero." Friday's appearance created the second myth, the noble savage being tamed, his coming, according to Tournier's reading, "bitterly disappointing"—a savage, not a peer, has broken Crusoe's solitude.[45] Tournier's Friday will be different, not there to be taught as in Defoe but prepared to teach Robinson, simply by example to show him the folly of what he had lost. (Tournier does not explain why Friday so easily succumbs to the civilization his pupil rejects when he decides to remain on Speranza.)

Tournier's version is fortuitous, for it points forward to some of the issues raised by the modern responses to solitude in the novels about to be examined: the philosophical doubts and ambiguities, the reassuring elements of a solitary existence, the disgust with society, the anxieties of Self, indeed the skeptical questioning of the autonomy of existence. Clearly Tournier's Robinson, unlike Defoe's Crusoe, assumes a mocking posture toward the Society that has agreed to "rescue" him, and his refusal to be rescued and instead to take his chances with nature and innocence (the cook's boy) are a critique of Defoe, clearly calculated. More than critique, however, Tournier's Crusoe is thoroughly modern. Gilles Deleuze has said it best in his interesting remarks on Tournier's novel: He sees Friday not as the Other but as a kind of "double," and Robinson "discovers (slowly) that it is the Other who disturbs the world . . . [and] was the trouble."[46] Making the Other the enemy would never have occurred to Defoe.

In 1978 Tournier published "La Fin de Robinson," in which Robinson has returned to England and, like his progenitor, has married and become rich. Eventually, however, he ages and succumbs to disillusionment, a drunkard, who tries unsuccessfully to find his island again. The aging Robinson discovers too late that his island was perhaps an idealization, like the "other island" of the original novel. This twentieth-century Crusoe, as we might have expected, comes to a sad end.

But the contrast between Defoe and Tournier is valuable precisely because it illuminates some of the crises that were to confront the modernists of the 1920s through the 50s. Defoe's Crusoe raises the issues that Tournier is prepared to deal with in ways that are significantly different, but Defoe recognized the problem and initiated the debate of solitary Self and Other. One is inclined to agree, then, that *Crusoe* articulates "the powerful existential theme of human solitude," especially as one confronts the novel's unrivalled grip on the world's imagination.

Chapter III ∼

"Soliloquy in Solitude": *To The Lighthouse*

> They had nothing to say . . .
> . . . I shall avoid that awkward space.
>
> Always, Mrs. Ramsay felt, one helped oneself out of solitude by laying hold
> of some little odd or end . . .
>
> —Woolf, *To the Lighthouse*

> The lighthouse as an image of loneliness has its limits.
>
> —Ira Sadoff, "February Pemaquid Point"
> (after a painting by Edward Hopper)

1

To the Lighthouse is probably the most analyzed of Woolf's novels, and over the years that commentary has taken a certain shape.[1] Most readers recognize that the novel is preoccupied with the difficulty of human communication and with the relentless striving for meaning and unity, especially by Lily Briscoe, whose painting (both the process and on the canvas) so dominates the narrative. And over the last five or six decades, as *To the Lighthouse* has generated increasing critical attention, most commentators have also been confident, as a recent biographer has written, that the novel "ends on a note of triumph." A number of critics, however, have become uncomfortable with that judgment and have suggested that the ending (indeed, the whole novel) is more indeterminate.[2]

The emphasis of this chapter is on demonstrating that *To the Lighthouse* is a novel spatially conceived and structured, so that space envelops characters and inhibits true communication with others, creating impenetrable solitude.[3] In addition, it will be argued that the ending is not merely inconclusive, but that one of Woolf's conclusions is that we must accept that the only insight we are granted is that the grander vision and unity we may seek are beyond us.

2

In assessing the shape of the novel of the future, Virginia Woolf wrote in 1927, the year she published *To the Lighthouse,* that "[the novel] will resemble poetry in this that it will give not only or mainly people's relations to each other and their activities together, as the novel has hitherto done, but it will give the relation of the mind to general ideas and its soliloquy in solitude" ("Poetry, Fiction and the Future.")[4]

In the long run she would be wrong, the novel returning to various forms of realism before its postmodern U-turn; but as she wrote this Woolf had in mind not only her own work, which was already approaching some of the changes she predicted, but certainly the work of Proust and Joyce as well. "Soliloquy in solitude" is achieved in large measure in *To the Lighthouse* through the twin-consciousness of Mrs. Ramsay and Lily Briscoe and, to a lesser extent, the consciousness of Mr. Ramsay. Far less than, say, Beckett, Woolf's "soliloquy" is still intensely bound to colloquy, whether in silent imaginary dialogue with those physically present—or absent, like the dead Mrs. Ramsay in the third section of the novel. So "people's relations with each other" remain an important part in Woolf's novel, despite the certainty that such relations are doomed. Her characters are not yet the amputated, hollow voices of *Malone Dies* or *The Unnamable;* there remains a critical need for company in solitude, whether such company is a dinner party for Mrs. Ramsay, silent "conversations" between Lily and Mrs. Ramsay through the medium of her vexing canvas, or the female repositories of sympathy for Mr. Ramsay for which he forages like a needy pet. None of these, of course, completely satisfies, but their very existence, however unattainable, creates the tension of *To the Lighthouse:* a painful yearning by people to connect, though barred from such connection by a spatial divide. A philosopher's view of monologue links it to the solitariness of language: the "[m]onologue of language, it speaks all alone. We, too, speak all alone—and we do it constantly. We call it thinking."[5] And, as in *The Waves,* Woolf "achieves for her characters an anonymity" parallel to "the waves" or, as in *To the Lighthouse,* the sea.[6] In her study of silence in Woolf's fiction, Patricia Ondek Laurence, focusing on the women in Woolf's novels, observes that they are "often present in this narrative space we are learning to read . . . [this] silence of gaps, gulfs, pauses, fissures, cracks, and interludes."[7] And we might add to the list unfinished thoughts and sentences cut short (Lucio Ruotolo has character- ized this as "the interrupted moment"[8]) of many "solitary scenes" that Woolf "structures" to "create a narrative space for the exploration of psychological silence or interiority. . . ."[9] These scenes are by their nature scenes of soli- tude, voluntary maneuvers to vacate the temporal of enforced events, de- fenses against the threat of intrusive penetration of privacy.

Woolf recognized the nature of solitude in all its complexity, often seek- ing it or having it imposed on her throughout her mental suffering; yet she (as do her characters) yearns to keep links to a world that so often seems shattered and inhospitable. As an artist Woolf understood the duality of soli- tude. Recognizing "the light side and the dark side" of the human soul, she concluded that "in company the light side of the mind is exposed; in soli- tude, the dark." While she agreed that "both are equally real, equally im- portant," she also knew that for the novelist it is more tempting to "expose one [the dark side] rather than another" ("How Should One Read a Book?" (*Essays*, 1926, 392). In March, 1925, the year she began writing *To the Light- house*, she reviewed *'Tis Pity She's a Whore*, and though marveling at the "world of tedium and delight, pleasure and curiosity . . . extravagant laugh- ter, poetry, and splendour" in the Elizabethan universe, she perceives miss- ing something we seek beyond the tumult that will give us "privacy," that we must turn to when the mind is "tired with company." What is it? "It is soli- tude," a respite during which the mind "explore[s] its own darkness" (*Essays*, 69). In September 1926 she sounds a similar note in an essay on a favorite, De Quincey: Novelists have tended too much to rely on reality, and thus "all that side of the mind which is exposed in solitude they ignore" ("'Impas- sioned Prose,'" *Essays*, 362). Or, as she wrote in an essay (1926) in which she observes that illness is an ignored novelistic theme (not as ignored as she thought) compared with "love," "battle," and "jealousy": "Those great wars which [the body] wages by itself, with the mind slave to it, in the solitude of the bedroom . . . are neglected" ("On Being Ill," *Essays*, 318). *To the Light- house* may not be a version of the "solitude in the bedroom" but it is a novel with hermetic scenes that virtually freeze-frame its characters in various poses of solitude, silently attempting to reach beyond themselves—mostly without success. Time merely "passes," as the title of Section II says with al- most deliberate banality; though cosmic events (the Great War) occur, those that touch the Ramsays are bracketed, not because they are seen as minor but precisely because they are not. Meanwhile, the spatial dilemmas of two September mornings fill up most of the novel's chronology, and essentially between Sections I and III very little changes among those who remain— solitaries remain solitary, and the unattainable remains unattainable despite the belated arrival at the lighthouse and the apparently triumphant completion of the painting.

In commenting on the novel in 1958, without benefit of letters or diaries, R. M. Adams identified the underlying problem of *To the Lighthouse.* Noting the novel's preoccupation with "the difficulties of communication," Adams acknowledges Woolf's attempt to "redeem" the novel's depiction of repeated failures at completion in the last two sections of the narrative. The arrival at the lighthouse and the ostensible completion of Lily's painting are certainly attempts at "rounding-off the novel." But, he argues, aside from the "obscurities of symbolism" in these final acts, the major problem is in the spurious relationship between the novel's ending and what preceded. Perhaps, he conjectures, Woolf means to convey that "in rare and lucky moments . . . understanding and communication are achieved"; but, considering how much Woolf stressed the difficulties of such achievement, it would be "meretricious to suggest that [the ending] is climactic." Rather, *To the Lighthouse* "wavers . . . unhappily between an arbitrary and a frankly irresolute ending; and, ultimately, it leaves us with a sense that the jump has not been clearly taken." In a harsh conclusion to his argument, Adams asserts that if Woolf believes communication is so elusive that she cannot clearly communicate its consummation, "her novel must be judged a symptom, not a triumph."[10] By sensing the "irresolute" nature of the ending, Adams has located a major issue; but the ending is not "arbitrary." The following sections suggest that Woolf understood her problem: the novel's ending(s) may be ambiguous, but they conclusively demonstrate Woolf's conviction that absolute endings, whether in life or fiction, may be impossible in part because the solitude to which we are assigned to play out our roles is impregnable.

3

Once again we are on an island (strictly speaking the novel takes place on the Isle of Skye); but the island where the Ramsay family and its companions enact their two Septembers, ten years apart, is an island quite different from Crusoe's. Where Defoe's hero was, for the most part, a solitary seeking to anchor his solitude by creating a sense of island-place, the Ramsays and their guests are solitaries enclosed by the island-space that envelops them and also divides them, each from each so that they collectively assume the characteristics of islands marooned on an island. The very place of "home" that Crusoe desperately seeks to construct is in Woolf's novel disassembled, so that Part II, which occupies ten years, describes in bleak detail the slow disintegration of a home into a neglected shambles of a house. When it is finally readied for yet another visit, it is no longer possible to reconstruct it: it is held together by unfulfilled yearnings and memories, and by the presence of absence, especially, of course, the present absence of Mrs. Ramsay.

Although it is common for artists to experience depression after completing a work—the dreaded white page or canvas—and although Virginia Woolf's battles with depression (and worse) accompanied her adolescent and adult life in repeated waves, it is nevertheless curious that her significant despair after finishing *To the Lighthouse* prompted her to recall it years later in her diary. "After Lighthouse," she wrote in 1934, "I was I remember nearer suicide, seriously, than since 1913"[11] (the year she completed *The Voyage Out,* her first novel). In September 1926, when she was finishing the novel, there are several references to her depression in her letters, which reveal that during the writing of *To the Lighthouse,* between 1925–26, she was interrupted by illnesses (most of them she labels "flu," not depression) on at least six occasions.[12] Twice in June 1926 she wrote disparagingly about the novel to V. Sackville-West: "My novel is very very bad: all my worst faults displayed"; she sees her "novel . . . glowing like the Island of the Blessed very far away over dismal wastes, and cannot reach land" (*Letters,* 272, 276); ten days after finishing *To the Lighthouse,* she regarded it "with complete indifference" (*Letters,* 296). The metaphor of not being able to reach land is fittingly spatial for a novel in which reaching land stands as the principal dilemma, from the aborted journey to the lighthouse in Part I to the actual journey, paralleled by Lily Briscoe's attempts to paint a second picture in Part III. Woolf's characters, as she sees herself, are adrift in spatial isolation, literally and figuratively at sea. Repetition does have its completions, but of what nature is debatable.

Despite the scraps of information in the diaries and letters one can only speculate about Woolf's state of mind while writing *To the Lighthouse,* and whether the actual process of composing the novel affected that state of mind or vice versa. Some dissenting voices aside, *To the Lighthouse,* once published, was well received and considered by many, including Leonard Woolf, her "masterpiece." Yet, as she recalls, the completion of the novel left her near suicide, a feeling stronger than any since finishing her first novel, although apropos *To the Lighthouse* she wrote, "I can never scrape through a book without disaster" (*Letters,* 378). In *Downhill All the Way,* Leonard Woolf reports that every aftermath of a completed novel was in some degree a crisis of "black despair."[13] Not only the finished novel, but its ending in particular, which gave her problems, seemed not to satisfy. It would appear that, like Lily, she had her vision, and it left her desolate. This leads one to ponder the ending (and it has been the subject of some debate) frequently admired for its symmetrical strategy whereby Lily finishes her painting apparently simultaneously with the arrival of the Ramsay party at the lighthouse.

One is expected to read these last sections as parallel events; they resemble the "spatial form" Joseph Frank explored in his provocative essay, "Spatial Form in Modern Literature."[14] *To the Lighthouse* is in several ways a "spatial" novel (as in its way, too, was the preceding *Mrs. Dalloway*); one observes incrementally how the solitude that envelops the characters *creates* the kind of spatial divide that makes communication between—and among—them virtually impossible. The lighthouse itself is a spatial beacon, a vertical stroke on the horizon, just as is that final stroke with which Lily in the end divides her canvas. It was always her preoccupation: "Yes, I shall put the tree further in the middle; then I shall avoid that awkward space." (84). But the "awkward space" is never avoidable; the movement of the tree and the final dividing vertical stroke placed through the middle of the canvas, create two spatial domains rather than one.

Part III is almost pantomime. The few words exchanged between Lily and Mr. Ramsay about his boots and the equally few words that pass between Lily and Mr. Carmichael are overwhelmed by the long wordless sections in which Lily confronts the dead and speechless Mrs. Ramsay and her canvas. Equally, with very few exceptions, the journey to the lighthouse is virtually silent. We absorb this part of the novel as a tableau vivant: two actions separated by the space of the sea, each ending on an island. Dorrit Cohn has noted the temporal aspect of Lily's consciousness in Part III: "narrated monologue" can reveal "a fictional mind suspended in an instant present, between a remembered past and an anticipated future." By allowing all "three of these time-zones" to converge in Lily's consciousness, Woolf achieves the necessary linkage to move the narrative forward.[15]

4

Much of what divides people from one another in *To the Lighthouse* is their inability to transcend themselves. Vanity leads them to chatter at times, to pronounce, to opinionate (for example, Mr. Ramsay and Tansley); so lack of vanity, where it may occasionally be found, calls attention to itself as a virtue. Lily, contemplating Mr. Bankes, muses: "I respect you (she addressed silently him in person . . . you are not vain; you are entirely impersonal . . .)."[16] The impassive "impersonal" is preferable to the intrusive personal, since the latter tends almost always to assume the posturing of the "petty, selfish, vain, egotistical" (24), and the meddling—even on occasion by Mrs. Ramsay herself. This silence that often pervades the novel is a symptom and consequence of what Woolf herself identifies as a principal theme—"the inadequacy of human relationships . . ." (40), and Mrs. Ramsay's own realization of the "pettiness of some part of her, and of human relations, how flawed they are, how despicable, how self-seeking, at their best" (42). And it is in Mr. Ramsay's solitude that these flawed human relations are most clearly manifest. Long past his intellectual prime, unable to get beyond himself (the letter "R," *R*amsay) in his quest for philosophical closure, Ramsay's isolation is at times almost self-lacerating:

> It was his fate . . . to come out thus on a spit of land which the sea is slowly eating away, and there to stand, like a desolate sea-bird, alone. . . . [H]e kept even in that desolation a vigilance which spared no phantom and luxuriated in no vision. . . . He was bearing down upon them. Now he stopped dead and stood looking in silence at the sea. (43–44)

Being, as his son explains a philosopher interested in "subject and object and the nature of reality," Mr. Ramsay defies "vision," and that defiance empowers him to mobilize his defenses against the visionary temper of his wife. It creates their collision course at the very start of the novel as his "Damn you" uttered at his wife is prompted by her visionary hopes for a journey to the lighthouse that cannot reasonably be expected to take place given the awful weather.

Lily, too, "liked to be alone; she liked to be herself; she was not made" for ordinary social intercourse. She recalls once having laid her head upon Mrs. Ramsay's lap "and laughed and laughed and laughed" at Mrs. Ramsay's self-deceptive certainty over matters "she completely failed to understand. . . ." Now she sees a different scene. Still "presiding" is Mrs. Ramsay, "but now with every trace of wilfulness abolished, and in its stead, something clear as the space which the clouds at last uncover—the little space of sky which sleeps beside the moon" (50). Thus separated, Mrs. Ramsay and Lily each occupies her space. It becomes clearer why Lily has more in common with Mr. Ramsay than may seem, and such affinity accounts for her obviously ambivalent attitude toward him, ranging from near-hatred to veneration. In her way, Lily, too, belongs to those interested in "subject and object and the nature of reality." Mrs. Ramsay is for Lily, like so many things in this novel, simply unattainable, whether in the flesh or on canvas. She is the receptacle, Lily feels certain, of "treasures," but they "would never be offered openly" (though they "would teach one everything"), "never be made public" (51). This thought comes to her even as she leans her head against Mrs. Ramsay's knee, and still "[n]othing happened. Nothing! Nothing!" The knowledge and wisdom Lily feels certain are in Mrs. Ramsay's heart are beyond reach: "How then, she had asked herself, did one know one thing or another thing about people, sealed as they were?" (51).

Yet Lily's enclosedness, like that of Mr. and Mrs. Ramsay, is never self-sufficient. None of them is content with his or her solitary state, for each seeks occasional escape from self-isolation. In Mrs. Ramsay it takes the form of "arranging," whether marriages, dinner, or making peace among her children; for Mr. Ramsay it manifests itself in his pursuit of sympathy, especially from women, which at critical moments compromises his stoic solitariness; and in Lily it shows itself in her ruminations about her attachment to Mrs. Ramsay, when she is alive and after she is dead. Mrs. Ramsay's double bind is debated openly; her solitude is both sought and nurtured, but with eight children, a husband and too many guests ("she asked too many people to stay" [6]), it is clear that she lives a life scarcely protected from intrusion. Her husband interprets her self-enclosure as pessimism, but she disagrees. Her 50 years are a "little strip of time": life itself remains an unanswered mystery, for "Life, she thought—but she did not finish her thought." In the end life is quite real after all, "she had a clear sense of it there"; but it was also "something private, which she shared neither with her children nor with her husband." As in other relationships described in the novel, this one too has its walls of separation: "A sort of transaction went on between them, in which she was on one side, and life was on another." Life for Mrs. Ramsay was an antagonist to be fought, not a timeline to which one could submit or over which one had control. Often "this thing that she called life [was] terrible, hostile, and quick to pounce on you if you gave it a chance" (59–60). To be "herself by herself" required her to retreat into her essence, to be "silent," "alone," and "invisible" (62).

Such pursuit of solitude is not altogether negative; indeed it becomes clear that Mrs. Ramsay needs, wants, and seeks such solitude when the realities of life overwhelm her. What becomes problematic is how to return to intimacy, how to reenter, as it were, from space to place, how to renegotiate a passage through that separation-barrier when it has served its purpose. "Always," Mrs. Ramsay "felt, one helped oneself out of solitude reluctantly by laying hold of some little odd or end, some sound, some sight"; but for Mr. Ramsay this did not always bring success. His wife's enclosure "saddened" him; "her remoteness pained him" (64). Their argument about whether they could go to the lighthouse the next morning is merely emblematic of an unbridgeable space between them, a "gap between the two clumps of red-hot pokers . . ." (68). Mrs. Ramsay seems spent. Her husband appears almost to be a stranger; she cannot even understand that she ever felt "any emotion or affection for him"; indeed her sense was of "being past everything, through everything, out of everything . . ." (83). Obviously they would never "know" each other: "human relations were all like that . . . and the worst . . . were between men and women" (92).

It is this state of mind and emotion that leads to that painful scene at the end of "The Window" (reminiscent of the last scene of Joyce's "The Dead"), during which the husband seeks sympathy and a verbal reassurance of love and the wife is simply unable to give it, unable to utter the words. The issue has been offered succinctly: "Woolf displaces the 'speaking subject' and speech or dialogue in the novel."[17] Though both husband and wife are aware of each other, silently "speaking" to each other, neither will give in to speech, and so they "had nothing to say" (119) and "the shadow . . . folding them in was beginning . . . to close round her again. Say anything, she begged, looking at him, as if for help." Their "crepuscular walls of intimacy" nevertheless allowed each to feel that they were communicating, though he felt her to be "heartless"; "she never told him that she loved him . . . she never could say what she felt . . . she could not do it; she could not say it" (122–124). The scene ends in her triumphant realization that without saying anything he knew that she did after all love him: "she had not said [it]"; yet "he knew" (124). It seems a pyrrhic triumph. Despite her smile of victory and reassurance, Mrs. Ramsay has not come any closer to knowing her husband nor he her; the earlier feelings of mutual isolation seem both stronger and more accurate; the present silent "reconciliation" is merely a coping mechanism that allows them to go on for yet another day. An articulated response remains impossible, especially when he comes for sympathy, for then Mrs. Ramsay "seemed to fold herself together, one petal closed in another, and the whole fabric fell in exhaustion upon itself, so that she had only strength enough to move her finger. . . ." (38)

Though both husband and wife have "communicated" through the space of silence, they are incapable of achieving emotional interpenetration. Nothing of sustaining power has passed between them. The darkness that initiates Section II reflects not merely the ominous harbinger of the coming war but the residual "shadow" of the Ramsay relationship, which owns an "immense darkness" (125) parallel to that of the world about to explode:

Did Nature supplement what man advanced? Did she complete what man began? With equal complacence she saw his misery, his meanness, and his torture. That dream of sharing, completing, of finding in solitude . . . an answer, was then but a reflection in a mirror, and the mirror itself was but the surface glassiness which forms in quiescence when the nobler powers sleep beneath? Impatient, despairing yet loth to go . . . to pace the beach was impossible; contemplation was unendurable; the mirror was broken. (134)

Solitude has no answers and, Woolf suggests, neither has human intercourse, since the latter has severe limitations. Stranded, then, on either side of the dividing line between the separation of aloneness and the separation of engagement, there is little space to exist, none really to live. And so Mrs. Ramsay dies between those enveloping brackets in a scene spatially rich in suggestion: "[Mr. Ramsay, stumbling along a passage one dark morning, stretched his arms out, but Mrs. Ramsay having died rather suddenly the night before, his arms, though stretched out, remained empty]" (128). Exceeding in impact any protracted death scene description, this brief account of a death already in the past projects a poignancy both effective and final. Mr. Ramsay is desperate to connect, and his outstretched arms grasp as for a ghost; but even in death the subject is denied his object, and the nature of reality—emptiness—is brutally confirmed. It is now his fate to be bracketed in living solitude without even the enveloping "shadow" of a relationship. Going to the lighthouse remains the only symbolic connection he can make; indeed we "perish, each alone." Mrs. Ramsay's death was already sealed when the darkness fell, when "[s]ometimes a hand was raised as if to clutch to something, or somebody groaned, or somebody laughed aloud as if sharing a joke with nothingness" (126).

5

Lily Briscoe's isolation is explored twice, once in Part I and again in Part III; once as she paints a living subject and again when she attempts to retrieve that subject's memory and paint it onto a new blank canvas. The artist in Lily has often been compared to Woolf herself, and a good deal has been made of their affinity. However, although Woolf takes Lily's painting seriously, she also makes it clear on several occasions that Lily was an amateur, that her painting was avocation not vocation, that even Mrs. Ramsay did not think much of it. Narrative time makes it easy to overlook that Lily's painting, on each occasion, takes up only a half day; though the first painting is obviously incomplete, the second is at least declared "done." This hardly accords with a comparison to the art of Woolf, who if anything pleaded all her life that writing be taken more seriously in her country and who labored long over every page. In no way does this diminish the importance of Lily's canvas and the artist's struggle with it, but these seem to be only symbolic of the ineffable nature of relationships. All the insurmountable difficulties that attended the relationship between Mr. and Mrs. Ramsay are reflected in Lily's attempts to understand Mrs. Ramsay (and her husband) and in her own ambivalence toward both these people in what constitutes a triangular figuration.

One cannot ignore the autobiographical stimulus that prompted Woolf's undertaking *To the Lighthouse*, with Woolf's parents being represented in large measure through Mr. and Mrs. Ramsay and surely a touch of Woolf herself in Lily. But like Septimus Smith in *Mrs. Dalloway*, Lily Briscoe is a necessary agent who brings into relief the novel's principal motifs. This does not devalue her importance, but she and her painting at times act more as devices rather than attempts to reflect on the nature of an *artist's* tribulations.

Lily Briscoe is not always an in-depth parallel to the aesthetic and epistemological dilemmas of the artist as Woolf herself experienced them. In some
way Lily is the "reflection in a mirror," and in the end perhaps that mirror
too is broken.

In Section I Lily faces the "mirror"—it is a window—in the desperate
hope that it reflects back to her sufficient meaning in the figure of Mrs.
Ramsay and her son James to create a sense of unity on canvas. By nature
Lily is a loner ("[s]he liked to be alone; she liked to be herself . . ." [50]);
isolated, she contemplates the painting before her, how to bring it off,
how to achieve balance. Perhaps the "line of the branch" might do it; or
she might "break the vacancy in the foreground" by inserting an "object"
like James; but with each possible move there was the danger of upsetting
the "unity of the whole" and failing at the very goal she hoped to achieve
(53). It is a dilemma poised to paralyze her. Like a chess player trapped
by the opponent (here the opponent is the unanswerable), every move she
might make threatens her with checkmate. This arrested state induces a
powerful conflict:

> She would move the tree more to the middle.
> Such was the complexity of things. For what happened to her, especially
> staying with the Ramsays, was to be made to feel violently two opposite things
> at the same time; that's what *you* feel, was one; that's what *I* feel, was the other,
> and they fought together in her mind, as now. (102; italics mine)

The particular moment of conflict is to be witness to the love between two
young people, which Lily sees as both absurd and "barbaric" but also "beautiful and necessary" (102–103). Lily cannot reconcile the *you* and *I*
dilemma: it is the agent of indecision, even failure. If the tree is moved in
one direction, it is toward "you"; moved in another, it becomes "I." So the
problem is to achieve the balance between Self and Other, where the one
can remain intact and yet be part of that remaining outside oneself. During all of Part I (and indeed, in a different way, Part III) Lily cannot fully
achieve that flexibility; indeed, in both instances she is overwhelmed by
Mrs. Ramsay's presence, which becomes her *you*. The movement of the tree,
then, that search for unity on the canvas, is more Lily's attempt to free herself and yet remain connected than it is an aesthetic search for unity *in* the
painting. For in the end, the painting is a reflection of her inner conflicts
between solitude and company, with the tree (or branch or line) serving as
the divider that stubbornly remains as the frustrating obstacle no matter
which way you move it. Lily remains insistent: "All must be in order. She
must get that right and that right . . ." (113). At dinner she had found an
answer that avoided the "awkward space": it was to move the tree. Yet to

place it directly in the center would ultimately prove no answer either—life, Lily will realize, is always decentered.

6

Lily opens Section III with the proper question: "What does it all mean then, what can it all mean?" (145). Having returned to the scene of her initial painting, Lily feels even more apart: "Sitting alone . . . she felt cut off. . . . The house, the place, the morning, all seemed strangers to her. She had no attachment here, she felt no relations with it . . ." (146). The repetition of Mr. Ramsay's mantra, "'Perished. Alone'" (147), now resonates more than it ever had. Staring at her new blank canvas brings forbidding new challenges: "The empty places. Such were some of the parts, but how bring them together?" (147). Essentially, ten years have not altered the dilemma of the "tree"; if anything, starting over with the subjects of the painting absent (Mrs. Ramsay is dead and James is on the boat headed to the lighthouse) unveils more problems, well beyond the recalcitrant tree—for example the widowed Mr. Ramsay, the remaining prompter of her memories, searching for sympathy again: "Still she could say nothing. . . . It was immensely to her discredit, sexually, to stand there dumb. . . . They stood there. . . . In complete silence she stood there. . . . But Mr. Ramsay . . . exerted upon her solitary figure the immense pressure of his concentrated woe . . . his desolation. . . ." (152–53) It is no accident that both resolve the impasse by descending from the vacancy of spatial silence to the real, the magnificently trivial compliment she offers to his splendid boots. Again subject, object, and the nature of reality win out to save the awkward moment in order to penetrate emptiness. But as soon as Mr. Ramsay leaves for the lighthouse, Lily is once more confronted by the canvas with its "uncompromising white stare," its "emptiness." All her plans were mental exercises; there was "all the difference in the world" between conceptualizing and "making the first mark" with the brush, for the critical problem was "[w]here to begin? . . . at what point to make the first mark?" (157). And, of course, at what point to make the last. (She anticipates what Beckett will diagnose as "aporia.")

Lily spends some hours toiling and in revery, hoping that she was right in believing that "[in] the midst of chaos there was shape; this eternal passing and flowing . . . was struck into stability" (161), but "the problem of space remained" (171). Lily's reveries either recall or imagine Mrs. Ramsay in varying moments. In one,

> Mrs. Ramsay sat silent. She was glad, Lily thought, to rest in silence, uncommunicative; to rest in the extreme obscurity of human relationships. Who knows what we are, what we feel? Who knows even at the moment of inti-

macy, This is knowledge? Aren't things spoilt, then, Mrs. Ramsay may have asked (it seemed to have happened so often, this silence by her side) by saying them? Aren't we more expressive thus [i.e., in silence]? (171–72)

One is tempted to argue that this is Lily's rationalization to make her peace with silence, and to some extent surely it is that. But subsequently, even more crucial, this is the beginning of her contemplating how this painting must end. For it, too, is subject to the rules of articulation. Ten years prior she had painted a mother and child abstraction, which no one understood. She seems to have taken up a more representational rendering in her second attempt, but it is doomed as well. In painting, as in life, perhaps silence and emptiness are better than being "expressive"? While Lily continues bravely "tunnelling her way" into the past and onto her painting (173), she seems to be getting further from, rather than nearer to, her goal. "Oh, Mrs. Ramsay! she called out *silently*, to that essence which sat by the boat . . . [my italics]." Almost in terror Lily discovers the bare drawing-room steps and wonders whether one could ever "express that emptiness there?" Everything turns into "curves and arabesques flourishing round a centre of complete emptiness." Once more she asks what she had asked at the start of Part III, "'What does it mean? How do you explain it all' . . ." (178–179).

Lily is caught in the vacuum between time present and time past, between presence and absence, which are both part of memory, and on no account can she articulate, whether with brush or words. Mr. Carmichael is close at hand, and sensing that presence, Lily wants desperately to tell him "everything." But her thoughts are "dismembered," rendering her speechless: " . . . no, she thought, one could say nothing to anybody" (178). The entire dialogue with Mrs. Ramsay is achieved "wordlessly": The subject's object is now twice beyond reach, though the wordless interchanges are more detailed, precisely because they can receive no verbal response: dialogue is now monologue. Lily continues to pursue the abiding questions of meaning. With Carmichael at hand, she thinks that perhaps if they both "demanded an explanation" there would be a resolution: "[B]eauty would roll itself up; the space would fill; those empty flourishes would form into shape. . . ." But her outcry, twice, "'Mrs Ramsay! . . . Mrs. Ramsay!'" produces only tears— "[t]he pain increased" (180). Lily's obsession with filling space is not, of course, concerned merely with her canvas; again the painting is a mirror image of larger issues of "space"—the emptiness of her life, the emptiness created by all those questions "'[a]bout life, about death, about Mrs. Ramsay'" (178) that weigh so heavily on her being. That is one reason she cannot achieve a "razor-edge of balance between two opposite forces; Mrs. Ramsay and the picture. (193)"

Is it the design, she thinks, is something "wrong" with it? The answer is probably no, for the design itself cannot solve this issue; Mrs. Ramsay inhabits an impenetrable world, a solitude that envelops her in life as in death, and it can never be in "balance" with a painting: It will always insist on mastery over it. Hence there was perpetually "something that evaded her when she thought of Mrs. Ramsay . . . (193), evasions that were critical in preventing closure. Now Mrs. Ramsay is out of reach; there is simply too much space.

7

As J. Hillis Miller has written, "The notion of ending in narrative is inherently 'undecidable'"[18]; and to corrupt Frank Kermode's title of his notable book, *To the Lighthouse* is a novel with a sense of no ending. Woolf's deep despair after completing the novel seems contrary to the conventional way that the novel's ending has been read. As suggested earlier, most critics have perceived the conclusion of the novel as the triumphant achievement of two "visions": the successful landing at the lighthouse by the three Ramsays and Lily's self-pronounced "vision" as she apparently completes her painting. Yet both endings fall short of visions. Arriving at the lighthouse creates some form of closure for Mr. Ramsay and James—for the former a belated sense of absolution perhaps, but for the latter disappointment, as no adolescent can experience the joy imagined by a six-year-old child. At best the experience is for James attenuated, and the compliment by his father on his steering skills of the boat, though welcome, is insufficient. The lighthouse appears as reality, "a stark tower on a bare rock," on which laundry is spread, though Woolf insists that "the other was also the Lighthouse, for nothing was simply one thing. The other Lighthouse was true too" (186). Nothing is ever one thing, but the insistence that the lighthouse of visual reality has its dream-like counterpart strikes a note of special pleading, a note of rebellion, perhaps aimed at Mr. Ramsay's unforgiving empiricism.

In James and Cam's eyes, Mr. Ramsay remains a "brute," a "tyrant," "egotistical." That is what they think of him, though what they see mostly is his isolation still enveloped in bitter solitude. When Cam studies his face, as they approach the landing site of the lighthouse, she wonders, "What was it he sought, so fixedly, so intently, so silently?" And what she sees is not clear: "He sat and looked at the island and he might be thinking, We perished, each alone, or he might be thinking, I have reached it, I have found it; but he said nothing." The *might* in this sentence (noted twice) is sufficiently ambiguous, and when Cam sees her father disembark as if "leaping into space" (an image with sexual implications) she exclaims: "There is no God" (207), making clear that such a leap is no supernatural leap of faith but, as it were, a desperate stab to fill the space of emptiness.

Lily Briscoe says that her painting is "done" and she has had her "vision." But both of these claims are ambiguous. After a morning of painting, it is possible that she has completed her canvas; yet "done" merely implies she has finished, not necessarily "completed" it. This may seem like a quibble, but the evidence is better than mere guesswork about the uncertainty of a single word. Nor are these readings of the endings pessimistic; they simply do not accord with the more or less cheerful readings of the novel's ending that have become almost *de rigueur.*[19] In "The Russian Point of View" (1919), Woolf herself cautions us to accept endings as they are, even when they are not really endings in the conventional sense: "let us never manipulate the evidence so as to produce something fitting" (*Essays,* 185). And in "Modern Fiction" (so titled when she first published it in 1919), she writes of the "Russian mind," which in literature she seemed to have valued above any other:

> More accurately we might speak of the inconclusiveness of the Russian mind. It is the sense that there is no answer, that if honestly examined life presents question after question which must be left to sound on and on after the story is over in hopeless interrogation that fills us with a deep, and finally it may be with a resentful, despair. (*Essays,* 163)

Resentful despair. Woolf would have it otherwise, despite her admiration for the "Russian mind," suggesting that the English tradition with its "natural delight in humour and comedy, in the beauty of earth, in the activities of the intellect, and in the splendour of the body" might be an alternative to "resentful despair." On the other hand, she was clearly drawn to the Russian habit of open-endedness and inconclusiveness, for instance the feeling that "nothing is solved" at the end of Chekhov's stories.[20] ("The Russian Point of View" [*Essays,* 1919], 184–85). As Woolf would have wished, the "evidence" should not be manipulated. In so following her caution, one can shape the argument that Lily's vision is that we *cannot* have encompassing "visions," that her painting is not completed but stricken, that "in extreme fatigue" the line she draws in "the centre" is more a cancellation of the painting than a triumph of vision. Lily realizes that any finality is elusive, that "always something . . . thrust through, snubbed her, waked her, required and got in the end . . . attention, so that the vision must be perpetually remade" (181). With caustic irony, T. S. Eliot referred to "visions and revisions"; and at some point Lily realizes that visions cannot be revised. Such a reading of the final brushstroke is not intended to be a perverse reversal of what has been the traditional reading. It is not difficult to extend out from the failure of communication among the dysfunctional people in the novel to an equal failure of communication—desperately sought—between Lily and her painting, the artist and her art: both kinds of relationships remain crippled. Of course, that final brushstroke is not without its achievement of completion. Since the painting was the creative bridge between Lily and Mrs. Ramsay, the completion of it (whether it meets Lily's intent or fails) finally severs the relationship with Mrs. Ramsay. In Platonic terms Lily is now thrice removed from Mrs. Ramsay: from the corporeal Mrs. Ramsay, from her creative vision of her, and from the attempted image of her on the canvas. Mrs. Ramsay's "soliloquy in solitude" has become Lily's, too: She is truly alone, and that in itself is a form of cancellation.

During her second attempt to paint, in Part III, Lily several times asks herself what it all means: "What is the meaning of life? That was all—a simple question; one that tended to close in on one with years. The great revelation had never come. *The great revelations perhaps never did come.* Instead there were little daily miracles, illuminations. . . ." [Italics mine] (161). We recall Mrs. Ramsay thinking, "Life, she thought—but she did not finish her thought"; and Mr. Ramsay cannot move beyond "R." Each recognizes that there are no final resolutions, that revelation (read: "vision") does not come in biblical proportions but at best in Joycean epiphanies. Just before Lily speaks the final words of the novel, she again "looked at the steps; they were empty," Mrs. Ramsay *was* dead; and "she looked at her canvas; it was blurred" (208–209). It is difficult to see how the sight of empty steps and a blurred canvas can equate with a triumphant "vision." It should never be assumed that Lily *resumes* painting; she begins, after a ten-year hiatus, afresh; in Part I it is true that matters of color and proportion are discussed, with Woolf's notions of painting deeply indebted to Roger Fry, Clive Bell and the currency, among the avant-garde, of "significant form." In Part III, however, while the problem of the "centre" remains, there is far less of that and far more of those elusive questions about the meaning of it all, questions that ultimately resist answers. It is this inability to achieve endings that forces Lily into those periods of revery, a Proustian *mémoire involuntaire,* preoccupied with resurrecting the powerful effects of remembering Mrs. Ramsay in hopes that thereby she will find meaning. But death has transfigured Mrs. Ramsay, as it has her painter, and in that sense it is virtually ordained that Lily cannot really "complete" the painting she had abandoned ten years earlier. At the end, Lily's solitude, as that of the three Ramsays landing at the lighthouse, remains intact, and verbal contact is still virtually frozen: "Incommunicability is in truth the most awful of solitudes."[21]

In her initial planning, Woolf intended to end the novel "in the Boat"; neither the actual landing at the lighthouse nor the completion of Lily's painting were contemplated. Her diary entry for September 3, 1926 is intriguing:

> The last chapter which I begin tomorrow is In the Boat: I had meant to end with R. climbing on the rock. If so, what becomes [of] Lily & her picture?

Should there be a final page about her & Carmichael looking at the picture & summing up R's character? In that case I lose the intensity of the moment. If this intervenes between R. & the lighthouse, there's too much chop & change, I think. Could I do it in a parenthesis? so that one had the sense of reading the two things at the same time?

I shall solve it somehow, I suppose. (*Diary*, 106)

And she did. She still did not feel satisfied with "Lily on the lawn," but she liked "the end" (*Diary*, March 21, 1927, 132). Clearly "the end" was to concentrate on the scene of the *uncompleted* journey, in "the Boat"; but she returned to the earlier idea of Mr. Ramsay climbing up on the rock, and then she recognized the importance of "Lily & her picture." That would be the end, not the boat nor Mr. Ramsay's ascent to the lighthouse, for she must have felt that the ambiguity of Lily's painting was stronger than the unfulfilled experience of reaching the lighthouse. Rejected, too, were the parentheses: Each event has its numbered section, or chapter, and the simultaneity of the last two events is clearly inferred. In *Writing Beyond the Ending,* Rachel Blau Du Plessis has made an interesting case for the "narrative strategies of twentieth-century women writers" (the subtitle of her book). In previous centuries writers of both genders felt compelled to follow the tradition of tying up their novels' endings with deaths and nuptials (Woolf makes the point in "Mr. Bennett and Mrs. Brown"). In *To the Lighthouse,* both deaths and nuptials occur decentered, not at the end. Marriage and death are positioned in the intervening hiatus of Part II: Prue dies in childbirth; Andrew dies in the war; Mrs. Ramsay dies at some point in that decade; and we hear that the Railey marriage has turned sour early in Part III. At the end, as Du Plessis argues, Woolf consciously goes against the convention: Lily renounces marriage, and there are no deaths to report. Lily, having first followed the "quest plot of artistic ambition" in Part I is, in Part III, finally able to understand the impossibility of the linear trajectory such a "plot" imposes. So at the end, Du Plessis concludes, the aesthetic problems Lily faced in Part I and at the start of Part III could not be solved by "aesthetic or formal means alone"; instead the solutions "lay in her vulnerability to feelings of emptiness and baffled desire." Du Plessis characterizes the two final events as "arcing and interconnected," and both as "journeys that had been becalmed until love, grief, and need were admitted."[22] So Mrs. Ramsay's death (and Andrew's and Prue's) become the enabling events for both Mr. Ramsay and Lily Briscoe. The only question is whether that enabling permitted real closure. Mr. Ramsay's landing at the lighthouse, rendered in "mid-flight," and Lily's final stroke on the blurred canvas as a divisive/dividing line of that canvas, made in a state of fatigue, raise serious doubts about the nature and extent of completion. Ruotolo, while accepting the ending as more conclusive than it is, mocks its meaning. James's successful navigation and Lily's completion of her painting are seen as "absurdly irrelevant," for "the end of each human effort remains inconclusive." Mr. Ramsay is silent as he reaches the lighthouse and "Lily . . . draws a line through the empty center of a painting destined to rest unnoticed and unappreciated in someone's attic."[23] This is only partially true because "irrelevant" trivializes what remains "inconclusive."

In categorizing writers who prefer inconclusive texts, R. M. Adams makes two lists. One of them includes Shakespeare, Cervantes, and Stendhal, who often create "ironic inconclusiveness"; from what he calls the "aspect of tonality" he is prepared to place Woolf in that group rather than "in that of the furious confused introspectors with whom her indecisiveness about indecision itself finally aligned her." Although "tonality" is imprecise, Adams's instincts are right: Woolf's inconclusiveness, certainly in *Mrs. Dalloway* and *To the Lighthouse,* is "ironic," and "open form," in both novels, achieves "a deeply recessed mirror vision in which the work of art itself occupies the foreground of its own picture."[24] In fact this perfectly describes the fate of Lily's "picture."

Perhaps one of the more convincing observations on the much-discussed problem of fictional endings is in Peter J. Rabinowitz's "End Sinister: Neat Closure as Disruptive Force":

> [O]ne of the major strategies that marks current Western interpretative practice is what I call the Rule of Conclusive Endings: we tend to guide our readings with the assumption that the author intended us to take the ending of the text . . . as a *conclusion*. . . . [W]hen we find texts that are "open" . . . the Rule of Conclusive Endings encourages us to interpret the openness *itself* as an essential part of the book. . . . [25]

This is salutary advice for reading *To the Lighthouse*. The motif of "soliloquy in solitude" virtually enforces us to be wary of a "conclusive" ending, for in this novel solitude is never transcended. Quite the contrary, the conclusion of the novel dovetails the description of "crisis"—"a moment of crisis, a flash-point, one of those brief instants in time when the primal isolation and helplessness of the human condition are revealed."[26] This signals neither "triumph" nor tragedy, but rather the freeze-frame in time and space that so often attends modern narrative, and that one suspects, Woolf learned more from Henry James than from Joyce.

8

In her essay on Defoe's *Robinson Crusoe* (see chapter II), Woolf had made clear her admiration of Crusoe's consistency of focus, whatever reservations she might have had about his fictional method. In facing this achievement of singleness of purpose (perhaps she might have called it "vision"), which she much admires, Woolf reveals her own desire to achieve such unity by exploring the solitude of soul through the "minds" (read: consciousnesses) of her major characters, especially in *To the Lighthouse.* Certainly her own method allows for such substitution: The focus is not Defoe's earthenware pot, but soliloquies of the soul mirrored in the mind, seldom articulated except to oneself and the reader, wedded in conspiratorial silence. As Auerbach observed in *Mimesis,* there are many ways of representing "reality" in fiction; in his chapter on *To the Lighthouse,* he attempts to put some definition to Woolf's method: "to put the emphasis on the random occurrence, to exploit it not in the service of a planned continuity of action but in itself." Thus stressing Woolf's deliberate randomness, Auerbach seems suspicious about the ending that has since been so assiduously constructed and deconstructed as unifying. When we have completed the novel, he suggests, "the meaning of the relationship between the planned journey to the lighthouse and the actual trip . . . remains unexplained, enigmatic, only dimly to be conjectured, as does the content of Lily Briscoe's concluding vision which enables her to finish her painting with one stroke of the brush."[27]

Woolf's artistic aims, the development of her art, what she admired and strove to emulate—all these issues have, of course, been widely debated over several decades. Still, what emerges from the little that has been offered about these problems in the context of the present discussion is more conflicted than many have conceded. Although clearly Woolf wished to give "voice" to the mind, she abhorred disorder in art (as in life), and she strove to achieve that elusive unity that perhaps all serious artists see as their objective. At the same time, then, that she admired the consistency of "perspective" in someone like Defoe, she rejected his means of getting there. The problem, therefore, was to discipline and harness what Auerbach called the "random," and although she achieved an external unity in *To the Lighthouse,* she was acutely aware that the last acts of completion—arrival at the lighthouse, finishing the painting—were not the grand visions of closure she had perhaps hoped she could attain when she began to write the novel. In an account of Woolf's "literary life," John Mepham writes that in the course of 1926, when *To the Lighthouse* was begun, Woolf "was at times almost unbalanced by her desire to catch her vision." Her ultimate recognition that, like Lily, such visions elude us must have devastated her, though her revisions of the manuscript show an acceptance that her "mystical visionary side" was suspect—especially in print.[28] In any case, both Woolf's act of writing the novel and Lily's act of painting her picture are solitary events. Blanchot says, "The work [of art] is solitary. . . . But whoever reads it enters into the affirmation of the work's solitude, just as he who [creates] it belongs to the risk of this solitude."[29]

One needs no postmodern perspective to allow that the open-ended closure in *To the Lighthouse* may be a greater triumph for the novel than the more neatly (and more superficial) double "visions" so many admirers seem compelled to insist on. Ruotolo believes that the "culmination" of Lily's "vision" is indeed that line "drawn through that 'awkward vacancy' in the center of her canvas." Between the first and second painting he discerns a shift: "In the course of a decade she has resolved first to fill and then to avoid that empty space." Again Blanchot perceives the dynamic: "To write [or to perform any creative act] is to enter into the affirmation of the solitude. . . . It is to surrender to the risk of time's absence."[30] It is "time's absence" that overwhelms Lily and her painting, perhaps a risk she had no idea was so emphatic in its consequences. Neither filling or avoiding space is accomplished by her final brushstroke, for space has no demarcations; it cannot be delimited, framed, caught, any more than time can. Space is eternally recreated: As soon as the brush moves in one direction, it creates "space" where it has vacated. The difference is subtle, but it is more accurate to speak of the ending as "inconclusive" than "incomplete." J. Hillis Miller, in his deconstructive reading of the novel, is in search of the narrator, who exercises considerable authority. "The voice of the narrator," he writes, "is subtly subversive of the thoughts and feelings of the characters." Yet Lily's final brushstroke is for him "the line that stands for the dead Mrs. Ramsay and substitutes for her, that replaces the missing shadow on the step cast by Mrs. Ramsay. . . ."[31] It would appear, however, that the 'subversion' is manifestly more ambitious, that Lily and her painting eliminate each other. In Poe's "The Oval Portrait," the subject of the painting dies when the painter is finished; in Woolf's novel, the painter, working with a physically dead subject, dies *with* the painting. Like so many scenes in *To the Lighthouse,* the last two assume the ambiguous and fragile line that Hamlet apprehends between *seems* and *is.*

So, too, this ambiguity attends the dark side of solitude, to use Woolf's own language: it, too, is never all-revealing. Like the dark side of the moon, there are times when we cannot see it at all. In one diary entry Woolf lamented, "Why is there not a discovery in life? Something one can lay hands on & say 'This is it?'" (*Diary,* III, 62; February 27, 1926). But such "discovery" evaded her in life and art; in *To the Lighthouse* it left her at the end with Cowper's lines from "The Castaway," which Mr. Ramsay utters, usually at those moments when he, too, seeks the certainty in the unfulfilled that he is accustomed to from the "subject and object and the nature of reality":

> No voice divine the storm allayed,
> No light propitious shone,
> When snatched from all effectual aid,
> We perished, each alone . . . [32]

These lines are more than Mr. Ramsay's mantra; as one recalls Woolf's observations that the solitude of Defoe's hero produces no fine sunrises or sunsets, no sublime Nature, no God making His divine appearance, one needs now to recall Cowper's stanza. For through Mr. Ramsay, Woolf also seems to realize that solitude, however contemplative its presentation, in the end has "[n]o voice divine... No light propitious": We exist and perish "each, *alone*" (italics mine).

Mr. Ramsay also repeats a line from Tennyson's "The Charge of the Light Brigade": "Someone had blundered." This unpredictable chaos we call life is always a blunder, Woolf concluded; together with Cowper's lament that we each die alone, we can locate the frustration and despair that *To the Lighthouse* apparently caused. Woolf chose the image of the envelope on several occasions; once, when thinking of clothes, she wrote that "people secrete an envelope which connects them & protects them from others, like myself, who am outside the envelope . . ." (*Diary,* III, 12–13; April, 1925). This oscillation between protection and connection clearly shapes the major theme in *To the Lighthouse,* and as protection had the stronger pull, it created, in the end, a novel of "soliloquy in solitude"—"To be silent; to be alone" (62).

Chapter IV 〜

O Altitudo! O Solitudo!
Exilic Solitude and Ambiguous
Ethics on *The Magic Mountain*

I love to lose myself in a mystery, to pursue my reason to an *O altitudo*.

—Sir Thomas Browne, *Religio Medici* (1643)

But if solitude is the stronghold of isolation where a man conducts a dialogue with himself . . . then we have the real fall of the spirit into spirituality. The man can advance to the last abyss.

—Martin Buber, *I and Thou*

Solitude can be the escape of the sick; solitude can also be escape *from* the sick.

—Nietzsche, *Thus Spoke Zarathustra*

As sickness is the greatest misery, so the greatest misery of sickness is solitude.

—John Donne, *Meditation*

From the earliest stories that found their full voice in the novella *Death in Venice* (1912) through the three major novels—*The Magic Mountain, Joseph and His Brothers,* and *Doctor Faustus*—to one of the last tales of loneliness, *The Black Swan [Die Betrogene],* Mann was preoccupied, even obsessed, with men (and sometimes women) who were on the outside, who did not fit, whose often solitary existence brought them little happiness and much sorrow. Most of the time he treated these figures sympathetically, for was he not in some measure, for all his public unsmiling face, one of them? Of course, there were always touches of irony and ambiguity, and nowhere are these more clearly the center of the portrayal than in the depiction of that voluntary expatriate, the self-exiled Hans Castorp, for whom solitude is intended to have a heuristic function. This unheroic hero and his fellow-patients, hermetically sealed off in a tuberculosis sanitorium, experience their solitude on top of that magic mountain, where solitariness was both an imposed and selected form of alienation from the flatland, that other, "healthy" society one left behind when ascending to this snowbound island of isolation. It will turn out that the thrice- orphaned Castorp will be thrice-exiled: once from the flatland and family to the enchanting mountain; and again from the mountain's medicinal function to the aesthetic, if decadent, realm of the East (for that realm can offer him nothing of the ethical). The third exile returns him to a "highly questionable" and ambiguous ethic as he is weaned from the mountain to return to the flatland, a released Ego making *a* choice.

Part of the attractiveness of exile is of its time: Castorp "belongs to that generation which had lost its way and its aim, and was therefore heir to the Romantic sympathy with death which expressed itself physically in disease." Such exilic solitude permits disease to be enriched (the air, we are told, is good in fighting the illness but also good for its prosperity). Illness "makes it possible for [Castorp] to experience unfettered adventures . . . and so finally he recognizes the morality of the Self losing itself, the will-less submission to illness and freedom."[1]

Beckett said that "art is the apotheosis of solitude,"[2] but Mann's portrayal of the outsider is not merely confined to artist-figures, though each of his solitaries certainly leans toward some quasi-artistic temperament.[3] Even in one of the earliest stories (1897), little Herr Friedemann comforts himself by playing his violin; and Thomas Buddenbrook falters because he struggles against the repressed artistic impulses that destroy his brother, Christian, and threaten his own upright burgher persona. Tonio Kröger of that named novella and Aschenbach of *Death in Venice* are, of course, the artist-figure solitaries in pristine clarity: Here Mann is unequivocal about the enormous cost of artistic solitude.[4] As in the much later version of the artist-solitary, Adrian Leverkühn, there is the suggestion, even a devil's dictum, that the hero, though capable—even desirous—of love, even permitted to experience it for very long. The price of art very nearly amounts to the abandonment of humanity. In *Doctor Faustus,* Beethoven's Ninth (with its "Ode to Joy" from that most genial of humanists, Schiller) is "taken back" by the hellish musical equivalents in the lamentations of a Faustus *("Höllengelächter"),* whose confessional account of his life in hell harkens back to the *Faustbuch* and Marlowe, but not to Goethe. As Fritz Kaufmann correctly observes, for "Mann the idea of the solitary genius is not merely a literary fashion"; it has its roots in "the blending of features of the Renaissance and the Reformation," in the evolution of "the Protestant concept of man in his frightful solitude before God and of the Renaissance individual from the medieval community."[5]

1

There are merging parallel motifs in *The Magic Mountain:* the inherent ambiguity of the state of solitude that pervades the sanatorium and its patients, especially Hans Castorp, and the principal force (other than the illness itself) that overcomes and eventually directs Castorp's life on the mountain and drives him into solitude. That solitude is enveloped in the ominous and threatening spirit of solitude itself—the dreaded East. It is reported that Mann said, "'There is much of the East in me . . . much heavy and sluggish craving after that form or no-form of consummation which is called Nirvana, or nothingness.'"[6] That East also beckons to Mann's hero, for far from being its victim, Hans Castorp arrives at the mountain both predisposed to be seduced by the East and even eager to pursue those seducers who embody the East in the novel. The first of these predates Castorp's arrival, reaching back into his childhood, to the Slav boy, Privislav Hippe—"the blending of Germanic blood with Slavic-Wendish, or vice versa"—revered if unapproachable friend and male counterpart to Clavdia Chauchat.[7] Toward the latter half of the novel, Mann characterizes Castorp's self-abandonment to Eastern lures as a falling into "self-narcosis," likening its spell to that most Eastern of potions: opium. Despite all kinds of premonitions and ominous warning signals to Castorp (especially from Settembrini) for him to resist these Eastern seductions, he increasingly surrenders to his "drang nach Osten" (this impulse toward the East), which is centered on, but by no means exclusive to, his pursuit of that representative from those distant geographical outposts of the deepest East, Clavdia Chauchat. It is this Russian woman with her "slightly Asiatic" eyes who embodies most, if not all, of the East's allurements and dangers.

And so Hans Castorp will discover that the enticements of the East serve as a defining measure of his alienation, however temporary, as he sheds the West imprinted in him (perhaps less deeply than he knew) when he arrives on the mountain. Further, it is the East that will define the ambiguity of his solitude, his need to be connected, contravened by his need to be "lost" in the abysses of the void that define the East in this novel: the far-away Daghestan (from which Clavdia Chauchat comes), the amorphous, vast, spaceless and timeless whiteness he encounters in "Snow." It would appear that nowhere does Heraclitus's line "[t]he way up and the way down is the same" apply more aptly than to Hans Castorp's journey from flatland to mountain to flatland. Like Zarathustra's, Castorp's journey "up" to the mountain is both down and inward; and while his descent after a seven-year stay (Nietzsche's "seven skins" of solitude must have been on Mann's mind) can hardly be called precipitous, the sudden departure down to the flatland engulfed by war is to a different level of nothingness—almost certain annihilation.[8] Zarathustra also ascends a mountain and, after due time, decides to descend: "Only now are you going your way to greatness! Peak and abyss—they are now joined together!"[9] Unlike Nietzsche, Mann deliberately does not endow Castorp with prophetic wisdom, but rather thrusts knowledge and insight upon him through the tedious research he undertakes, either by means of book learning or as a listener to the endless disputations between Settembrini and Naphta.

It is obvious that, among other things, *The Magic Mountain* is about solitude, both its siren song, to which Castorp quickly falls prey, and its deep and melancholy diseases that infect not only his lungs but his spirit. And who would understand solitariness and isolation better than he who embraced both Schopenhauer and, however uneasily at times, Nietzsche? After all, Schopenhauer insisted that the *principium individuationis* was the principal evil of our existence, this ego-oriented preoccupation with individuality. Once we tear away this "veil of Maya," we can, according to Schopenhauer, take on the sufferings of others and penetrate to the thing-in-itself. For, in Mann's interpretation of Schopenhauer, "Such is the conviction of . . . unenlightened egoism: absolute prepossession with the *principium individuationis.* To see through this principle, to divine its illusory, truth-shrouding character; to begin to see that the I and the you are indistinguishable . . . is the beginning and the essence of ethics.[10] Applied to *The Magic Mountain,* this is a tricky premise. In order to divest himself of the principle of individuality, Castorp must first recognize what it really is. His "unenlightened egoism" is a central participant in his ultimately self-enforced solitude. When at last he renounces his longing for Clavdia Chauchat, and when his remaining time on the mountain becomes a state of habituated exile rather than therapy or "research," he begins to penetrate a certain "ethical" dimension. Ultimately, such an ethic is not manifested in his decision to go to war, but in his decision to *go;* not a surrender of individuality for some communal duty, but a recognition that "[f]reedom, like the will, was beyond and on the other side of the phenomenal. . . . [Freedom] lay not in doing but in being, not in *operari* but in *esse.*"[11] Participation in the conflagration is, of course, a kind of "doing"; but freedom for Castorp lies in his decision to leave the mountain, which puts an end to his "aesthetic" solitude and to "unenlightened egotism." What freedom generates is another matter, but the ability to make a choice is ethical.

2

"There are lacunae in 'The Magic Mountain.'"[12] While it is perhaps odd to think of a novel so densely written and conceived as having "lacunae," the term is obviously metaphorical and most aptly describes those spaces in the text into which no amount of verbal sparring, no philosophical dialogue, no cosmic speculations can penetrate. Indeed it is these lacunae, these silences, that create a kind of metaphysical emptiness, a deep solitude in which the text itself is embedded, serving as a bulwark against the onslaught of words and ideas that swirl, like the mountainous snow, through so much of Mann's book.

And within this structural solitude is the solitude of the personae and their lives. Both in the life of its hero, Hans Castorp, and in the lives of his fellow-patients, solitude is the accompanying condition (or consequence) of their collective illness. As a disease, none fitted Mann's purposes of depicting isolation from the world better than tuberculosis; indeed the Berghof is in certain respects a perfect parallel to a monastery/nunnery. The patients have come to this isolated mountain retreat from "down there" to live what we are repeatedly told is an "hermetic" existence. True, some are more cut off from the world than others; some resist their sealed-up lives; some return periodically to the "flatland" for respites. But the thrice-orphaned Hans Castorp (that is what he calls himself when his uncle, the last male relative, dies) becomes the consummate isolate. Ultimately he severs all relations with the other world: He ceases to read newspapers, has little or no contact with what family is left, stops ordering his beloved Maria Mancini cigars from "below," and increasingly becomes self-absorbed and isolated, even from his own companion sufferers. Indeed, as Hofrat Behrens predicts from the start, Castorp has a "talent" for illness that makes him a perfect patient; even when pronounced well enough to leave, he resists. And in time he develops a superiority and contempt that allow him to use his isolation as a basis for small, but significant, acts of arrogant, high-handed behavior. His isolation, cultivated and flaunted, begins to convey a stern message: "Watch out! I am no one to mess with; my space is mine, and no one is permitted near it." For a time, Mann endows him with a Nietzschean harshness: "'One must learn to *look away* from oneself in order to *see much:* this hardness is necessary to every climber of mountains.'"[13] From convivial and polite innocent, Castorp becomes something of an intellectual and social snob, a harsh judge of his fellow patients. Such snobbery is no longer that earlier more charming bourgeois sense of rectitude (everyone should wear a hat in order to be able to take it off in reverence when necessary), but a contemptuous, sometimes sneering, attitude of righteousness. Only *he* will defy the rules and ski the mountains (almost at peril of death); only *he* will play the third party in that morality play of Peeperkorn and Clavdia Chauchat; only *he* will become the proprietor of the gramophone and its records; only *he* will take the risk of first raising the ghost of his cousin, Joachim, and then abruptly terminating the séance. Such behavior signals an inherent impatience that becomes a source for turning Castorp into a solitary malcontent. Nietzsche's description of an hypothetical "striver" comes uncomfortably close to the developing character of Hans Castorp:

> A man who strives after great things, looks upon everyone . . . either as a means of advance, or a delay and hindrance. . . . His peculiar lofty *bounty* to his fellow-men is only possible when he attains his elevation and dominates. Impatience, and the consciousness of being always condemned to comedy up to that time . . . spoil all intercourse for him; this kind of man is acquainted with solitude, and what is most poisonous in it.[14]

But this, too, would be an unfair description of Castorp, even at the end, for he preserves compassionate impulses and cares deeply for those he respects or admires: his cousin Joachim, Clavdia Chauchat, Peeperkorn, even Settembrini. So the case of Hans Castorp's state of solitude—like so much else on the magic mountain—is ambiguous.

Still, all the accompanying fetishes of illness on the magic mountain necessitate a variety of solitary acts. There are the daily rest cures taken on one's balcony, sealed (hermetically) in one's mummylike blankets; the measuring of one's temperature; the occasional necessity for privacy to cough into the "Blue Peter"; and, of course, the state of becoming moribund and facing that final solitary act, death itself. Yet again all this is counterbalanced by a conviviality, however forced it may be, among the patients. Transcending their aloneness, their solitariness, they seek each other out in a variety of social and sexual liaisons that create a kind of counterculture both to the flatland and the prescribed culture of the sanatorium with its rules, habitually violated. We hear of games played, of riotous behavior, of overeating and too much drinking, of excursions to waterfalls, of parties, séances, sexual affairs. By and large, these violations are known to the establishment and are most often winked at as necessary outlets. Perhaps reactions of defiance, these desperate attempts to normalize the life of illness bespeak something communal. To be sure it is not the sort of community envisioned by Settembrini or Naphta, or that dreamt of by Hans Castorp in "Snow," but it is community of a kind. All the patients appear to be in solitude for company; their perspective of solitude and the attempts to ameliorate it exempt no one, not even Castorp, though he carries out this ambiguously exilic existence in a way unique to himself.

A major component of solitude is time: how the individual fills it, or makes attempts to *ful*fill it; how time is separated out from spatial intrusions, so as to isolate the flow itself unhindered by clocks or calendar constrictions. Again illness suits itself to temporal isolation, especially such extended isolation as is meted out to so many of the patients on the magic mountain. And with a loss of so-called normal indicators of time, we become ensnared—seduced, as Settembrini asserts—so that we adopt a uniquely different view of life. For Settembrini, the slovenly, loose, vague, unstructured, dangerous, and even demonic nature of this acquired worldview (which he resists), comes from the East; it is palpably contrasted to the perceptions of a normal, measured, sane sense of time championed in what is considered by Settembrini the civilized West. Among many Modernists, this fear of the East was common: Yeats placed unflattering "vague Asiatic immensities" in contrast to Phidian "measurement"; Eliot envisioned "hooded hordes" threatening western civilization; Hesse asserted that *The Brothers Karamazov* was the "cause" of Europe's "Untergang"; and, in *The Magic Mountain,* Mann plays out the contrast in so many ways that the subject commands attention.[15]

For it is Asia and the West and their respective perspectives of time that define, insofar as this is possible, the nature of solitude and its often ambiguous role in Mann's novel. In his critical chapter on the narration of Time ("A Stroll by the Shore") Mann writes:

> The diaries of opium-eaters record how, during the brief period of ecstasy, the drugged person's dreams have a temporal scope of ten, thirty, sometimes sixty years or even surpass all limits of man's ability to experience time . . . with images thronging past so swiftly that, as one hashish-smoker puts it, the intoxicated user's brain seems to "have had something removed, like the mainspring from a broken watch." (532)

This description, reminiscent both of De Quincey and Baudelaire (who translated him), embodies the full meaning of the somnambulant atmosphere of the novel. Mann's emphasis on time and space echoes De Quincey (and Baudelaire), especially the temporal and spatial distortions that Castorp experiences almost from the start. "Space and time," writes Berdyaev, "which determine the life of our objective world, are the real source of solitude as well as the illusion of transcending it." Freud, taking the phrase from a correspondence with Romain Rollandy, called them our "oceanic feelings," and in "The Unconscious," Freud writes that the "processes" of the unconscious "are not ordered temporally . . . they have no reference to time at all." Freud also takes up timeless states induced pharmacologically.[16]

Dreams that mark a duration of great length when in fact they may be very brief in *real* time parallel, as Mann points out, the long narrative time of the first three weeks, three months, the first year of Castorp's stay. "Snow," which occurs two-thirds into the novel, occurs in the *second* winter of Castorp's stay—he will remain five more years. Those dreams that "surpass all limits of man's ability to experience time" are also described by De Quincey: " . . . I sometimes seemed to have lived for 70 or 100 years in one night; nay, sometimes had feelings . . . of a millennium passed . . . of a duration far beyond the limits of any human experience.[17]

Whether Mann's echo is direct or accidental is of no importance; what is clear is the common druglike experience of enchantment. Castorp often behaves as if under the spell of opium, and his sojourn on this magic mountain is like a long dream fugue, like "L'Après-Midi d'un Faune," which becomes one of his favorites after he assumes control of the gramophone records. But enchantment has many faces. Offering its lures all too readily, the magic mountain's enticement is one elongated dream, a timeless vista where one may not merely forget but, as Mann suggests in "Walpurgisnacht," play the pig like Odysseus's men stranded on Circe's island. Though Hans Castorp sheds no tears for home and makes no effort to return until the war awakens his sense of "duty," and, as has been said, his opportunity to make a choice, his journey has many parallels with Odysseus's (though there is no evidence that Mann as yet knew of Joyce's *Ulysses,* published two years earlier than his own novel). Castorp's odyssey is also long and full of seductions; it has its own Hades, and it ends in battle. Mann was certainly not averse to envisioning the epic or mythic.

In his metaphysical quests, his "research," Castorp operates like a solitary, a captive of narcotic trance. Of course, Settembrini and Naphta are the putative father-teachers, but each has an agenda; cousin Joachim has no inclinations toward philosophizing and Clavdia Chauchat, if anything, is the anti-philosophe, while Peeperkorn is incapable of formulating coherent sentences. Krokowski may be the analyst of the psyche, but about Castorp's analytic sessions we hear nothing; Behrens's jovial public mask covers deep private grief, revealing little of what he thinks or feels. So Castorp's isolation is fairly complete, and one of the few connections with the flatland is his beloved Maria Mancini cigar: "Did not Maria act as a kind of connection between him, a man withdrawn from the world, and his former home in the flatlands?" (381). As Freud did *not* say, sometimes a cigar is *not* a cigar: this religious, feminine-named phallic object links Castorp not merely to the flatland but to Clavdia Chauchat, for it ultimately serves as a rival's symbol to the cigars that Behrens sports.

When Castorp contemplates Joachim's departure, it causes him fear and anxiety: "Can it be that he'll leave me alone up here . . . ?" (408); but in the end, Castorp reacts as he did when Clavdia Chauchat left: "It was all of no interest to Hans Castorp . . ." (415). His often indulgent self-isolation, masked as inhibition, irritates the sense of urgency Clavdia expects from a pursuing lover. Twice in the novel—during Walpurgisnacht and during her talk with him about Peeperkorn—she reproaches his failure to declare himself sooner: "'I was annoyed by your detachment . . . '" (589). Although a certain reserve in young Castorp played a role in his sideline passion, it is apparent that his cultivated sense of isolation was deliberate. Also he knew that surrender to Clavdia signaled a much broader giving in to impulses better kept at some distance. Here is what he tells Peeperkorn: "For the sake of [Clavdia's] love and in spite of Herr Settembrini, I subordinated myself to the principle of irrationality, the principle behind the genius of illness, to which, admittedly, I had long since . . . submitted myself and to which I have remained true up here. . . . [The] flatlands is entirely lost to me now, and in its eyes I am as good as dead" (601). With the death of Joachim and Peeperkorn, and the final departure of Clavdia Chauchat, Castorp's solitude takes on a more "jaded" aspect, and the word is Behrens's who correctly diagnoses: "'Castorp, old pal, you're bored'"(616). Castorp succumbs, like others, to the "demon" called "stupor"; he begins to play solitaire obsessively until the solitary ritual of music-listening on the newly acquired gramophone, for which he has anointed himself guardian, "rescued . . . [him] from his mania for solitaire . . ." (626). Still he maintains his "good nature," which makes him the "confidant" of individual fellow-patients; yet "sadly [he was] unable to find a hearing among the easygoing majority" (622). Uncle Tienappel's death creates finality: Castorp feels orphaned a third time, though he also experiences a new freedom that finally liberates him so he can sever his last link with the world below, those Maria Mancinis, which are replaced by a local Russian brand, maintaining at least a faint link to Clavdia Chauchat.

So Castorp's ambiguous solitude, accompanied by an equally ambiguous freedom, make him increasingly sensitive to time. Now "he no longer carried his pocket watch. It had stopped, having fallen from his nightstand . . . [and] he had long ago dispensed with calendars. . . . It was his way of honoring the stroll by the shore, the abiding ever-and-always, the hermetic magic, to which, once withdrawn from the world, he had proved so susceptible . . ." (699). (The broken watch recalls Mann's description of the opium dreamer's brain, which feels as if something "has been removed, like the mainspring of a broken watch.") At the very moment, then, of Castorp's highest achievement of "freedom" (from time) and isolation (in space), of dreaming "anonymously," the abstract "communal" call of nation and war shakes him loose from his self-narcosis to navigate the dubious and even more ambiguous battlefield, all too much time-oriented and space-specific. It will turn out to be the novel's final irony.

3

From the moment Hans Castorp arrives at the Berghof, he senses that he has entered a new dimension where "Space, like time, gives birth to forgetfulness . . ." (4). This dreaded Lethe, which Settembrini cautions against so vehemently and so often, begins to assert itself in small matters and ends in the wholesale forgetting of that other world, the flatland. Some, like cousin Joachim, experience the "everlasting, endless monotony" (14) impatiently, something to endure; but Hans Castorp will be a sojourner at the Berghof for years until even he begins to feel that sense of stagnant monotony. For a long time he relishes the routine of the patient, eager for just that respite from the world, although he cannot consciously know that three weeks will turn into seven years. His "talent" for illness quickly asserts itself, and it takes no time at all for the casual visitor to become a professional patient, transformed into "a veritable mummy," taking his rest cures even before an official diagnosis exiles him to three weeks of solitary confinement in his bed.

Late in the novel, after Clavdia Chauchat's return to the Berghof, her arch-enemy, Settembrini, tells Castorp, not without sarcasm: "Of course, your weakness for things Asian is well-known" (575). There is little doubt that the major element of this "weakness" is his hopeless surrender to Clavdia Chauchat. Yet Castorp often displays many of the characteristics Settembrini associates, in a state of dread, with the East. One reason, argues Settembrini, why the Berghof attracts so many patrons from the East is that their lifestyle, already predisposed to languor, needs little adjusting. From all the arguments about the vastly superior culture of Western Enlightenment compared with Eastern chaos and irrationality, one can single out the following as the most inclusive indictment Settembrini offers:

> two principles were locked in combat for the world: might and right, tyranny and freedom, superstition and knowledge, the law of obduracy and the law of ferment, change, and progress. One could call the first the Asiatic principle, the other the European, for Europe was the continent of rebellion, critique, and transforming action, whereas the continent to the east embodied inertia and inactivity. (154)

However sweeping such a map of antinomies may read, it accurately reflects some of the contending forces within Hans Castorp. While he, too, strives for "freedom" it will turn out to be not the active Faustian spirit (which Settembrini clearly has in mind), but that ambiguous and contingent freedom of Dostoyevsky, Nietzsche, and Freud, in danger—if one is not careful—more of imprisoning than liberating the Self. The freedom of "negative capability," vouchsafed to Castorp in his solitude in the snow, is a heavy burden. "'I do believe,'" Castorp tells his cousin Joachim, "' . . . that [Settembrini's] freedom and courage are somewhat namby-pamby concepts'" (379). Indeed, he then repeats what Clavdia Chauchat had once asked (in French): Does Settembrini have sufficient courage to *"de se perdre et meme de se laisser desperir, que de se conserver?'" [lose himself or to let himself be ruined?]* (379). As it concerns Settembrini the question is rhetorical; just as clearly Castorp implies that *he* may have such courage. What Clavdia Chauchat had said during Walpurgisnacht, *"that one ought not to search for morality in virtue . . . but in just the opposite . . . in sin, in abandoning oneself to danger . . ."* (334) has not been forgotten. When Clavdia returns with Peeperkorn, Castorp means to prove that point to her, for had he not already "lost" himself by waiting for her return? In a manner of speaking, had he not "ruined" himself, abandoned himself to danger? "We had a folk song in school, that went, 'The world is lost to me now'" he tells Clavdia. "That's how it is with me" (584). Therefore, he cannot lend her a postage stamp, for he has no contact with the world below: "I have no feeling whatever for the flatlands anymore . . ." (584).

4

Who, then, is this young man with this "weakness for things Asian"? Deep into the novel Naphta argues that "[i]llness was supremely human," while Settembrini retorts that "[i]llness . . . was inhuman" (456). This difference between their concepts of illness and death creates the center of their antagonism, but Castorp arrives at the mountain much more sympathetic to Naphta's position than to Settembrini's. He has a reverence for death that reinforces his talent for illness; he refuses to accept the humanist's assertion that illness is not "elegant . . . [or] venerable," that "illness is rather a *debasement*," that "illness and despair are often only forms of depravity" (96–97, 218). True, these views are encoded in Castorp's primal experiences (his *"Urerlebnisse"*), the death, in quick succession, of his parents and grandfather—and his position will be reinforced by more experiences as an adult patient at the Berghof. Nevertheless his whole nature, like that of many of Mann's characters, is inhibited, repressed, coiled; these are his protective denials, so that he is ripe for a version of Dionysian rebellion. The affinities he feels for the dead and dying, translated for a time into his ritual visitations with the moribund, are clearly in concert with his desire for a solitude that beckons to him from his own inner need to be ill and thus severed from his "health" of the flatlands. Falling in love with Clavdia Chauchat is in all ways contrary to his upbringing: her bitten fingernails, her Asian-slit eyes, her unkempt appearance, her unladylike entrance into the dining room: these are the very features that attract. It is a classic case of reaction-formation.

Castorp's almost immediate attempts to distance himself from family are a conscious break with exterior ties in order to clear the way for the searching *interior* inquiries to come. In addition to asking *What is life?* and *What is time?*, he will also ask *Who am I?* For these questions, his illness and the sanatorium provide the perfect condition and venue: "'Contemplation, retreat—there's something to it . . . One could say that we live at a rather high level of retreat from the world up here. . . . To tell the truth, my bed . . . my lounge chair . . . [have] made me think more about things than I ever did in all my years down in the flatlands . . .'" (370). Castorp's seemingly uncharacteristic behavior during Walpurgisnacht (he is slightly tipsy), which includes the first public rejection of Settembrini and a carnal consummation with Clavdia Chauchat, is the first clear indication to himself of his surrender to the spirit of the East. On his knees, speaking a better French than he has a right to, his biologically worded *blazon* of his conquest is absurd and significant. It is not only that he must express his passion in a neutral language (as has often been noted); in addition the comic disguise of scientific terminology for love language transforms a passionate longing for body into a feat of accomplished displacement. This gentlemanly, cultivated Western exemplar pursues his conquest from the East within the linguistic context of a covert military maneuver and displays Mann's penchant for injecting humor at critical moments. As each passionate description of Clavdia's body parts is couched in the textbook language of biology and related sciences, the total impression takes on the characteristics of unbridled Eastern passion wrapped (and trapped?) in a Western exterior. Mann slyly refuses to recount what later in the evening becomes, at last, a consummation.

Chauchat's absence, however, does not generate any pining. At one point Castorp declares himself relieved to be distanced both from Settembrini (who has moved to the village) and Chauchat. What he cultivates is a solitude that will culminate in his dangerous excursus into the void in the section "Snow." Again Berdyaev's remarks fit: "The Ego's failure to establish a relationship with the We, and the acute and anguished sense of solitude resulting therefrom, brings to life the personality's growing consciousness of itself."[18] Such self-consciousness leads Castorp paradoxically to negate himself at the same time that he becomes oppressively conscious of the ownership over that Self. That paralyzes him, so that when Behrens pronounces him cured and fit to leave, he refuses: "a departure seemed impossible, because . . . he had to wait for Clavdia Chauchat . . . (413), which is obviously not the whole story. And so Castorp indulges in the first of many self-deceptions that will keep him on the mountain for seven long years.

5

Despite the ironic turn of Castorp's dream vision in "Snow"—namely, that he forgets it by the time he returns "home"[19]—this section remains pivotal, as Mann himself insisted. For the dream vision is not all that informs this

episode. Castorp's rebellious initiative to go skiing and contravene the sanatorium regimen is initially applauded by Settembrini; but even he cautions
against the folly of skiing off into the unknown, what turns out to be Castorp's *descensus averno.* But that journey into the unknown whiteness is a
semi-conscious immersion into the "destructive element."[20] The ensuing
experience of his encounter with the blizzard generates not only his ambiguous solitude, but the choices between life and death that lie beneath it.
The dare he offers the void of whiteness embodies all the features of submission to a spaceless, timeless surrender to that very East that so horrifies
Settembrini. "Snow" has been criticized as a sudden insight unprepared for
or an event that settles nothing, since Castorp remains for years after his experience. Neither criticism is justified: Though the section appears late in
the novel in terms of page counting, it is still relatively early in Castorp's
stay, and its emphasis on solitude and surrender to irrationality has been
amply prepared for from the first week, when Castorp's solitary walk ends
up in a swoon and a hefty nosebleed. In addition, the fact that much real
time (as opposed to narrative space) elapses after the episode is in no way
anticlimactic; Castorp's forgetting is partly a function of allowing Mann the
space for further developments of the same themes of solitude and surrender. After his confrontation with the snow, which evokes in him the images
of the dunes (and by extension the sea) of his homeland, Castorp scales
back his domain. He becomes like the sisters whom Cocteau describes in a
quotation cited by Auden in *The Enchafèd Flood:* "Mes soeurs n'aimez pas
les marins: / La solitude est leur royaume" (My sisters do not love sailors: /
Solitude is their kingdom").

Shortly before "Snow," Uncle Tienappel flees from the snares of the magic
mountain, and for Castorp this has special significance. His uncle's arrival
evokes no conversations about home and family: They "said nothing about
personal or family affairs . . ." (423). When only days later Tienappel beats a
hasty retreat, it signals finality: "And that was the end of the attempt by the
flatlands to reclaim Hans Castorp . . . [;] for him, however, it meant freedom
finally won, and by now his heart no longer fluttered at the thought" (432).
This freedom is quickly translated into the purchase of skis and his determination to learn how to use them. And that "permitted him the solitude he
sought, the profoundest solitude imaginable, touching his heart with a precarious savagery beyond human understanding" (466). Observing people ski
and sled inspires in Castorp a new admiration, a "sense of dignity" he recognizes in activities that made for a "deeper, wider, less comfortable solitude
than that afforded by his hotel balcony . . ." (468). This mummy has un-
wound itself and is now prepared for his own "deeper, wider" experience.

As he skis away from familiar markers, he is soon "deep in his solitude,"
headed for the "icy void" (469). We learn that Castorp has "secretly" been

trying to get lost, fearful but with "defiance" until he is "staring into nothing, into white, whirling nothing" (474). (Now he resembles Wallace Stevens's "Snow Man" who "listens in the snow / And, nothing himself, beholds / Nothing that is not there and the nothing that is.") Lost in the sudden snowstorm he faces self-annihilation, a gradual death, "self-narcosis"—a condition described as "highly ambiguous" *[zweideutig]* (475–476). Everything hangs in the balance: either surrender to "self-narcosis" or engage in the battle, stay awake, move, fight your way from dream-death back to life: "All this came from those ambiguous attacks, which he fought off only feebly now. The familiar blend of languor and excitement . . . had grown so strong in both component parts that it was no longer even a question of his taking prudent action against such attacks. . . . [H]e came to excuse his own inertia in fighting off such attacks of self-narcosis *[narkotischen Ausfälle]* . . ." (476). Although Castorp nearly succumbs, eventually he musters sufficient strength to engage his will to live. Before that, in that twilight between death and life, he has his dream-vision, "anonymously, communally," each word descriptive of an aspect of ambiguity. What he dreams has often been described and analyzed; suffice it to say that the duality central to the dream (the Arcadian vision disturbed by death and terror not far off) is neither new nor startling. For Hans Castorp the dream validates what had not revealed itself to him clearly, namely not only the existence but the necessity of ambiguity. It becomes Mann's version of Keats's "negative capability": "Man is the master of contradictions" (487).

Back from his excursion, the dream already fled from memory, Castorp does not yet quit the hermetic mountain for the flatland world. He will remain many years more, and in that expanse of time he will become increasingly prone to isolation, moodiness, and a mummification quite different from the kind that required wrapping oneself in blankets. But the essential difference of this solitude from that before "Snow" is that now he has a grasp of its necessary ambiguity, and for years he will live comfortably within it, rather than feel it as a tug-of-war between contending forces. Internal strife is transformed into a balancing act, and he, too, becomes a "master of contradiction." Castorp warms to Naphta's word "hermetic"; it strikes him like "a magic word with vague, vast associations" (501). Indeed, "hermetic" fittingly describes Castorp's remaining years on the mountain. Settembrini notices a new kind of silence: "'Wordlessness isolates. One presumes,'" he urges, "'that you will seek to break out of your isolation with deeds'" (508). But he may misunderstand; and in fact we hear no more of any skiing excursions. Henceforth Castorp will spend his solitary time in safer surroundings; one kind of "icy void" has been encountered, if not conquered. Still, more than before "Snow," Castorp falls under the spell of "self-narcosis"; all latent inclinations toward Asia become manifest. Slowly, inexorably, Castorp is absorbed into the final "stupor," where "anonymous" and "communal" no longer stand as equal ends of a single antinomy, but where they collapse into each other as willful, if domesticated, inertia, waiting, it would appear, for a proper signal to break the spell:

> In the depth of his solitude, of his hermetic existence, man grows acutely aware of his personality, originality and singularity. He also longs to escape from his solitary confinement, to enter into communion with the Other Self . . . the Thou . . . the We. The Ego longs to escape from his prison-house in order to meet and identify itself with another Ego.[21]

Obviously, dodging shells on the battlefield is not exactly the proper venue for experiencing such a transformation, but at least the Ego has gained release from what had come to feel like a "prison-house." So any condition that permits decision and choice is—however ambiguously in this instance—an ethical act. All this begins with Castorp's systematic renunciations: first, of course, comes the renunciation of family and flatland; then Settembrini, Joachim, and Clavdia; time and space, too, are renounced. The last and most difficult renunciation is the illness itself.

The principal argument of this chapter so far has focused on the undulations of Hans Castorp's exilic solitude (which resemble the upward and downward fluctuations of his fever chart) and the ambiguous parabolas of his journey from the aesthetic realm to the ethical. These are shaped by Castorp's inclinations, his fastidious burgher upbringing notwithstanding, to pursue the irresponsibility inherent in his perception of the infinite and timeless East, where Western individual and communal certitude succumb to Eastern anonymous timelessness and, one must add, from Castorp's perspective, slovenliness. The Spenglerian Faustian view is, after all, infinite too, but infinite action, not Eastern superfluity, inertia, the "Underground Man." Castorp's solitude, however ambiguous, has taught him both the reward and pain of solitude and the self-consciousness it engenders. In the end, Castorp loses himself, at great risk, in order to be positioned for "recurrence" to a former self both chastened and enhanced. Like Sir Thomas Browne in the epigraph to this chapter, he had lost himself in a "mystery" to pursue his reason; and he had reached his "O altitudo!" Octavio Paz confirms Berdyaev: "Hence the feeling that we are alone has a double significance: on the one hand it is self-awareness, and on the other it is a longing to escape from ourselves."[22] Thus, it is the same with Hans Castorp. Like Joseph in the pit, "he actually experienced a sort of joy . . . the pleasures of enlightenment, almost like the relief which laughter brings, had illuminated the dark terror in his soul." Castorp's "dark terror" is less obvious, yet he too spends seven years in a kind of inverted pit. For a time, also like Joseph's, his pit is "deep" and "return to his former life" is "inconceivable" and impossible.[23] His exilic solitude releases his pursuit of the East that embodies both drives: self-awareness and the desire to escape it. Self-awareness can only be achieved by contrast, on alien territory, and for that purpose the East (transplanted onto the mountain) served him well. Yet, self-awareness, itself a form of solitude, eventually can become sufficiently dangerous to prompt an exit that reunites the Self with the world. As Nietzsche said *(Beyond Good and Evil #146),* "If you stare long into the abyss it will stare back at you." Or, as Zimmermann wrote, "Retirement from the world may prove peculiarly beneficial . . . [in] youth . . . to lay the foundation of the character"; but also, "Solitude . . . is equally unfriendly to the happiness and foreign to the nature of mankind."[24] Solitude exacts its price, and of that Castorp becomes keenly aware. Where Castorp perhaps departs from the Schopenhauerian "denial of the will to live" and sides instead with Nietzsche's "eternal recurrence" is in his refusal to surrender forever the Ego he had so willingly put at risk of being "lost" in "Snow." It is also the juncture at which he abandons his quest for the East. The critical moment of his transformation occurs during the séance, which he aborts when Joachim's ghost appears. The event is "highly questionable" for many reasons, but chief among them appears to be its challenge to Castorp's life-wish that has hung on with surprising tenacity while so many around him, most notably Joachim and Peeperkorn, have successfully implemented their death-wish. Settembrini's *placet experiri* has unintentionally brought matters to a dangerous juncture, and Castorp abruptly ends the session and does so decisively. Seeing the apparition, he asks for forgiveness, and for the second time in the novel (the first was at Joachim's death) "tears came to his eyes" and blinded him momentarily. Then, reminiscent of Settembrini's gesture when he first visited Castorp in his darkened room, Castorp "with a flick of his hand . . . turned on the white light." Against the loud protestations of Krokowski (principal thief of the Self), Castorp reasserts his "doing" by firmly reestablishing his "being": "Hans Castorp walked over to Krokowski . . . tried to say something, but no words would come from his lips. With a brusque, demanding gesture he held out his hand. Taking the key, he nodded menacingly several times directly in the doctor's face, turned on his heels, and left the room" (672).

The vision of Joachim in a World War I helmet (which has drawn the attention of critics) appears to confirm for Castorp the untenability of existing in timelessness and time simultaneously. In his study of the modern Self, Charles Taylor concludes that *"The Magic Mountain* presents two radically incombinable modes of time-consciousness, one which approaches timelessness and one which is constituted by the calendar of real events. . . ."[25] Joachim's apparition, though one of time future, nevertheless has the effect of an urgent time present. What serves here as the trigger for Castorp's descent (the outbreak of war) is prefigured in real time; and despite Castorp's abrupt termination of the event, it has had its intended impact. Eastern timelessness in any form is no longer an option. Ironically, then, the unreal has validated the reality to come. Naphta's death, which occurs in the next section, is now ordained, for Castorp has opted for life after all—if not for Settembrini's rational sentimentalization of it, life nevertheless.

During the course of his experience of near annihilation in the snow, much is revealed to Castorp, not all of which he forgets: After all, life is a continuum, and "Snow" is rooted in Castorp's *Urerlebnisse*. He and Clavdia Chauchat become bound in a common friendship formed to protect a helpless Peeperkorn, and he tells her, "'There are two ways to life: the one is the regular, direct, and good way. The other is bad, it leads through death . . .'" (587). This colloquy is a defining moment for Castorp, for it sets in motion what Nietzsche called the "great emancipation," this "will to *free* will," which does not come without its burdens. For, Nietzsche observes, "how much disease is manifested in the wild attempts . . . by which the liberated and emancipated one now seeks to demonstrate his mastery over things!" Emancipation makes him suffer the "dangerous tension of his pride," precisely what Castorp begins to display. Indeed, in Nietzsche's words, "Solitude [now] encircles and engirdles him . . . that terrible goddess and *mater saeva cupidinum* [wild mother of the passions]—but who knows nowadays what *solitude* is?"[26] This new ambiguity, though Castorp perceives it clearly, continues to dominate his life on the mountain long after Peeperkorn is dead and Clavdia Chauchat has left for good. We may believe he resolves it when he breaks the spell and joins the mass exodus for the embroilment of war. Yet, the road that Castorp finally takes is more open to question than it may appear. Singing the favorite Schubert *Lied* (about love and death) on the battlefield, where his creator gives him precious little chance of survival, is Hans Castorp following the "good" road to life—"regular" and "direct"? Or has his "weakness for things Asian" won out (even if not willed) against all odds? Despite his hard-earned "freedom" and his choice of life over death, has his creator, by dispatching him into the hopelessness of the battlefield, hurled him from the enchantment of one irrationality to the seduction by yet another, Yeats's "irrational streams of blood"? At best, these questions leave the reader in a state of uncertainty. The solitude Hans Castorp experienced on the mountain had, of course, its own quality; but isolated as a single soldier on the confused field of battle, he remains the solitary, however different from his "hermetic" life on the mountain. What Zarathustra says at the beginning of *his* "Homecoming," his descent from the mountain, parallels Castorp's homecoming as well: "O solitude! O my *home,* solitude!"[27]

6

Perhaps no discussion of *The Magic Mountain,* especially when it highlights the problematic of solitude, is complete without noting Mann's last major postwar novel, *Doctor Faustus.* Although the two works are separated by more than two decades, and composed in different countries, Mann's preoccupation with the estrangement of the human reaches a kind of apogee in his Faust tale. Adrian Leverkühn remains totally the "Unpolitical Man": Nothing that happens "outside" disturbs or intrudes his artistic solitude. Born in 1885 (the year of Mann's birth), he has his encounter with the Devil in 1911 and is promised the usual 24 years of reward (in his case, creativity), which would have brought the bargain to an end in 1935. But in 1930 he suffers a complete mental collapse and thus is cheated of five years. Why? Because Adrian, explicitly forbidden to love (Devil: "'You may not love'"), cannot resist his little nephew, Echo. Once his love for this young child is openly offered, the boy dies a horrible death, and the artist feels the heavy burden of guilt as if he had murdered the child.

Baudelaire, and many after him, had saluted the artist's urgency for solitude: "The man of genius wants to be *one,* and therefore solitary"; and he mocked the urge to love, "this horror of solitude, this need to lose his *ego* in exterior flesh . . . man calls grandly *the need for love.*"[28] Leverkühn had thought likewise, but Mann refuses to permit even genius that bargain. Serenus Zeitblom, the narrator, launches the novel with some musings on love:

> But love? Whom could this man have loved? A woman at one time—perhaps. A child toward the end—that may be. And a lightweight dandy, a winner of every heart in every season, whom, presumably, just because he was fond of him, Adrian sent away—to his death. To whom might he have opened his heart . . . ? That was not Adrian's way. He accepted others' devotion—I could almost swear often without even realizing it. His indifference was so vast that he hardly ever noticed what was happening around him. . . . I might compare his isolation *[Einsamkeit]* to an abyss. . . . All around him lay *coldness.* . . . [29]

Any Devil's visitation would be a memorable event; Mann accentuates it by making this Devil a chameleon who unobtrusively changes his appearance as he carries on his disputations with his willing victim. To begin with, this Mephisto is thoroughly modern, and despite Mann's questionable attempt at a form of medieval German, what he says is of the moment. He understands all too well Leverkühn's desperate desire to move beyond the canon of masters and perceives the "anxiety of influence" besetting the modern artist. So naturally, the devil's irresistible bait is to offer creativity, to "break through the laming difficulties of the age" in order to attain "a barbarism, a double barbarism, because it comes after humanitarianism . . ." (259). With such promises, the human as well as the humane are banished: "Love is forbidden you insofar as it warms. Your life shall be cold—hence you may love no human" (264). When later the artist's friend insinuates himself into his life as lover, the narrator laments that this incursion was a "a cheeky plot of confiding familiarity against lonely solitude," and comments on "solitude's defenselessness against such wooing . . ." (370). Only once, and rather half-heartedly, does Leverkühn show an inclination to end his hermit life *(Einzelgängerei),* when he sends his friend as intermediary, bearing a proposal of marriage to a young woman. In his plea he uses repeatedly—as the friend caustically notes—the words "human" and "human being." Leverkühn is hurt: "' . . . don't you find it cruel to inform me that I am what I am only out of inhumanity and that humanness doesn't suit me?'" (457–458). Yet the narrator, who, by his own admission, could not possibly have overheard this conversation, needs to convince us as readers—and he does so defensively to secure our trust—that it must have occurred as he reports it. Perhaps. In any case, the love for Echo, which is his last chance to bestow real love, ends with a double punishment: Not only is the boy cruelly killed by ravaging disease, Leverkühn himself falls into madness; the "echo" of illness and death has come back to avenge itself. Not long after Echo's death, Leverkühn composes his revenge-piece, "The Lamentation of Dr. Faustus." This dark work has been described as being "essentially about cosmic solitude as the condition of humanity"[30]: Whatever persona, or Ego, Leverkühn may ever have possessed is dissolved into a kind of Pascalian human emptiness, inspiring the dread the heavens once had.

In *The Magic Mountain* love, according to Dr. Krokowski, was a mere displacement of disease, and Castorp took that somewhat seriously, carrying with him the talisman of his beloved's chest x-ray, probably even into battle. By the time we reach *Doctor Faustus,* love has become a "sin" and one ironically against the Devil. As early as *Death in Venice,* of course, homoerotic love was a sin that exacted the hero's life, but love as a sin against the Devil carries with it an absurdist irony that Mann obviously relishes. How often are any of Mann's characters permitted real love (as distinct from infatuation or carnal passion)? Sometimes they are passionate, but it is unrequited, and such passion is soon spent with a price as high as life itself.

On the magic mountain, did Hans Castorp ever experience love? Was he capable of a relationship that penetrated *his* solitude, exposing *his* Ego to some Other? Mann ends what he calls his "hermetic story" with a rather cosmic question: "And out of this worldwide festival of death [the war], this ugly rutting fever that inflames the rainy evening sky all round—will love someday rise out of this, too?" (706). In the penultimate sentence to *Doctor Faustus,* Mann, in the voice of a "solitary man," the narrator, also asks a question: "When, out of uttermost hopelessness—a miracle beyond the power of belief—will the light of hope dawn?" In the latter question, "light" has replaced "love" as the revealing sign, almost as if there were no hope for love remaining; as if, that is, the world would have to be recreated. In *The Magic Mountain,* the hope that love releases one from the "prison-house" of solitude is, however faint, a possibility. Or perhaps T. S. Eliot's line from *The Waste Land* resonates with the protagonist: "There is not even solitude in the mountains . . ."

Chapter V ∼

Solitude of Questionable Freedom in Cartesian Antagonists: Sartre and Camus

Is this what freedom is? . . . I am free: I haven't a single reason for living left. . . . Alone and free. But this freedom is rather like death.

—Sartre, *Nausea*

. . . his body had served him forth fully, had opened him to the world, but at the same time, it lived a life of its own, detached from the man it represented.

—Camus, *A Happy Death*

"Cartesian" is one of those stubborn concepts we have encoded into our critical thinking and have applied, loosely to be sure, to any mind/body dualism, especially as it may occur in philosophy or literature. Two philosophers have recently attempted to clarify and correct what they have called the "Cartesian Legend." First they summarize that legend's major points: "It is common knowledge that Descartes was a Cartesian Dualist. . . . As everyone knows he held that there are two worlds, one of mental objects and one of material things. . . . The mental objects are 'states of consciousness' . . . the material objects are . . . bits of 'clockwork.'" We perceive the "'inner world'" by means of "introspection"; the "'outer world'" is apprehended by "the five senses." Although Body and Mind are "independent," they are nevertheless held together by "causal interaction." The authors suggest that such a reading of Descartes, especially among Anglo-Americans, perpetuates the "legend," and they proceed to demonstrate what, in their view, Descartes really meant—in short to undo the damage of the "legend" and to posit a more accurate account of "Cartesian."[1] The problem, of course, is that the "Cartesian Legend"—assuming the authors are correct—is what, for better or worse, the culture has absorbed, and so one can with some degree of certainty use it when dealing with Sartre and Camus. Surely they, too, must have seen Descartes' dualism as the "legend" describes it. It is in that spirit that the term "Cartesian" is invoked in the chapter title.[2] Sartre's Roquentin and Camus's Meursault are "Cartesians" in the sense that each divided body from mind and further subdivided "introspection" and "inner world" from "five senses" and "outer world," which is not to say that either Sartre or Camus were Cartesians. As one critic has remarked, despite Sartre's rejection of Cartesianism, Roquentin's is a "kind of negative Cartesianism, it is [his] horror of existing, even more so his horror of thinking which, itself a thought, causes him to exist."[3] In their solitary states, Roquentin and Meursault experience, from a judgmental perspective, a negative solitude; in various ways and for differing lengths of time, these figures are in a state divided, their solitude initially negating, severed from external awareness. However, their partial success in attempting to seek and understand any "causal relation" forms a critical juncture in the works they inhabit and constitutes, in the end, a form of affirmation, though this is perhaps more specious in Sartre's novel than in Camus's. Roquentin and Meursault are *an*tagonists[4] rather than *pro*tagonists, in this sense: Each counterattacks, each opposes a world that seeks to, or has already, destroyed him, at least as they interpret the lurking, menacing forces they seek to hold at bay. Roquentin appears to achieve a point from which to contemplate a new start, an ending that has been criticized[5]; Meursault can define his happiness only within the context of his impending execution. Yet both achieve an affirmative, if attenuated, solitude: They affirm the necessity of solitude as a preexisting condition for what they imagine as freedom.

Nausea

1

In his recent biography of Camus, Olivier Todd reports that Camus thought long about his review of Sartre's *La Nausée,* published in the weekly *Algér-Republicain* on October 20, 1938. At the end of July, according to Todd, Camus wrote his friend Lucette Meurer, "'I read . . . *La Nausée* . . . and I have a lot to say about this book. It's too close to a certain part of me . . . but that's exactly the part I want to react against.'"[6] Four years later, when Camus published *The Stranger,* one can understand this comment even better, for the two novels, important in how they differ, are equally of interest in where and how they approach similar states of crisis. Roquentin and Meursault may not be twins or even brothers, but they are close first cousins, related in their solitariness, their sense of exclusion, difference, and calculated *in*difference. Both writers, though perhaps standing on opposite sides of the shore, understood, experienced, analyzed, and dreaded the potential emptiness of existential solitude. Both were familiar with Kierkegaard's *Concept of Dread.* Their initial friendship, their public quarrels, and Sartre's posthumous reconciliation with Camus were all predictable for two men who understood each other better than any differences might suggest. And since the first English edition of *The Stranger* was not published until after the war (1946), we tend to forget how close on the heels Camus's novel (published in 1942, but completed in 1940) followed Sartre's (1938), especially since Camus had begun to think of *The Stranger* as early as the late 1930s. Indeed, two months *before* Camus reviewed *La Nausée,* he wrote down, in his *Carnets,* the first sentence of *The Stranger,* for which he had projected such titles as *A Happy Man, A Free Man,* and *A Man Like Any Other.*[7]

What was that "certain part of [himself]" that Camus found so close to him in Sartre's novel? In his review, the young critic, who had not yet met Sartre, confidently asserts that "a novel is never anything but a philosophy expressed in images," and that in a successful novel "the philosophy has disappeared into the images." In *La Nausée,* Camus argues, the author has broken the balance between philosophy and image: "the theories do damage to the life." Moreover, this has the result of making the book more a "monologue" than a novel: "A man judges his life, and in so doing judges himself." (Ironically this is precisely what Camus himself attempted in *The Fall.*) Camus also censures the apparent pessimism of the novel—"[l]ife can be magnificent and overwhelming—that is its whole tragedy"; "to live with the feeling that life is pointless gives rise to anguish . . . and the revolt of the body is what is called nausea." Yet, Camus also offers some guarded approval. Comparing Sartre to Kafka, he praises the book's "painful lucidity" and struggles to strike some balanced interpretation of the intention and ending of the novel: "The realization that life is absurd cannot be an end, but only a beginning. . . . At the end of his voyage to the frontiers of society, M. Sartre does seem to authorize one hope: that of the creator who finds deliverance in writing. . . . From the original doubt will come perhaps the cry, 'I write, therefore I am.'"[8] These brief passages by a 25 year-old newcomer who had not yet published his first novel (or much else) are remarkable in that they raise some of the important issues that have pervaded the reaction to *La Nausée* since. Is the novel a novel or does philosophy penetrate its pages; indeed, is it a preface to the major work, *Being and*

Nothingness? Is it an invented narrative or a thinly disguised autobiograph-ical monologue? Does the novel's ending suggest the redemptive hope of creative beginnings, or is it an ironic afterthought tacked on with a smirk?[9] Three definable readings of the novel evolve: the optimistic-redemptive, which sees the hero's future as a creative force, a writer of fiction; the pes-simistic, which takes "nausea" literally; and the indeterminate and ambigu-ous, which attempts to balance the two to claim that Sartre suggests an ending with a potential future without defining the outcome. Some critics, like Iris Murdoch, see the novel as almost pure philosophy: "It [*Nausea*] is an epistemological essay on the phenomenology of thought. . . ."[10] But all three readings agree on Antoine Roquentin's solitude: It is a form of self-exile from society, an "Entfremdung" that throughout the novel is articu-lated as embittered aloneness (and loneliness) of a man who discovers the ultimate challenge: the consciousness of his own existence. And it is, finally, the struggle of one enveloped by the devouring perception about the exist-ing world that surrounds and threatens him, much like the cannibals who began to surround and threaten the benign solitude of Robinson Crusoe.

Roquentin's isolation is shaped by an inversion of his relationship to the phenomenological world, so that his solitary state makes him more a victim-object than an experiencing subject. Essentially, he feels that all the layers that relate us to the world are stripped away, confronting him with an un-mediated world of objects. And it is not so much that he is isolated from so-ciety, but rather that he experiences society as having distanced itself from him. Looking into the mirror only distorts and disturbs, so Roquentin looks for different venues. "A little more and I would have fallen into the mirror trap," he writes. But as he avoids it he falls into the "window trap," that is, surveying the world from his window with a transfixed consciousness. What is really out there is, as he realizes, "the future": "I can *see* the future. It is there . . . hardly any paler than the present." But the real dilemma is, "Why does it have to be fulfilled?" (49–50). For the unfulfilled future poses a threat, makes demands, arouses the need for choices, and terrorizes one with fear of failure. Like closed doors, the future hides unknown monsters of ex-istence: Which door (which future) lies behind the unopened door?

All phenomena take on an anthropomorphic quality, and with their abil-ity to intrude, the "things" surrounding Roquentin define him as the im-mobile object. So it is not that he feels "nausea" within or outside him, but that he is somehow enmeshed in the nausea, that the nausea has appropri-ated him: "The Nausea isn't inside me: I can feel it *over there* on the wall. . . . [I]t is I who am inside *it*" (35). This awareness of being both subject and part of the object is both disturbing and disorienting. Experiencing isolation fully within society, Roquentin perceives himself imprisoned within *things* without fully losing consciousness of self—hence the dissociative terror that often grips his existence. The feeling conveyed is that he has been abducted and raped by an overbearing reality, or what he prefers to call "existence" ("gelatinous subsidence"); this is not the feeling of the outsider, viewing the world of phenomena either with the regret of having been banished or the contempt of superiority. Indeed, his state bears an uncanny resemblance to the various versions of the film *The Invasion of the Body Snatchers,* in which individuals are trapped in the gooey, fructifying mass that envelops and destroys those it seeks out, pursues, and ensnares: "I am suffocating: existence is penetrating me all over. . . ."[11]

This inversion, where phenomena are purely external and never internalized, is expressed at various points in the novel, but probably nowhere more forcefully as in the early episode: his journey into the icy clarity of Hell at the Boulevard Noir, where he observes the fate of the charwoman, Lucie. He first enters the "black hole" where "nothing is alive," where there is a purity of silence: "The Boulevard Noir is inhuman. Like a mineral." The dark purity leaves him happy and temporarily displaces his nausea—it is "over there." Then he sees Lucie, having quarreled with her lover who has abandoned her, and who is "suffering with an insane generosity" he envies. The episode is a critical juncture of the novel because Roquentin recognizes that the simple woman's suffering is an expression of "being," whereas his own life, he begins to understand, has been a "nothingness"—void of any "adventure."[12] "After all," he comments, " . . . I for my part have been much too calm these last three years. I can receive nothing more from these tragic solitudes, except a little empty purity . . ." (42–45).

After his brief sojourn in a purity that turns out to be less than satisfying and more revealing of his own "tragic solitudes," Roquentin approaches his future with a doubt and skepticism that now belie the more simplistic certitude with which he began: "For my part I live alone. I never speak to anybody, I receive nothing, I give nothing" (16). Although he felt "dead" and "empty" from the start, he had hoped, as the Boulevard Noir episode shows, to refine his solitude into a pristine separateness, to find within solitude a kind of liberating inhumanness. This has failed. For the remainder of the novel, Roquentin needs to come to different terms with solitude, and where he had early on claimed to be a mere "amateur" at being a solitary, by necessity he must now make an attempt to become the professional.

To that end, Roquentin reinvents himself to fashion a strange mixture of the active and passive, the real and imaginary, the participant and observer. In a curiously predictive remark pointing to the ending, he notes, "it is *I* who am piercing the darkness. I am as happy as the hero of a novel." This happiness comes when he discovers that the "adventure" he has been seeking may indeed be his very existence itself. Experiencing something like the nausea, but also its "opposite," he discovers that "*it happens that I am myself and that I am here . . ."* (82). Like a fictive hero, he has at least discovered an identity, though that is far from the optimistic view of having traveled from "solitude to salvation."[13]

Reminiscent of Gogol, Dostoyevsky, or Kafka (among others), the novel proper begins with an almost supernatural suddenness: "Something has happened. . . . It came as an illness does, not like an ordinary certainty . . ." (13). When the nausea announces itself as that "something" that has happened, the initial response is natural enough: attempt to puzzle through its nature—what is it?

This malady that Roquentin has named "nausea" has, of course, occasioned the normal debates, which Roquentin himself helps to stimulate, as to what it really is. Is it revulsion with all outside himself, or is it really a potentially liberating phase in his journey toward self-making? Is nausea a terror that feeds, perhaps creates, his dissociative pathology, or is it a defining condition that comforts and helps his desire to search for total separateness? "Nausea," writes one critic, "is the disgust we experience in the face of that total absence of necessity, either interior or exterior, and the freedom which characterizes existence." But this disgust "soon changes to horror and dread."[14] Or, nausea is an "'état d'âme'" manifesting itself in "fantastical visions, in states of '"fascination,'" "'illumination,'" or "'extase,'" owing something to the Romantic and later Baudelairean ennui, Sartre substituting a scholar-historian for the sentimental hero or the poet.[15] Others have approached the novel's nausea more psychoanalytically: "it describes how a man . . . comes suddenly to doubt not only the purpose of his existence, but also its very reality." Roquentin's demise is seen as a "kind of Laingian collapse, a secular dark night of the soul, resulting in . . . a radical rediscovery of the self": Roquentin's is the "introvert's breakdown."[16] Henri Peyre views the novel as "ironic" and focuses on Roquentin's oppressive feelings of "contingency" as the source of his nausea; the title, incidentally had been suggested by the publisher. Sartre's previous suggestions included *La Légende de la Vérité* (certainly ironic) and *Mélancolie,* neither of which invokes the distasteful connotations of *Nausea.*[17] Still others have regarded nausea as the metaphysical component of a philosophical novel. In such a reading, the real struggle is between the "*en soi*" and the "*pour soi*"— human consciousness and that of which it is conscious. What Roquentin's nausea amounts to is the "experience of his body as an inert demonstration of futility. . . ." Consciousness, as it "aspires toward purity" (see the episode of the Boulevard Noir), is "irremediably trammeled by the limitations of . . . duality, of the world, time, and the flesh"—again the contingency issue seen from the perspective of self-consciousness.[18]

In time, Roquentin learns that what he must master is not the nausea, but his relationship to it. Is his solitariness an inhibiting force to that end? Victor Brombert sees *Nausea* in the tradition of Malraux "and the later Existentialists," all "haunted by the loneliness of the self (*solitudes des consciences*). . . ." Roquentin's is a "visceral experience of alienation and absurdity" as he realizes that the "absence of essence condemns man to freedom," a condition that overwhelms this, Sartre's first hero. Indeed, this freedom inverts itself to imprisonment and immobility.[19] Perhaps, Roquentin muses, it is impossible to understand one's own self; or, as he is wont to, he uses his own condition to conclude that a solitary may be deprived of self-reflection: " . . . perhaps it is because I am a solitary? People who live in society have learnt how to see themselves, in mirrors, as they appear to their friends. I have no friends. Is that why my flesh is so naked? You might say—yes, you might say nature without mankind" (32). Yet what Roquentin is forced to confront is that nature and mankind cohabit, that he must understand his solitude without being self-referential and yet without simply capitulating to society. It will be a daunting challenge, even for this "happy" hero of a novel within a novel. Sartre reveals a consistent preoccupation, one that *Being and Nothingness* explores throughout: "How [one can be] his own foundation . . . to reach . . . self-identity of the object, while yet remaining sufficiently distinguished from this self to be conscious of it"[20]

2

Roquentin's discovery of his existence is almost filled with a childlike ecstasy—"Existence, liberated, released, surges over me. I exist. . . . It's sweet, so sweet . . ."(143). And the two word "Tuesday" entry is as succinct as it is provocative: "Nothing. [I] Existed" (149).[21] Yet this existence-discovery is not at all simple, nor does it provide any solutions; indeed, it raises more epistemological issues about selfhood and objective reality: "Things are entirely what they appear to be and *behind them* . . . there is nothing" (140). This insight is Roquentin's reward after walking through the Portrait Gallery, where he is absorbed by the faces of the self-satisfied burghers of the town and as he leaves the gallery, utters the famous "farewell, you beautiful lilies, our pride and *raison d'être,* farewell, you Bastards" (138). Obviously the two incidents—"Nothing. Existed" and the visit to the Gallery—are not unrelated. Roquentin's perusal of the fine citizens of Bouville is, after all, a kind of one-dimensional viewing of "things" behind which there turns out to be "nothing": nothing but existence itself. Put bluntly, what you see is what you get, and there are no metaphysical secrets "behind" the things you confront—everything is an unmediated reality. The "blinding revelation" turns out to be that "it is *I who* pull myself from the nothingness to which I aspire . . ." (145), pushing a knife point into his palm to test his own existence. Inexorably it becomes increasingly clearer to Roquentin that it is existence itself that is his barrier to freedom: "Everything is full, existence everywhere, dense and heavy and sweet" (149). The contingency of such existence is self-imprisonment, for the cycle seems almost punitively circular: "I exist—the world exists—and I know that the world exists" (176). Caught in this inescapable drama of multiple existence, Roquentin appears unable to fashion any genuine solitude: "if I exist, *it is because* I hate existing" (145). Perhaps the most definitive statement about his existence is a kind of self-conscious parody of the Cartesian formula, which at the same time poses serious questions: "I am, I exist, I think therefore I am; I am because I think, why do I think?" (146). An enlightening gloss on this conundrum is Wolfgang Holdheim's essay in which he parses it (and surrounding passages) with rewarding care. Georges Poulet, he reminds us, saw the whole novel as a "parody of the *Discours de la Méthode*," but Holdheim rejects this as exaggeration. Fixating on the disconnected (e.g., his living hand), Roquentin is a "tormented Cartesian . . . the Western intellectual who is condemned to live with his Cartesian heritage," unable to disengage himself from "the principle of subjectivity. . . ." Even at the end of the novel, Holdheim believes, Roquentin has failed to detach himself from the "*ego existo.*"

Philosophically, Holdheim sees *Nausea* as "an existential-narrative modification and correction of its author's speculations of that time." And as literature, he argues for a more nuanced "redetermination" of *Nausea*'s place in modern fiction. Rejecting (correctly) the notion that *Nausea* is the first modern novel to lay bare the unmaking (or unmasking?) of selfhood (a claim forwarded by the *Pléiade* editors, who rely on Lucien Goldmann), Holdheim sees a continuation of what began as early as Kierkegaard, and, more near to Sartre, in Gide. This all points toward a marriage of philosophy and literature that in turn shapes "postmodernism's modalities. . . ." (He might well have mentioned Poe, Gogol, and Dostoyevsky.) Essentially Holdheim perceives Roquentin's conflictual existence as a desire to be an "object" while retaining his "cogito" as a reminder of his need to be a "subject." And to some extent, that *is* the issue of the novel.[22] Others concur: "By requiring a suspension of disbelief, Descartes' method of doubt also destroyed the connections. He, too, moved toward substances." Whereas Descartes' "doubt," however attenuated, "led to the uneasy separation of mind and body," Sartre's introduction of "nausea" leads in a parallel but different direction—it "separates [Roquentin], or at least his consciousness, from the object of disgust." And while this may for a time be self-protective, in the end Sartre will move beyond the "crude existence" into which his hero has transformed the world. Rather than a Zarathustra, Sartre presents us with an "Ecce Homo": Sartre "unmasks Roquentin."[23]

True solitude would need to negate at least the world's existence or his knowledge of that existence. Yet, this would bring him back to the pure and icy "black hole" of the Boulevard Noir, and that, too, was in the end of no avail. Roquentin is trapped in a form of existential claustrophobia: On one side is the world of repulsive things ("that ignoble jelly"); on the other is his superfluous self ("My thought is *me*"). The inability to mediate between these alternatives shapes his apparently unresolvable dilemma, which at last he finds "absurd." If the world is too much with him, it would seem simple enough to retreat into himself, as solitaries have always done; but such self-immersion only brings more dissociative anxiety, like the fixation on his hand: "It is alive—it is me" (143); but, as in Keats's "This Living Hand," the experience is fragmented, synecdochic. The infamous chestnut tree in the novel becomes the image and metaphor of ever growing existence that penetrates, suffocates, and makes all differentiation impossible: "I couldn't stand things being so close any more" (181). If his own singularity is undefinable, Roquentin comes to the inevitable conclusion that all is *de trop*—all including himself is "superfluous" (184). "I dreamed vaguely," he recounts, "of killing myself, to destroy at least one of these superfluous existences" (184). "So the adversary of *Nausea* . . . is being, the *en-soi* in so far as it is full of itself. . . . It is life in its absurd proliferation." This further inhibits the often longed-for experience of pure solitude, for, like Baudelaire, Roquentin is "the man who never forgets himself," hence his failure of attaining freedom. All he can achieve is "impasse" or a "petrified consciousness."[24] Such a view of the novel may exaggerate the paralysis that stalls discernible development, but essentially it is correct in emphasizing the overwhelming nature of "existence" that indeed forces Roquentin to abandon more than he attains. He must shed himself to the core before permitting himself any thoughts of a possible future. When he realizes that the Autodictat is also a solitary except that he does not know it, he begins to understand that *conscious* self-sustaining solitude may be out of reach. Almost boastfully the Autodictat asserts, "'I no longer *feel* alone'"; "'But naturally . . . I don't have to be with anybody'" (167). This illusory conclusion leads the Autodictat to his spurious "humanism," to the position from which he embraces the whole of humanity with his "love." But his love is, in the end, really reserved for little boys, and Roquentin takes note of this both with pity and revulsion, for he now understands the expansive nature of self-deception (what Sartre later called "bad faith").

Roquentin's relationship with Annie, now living in Paris, is a memory, but in a final attempt to connect and recover, he goes to Paris to see her again. Predictably there is no reciprocal response: Annie suggests she is outliving herself, and by the same token outliving him. Both have undergone parallel travail: "There are no adventures—there are no perfect moments . . . we have lost the same illusions, we have followed the same paths" (213–214). In this final failure lives the specter of a wasted life, though he is only 30—"My whole life is behind me" (222). In *The Myth of Sisyphus* Camus writes: "Yet a day comes when a man notices or says he is thirty." While announcing his youth, he also "situates himself in relation to time," conceding that he "belongs to time, and by the horror that seizes him, he recognizes his worst enemy."[25] So it is with Roquentin, for whom the future has, for now, truly disappeared. As an ironic defense against creative living, he finds the explanation in his revulsion against existence: "I don't want to do anything; to do something is to create existence . . ." (245). Perhaps this is why Roquentin's final musings about writing a novel have seemed to many critics a tacked-on ending, an unprepared for reversal, an ironic spoof, or an ending *il faut de mieux.*

In any case, *Nausea,* though not yet the expression of Sartrean Existentialism that some have attributed to it, reveals Sartre's preoccupation with several major themes that will be developed both in his philosophical and creative work: our aloneness, our necessary acceptance of that condition, and our coming to terms with the freedom that we must carve out of chaotic "existence." Certainly Sartre was "imbued with an awareness of man's solitude and responsibility in the world. . . ." And while Edith Kearn is correct is emphasizing Sartre's positive and eventually antinihilistic position, an "affirmative acceptance of life . . . ," it is amply clear that in this first novel, Sartre had not yet reached that point, and *Nausea* is as bleak an account of solitude and its failures as we have. Roquentin did not have—as Sartre did not either in 1938—a "moral answer" to life.[26] His disquietude arises from many sources, perhaps chief among them his realization that the "things" that constitute the world of phenomena "*can be almost anything,*" that their instability and mutability make them dangerous and necessary to conquer.[27] Perhaps the most interesting characterization of the novel's "horizontality" is Pollmann's analysis of the style: "The brief sentences follow one another loosely, formally expressing the disconnectedness and isolation . . . of their content." The experience of the "objectness of things" is so removed from himself, that he cannot internalize it.[28] Such a view of the flat (or "horizontal") progression of the novel appears to be the most convincing response to those who read a vertically linear development of awareness. This is not to deny, of course, that Roquentin achieves progressive insights; but these are not in the tradition of "Steigerung" as in a *Bildungsroman,* but rather spasmodic and uncertain responses to continual failures of expectations. Once Sartre has devised the means of making our solitude serve matters outside itself, and once he has moved from dread of freedom to the joy of its potential of self-making, the "nausea" of this first novel disappears.

The Stranger

[On the canvas] . . . completely blank . . . Jonas had merely written . . . a word that could be made out, but without any certainty as to whether it should be read *solitary* [solitaire] or *solidary* [solidaire].

—Camus, "The Artist at Work"

This Descartes of the Absurd . . .

—Sartre, "Tribute to Albert Camus"

In *The Enchafèd Flood,* W. H. Auden writes of the sea and the desert:

> As places of freedom and solitude the sea and the desert are symbolically the same. In other respects . . . they are opposites. E.G. the desert is the dried-up place, i.e., the place where life has ended, the Omega of temporal existence . . . nothing moves; . . . everything is surface and exposed. The Sea . . . is the Alpha of existence, the symbol of potentiality.[29]

Most of the action in Part One of Camus's novel takes place by the sea and the sand, and the sand becomes the desert, in Auden's sense, whereas the sea is indeed Meursault's salvation. It is by the ocean that he meets Marie, the former typist, the only person in the novel who genuinely comforts him. In the water they touch, they kiss, they "tumbled in the waves. . . ."[30] The sand, of course, is the beach of Part One ontologically altered into the desert of Part Two, where Meursault's life comes apart when he shoots the Arab. This transformation of beach into desert—"the place where life has ended"—is ultimately so perceived by Meursault, and ironically by inverting the two places: "For two hours the day had stood still; . . . it had been anchored in a sea of molten lead" (58). And on that beach turned desert, Meursault's physical life—his freedom—has indeed ended.

1

To understand some of the conundrums *The Stranger* has offered up, the posthumously published *A Happy Death* (*La Mort Heureuse,* 1971) serves as an interesting predecessor,[31] if not quite a "preamble to *The Stranger*" as the American paperback cover quotes from *Time*. In fact, the two novels are quite different, despite the similarity of the names of the heroes (Mersault and Meursault) and despite the murder that both men commit. Plans for the novels almost overlapped: Notes for *A Happy Death* were already written in 1936 and work on that novel continued until 1938; concurrently Camus was beginning to conceive *The Stranger*. How the confusion and explicitness of the first novel developed into the sparse clarity and implicitness of the second is one of those inexplicable events of rapid artistic maturity that cannot be easily explained. For example, in both novels we have solitary heroes, but whereas the word "solitude" finds its way into *A Happy Death* 17 times, Camus, "pushing to the extreme the logic of [Mersault's] solitude . . ."[32], never uses the word in *The Stranger,* where its condition is clearly even more urgent. Camus had learned how to show rather than name, as if somewhere between the writing of the two works he had read Mallarmé's warning that (in the words of Arthur Symons on Mallarmé) "to name is to destroy, to suggest is to create." (Actually he was reading, among others, Sorel, Nietzsche, Kierkegaard, and Spengler.) The most frequent expressions to suggest solitude for Meursault are "I didn't say anything," "silence," "I didn't answer," and "No." How these work in the story will be detailed below. *The Stranger* is not a symbolist novel in any strict sense, but its allusiveness, despite its clarity of language, accounts in great measure for some of the mysteries that have given rise to so much speculation as to its ultimate meaning.

In contrast, *A Happy Death* makes itself understood (even when its aim is confused), and those many references to solitude make clear that the solitariness of his hero was focused in Camus's creative vision: "[I]t is a question of a slow conquest of happiness, which cannot be obtained without asceticism and detachment"—and, one must add, a high dose of *amour de soi*.[33] Camus's handling of the question of solitude in the discarded novel and in the one he published is relevant to both. Aside from their obvious similarities of name, their acts of murder, and their deaths, the heroes of these books share certain other experiences. For example, both lose their mothers, and Mersault "had to abandon his studies and take a job [when his mother took ill]." Until his mother's death he had continued "to read, to reflect" for ten years.[34] When Meursault's "boss" asks him to transfer to Paris after *his* mother's death, he refuses, commenting, "I had no ambition. . . . When I was a student, I had lots of ambitions like that. But when I had to give up my studies [presumably when *his* mother became frail] I learned . . . that none of it really mattered" (41). The difference between the account of Mersault's and Meursault's earlier lives is revealing. In *The Stranger,* where such matters are only hinted at, it is quite clear that Meursault has had a very different background to the life we enter when the novel begins, one in which he, too, read and reflected. Like his predecessor, he was forced to give up that life but, unlike him, he also surrendered what had sustained it (reading, reflection). No wonder Camus was most upset by those who saw Meursault as some sort of moronic, unthinking automaton, for here was someone who had known the life of reflection and deliberately exchanged it, in self-defense, for a life of immediacy. Another diverging parallel is the murder that occurs in both novels. In *A Happy Death,* Mersault kills his victim (Zagreus) with premeditation and with at least several motives, one of them robbery; in *The Stranger,* the killing is nearly accidental, spontaneous, perhaps again in self-defense, and certainly without any discernible motive. While the first victim is well known to the killer, the second is a mere stranger, like the murderer himself. Both Mersault and Meursault (like Roquentin) dislike Sundays: They are generally a boring routine in preparation for the new week; both are drawn to sea and sun (as Camus himself was); and both refuse to utter the word "love" to their women. Though these details are somewhat superficial, they are sufficient to establish at least a kinship between Mersault and Meursault, while admittedly their differences are greater than the dropped "u" in the former's name. But that "[t]he hero grows in that solitude he imposes on himself or which is imposed upon him, grows to the point where it dominates his anguish and attains tranquility" is applicable only to *The Stranger.* When he was 24, Camus published *The Wrong Side and the Right Side* and placed "The Death of the Soul" before "Love of Life," although the two essays were written in reverse order. Philip Thody comments that Camus's decision "suggests that an upsurge of happiness can follow closely after the experience of . . . solitude."[35] That is precisely what happens in *The Stranger,* although Meursault's "upsurge of happiness" remains highly contingent.

Camus fails to make the case he intended in *A Happy Death,* that Mersault searches, with success, for the freedom of solitude that brings happiness. Instead his hero emerges as a narcissistic, lost murderer, whose act of killing a crippled man seems a conscious and cruel dare to himself, an unintended parody of Raskolnikov's tempting of the moral structures.[36] What Camus is later able to show in unmediated action in *The Stranger,* he labors to describe in *A Happy Death:* "Today, in the face of abjection and solitude, his heart said: 'No.' And in the great distress that washed over him, Mersault realized that his rebellion was the only authentic thing in him, and that everything else was misery and submission" (53). Sitting in cafés (like Hemingway's loner in "A Clean, Well-Lighted Place"), he seeks out the "herd warmth which is the last refuge against the terrors of solitude and its vague aspirations" (51). Here the operative word is "vague," for Mersault has only vague ideas, not only about solitude and what it may bring him, but about freedom and revolt as well. After the murder, having fled to Switzerland, he does experience a flood of pleasure—"dreadful pleasure"—at the prospect of so much "desolation and solitude," but it is more titillating than informed. What lies ahead seems to be a form of adolescent thrill, anticipating the "shameful and secret countenance of a kind of freedom born of the suspect, the shady" (59). Something of the melodramatic surfaces in sentiments such as describing his nausea and "inhales all the alien solitude the world could offer him" (63). When he moves on to Prague, he becomes even more depressed (as Camus had) and aware of his "desolation," and of "a solitude in which love had no part" (68). Longing for sun and women (in the midst of gray Prague), Mersault weeps, and within him "widened a great lake of solitude and silence," which is the prelude to his "deliverance" (71). Rootless, a "miserable wretch," Mersault now feels "poisoned by solitude and alienation" and returns home to seek solace in the three women and his wife, Lucienne, who now serve his needs like harem girls. Like Roquentin, Mersault faces himself mirror-like; his "passion" now was "[t]o lick his life like barley sugar," to be as self-indulgent as he could be. At last it seems he has found the way, in the Narcissus pool: "This presence of himself to himself . . . even at the cost of a solitude he knew now was so difficult to endure" (83). So solitude becomes a "tender meditation," but only briefly. Soon the "release" he had sought turns to dismay again, and the "solitude he had sought so *deliberately* seemed even more disturbing . . ." (110; italics mine). But cultivating solitude is a doomed project, and weary of it, he summons his wife, Lucienne, "recover[s] his complicity with the world," and takes "refuge in humanity"; but, after two days, he is bored with Lucienne and is back where he began (113). Camus searches for a way to have his hero accept solitude, and only near the end of the novel does he appear to at least force the issue, not without delusions of grandeur and ambiguities: "Only today did his solitude become real, for only today did he feel bound to it. And to have accepted that solitude, that henceforth he was the master of all his days to come, filled him with the melancholy that is attached to all greatness" (135). What Mersault feels he has accomplished is "man's one duty . . . only to be happy." Yet that happiness is painfully contingent and, Camus must have sensed, empty. It has no relationship to love or to the world ("a landscape"), it is "nothing but an infinite waste of solitude and happiness . . ." (150). Such solitude is a personification of Cartesian splintering, the body "is detached from the man it represented" (149), and absent an integrated and holistic effort failure is inevitable. In the pursuit of solitude, Mersault, like Roquentin, remained essentially an "amateur."

2

In his now famous preface to the American textbook edition of *The Stranger*, Camus nearly turns Meursault into an Ibsenesque hero, someone like Brand or, more likely, someone out of *The Wild Duck*. In reaction to the figuration of Meursault as an unfeeling and undirected figure, Camus almost overstates the case: "For me . . . Meursault is not a piece of social wreckage. . . . Far from being bereft of all feeling, he is animated by a passion that is deep because it is stubborn, a passion for the absolute and for truth."[37] Of course, unlike Ibsen's "idealists," Meursault's search for truth—though in one sense equally self-destructive—is not rooted in a false sense of the absolute, but rather in assuming a modality of refusal to institutionalized cant. It is, Irving Massey has concluded, the modern mirror-image of quixotic idealism—Camus's "brave if imperfect embrace of objectivity." Since it would appear that all ideals are false, reality itself becomes the ideal worth fighting and dying for: "Meursault plays the Quixote for the modern world, the martyr and redeemer incomprehensible . . . refusing at the cost of his life to compromise . . . his ideal of experience un-contaminated by prefabricated generalizations."[38]

Commentary on *The Stranger*—as happens with notably ambiguous works—has created a critical internal food chain: Interpretations have fed on one another, either by enlarging on a predecessor or, frequently, by oppos-ing and striking out in new directions. The result is an impressive bibliogra-phy and very little agreement. Nearly 60 years after its publication, there is scarce evidence of any common ground on the novel's meaning, though the many views proposed offer a kind of key to the problems this brief novel has generated.[39] The title itself (whether translated as *The Outsider* or *The Stranger*) has perhaps made Meursault's "solitude" seem so obvious that ex-tensive analysis of that aspect of his state has seemed superfluous. Solitude, however, was an important thematic strain in Camus's life and work, from beginning to end, and it will not be difficult to focus on that issue as both singular and determining of the novel's meaning. Camus's style has been scrutinized carefully, but Barthes's observation that he "achieves a style of ab-sence"[40] goes to the heart of that issue. What is absent is any continuum be-tween a past and futurity, so that Meursault is virtually an isolated phenomenon in his own narrative. Further, almost everyone has taken note of the structure of *The Stranger:* its two almost coequal parts are neatly or-ganized, the first part offering Meursault before the murder on the beach and the second his incarceration, trial, and impending execution. Such structural balance helps Camus to represent two distinct experiences of soli-tude in his hero's life: In the first part Meursault is with others (however tan-gentially) but isolated from himself; in the second part he is with(in) himself, but isolated from others. This later isolation is, of course, in part in-voluntary, he is imprisoned; but a second and more complex isolation de-velops that comes to a kind of apotheosis in the final pages. The two parts of the novel confront each other: the "balance" between them is ultimately more technical than substantive; put another way, the second part is a re-sponse to the first, and Meursault evolves almost as if he were in debate with the man who empties his pistol with five shots at the end of Part One.

3

Even more promising than *A Happy Death,* the best entrance to *The Stranger* is forward to a late volume, *Exile and the Kingdom* (1957)—a series of sto-ries about silence and solitude—especially its penultimate tale, "The Artist at Work." Camus's interest in the theater apparently prompted him to cre-ate "scenarios" of his prose, and one that survives is for "The Artist at Work." This scenario is divided into two parts, each with five "sections" sketched out in brief. Both the tone and actions of this scenario are, according to the editor, more "brutal" than in the story; and the "bitterness" gives way, in the final story, to "a bantering sort of irony. . . ."[41] Nothing in Camus conjures up Kafka more directly than both this scenario and the story that finally emerged. In the scenario, the scenes outlined are often Kafka-like comic, and the behavior of the artist, who is called Jonas in the story, is bizarre and conflicted in a manner that is reminiscent of, say, Georg Bendemann of "The Judgment" or Gregor Samsa of *The Metamorphosis*. At the very least, the artist of the scenario and Jonas of the story find themselves increasingly trapped and suffocated by their families and forced into choices that can only lead to self-destruction. In the scenario, the artist is more explicitly aware of how fame and family are destroying his artistic integrity, as a look into the mirror reveals the truth and ends in a violent reaction, a gesture of overt rebellion. In a panic, the artist displaces his family: He builds himself a "studio" out of reach, pushes the furniture aside, does not take food or communicate with anyone, escapes into a world of "silence," and working feverishly on huge canvases. Painting becomes an increasingly solitary, obsessive, and hysterical act. When his wife dies, the painter steps down from his ladder, returns to his apartment from what in the story becomes an attic-like studio (shades of Ibsen's *The Wild Duck*), but only briefly to kiss her dead face before returning to his canvas to paint it.

The named painter in the story, Jonas, is an insouciant man who never quite realizes the insincerity of the dealers and students who surround him. But, like the man in the scenario, he becomes increasingly more reclusive from everyone, including his family, as his confused psyche comes under assault. The artist at work becomes the man out of touch: his solitude, self-created, turns into an exilic experience in his own quarters. Only his children still fill his "empty solitude," but soon, "even in the moments of solitude," he has difficulties painting. In a final move of desperation, he builds himself his studio loft, where he begins to sleep and eat and, he says, to paint. Physically emigrated from his family, Jonas, not his wife, dies. Just before that, however, he is happy to hear the sounds of the connectedness he had foresworn: "The world was still there. . . . Jonas listened to the welcome murmur from mankind." Like Henry James's artist in "The Madonna of the Future," Jonas leaves an empty canvas—except that he has inscribed his dilemma on it, so clearly that but for a single letter it could not be made out: Was it "soli*t*ary" or "soli*d*ary"? Such a conflict between the need for solitariness and the equally urgent need for solidarity with others dominates Camus's fiction (and his doctrinal essays) from *A Happy Death* through *The Fall*.[42] The absolute necessity for solitude as a condition for creative and moral cleansing and the equally challenging urge to be in solidarity with the all-too-human crystallize the paradox that governs any understanding of *The Stranger*.

4

That Meursault had once been a different person from the one we encounter is not speculative: He tells us directly. Aside from the passage about "having to abandon his studies," when the lawyer at the beginning of the trial asks whether he had experienced any sadness the day of his mother's burial, he responds by first confessing that the query took him by surprise. Then he reflects: "I had pretty much lost the habit of analyzing myself and [told him] that it was hard for me to tell him what he wanted to know"; he follows up with the Dostoyevskyan echo that "[a]t one time or another all normal people have wished their loved ones were dead." And the last-resort explanation of this self-made Cartesian antagonist is that his "physical needs often got in the way of [his] feelings" (65), that his "homeland," at least momentarily, is his "sensations," that "interiority has emigrated from the soul to the body."[43] We do not know how far Meursault's studies took him (it is too often assumed he is on a level with the *pied-noir* culture in which he lives), but clearly his comments are evidence of intelligence and reflection. Much debate has engaged such issues as when Meursault "wrote" the story he narrates, what tenses he uses at what point, whether he tells his story by way of a diary, novel, or *récit*. What is certain is that his account, however much it is in the present, is recounted with a knowledge of an anterior life to the events told, that the consciousness of that past life informs the tone and tenor of the chronological details from Maman's death to the eve of his execution. Such an anterior life can only be surmised from what Meursault says, and he says little about it. Yet, in critical spots there are what cannot be accidental hints. For instance, the picture of a man unconscious to feelings is largely promoted not by the prosecution, but by Meursault himself, who provides a self-image to buttress the prosecutor's accusations. What he hides from the others, but not the reader, are his truer feelings. The solitude of silence itself becomes a powerful instrument of his official undoing. For example, in the fifth paragraph of the narrative, he tells us that he had "wanted to see Maman right away"; when the residents of the home sit facing him, he has the "ridiculous feeling that they were there to judge [him]"; walking in the funeral procession, remarking the peaceful countryside, "I was able to understand Maman better"; when Salamano wails about his lost dog, "I realized he was crying. For some reason I thought of Maman"; in turn Salamano said "he knew me and he knew I loved [Maman] very much"; and when the prosecutor mercilessly impugns him for not having wept at his mother's funeral, "for the first time in years I had this stupid urge to cry"— and "years" surely does not refer back to his childhood (4, 10, 15, 39, 45, 89–90). All these exculpatory thoughts—and they precede his final tender feelings about his mother—remain dormant in Meursault's well of silence.

This refusal to explain his feelings (reminiscent of "Bartleby the Scrivener") amounts to a form of affective self-imprisonment, a solitude that pervades both parts of the novel, though most references have been taken from Part One. In addition, as readers have noticed, he feels guilty (along with being judged) well before he is on trial: "Besides, you always feel a little guilty" (20), whether toward the director of the Home, his mother's fellow residents, the boss, or Marie. Pollmann's otherwise useful horizontal/vertical schemata fails him when he insists that Meursault had fashioned for himself a unity prior to the murder that, once it is committed, falls apart and forces him into a "verticality of differentiation and reflection. . . ."[44] No doubt that Meursault's pre-murder Self was comforted by his "horizontal" routinized existence; but the reconstitution of the Self that occurs in prison and at the trial cannot be a wholly new discovery of "verticality": Meursault recovers his past that adds to the urgency of the present, formulates the apparent resolution of the final paragraphs. And there may be reason to conjecture that the additional four shots—perhaps even the first shot—are reality-based pretexts for a recovery of a Meursault more responsive and tender than the naysayer who reveals himself, especially in Part One. What has frequently been called the "lyricism" of Part Two is embryonic in Part One. As Camus himself said, "the last pages of a book are already contained in the first pages."[45]

On a higher level of abstraction, Meursault's life, beginning in Part One, seems remote even from himself. His routinized existence, somewhat deliberately chosen perhaps as a maintenance of "balance," is gradually compromised by events to which passivity has been the willing gatekeeper. Like Roquentin, but less imaginatively and dramatically, Meursault begins to feel himself spectator of his own life and fate. That vexing question about the four additional shots, troubling the lawyer, Examining Magistrate, and readers and critics, appears to be resolved to some extent when we recall Meursault's admission that he waited "a few seconds" after the first and fatal shot to fire them. For it is these four shots, not the first, that Meursault specifically singles out as those "knocking four quick times on the door of [his] unhappiness" (59). In effect, then, these additional shots have nothing to do with the dead Arab; they are the exclamatory "knocks" against a door now shut from without as well as from within. Deprived of his freedom, which has been described perhaps somewhat misleadingly as "the freedom of non-involvement, of non-commitment . . . ,"[46] Meursault struggles with but overcomes minor crises: the absence of women, tobacco, initial sleeplessness. Eventually he finds himself trapped in a kind of "vestibule" (not yet the well-defined one of Jean-Baptiste Clamence of *The Fall*). The first day in court he has the distinct impression that while everyone is comfortably settled in familiar routines, he was "odd man out, a kind of intruder" [the original is *de trop,* Roquentin's phrase] (84). In addition his "fate was being decided without anyone so much as asking [his] opinion" (98). And when the lawyer uses the first person in presenting Meursault's case it fosters Meursault's perception that "it was a way to exclude me even further from the case, reduce me to nothing, and, in a sense, [for the lawyer to] . . . substitute himself for me" (103)—all reminiscent of Joseph K's astonished confusions in parts of Kafka's *The Trial,* with which Camus was, of course, very familiar.

A sense of being apart from rather than a part of events is, in Meursault's case, close to dissociative solitude, and it prepares for the two major concluding events: his enraged quarrel with the priest and his apparent reconciliation with the universe in which he is soon to be executed. While it may be tempting to conclude that, at the end, Meursault experiences an existential epiphany that provides him peace, the evidence points to something less. Some have crafted this stranger into a hero at the end: "A hero, Meursault becomes a stranger in solitude, he is alone within his narrative; he has even become a stranger to that narrative"; and "Meursault undergoes solitude. He as yet is not assuming it. . . . It is the solitude of the hero that he is going to claim."[47] But if Meursault is estranged from his own tale, it is not he but his maker who moves to distance himself; and "the solitude of the hero" hardly accounts for the man who desperately needs the spite of others to face his death. Maurice Blanchot shrewdly observes that "[t]he journal—this book which is apparently altogether solitary—is often written out of fear and anguish as the solitude which comes to the writer on account of that work." Doubtless, from all we know, that would apply to Camus at the time of writing *The Stranger;* and that equation translates itself to Meursault. "When I am alone," Blanchot writes, "it is not I who am there, and it is not from you that I stay away, or from others, or from the world." Such solitude is not Romantic self-consciousness but the final expulsion of the "I": as in Beckett, the "I" has essentially been eliminated from any stable self-identification that necessarily clings to the world of others. Instead, as Blanchot observes,

> it happens that this masterful possibility to be free from being, separated *from* being, also becomes the separation of beings: the absoluteness of an "I am" that wants to affirm itself without reference to others. This is what is generally called solitude. . . . It can be experienced as the pride of solitary mastery. . . . Or solitude may disclose the nothingness that founds the "I am." Then the solitary "I" sees that it is separated, but no longer able to recognize in this separation the source of its power.[48]

This *almost* describes Meursault's state in the final pages of *The Stranger;* his last wish, however, still concerns those others, that crowd he envisions at his execution. His desire to be in relation, even if such relation is confrontational, exposes a powerful need *not* to achieve total isolation. This crowd,

Meursault hopes, to make him feel "less alone," should greet him with "cries of hate" (123), just as Baudelaire had insisted that only when he had inspired "universal hatred, [he] shall have attained solitude." For Baudelaire and Meursault, both genuine solitude and its partial alleviation required the defining hatred of the Other.[49]

Camus was often irritated with the random use of "absurd." In a 1950 essay, "The Enigma," he complains that like the word "existential," "[t]hey've chosen the cliché: so I'm absurd as ever"; but the "absurd" is only a "point of departure" because "there is . . . no total nihilism." If one deprives the world of "all meaning" one deprives it also of all "value judgments. . . ." And a "[l]iterature of despair is a contradiction in terms."[50] Although one may argue that this follows by nine years the publication of *The Stranger*, it is clear both from the text and Camus's own comments that such was already his view, if less developed, in his first published novel. Meursault is neither an unthinking fool nor a philosophical nihilist; he is human, all too human. As nearly all of Camus's major figures, Meursault may indeed be tempted by "the lure of solitude," but this gives way to "the need to live *with* others," to allay "anguish" and spiritual impoverishment. That was Camus's own dilemma, as recent biographers and critics have concluded: "'Being with' another seems so necessary . . . that Camus's thought was drawn toward it as if by magnetic attraction."[51]

5

Just as in *The Myth of Sisyphus* Camus rejected suicide as a response to the Absurd, so in *The Rebel* he rejected murder. Meursault, though he has a glimpse of his "absurd life" (113) almost on the penultimate page of his tale, is not the rebel Camus defined much later. It is doubtful that "indifference [in Part Two] becomes less alienation and more a protest . . ."[52]: In neither section of the novel, before or after the murder, is Meursault's "protest" an articulation of mere "indifference." If anything, his "alienation" is increasingly transformed into his divorce from continuity, indeed from time itself, which repeatedly in Part Two, in prison, he says he "kills."

As for the murder itself, Camus never justifies it in *The Stranger* as he had implicitly done in *A Happy Death*.[53] To be reminded not to ignore Meursault's crime (as we can not shrink from murder in Dostoyevsky's novels) is salutary; but to suggest, as some have, that Meursault is basically an indifferent criminal unworthy of our or the court's mercy is to disfigure Camus's novel beyond recognition. Meursault's seemingly insouciant reason for the shooting of the Arab, "[it] was because of the sun," is greeted with laughter by the spectators in the court and with sometimes quizzical exegeses by critics. But Meursault's explanation may be more than a non sequitur. It is ironic that the overarching sun—which completes the design of sun, sky and ocean that Meursault (and Camus) so much loved—is in the course of the novel both the pleasure and the bane of his existence. On the way to and during the funeral, the sun is merciless; with Marie it is pure pleasure; in the court it creates stifling heat; in prison he remembers and misses its light; and at the time of the killing it deadens the senses. As the unbearable aspect of the natural world that had always been his comfort, the sun becomes not reassuring warmth but oppressive weight. Camus himself describes Meursault in his preface as "a poor and naked man enamored of a sun that leaves no shadows." On the level of logical causation, Meursault's explanation of the murder is absolutely honest, for "the Arab drew his knife, and held it up to [him] in the sun. The light shot off the steel. . . ." Believing the man was about to attack with "the [knife, which] was like a long flashing blade cutting at [his] forehead. . . . [a] dazzling spear . . ." (59), Meursault pulls the trigger. Yet despite the logical elements of the episode, the encounter describing the killing is Pascalian: In a state of total isolation, the human stands in the face of the cosmic and is overwhelmed. Camus simply permits the moment to stand as perceived by Meursault; he makes no authorial effort to explain.

On this score Sartre, ever the philosopher-writer, contradicts himself in his review of *The Stranger* on the same page: "Although the absurdity of the human condition is its sole theme, it is not a novel with a message . . ."; "Thus, the very fact that Camus delivers his message in the form of a novel. . . ."[54] *The Stranger* is not a roman à clef: it is, among other things, a modern account of solitude, both enhanced in depth and destructiveness by the self-conscious choices of a man attempting to live a life without either the burdens of the past or the fantasies of the future. As Camus's Caligula says: "Solitude! What do *you* [Scipio] know of it? Only the solitude of poets and weaklings. You prate of solitude, but you don't realize that one is never alone. Always we are attended by the same load of the future and the past" (*Caligula,* Act II).[55] A life without past or future is fatal: It is disabling rather than enabling. In the final pages, Meursault tells us, "I never really had much of an imagination" (112–113). But this is a failure in self-analysis, for no reader can take that judgment seriously except as an ultimate irony Meursault inflicts on himself and on us. For lack of imagination is a wish fulfillment denied. His claim that he lacks imagination is made at the very moment when his imagination is furiously, and perhaps for the first time in a long while, contemplating the guillotine, its mechanism, the appeal, the certainty of death. At the instant of realizing the punitive present, Meursault remembers his past (Maman) and envisions his future (death).[56]

The Rebel was the final cause of the split between Sartre and Camus, because in it Camus's political views decisively shifted against tyranny, especially the Stalinist tyranny. In this volume he becomes the so-called "humanist" whom Sartre derisively rejected; but Camus's attack was quite simple: If "solidarity" among humans is a goal, then it cannot tolerate murder, for that act creates the ultimate and "most desperate sensations of solitude," or "that other kind of solitude called promiscuity." In retrospect some of what Camus says in *The Rebel* is both a self-critique and an explanation of *The Stranger*. If an individual is responsible only to another individual, Camus argues, he ceases to be "justified in using the term *community of men*. . . ." Further, if a single man is removed from "the society of the living," it is sufficient "to automatically exclude" the person responsible for that removal. Murder can never be the concomitant of rebellion:

> For it is now a question of deciding if it is possible to kill someone whose resemblance to ourselves we have at last recognized and whose identity we have just sanctified. When we have only just conquered solitude, must we then reestablish it definitively by legitimizing the act that isolates everything? To force solitude on a man who has just come to understand that he is not alone, is that not the definite crime against man?[57]

Meursault, having killed, does at the end recognize that "he is not alone": Memory reawakens the company of the past and the prospect of the guillotine fixes his attention on the company of the future. While the final paragraphs of *The Stranger* are subject to several readings, the figure of a man upon whom "the definite crime" of solitude has been inflicted is not inconsistent with his apparent acceptance of that inevitability. In the Kierkegaardian sense Meursault is perhaps beyond dread; as an alienated man he is stranded in the solitary confinement between the irretrievable past and the unstoppable future.

Both *Nausea* and *The Stranger* were first novels. Five years after *Nausea*, Sartre published his major philosophical work, *Being and Nothingness;* and a year after *The Stranger*, Camus published his moral treatise, *The Myth of Sisyphus*. But the impulse to read the novels as parallels to these proximate volumes, though tempting, is probably best avoided.[58] Perhaps one can speak in very loose terms of "existential solitude," or "absurd solitude," but that would encompass a much larger field and engage a more impressive scale than the initial fictional works of Sartre and Camus. As with most accounts of "existentialism" or the "absurd," one would be obliged to reach back, at the very least, into the nineteenth century—to Kierkegaard, Dostoyevsky, and Nietzsche. Both Sartre's Roquentin and Camus's Meursault are exemplary modern solitaries, each testing out a life of solitude that fails to bring them what they had imagined. Indeed, quite the contrary: Roquentin ends in desperate isolation, finding the need (if not the solution) to relate to Other strengthened; Meursault, of course, concludes with his desperate wish for a hateful crowd that will make him feel less solitary and, by confrontation, help to identify him in his defining moment: death.

Each of these antagonists attempts to achieve freedom. Initially they fashion versions of hermetic solitude: in the case of Roquentin by focusing on an encroaching "existence," and in the case of Meursault by focusing on the threat from the Self. Each also attempts to untangle the complex intertwining of body and mind that so predictably implicates us in an endless series of decisions and choices. Neither attempt can be lastingly successful. Freedom through solitude encounters the opposition that La Bruyère called this "great misfortune of not being able to be alone," the epigraph to Poe's story, "The Man of the Crowd," about a man who, Poe writes, "refuses to be alone." Dividing body from mind yields no easy success either: No sooner is body free when mind counteracts with its disorienting power; no sooner is mind free when body counteracts with its irrepressible urges. Both states are inhospitable. At the very least, this dynamic—though it works better for Meursault than for Roquentin—bestows a highly questionable freedom. "Surely it was no simple play on words that made Camus say, solidarity-solitary"; and the same polarity applies to Sartre. In an ironic reversal, "whereas the masses (or mass) isolate(s), solitudes create solidarity with the common-place . . . of dislocation . . ."[59], whether such dislocation is called "existence" or the "absurd."

Although the mystery of reconciling solitary/solidary remains unsolved for both Roquentin and Meursault, their isolation deepens their understanding of—if not their conciliation with—what they have been severed from. Each has a heightened sense that "solitude creates solidarity," even if it is not entirely clear with whom or what such solidarity can or should be formed. Contrary to expectation, self-consciousness of isolation focuses on the object by delineating what is separated from the "I." Awareness of Other, however, shapes the subject, like Keats's "sole self" who "darkling" listens to the tempting world that would seduce him from earthly solitude to eternal solitude. It is the condition that Blanchot defines as being "absolutely 'denatured,' the absolutely separated . . . the absolutely absolute." It is an affirmation at the cost of "denying being" and "all-encompassing community of men," a choice that can be made only with the full knowledge of such an exchange.[60] That is what distinguishes the modern solitary from the nineteenth century's (progeny of the Romantic), for the latter was able to retrieve, or at least desire, "community" without being devoured by it. In the midst of scorn and humiliation, Dostoyevsky's Underground Man still laments, "I longed at that moment for a reconciliation. . . ." In the end, neither Roquentin or Meursault (as Beckett, too, insisted in the trilogy) can indulge that luxury of desire. What Sartre's Roquentin says about himself also applies to Meursault: Both remain "amateurs" at solitude.

Chapter VI ∾

As They Lay Dying
"Rotting with Solitude":
Endgame in Beckett's Trilogy

. . . oh it's only a diary, it'll soon be over.

—Beckett, *Molloy*

When I think . . . of the time I wasted . . . tottering under my own skin and
bones, rotting with solitude and neglect, till I doubted my own existence. . . .

—Beckett, *The Unnamable*

The island, I'm on the island, I've never left the island. . . . The island, that's
all the earth I know.

—Beckett, *The Unnamable*

Never once a human voice.

—Beckett, *Molloy*

1

Beckett's treatment of solitude, throughout his work, pushes the issue
of the solitary state to its limits: a Self without identity, with crippled
or amputated body parts, a consciousness (barely), and words. It is
difficult to imagine taking exilic solitude beyond this, except to begin again
with variations of previous versions. In Beckett's three-part novel, *Molloy,*

Malone Dies, and *The Unnamable*—commonly referred to as the "trilogy"—
all the narrators lie dying, "rotting with solitude," or living out what one
critic, quoting Husserl, calls "'das einsame Seelenleben' [the solitary life of
the soul]."[1] The Unnamable insists, with bitter wit, that whatever may happen to the body, the soul survives, it "being notoriously immune from deterioration and dismemberment."[2]

To engage the trilogy, the most productive strategy pointed to a selection
of a number of thematic strains as identified by accompanying images (and
metaphors); the criterion was that these thematic strains forward the argument of the narrators' (the ubiquitous "I" in the trilogy) often ambiguous
monologue(s).[3] For the trilogy at least, the most efficient way to demonstrate its cohesive interrelationship (the inherent intertextuality of all three
novels) is to identify these thematic strains as they weave through the three
novels. Those that emerge as the most suitable in carrying the argument of
the three narrators forward in a unifying fashion are: (1) the "I"'s stratagem
of creating and surrounding himself with "puppets" (comprising almost all
of the invented characters in the trilogy) through whom he can express his
ambiguities, and whom he appears to create to assemble that "company" he
hopes will assuage his solitude; (2) reflective commentaries on light and
darkness, which modulate his ever contentious relationship both with himself and the phenomenal world, the inside and outside, the subject and the
object that are divided by a vulnerable membrane he calls the "tympanum";
(3) the image of the island (often so reminiscent of Crusoe's), which at crucial points in the trilogy clarifies the terrible isolation that only endless pup-
pet-creating and endless talk can make bearable. Equally functional
throughout the trilogy are the repeated revelations of the "I"'s' aloneness an-
nounced by the word "alone" (often in sequences of two or three, like the
Ancient Mariner's) and his use of what he calls "aporia," which modern dic-
tionaries define as "an affectation of being at a loss of where to begin, or
what to say." Surely no better definition can reveal to us the true nature of
the narrator's problem, and this holds true not only for the opening words
of *The Unnamable*—"Where now? Who now? When now?"—but for the
entire trilogy.[4]

Each volume is an extended version of aporia, for where to begin and what
to say being the questions, what more appropriate response than the para-
graphless first part of *Molloy;* or the progressively disintegrating structure of
Malone Dies, which leaves us not in mere doubt, but in contrived confusion;
and the contradictory dialogue with himself in which the Unnamable delights at the reader's—and his own—expense. The overlapping narrators are
in part the consequence of what Beckett calls his "old "aporetics" approach,
in which characters are seemingly invented, uninvented, reversed: "I don't
know" (*MD* 205). Charlotte Renner has called the three narrators a "narrat-

ing chorus"; in Beckett's fiction "narrating characters do not merely collaborate; they coalesce." So, for example, we begin *The Unnamable* with all of the "paired personae [having] dissolved into a single narrating mind. . . ." Or as Philip Solomon describes the narrators' "coalescence": "Both [Molloy and Moran] can be considered . . . 'vice-existers' of the Unnamable, who will later . . . take their place among the dead satellites that encircle him."[5] Of course these observations do not imply that there are no differentiations among the major narrators; it may be more useful, therefore, to conceive of them not as interchangeable but as evolving in response to their circumstances, which do differ. This is achieved by means of a continual verbal parrying from all three in which the object is always to move from one point to its opposite; that is, to ensure that the reader never settles down in certainty, that aporia continues to reign. One commentator writes, somewhat unconvincingly, that Beckett is "the last romantic, asserting his artistic allegiance to what is invisible and mysterious and forever beyond the text."[6] What differentiates the "invisible and mysterious" in the Romantic text from Beckett's is that the latter was committed to believe the aporetic, which the Romantic often contrived.

One way to describe Beckett's narrators, then, is to say they are well schooled in the language of antinomy, and Beckett's language has for some time been a focus of his critics.[7] Difficulties of plot and structure (what there is of either) have often been linked to language and how he came to use it, both in French and English. One critic has gone so far as to identify language as the "central protagonist" in Beckett, and interpreted his search for a new way of expression as the pursuit of a "metalanguage." Beckett's is a "language of negation": "Unanswerable questions, defeated negations and affirmations, aporias—these are what keep the text going."[8] Yet for all of Beckett's "negation," embedded in a carefully crafted language of antinomy, his rhetorical structures lead to endings—perhaps one might better call them upendings. What Gabriel Josipovici calls "our human hunger for a *telos*," the kind of ending that justifies what preceded as making sense, was a product of the nineteenth century, vigorously challenged by Kierkegaard and Nietzsche; Beckett dramatized their objections.[9] Molloy pointedly says that he has completely lost any sense of direction. Finality of meaning, then, is quite another matter, for Beckett resists: "Inscribed in Beckett's trilogy is an obstinate refusal to mean; signs are to be self-referential, their employment no more ambiguous, no less arbitrary than a train-signal."[10]

In all three novels, Beckett's monologist is indisputably a solitary, but his outpouring of words is aimed at both revealing and concealing, simultaneously, his intolerable aloneness, which he frequently belittles, mocks, even denies. This has been imaginatively called a "process of regression" in *The Unnamable* (though it applies to the whole trilogy), which "becomes more and more apparent as the voice continues speaking of and denying the relationship between itself and . . . subsequent impersonations, with every affirmation a denial, and every denial an unwilling affirmation."[11] Molloy prevaricates: "And once again I am I will not say alone, no, that's not like me, but, how shall I say, I don't know, restored to myself . . . [to] senseless, speechless, issueless misery" (*M* 10). As for Malone he simply denies himself: "But what matter whether I was born or not, have lived or not, am dead or merely dying, I shall go on doing as I have always done, not knowing what it is I do, nor who I am, nor where I am, nor if I am" (*MD* 256–257). And the Unnamable, with a prefiguring trace of Camus's Jean Baptiste Clamence, mocks: "a world without spectator, and vice versa, brrr! No spectator then, and better still no spectacle, good riddance" (*U* 430).[12] In his introduction to the most recent edition of the trilogy, Gabriel Josipovici reminds us that "all fiction is monologue" set down by the author in "the solitude of his room"; and that the "disgust at the uselessness of words" is prefigured in such writers as Hölderlin and Kafka, who were horrified at the thought of not creating expressions of the muses, but "indulging [themselves] in solitude." Actually, Josipovici believes that Beckett was able to avoid first person narration since "it seemed to close the gap completely between fiction and memoir—the very reason . . . it was chosen by Defoe." For Beckett, the "error" of merely using an "I" to tell the story consisted of creating "a first-person narrator with the clarity and control of a third person. . . ." However, what would happen if one created a first-person narrator "who was as confused and incoherent as the author himself felt . . . ?"[13] Perhaps "confused" and "incoherent" go too far; Beckett was in control and whatever confusion and incoherence he created were by design.

<h2 style="text-align:center">2</h2>

Conrad's *Heart of Darkness* (1902) bears comparison with Beckett's trilogy on a number of issues: the binary narration that creates doubling: the quest journey, the interior pursuit of Self; the horror of decay and death; the disembodied voice; especially in *The Unnamable*. But it is another Conrad novel that strikes an even closer chord: *Victory* (1915). Here perhaps the contrast is more striking than any resemblances, though underlying themes attract attention: Axel Heyst, the protagonist of *Victory*, is a solitary steeped, like Conrad, in a humorless, pessimistic (even misanthropist) and corrupted Schopenhauerian philosophy. (Harold Bloom has suggested that Beckett has a "profoundly Schopenhauerian vision").[14] Heyst's retreat from the world is temporarily relieved by an unlikely love affair, its dénouement occurring in isolation with a Liebestod. What generates our interest is Conrad's romanticism, however stoic the novel's intention, as compared to Beckett's sardonic humor and relentless rejection of anything resembling Conrad's insistence on humanistic tragedy. Where Axel Heyst clearly suffers in his solitude, the collective "I"[15] of the trilogy—despite reservations—almost revels in it. As we shall see, this does not imply that Beckett's "I" in any of the three novels is in an ordinary sense "happy": He is simply immune to the vulnerability of which Conrad's hero is fatefully (and fatally) a victim. And this may show us where we have arrived with the state of solitude, namely, as a critic has recently offered, at "the end of modernity."[16]

Still, there is much that Beckett would recognize in Conrad's novel. In his author's note, Conrad speaks approvingly of our "power of endurance" as well as our "capacity for detachment"; and he ventures that the "most pernicious habit" formed by "civilised" humans is the "habit of profound reflection. . . ." Whenever Conrad faces the dark, his prescription for survival is "work"—engagement with the details of daily life. Heyst, however, is caught in "persistent inertia"; he was not a "traveller" for he never departed; and despite his woeful state, he pursued what a "utopist" is likely to pursue: "chimeras." His "Hermit" existence is "floating," "unattached," and he had in fact always had a "taste for solitude." When he rescues an equally lonesome woman from an ugly situation, he takes her to an island, where "disenchanted with life," he felt safely "back [in] his solitude." Yet, despite his decision to remove himself from the world, he "felt irrationally moved by his sense of loneliness," so that he envisions himself a kind of Adam who takes an Eve and names her Lena. Son of a pessimist philosopher, whose bitterness he inherits, Heyst will "drift . . . like a detached leaf . . . in the wind. . . . He became a waif and a stray." He recognized neither friend nor enemy, and "alone on the island [he] felt neither more nor less lonely than in any other place, desert or populous." Like Beckett's "I," Heyst's "spirit . . . had renounced all outside nourishment, and was sustaining itself proudly on its own contempt"; but he had those "moments of doubt that will come to a man determined to remain free from absurdities of existence. . . ." Those "absurdities" arrive in the end through the agency of the three intruders who shatter Heyst's paradisiac dream of blissful solitude with his lover: "The outer world had broken upon him. . . . [The island] was no longer a solitude where he could indulge. . . ." For "I am the world itself come to pay you a visit," says their leader; "I am a sort of fate that waits its time." The Beckettian "I" has his visitors, too, even one who hits him on the head to roust him from his isolation; others who stand vigil and observe suffering with mockery. But Beckett's creation has better defenses than Conrad's Heyst because he was never one to create those illusions upon which Heyst built his foundationless existence:

> It was the very essence of [Heyst's] life to be a solitary achievement . . . accomplished not by hermit-like withdrawal with its silence and immobility,

but by a system of restless wandering, by the detachment of an impermanent dweller. . . . In this scheme he had perceived the means of passing through life without suffering and almost without a single care in the world—invulnerable because elusive.

That, of course, at least for Heyst, was illusory. Heyst needs some form of love, but his Lena is not Molloy's Lousse. Beckett's "I" likes to think of himself as being nearly invulnerable because he is determinedly elusive: whether he hides in the forest, journeys in the dark on evasive paths, or is rooted to his bed. Convinced that he lives and dies on his terms, he defies as well as defines the world, no matter what orders from above may bring him to physical decay or mental distress. Conrad mines melancholy, Beckett offers defiance. Both invoke suffering for their solitaries, but for different reasons: Conrad has the world destroying idyllic solitude and innocence, whereas Beckett has taken solitude to its limits, devouring the "I" piece by piece, a form of autocannibalism.

The trilogy ends with the tenacious, if somewhat ambiguous, "I will go on"; *Victory* ends with the narrator, on discovering the joint funeral pyre, sadly exhaling, "There was nothing to be done there. . . . Nothing!"—the last word of the novel. It is the "there" that distinguishes Beckett from Conrad, the situating of a locus still recognizable in time and space, with beginning and end, and coming fittingly *at* the end.[17] "Nothing to be done," we recall, are the *opening* words of *Waiting for Godot* (having already appeared some years earlier in *The Unnamable*). Nothing can be done because those matters about which something might, or ought, to be done have themselves become elusive. Like Mann's Leverkühn, the Beckettian "I" has forsaken love: "But it is only since I have ceased to love that I think of these things and the other things" (*M* 24), and those "things" are what compose his isolation.

Even the body, "like the body of a failed act of birth," is literally fragmented: "[B]odies in the trilogy are rarely expressive of any organic wholeness. . . . They, too, are marked by the same disruptive lack of unity as the name."[18] Preoccupation with body parts, as in *Nausea,* often expresses the subject's panic, creating dissociation anxiety, body separated from mind. In Beckett, such feelings are sometimes converted to a bemused Kafkaesque reality: We are forced to *believe* in these amputated bodies just as Kafka refuses to allow any evasive willing suspension of disbelief as to the reality of Gregor Samsa's insecthood. The collective "I" of the trilogy incrementally loses parts, in the final volume all protruding ones, even penis and nose. All narrators in the trilogy have problems with their feet (even when they travel, as in *Molloy,* they travel nowhere), requiring crutches or bed rest. But it is the hand, which has fascinated several of our authors, that is dominant: It is that body part that grips, loves, plays—and writes, that can both extend and hold on to life or lose its grip. In the depths of the X-ray chamber, Hans Castorp is permitted to "view his own hand through the fluoroscope. And Hans Castorp saw exactly what he should have expected to see . . . his own grave." Intimations of mortality. For Roquentin, his hand is not death, but intimations of existence: "It is alive," he says, not without a mixture of anxiety and reassurance, "it is me." For it is true that "reporting the self is a doomed and potentially infinite literary experiment, just as telling stories is a continual return to the self."[19] But Beckett's Malone finds neither mortality nor existence, only dissociation: "I have no arms, they are a couple, they play with the sheet, love-play perhaps . . ." (*MD* 71–72). This insistence on fragmentation may not destroy Self (which remains in consciousness), but it does destroy identity. Many commentators on Beckett's trilogy make no distinction between "Self" and "Identity," but it is crucial to do so. Beckett stresses that consciousness suffices to keep intact what might be considered a marginal Self, whereas identity is a Self with memory that can place its existence temporally, spatially, and longitudinally in relation to the world surrounding it. Identity knows where, how, and why it is; Self knows only *that* it is. In a Jungian interpretation of the trilogy, a critic concludes that "[i]n essence *The Unnamable* is a vision of hell, the hell of being tormented by one's own thoughts and especially by the thought that the Self can never be defined."[20]

Although Wylie Sypher's judgment that Beckett's "nihilism" completes "the last phase of anti-literature" begun in *Rameau's Nephew* and continued in Dostoyevsky, Gide, and Kafka is typical of a certain apocalyptic approach to Beckett, on the question of Self and identity he gets it right. In *The Unnamable,* he comments, that the "self has shriveled, the human remains. . . . [W]e have an existence . . . after we have lost an identity. . . ." Sypher sees all of Beckett's novels (at the point of his writing) as "studies in the extreme attrition of personality, an advanced stage of entropy in the self"; and "existence" presupposes a "self," however "shriveled." The Unnamable's "nothingness strangely keeps its tinge of pain, doubt, solitude, despair," a posture Wylie calls "a defensive humanism" (the subtitle of his chapter on Beckett) "gloomily qualified."[21] What the "tinge of pain" reveals is the "I"'s insistence on his humanness, what Ihab Hassan calls "the solitude of consciousness,"[22] more than some "defensive humanism"; Beckett would have disavowed that phrase. Dennis Brown argues that poststructuralism "does not so much fragment selfhood as abolish it altogether, save as signifier," adding that nevertheless Beckett has continued "that self-aware deconstruction of selfhood we associate with Joyce and Eliot."[23] Up to a point this is true; but there is a major distinction between "self-fragmentation" in the classic moderns and in Beckett. In, say, Eliot, the "I" keeps a narcissistic vigil over its own disintegration, has an awareness that calls attention to itself, and thus is never really successful in achieving authentic self-annihilation. When Eliot writes,

"These fragments I have shored against my ruins," the "ruins" remain the self-conscious ruins of a Byron ("To meditate amongst decay, and stand / A ruin amidst ruins" *[Childe Harold's Pilgrimage]*), where the woe we are invited to behold is extended by the Self. For Beckett, the "I" is always a moving, shifting, evasive target intent on escaping not only the reader's ability to name, but avoiding any self-conscious power that can identify and judge. Beckett's choice of displaying "ruins" is loss of bodily dimension. He is a traveller in "muddy solitudes" (*M* 190). As Alain Robbe-Grillet has noted, the parade of characters in the trilogy "occupied the sentences of the novel"; they were "there to deceive us," present "in place of the ineffable being who still refuses to appear there, the man incapable of recuperating his own existence, the one who never manages to be present."[24] Malone's sense of impending death finally feels as if he is being born "into death. . . . I shall say I no more" (*MD* 323).[25]

And in each succeeding volume of the trilogy, the "I" has fewer body parts, until the Unnamable is so amputated (his infected leg is actually cut away) that all that remains is a torso. Such progressive diminution allows for no ruminative reverie such as was granted that other bedridden writer, Proust, about whom Beckett wrote his first book; Beckett's "I" is haunted. By the time we have reached *The Unnamable* Blanchot sees that "narrative has now become struggle"; and that this novel renders the "malaise" of a man drifting between "existence and nothingness," trapped in limbo, "incapable of dying and incapable of being born . . . an endless dying"[26]—which, one would agree, is the same as an endless living, an endless solitude.

3

"Solitude," wrote Conrad in *Nostromo,* " . . . becomes a state of soul in which the affectations of irony and skepticism have no place." It is a measure of the distance between Conrad and Beckett, for in the latter, solitude entrenches itself and can function only within the "affectations of irony and skepticism." The Beckettian solitary, especially in the trilogy, can survive only when camouflaged as the ironist and the skeptic, for without these (dis)guises he could not cope for long, perhaps not at all. He turns himself into perhaps the most successful chameleon in fiction ("Chameleon in spite of himself, there you have Molloy, viewed from a certain angle" [*M* 30]).

Readers of the trilogy have remarked on the repetitions and contradictions that occur with regularity in all three novels[27]; and many critics (especially in the last two decades) have offered ingenious postmodern exegeses built on deconstructive or poststructuralist foundations. While such explanations of Beckett's strategies are often useful, there are prior questions that need to be addressed, and while they may often seem self-evident, they are not.[28]

One of the issues in the trilogy is how the "I" responds to his condition, which in all three novels is ultimately desperate. Evidence in the texts suggests that the "I" is not only accepting of his state, but is defiantly proud of it, a misanthrope who gives the world the finger and detests pity, for himself or others. Early commentary on the trilogy seized on the despair of the three novels by declaring, for example, that in *The Unnamable* "the journey to solipsism is completed"; that "Beckett's image of the Absurd Man is developed in breathtaking fashion in his trilogy"; and that "Beckett's Absurd Man is the image of man cut off from humanity and imprisoned in an absurd world and unnamable self. . . ."[29] What was often ignored was the nastiness, however repaired, with which Beckett endowed his narrators. Molloy and Moran are murderers, Moran is a sadistic father, Malone is an unrepentant misanthrope, and the Unnamable a limbless torso with an often poisonously sarcastic voice. Malone vows, "I forgive nobody. I wish them all an atrocious life and then the fires and ice of hell . . ." (*MD* 204). And the Unnamable plays with the reader (several readers have suggested the trilogy is full of "games"), making us feel pity when suddenly he undercuts it with a smirk. In fact his last words, which have become canonized in the Beckett world of readers and critics, are an exemplary instance of ambiguity: "I can't go on, I'll go on." Is this an affirmation to endure and prevail over his miserable state? Or is it one of those give and take back statements, with the final "I'll go on" an ironic counterpoint to the "I can't go on," a sly message to the reader that says, perhaps mockingly, No, I'm not done, you're not rid of me, the silence of "the end" is only white space on a page, but there is more?

In an interview with Israel Shenker, frequently referenced, Beckett claimed that "[t]here's no way to go on" beyond the trilogy, but he did go on, beyond the *Textes pour rien,* which in the same interview he considered to be a failure. Still, the interview led to such apocalyptically titled essays as Leo Bersani's "Beckett and the End of Literature" (1970), after Robbe-Grillet (*Pour un nouveau roman,* 1963) had declared an end at least to the formal novel as we knew it.[30]

At best, the Unnamable's last words are ambiguous. For all that is solipsistic, nihilistic, mocking, and clearly anti-"humanistic" in the trilogy,[31] the "I"'s predicament in all three novels is also an unmistakable invitation for us to behold an abandoned human being "rotting with solitude" and crying out from the deepest despair of suffering, a *de profundis clamavi* as powerful as any that emanates from, say, Baudelaire or Rimbaud. For the Unnamable, his crime, he says, is his punishment; he is in a dungeon, and if there may be others there with him, "perhaps . . . [they are] companion[s] in misfortune . . . they loathe me . . ." (*U* 422)—precisely what Baudelaire had defined as proper solitude and Meursault had envisioned as his triumphant death. Although the ironist and skeptic are fused in the "I," neither quality cancels "human, all too human." Indeed, like Nietzsche, who remade himself into the champion of pitilessness, Beckett's solution (if that is the right word) to his dilemma, at least in the trilogy, is what the Unnamable, on the first page of that novel, calls "aporia": "What am I to do, what shall I do, what should I do . . . how proceed? By aporia pure and simple? Or by affirmations and negations invalidated as uttered, sooner or later?" (*U* 331) The *Oxford English Dictionary*'s definition is more suggestive than the modern: It cites a 1751 passage defining aporia as "a figure whereby the speaker sheweth that he doubteth, either where to begin for the multitude of matters, or what to do or say in some strange or ambiguous way."

This definition precisely (or better than anything else) reveals at least one passage leading to an understanding of the ambiguous figure of Beckett's solitary. Christopher Ricks has sized up Beckett's ambiguity about solitude with precision: "'The wish to be alone' is set against—even while it cannot but concede as it passes—the wish to *be*. Or not to be. Period. Will one ever be alone except in the grave?"[32] Beckett's isolates create, quite literally, their own "company," their Others, to populate their solitude. These are some of the "puppets," those characters that fill the trilogy: Moran, Mahood, Macmann, Worm, Sapo, Lemuel, the Lamberts, and countless others, even the mysterious Youdi in *Molloy*, or the "master" and "they" in *The Unnamable*. Such invention constitutes some of the character-doubling, searches without end, seemingly aimless journeys, for these offer not merely an evasion of death but an amelioration of solitude. Most of these created figures are what the Unnamable calls his "puppets," and *he*, the "I," is their puppeteer. "I shall not be alone . . . I am of course alone. Alone. . . . [But] I shall have company. In the beginning. A few puppets. Then I'll scatter them, to the winds, if I can." That "if I can" is not an afterthought. About 40 pages later, he seems more confident: "I'll scatter them, and their miscreated puppets," and the "their" seems to have shifted the creation of the puppets away from himself to the "they." Forty pages after that, the necessity of puppets is put to the question: "Are they really necessary that he [the "he" refers to the unborn Worm] may hear, they and kindred puppets?" (*U* 332, 370, 410). The failure to give Worm life, for he remains a kind of homunculus, may be open to a number of surmises, but it constitutes a dilemma for the narrator: are his puppets necessary to keep him company in his solitude? Or do they remain stillborn because his aloneness cannot relate any longer to any Other, even invented puppets? There was a time when Malone felt he had time to "frolic . . . in the brave company I have always longed for, always searched for, and which would never have me" (*MD* 219), but for the Unnamable that time, that hope, is no longer possible. After Mahood has left him, the Unnamable laments, "I'm alone. . . . I invented it all in the hope it would console me, help me to go on. . . . All lies" (*U* 357). Worm is the Unnamable's Friday—"I gave this solitary a name . . ." (*U* 385), but he remains un-born. But Malone is like a child, protective of inanimate objects, for they substitute for humans: "And but for the society of these little objects . . . I might have been reduced to the company of nice people"—a stone, a horse chestnut, a cone, all are in his deep pockets to be fingered for reassurance, talked to with love, discarded for new ones when no longer in favor (*MD* 282). Molloy had his sucking stones.

Sometimes Malone felt abandoned, "alone, back alone, as alone as when I went . . . ," as he is "all alone, well hidden, [playing] the clown, all alone . . ." (*MD* 269, 220). By the end of the trilogy, the "I" has been re-duced to the essence of aloneness: "I'm alone . . . talking alone, listening alone, alone, alone, the others are gone, they have been stilled. . . ." Since "[p]ast happiness" had disappeared from his memory, he "invents obscuri-ties," but effectively memory has evacuated his being—"I . . . feel nothing, I know nothing . . ." (*U* 470, 334, 349). In fact, the Unnamable is never quite certain who he is: "it must have been I, but I never saw myself, so it can't have been I . . . how can I recognize myself who never made my acquain-tance . . . (*U* 457). This repeated allusion to uncertain identity is critical to understanding the collective "I"'s skeptic disposition. "My concern," says Malone, "is not with me, but with another . . ." (*MD* 221). While there are Gogolian comic possibilities in an identityless narrator ("to have no identity, it's a scandal" [*U* 432])—and Beckett exploits them—the major impact of an unrecognized self is far from comic. Not only does this repeated motif underscore the narrator's isolation from others, it also suggests an altogether more frightening discovery, the isolation of Self from Self, which again cre-ates a "tympanum" between subject and object, positioning the "I"'s place between them, proscribing what defines his annihilation. Beckett resisted the whole traditional subject–object relationship, the efficacy of epistemo-logical reassurance.[33] Roquentin and Meursault are at least self-reflexive; Beckett's "I" has neither external nor internal referents. In this sense his soli-tary state nearly eliminates solitude, for one is in solitude from someone or something that, from the position of that solitude, can be named. Yet, the Unnamable refers not only to the person, the narrator, but to his lack of ref-erence, to that outside that cannot—like himself—be named.

Close to the end, the Unnamable makes an important hypothetical dis-tinction: "if it's I what it is, and it's not I who it is, and what it is, I see noth-ing else for the moment . . ." (*U* 446). A differentiation between "what" and "I" may appear arbitrary, but nothing in Beckett is accidental. "What" is ob-ject; "I" is subject. By asking whether the "I" is the "what" while the "who" is the 'not I,' Beckett invokes an epistemological conundrum: Can the ob-ject appropriate the subject's perspective? Can the phenomenal overwhelm, even obliterate the "I," as Sartre said existence obliterated Roquentin? The

Unnamable's repeated questioning of his own existence, his physical deterioration, and his skeptical monologue all suggest that Beckett is describing just that, a devouring world that strips the ego of any certainty of its own existence or identity.[34]

Moran notices the "great changes [he] had suffered and . . . [his] growing resignation of being dispossessed of self." He also remarks that "[a]ll is dark, but with that simple darkness that follows like balm upon the great dismemberings." What dismemberings? "One does not ask. There somewhere man is too, vast conglomerate of all nature's kingdom, as lonely as a bound" (*M* 168, 123–124); this desperation is reminiscent of Josef K's last thoughts before being led to his assassination in the quarry. Using "bound" as a noun, short for boundary, Beckett achieves a fortuitous double meaning, for is he not truly bound within the tympanum (like all two-sided boundaries) that separates him—as all the narrators in the trilogy—from self *and* world? Moran, that originally punctilious antithesis to the dilapidated Molloy, wonders that his quest for chimeras does not make him suspicious, but "[n]othing of the kind. I saw it only as the weakness of the solitary . . . admittedly to be deplored, but which had to be indulged in if I wished to remain a solitary, and I did, I clung to that . . ." (*M,* 128). Horrified by "fancy," Moran nevertheless sacrifices his usual calm demeanor to be "haunted and possessed" by these illusions that preserve his solitude; eventually he pays a price. He loses his identity and becomes Molloy, the stalking horse of his quest; the hunter, as a precondition of self-defining, needs himself to become the hunted. Moran never knows what to do with Molloy if he finds him, because he has already found him at the very start. When Moran tells the story of Macmann he is also telling his own (and Molloy's): "But space hemmed in on every side and held him in its toils, with the multitude of other faintly stirring faintly struggling things . . . and the trapped huddled things changed and died each one according to its [own] solitude" (*MD* 317–318).

Posturing as a fearless, defiant, manipulative savant, the Unnamable is also afraid, aware of his vulnerability to the onslaught of language: "And yet I am afraid, afraid of what my words will do to me, to my refuge . . ." (*U* 344). Words can invade his "refuge" and destroy his solitude. Words create, but words undo; words prolong life, but words also extend suffering. Silence is death. The Unnamable's fear is both being egoless and being identified as nameable, as both conditions bring the burdens of identity: responsibility, guilt, and moral choice. For that reason he ponders his ambivalence toward the mysterious "they": "Do they believe it is I who am speaking? . . . To make me believe that I have an ego all my own, and can speak of it, as they of theirs." Though the collective "I" in Beckett's trilogy may at times search longingly for his ego, its accompanying identity is a demon from which he makes every effort to escape. "For to go on means going from here, means finding me, losing me, vanishing and beginning again. . . ." Safer to stay in his "refuge." Wishing for anything else is merely mock heroics: "Ah," muses the Unnamable, "if I could only find a voice of my own, in all this babble, it would be the end of their troubles, and of mine," but he concedes only a few pages later that he is "[his] own destroyer," that he "feel[s] nothing" (*U* 395, 344, 397, 405, 417). All this evasion from Self is what Molloy calls, with supreme irony, "the tranquillity of decomposition," for "to decompose is to live too . . ." (*M* 24). For all the same reasons, especially for the solitude that bestows a costly freedom, Malone denies that he is self-oriented: "My concern is not with me, but with another . . ."(*MD* 221). As for Molloy, the solution was multiplication: "there were three, no, four Molloys" (*M* 129). So while these narrators make every attempt to evade themselves, what Beckett succeeds in conveying is that however removed from identity, indeed, the more one flaunts its absence, the more one is caught in the depths of a despairing aloneness or solitude.

The search for company, however misguided it may be, begins with Molloy. As the two mystery figures, A and C, pass across Molloy's vision, he is tempted "to get up and follow [one of them], perhaps even to catch up with him one day, so as to know him better, be myself less lonely" (*M* 7). And here is Molloy's description of his original mission: "And so at last I came out of that distant night, divided between the murmurs of my little world . . . and those so different (so different?) of all that between two suns abides and passes away. Never once a human voice . . . But I shall not always be in need. But talking of craving for a fellow [human being] let me observe that . . . I resolved to go and see my mother" (*M,* 12–13). And that quest, of course, turns out to be his undoing. Not only does Molloy never find his mother, but we discover that he has had anything but a loving relationship with her; his thoughts are matricidal, and his search for her lands him, in the end, in a ditch after a lonely and fruitless trek through dark forests. When we first meet him he has somehow come to rest in his mother's bed in a place that resembles, as do the venues of the succeeding two novels, a hospice or a madhouse. The remaining narrative is an account of how he managed to end up in such strange circumstances.

Wolfgang Iser is struck by the use of contradiction in the trilogy: "The sentence construction in *[Molloy]* and in the subsequent novels is frequently composed of direct contradictions. A statement is followed by the immediate retraction of what has been stated."[35] A number of convincing explanations have been offered to account for this contradiction-strategy; but while the contradictions are often sly, they signal a genuinely ambiguous state of mind in the collective "I." Can the "I" survive his solitary state despite the odds that are so starkly set against him? Molloy says, "I misjudged the distance separating me from the other world . . ."(*M* 53). If the "I" awaits death (and not only Malone "dies"), what mechanism is available to transcend irony and skepticism, to permit him to reveal himself through the tears that the Unnamable continually wishes to assure us are not real? ("Ah yes, I am truly bathed in tears" [346]). "Overcome," he commands himself in his "solitary confinement," among many things, "the fatal leaning toward expressiveness.... Doubt no more ... carry on cheerfully as before" (*U* 447–448). All exertions toward these wishes fail. He may shut his door against them, those mysterious "others" who watch him; but at once he offers the opposite, "I'll find silence, and peace at last, by opening my doors and letting myself be devoured, they'll stop howling, they'll start eating ..." (*U* 448)—Crusoe's nightmare. A good deal has been said about Beckett's Cartesianism (after all, he wrote his MA Thesis on Descartes), some seeing signs of a rejection and satire of Descartes, others some form of adherence.[36] Of one thing we may be certain: Beckett envisioned and accepted duality, and this helped him to communicate his narrators' peculiar tendency to fall into contradiction: "[P]erhaps that's what I am, the thing that divides the world in two, on the one side the outside, on the other the inside ... I'm neither one side nor the other, I'm in the middle ... I've two surfaces and no thickness ... I'm the tympanum, on the one hand the mind, on the other the world, I don't belong to either ..." (*U* 439). This "tympanum," this membrane, is vulnerable to both sides it faces: its own mind, or consciousness, and the world that always impinges. Like Roquentin and Meursault, this "I" is frequently dissociated from self; only in Beckett is such dissociation *in extremis,* "alone and mute." The "I" can no longer be certain whether he is in hell or paradise, "the light of paradise, and the solitude, and this voice ... of the blest interceding invisible, for the living, for the dead, all is possible" (*U* 411).[37]

Often the narrator seems to be eager to get done with life and is prevented by the mysterious "they." On the first page, Molloy tells us that "What I'd like now is to speak of the things that are left, say my goodbyes, finish dying. They don't want that" (*M* 1). Like his brethren, Molloy is lame: Collectively the narrators are increasingly disabled so that their imprisonment is mandated by physical limitation: it is imposed solitude. As he recounts what he can recall about how he ended up in his mother's bed, Molloy describes himself as without identity, homeless: "no papers ... nor any occupation, nor any domicile ... (*M* 20). Detained by the police, mistaken for a vagrant or criminal (like Mann's Tonio Kröger), Molloy begins his journey already lost: He cannot recall his own town, his mother's name, or sometimes even his own. In some ways, he walks and cycles as his own "double," or, perhaps more accurately, a part of himself, like Gogol's nose.

There are times, Molloy concedes, when he forgot not only "who I was, but that I was, forgot to be." Mostly, he says, he stayed in his "jar," where sealed and "well preserved," he cogitated on his own existence (*M* 52). That motif of loss and recovery of Self dominates the trilogy, and is parodied by losses of such items as sticks, notebooks, and pencils. Malone expects to be "quite dead at last," but through his puppet, Sapo, he creates a metaphor of return, for Sapo loves the "flight of the hawk": "He would stand rapt, gazing at the long pernings, the quivering poise, the wings lifted for the plummet drop, the wild reascent, fascinated by such extremes of need, of pride, of patience and solitude" (*MD* 217). And the Unnamable understands that "to go on means going from here . . ." (*U* 344). And one step toward self-retrieval, at the end of *The Unnamable,* is to cease inventing stories of puppets by scattering them. "Perhaps I'll find traces of myself by the same occasion" (*U* 370). Kenner has said it best: "*The Unnamable* is the final phase of a trilogy which carries the Cartesian process backwards, beginning with a bodily *je suis* and ending with a bare *cogito.*" Existence precedes all.[38]

4

"What rubbish," says the Unnamable, "all this stuff about light and dark. And how I have luxuriated in it" (*U* 348). Malone uses an oxymoron: "dark light, if one may say so . . ." (*MD* 270). This is elaborated in *The Unnamable,* when the narrator fancies himself as the source of the "faint light that enables me to see," and asserts that "[t]here is no night so deep . . . that it may not be pierced . . . with the help of no other light than that of the blackened sky . . ." (*U* 341). Throughout the trilogy light and darkness are dominant motifs and images; while the first sometimes betokens the comfort of solitude, the second embodies a longing for the abandoned world of others. Even Molloy makes "insane demands for light" (*M* 33), though he also tells us that he avoids the sun: "The Aegean, thirsting for heat and light, him I killed, he killed himself, early on, in me" (*M* 29). Malone sometimes consoles himself within his own created protectiveness of dark solitude: "I feel the old dark gathering, the solitude preparing, by which I know myself . . ." (*MD* 214).[39] Both Molloy and Moran travel at night, mostly to evade detection (though from whom or what, it is never certain); and it is in this dark forest that Molloy encounters one of his look-alikes, the charcoal burner: "A total stranger. Sick with solitude probably" (*M* 92), like himself. He kills him. At the end of his quest, half dead, Molloy arrives at the edge of the forest: "I saw the light, the light of the plain. . . . I lapsed down to the bottom of the ditch. . . . Molloy could stay, where he happened to be" (*M* 100–101). Deliberately he makes no effort to save himself; those who bring him to his mother's house and lay him on her bed are again mysterious ones whom he neither knows nor asks for aid. One solitude, then, is by choice; the next is imposed. After his initially optimistic departure on his journey, Molloy's "subsequent contacts with society," remarks one critic, "will be marked by hostility and thus by an absence of light."[40] On his return journey to his home, which has been neglected and is in shambles, near it he meets a stranger with an unlit lantern; the house is "in darkness"; fallen into a deep depression, ready for death, Moran says he "shall never light this lamp again" (195, 198, 199).

Malone, on the other hand, is not always happy with the dark of his subsequent dungeon-like imprisonment: "I can scarcely even see the window-pane, or the wall," which conspire to create angles so that their meeting place "often looks like the edge of an abyss." At times, Malone needs and asks for light, for "there is never any light in this place. . . ." Then again: "A bright light is not necessary, a taper is all one needs to live in strangeness . . ."(*MD* 236, 207). The concluding words of *Malone Dies* are fragments that echo both Lear's lament and Goethe's dying wish (which is reported to have been, "More light!"):

> or light light I mean
> never there he will never
> never anything
> there
> any more (*MD* 328)

As for darkness, Malone knows its overwhelming power: "I feel the old dark gathering, the solitude preparing, by which I know myself. . . ." So he "want[s] as little as possible of darkness in [Sapo's] story." A "little darkness . . . is nothing," it passes; "[b]ut I know what darkness is, it accumulates, thickens, then suddenly bursts and drowns everything." Besides, Sapo's story is intended as a foil; when Beckett first implies that he is friendless, he takes it back: "The dolt is seldom solitary" (*MD* 214, 215). Malone's process of dying is itself a loss of light, of course, and a gathering darkness. What there is of light is never direct, never natural; the opaque barrier between his sight and light is again a kind of "tympanum" separating awareness from objectivity. "The light," Malone observes, "is there, outside . . . but it does not come through . . . a kind of leaden light that makes no shadow. . . ." His almost surrealistic perceptions of his relationship to physical phenomena separate and isolate him in what he describes as a void, one he desired: "What I had sought, when I had struggled out of my hole . . . was the rapture of vertigo, the letting go, the fall, the gulf, the relapse to darkness, to nothingness. . . ." In the process, however, light will not penetrate his life again: It refracts through a "narrow opening," and it has no "steadfastness. . . . [I]t entered and died . . . devoured by the dark. . . . For the dark had triumphed." And the dark is linked to silence, "that silence, which like the dark, would one day triumph too. And then all would be still and dark and all things at rest for ever at last" (*MD* 250, 221, 230).

5

What differentiates the collective "I" narrator in Beckett's trilogy from Defoe's Crusoe is, of course, much more than the distance that nearly two-and-a-half centuries inevitably creates. Volcanic disruptions reshaped the geography of the Self, and our concept of it, in the interval between the novelist who was perhaps the first realist—at least in the English tradition—and the writer who stands at the crossroads of modernity and postmodernity: Beckett. Arguably, Defoe's realism came under the Cartesian spell; Kenner seems to think so when he asserts, if rather grandly, that "[i]t is Descartes who leads the Western mind to the place where realistic fiction . . . becomes a focal mode of art."[41] Hence the Self's survival is linked to a world of objects despite the increasingly weakening vision perceiving those objects. In his own way, Beckett is a supreme realist; the growing separation between what objects are out there and our ability to see them in no way denies their existence: It only affirms, painfully, our fading ability to see, our loss of light, our deepening solitude.

Beckett seems to have positioned himself to challenge Donne's "No man is an island entire unto himself," with all the sentimental communalism that phrase had gathered by the middle decades of the twentieth century. And he almost succeeded. But his occasional references to "island," and many of the previous passages already cited, also betray his own ambiguous sense about total self-annihilation. From certain perspectives, the narrator(s) of the trilogy are, like Robinson Crusoe, drunk with freedom and terrified by its ultimately isolating consequences. Indeed, the collective "I" is, like Crusoe, essentially an orphaned castaway, condemned to solitary confinement, involuntary solitude, and made to rely on himself, to improvise and innovate just to survive. And despite the undulating perspectives that Beckett manipulates in his narrators, his prose confronts the reader with a directness that Defoe might have appreciated; a hard, almost minimalist simplicity that Beckett's friend Joyce so much admired in Defoe. "The tone [of the trilogy]," writes Josipovici, "is factual, reportorial even."[42] But where Defoe's directness empowers certainty (though he has his moments of doubt), Beckett's trips over itself—often with ironic and comic results—in repetition, contradiction, paradox, uncertainty: "aporia." Describing a balancing act on his crutches, Molloy begins with a carefully crafted description of how he moved with them, only immediately to undercut it: "how could I press my feet together, with my legs in the state they were?" Well, he teases, "I pressed them together, that's all I can tell you. Take it or leave it. Or I didn't press them together" (*M* 93).

Like Crusoe, the collective "I," especially Molloy, is a careful gatherer who occasionally takes time to enumerate his inventory: "For where do you think I hid my vegetable knife, my silver, my horn and the other things I have not yet named, perhaps shall never name" (*M* 78). Malone is equally enamored of objects: "my exercise-book, my lead and the French pencil . . ." (*MD* 290). Molloy's description of how he manages to ride a bicycle with crutches might well come from *Crusoe:* "I fastened my crutches to the crossbar, one on either side, I propped the foot of my stiff leg (I forget which, now they're both stiff) on the projecting front axle, and I pedalled with the other" (*M* 13). Only the parenthetical sentence marks a difference, and a telling, "aporetic" one. As a precaution, also like Crusoe ("I barricado'd my self round"), Moran builds himself a shelter, "the shelter, which I was beginning to think of as my little house . . ." (*M* 167). Although both Crusoe and Beckett's collective "I" pride themselves on lucidity and reason, both are in fear of being devoured, both dread wild beasts. Crusoe's fear is clearly based on a real threat; Beckett's narrators tend to identify their own inner state with beastliness, so that the Self images forth a self-devouring fantasy. Already in *Molloy,* the narrator "lives in menaced solitude."[43] "Live and invent. I have tried," says Malone. "Invent. . . . While within me the wild beast of earnestness padded up and down, roaring, ravening, rending. . . . And all alone . . ." (*MD* 220). And the Unnamable expresses his frustrations and inhibitions that have led him to identify with the beast: "I . . . seek like a caged beast . . . born in a cage and dead in a cage . . . with nothing of its specifics left but fear and fury . . . fear of the sounds of beasts, the sounds of men . . . in the daytime . . . at night . . ." (*U* 443). Beasts, like everything else on the island, are perceived by Crusoe, the subject, as objects; even the single footprint in the sand becomes the frightening part for an even more frightening whole. For the Unnamable, the beast, an inner phenomenon, fuses as subject-object, perceiver and perceived so that the horror that Defoe permits Crusoe to feel is replaced—or better, disguised—by Beckett with a submerged terror posing as grim humor and bemused acceptance.[44] The "I" writes his stories and "diary"; his pencil (which at one point is lost, just as Crusoe's pen runs out of ink), his notebook, his stick, and crutches are talisman-like survival objects that resemble some of Crusoe's "Provisions, Ammunition and Stores."[45] Each house, each room, each bed becomes, in descending order, a narrower island for Beckett's narrators; and even the forests that Molloy and Moran roam are sanctuaries with boundaries that separate them from encroachment. For Malone, the island is a mere fantasy: "A last effort. The islet. The shore facing the open sea is jagged with cracks. One could live there, perhaps happy . . . but nobody lives there" (*MD* 326). It remains for the Unnamable to offer the most poignant reflection on his imprisonment:

The island, I'm on the island, I've never left the island. God help me. I was under the impression I've spent my life in spirals round the earth. Wrong, it's on the island I wind my endless ways. The island that's all the earth I know. I don't know it either, never having had the stomach to look at it. When I come to the coast I turn back inland. (*U* 372)

And therein, of course, lies the crucial difference from Crusoe who, one recalls, makes every effort to explore his island and, after years of comforting solitude, begins to seek escape from it to reach his human others.

Until he meets Friday, Crusoe is truly alone; at the beginning of his stay on the island, his everyday struggles to eat, sleep, and merely to hang on to life occupy him day and night. While it has been argued here that he does not, as some critics have said, lack imagination, his early focus is admittedly not on reflection so much as on survival. When he undergoes his conversion, begins to doubt his freedom as a liability, discovers the footprint, meets the savages, and rescues Friday, then one begins to take notice of the developing conflicts that redirect his thoughts from remaining King of his Island to escaping its loneliness. Beckett approaches his isolates quite differently. Their process of doubling, of creating characters and stories, of searching for what cannot be found, of traveling to dead ends—all this is designed to stay not only death but the solitude that precedes it. While technically as abandoned as Crusoe, Beckett's collective "I" is able to invent many Fridays, whom he can possess or dismiss at will. Crusoe's sturdy sense of Self that shapes his identity, though it has its crises of instability, is ultimately his salvation; Beckett's narrators have been neutered, figuratively and literally, and (Wittgenstein notwithstanding) pure mind and pure language are neither of them sufficient to maintain a consistent voice, a stable identity, a Self in which body and mind can remain unified. Crusoe exemplifies a "classic and consistent self." His rebellion against his father, his shipwreck, his solitariness—no one of these conditions changes his sense of "self-identity," which remains "coherent" and enables him to overcome his challenges with a steady ego. Seen from a postmodern perspective, there may indeed be an "extraordinary insouciance" in his role as "chronicler,"[46] something Virginia Woolf had already noted and commented on (see chapter III).

Despite whatever opposition Beckett harbored against Descartes, ironically and paradoxically, the trilogy validates Descartes' dualistic architecture of the human, though throughout the trilogy there are valiant attempts to subvert it. Crusoe hides from *real* savages and *real* beasts; the beasts in the trilogy, no less real of course in the imagination, are too interchangeable, too domiciled as inner demons to become objective targets. Whereas Crusoe slays his enemies, Beckett's collective "I" can merely dream of murder, or invent it in his puppets, from his Oblomovian position of reclining in the bed that becomes his living grave.[47] "It is true," says Malone, "I had to wish to leave my bed" (*MD* 290). What keeps the Unnamable in bed, aside from physical limitations and "they" who appear to guard him, is his own sense of futile circularity: "For to go on means . . . finding me, losing me, vanishing and beginning again, a stranger first, then little by little the same as always, in another place, where I shall say I have always been. . . ." (*U* 344).

6

The narratives of the collective "I" of the trilogy convey the bitterness of betrayal, a sense that the "I" has been wronged by life, by enemies beginning with birth itself: The three novels constitute an ontological plaint. Yet, tempting as it may be to see all affirmative and self-accusing comments as mere cynical posturing, there are moments when the "I" appears to be genuinely reflecting on his own role in his misery, not as a mere victim. In one such passage, with a deliberate reference to Hamlet (who, after all, was also wavering between feeling the victim and the self-destroyer), the Unnamable says: "Slough off this mortal inertia, it is out of place, in this society. They can't do everything. They have put you on the right road . . . now it's up to you . . ."(*U* 380). But all these narrators are well beyond self-redemption: Malone thinks he may be have died already, the Unnamable has, he believes, lived in a "coma." These personae occupy a territory well outside the perimeters where one may change course and go to a future: They are condemned to a form of ceaseless existence. Malone says it best when he muses, "But what matter whether I was born or not, have lived or not, am dead or merely dying, I shall go on doing as I have always done, not knowing what it is I do, nor who I am, nor where I am, nor if I am" (*MD* 256–257).

Critics have struggled with the antinomies in the trilogy. For that sense of having been betrayed brings its own countering reaction: "What is . . . predictable is that the isolated individual—who has been brought into existence by his separation from his community—will respond in kind"—that is, with violence directed at others. This at least brings a semblance of explanation for murders, sadistic behavior toward a son, or matricidal thoughts. As with "solitude, this violence is not so much an attribute of his self as it is his essence." But it is difficult to agree that this "interplay of affirmation and negation" does not produce a "dialectical tension," but a "synthesis" that "renders these oppositions ephemeral."[48] Quite the contrary: The tension between solitude and violence (even if sometimes it is merely the thought of it) emphasizes the "I"'s entrapment and provides the narratives the power to continue. Kenner calls it "heroism without drama" in a book virtually emptied of plot and character.[49] Comparing Crusoe's redemptive episodes of conversion to the "penance" Molloy or Malone talk about, one critic notes the difference as sharply defined: If *Crusoe* is a Puritan conversion story leading to redemption (at best an "if"), "In the trilogy . . . it is just the opposite," for Beckett "has created a *via dolorosa* in reverse," in which "decrepitude and disintegration" point toward the "downward path," mocking the Pilgrim's Progress trajectory that leads from the Slough of Despond to the Celestial City.[50] It is most dangerous, however, to elevate the trilogy into some metaphorical realm out of bounds of reality. Beckett's scatological references are not arbitrary naughtiness: They remind us what we cannot forget, the essence of being human. Josopovici says it of Molloy, but it applies to all the narrators of the trilogy, that they are "obsessed" with "reality."[51] Beckett challenged, perhaps consciously, Eliot's "Human kind / Cannot bear very much reality," for bearing reality is what the trilogy is all about. Malone calls it "[m]ortal tedium" (*M* 247), and only in solitude can such mortal tedium be endured; solitude, Conrad said (again in *Nostromo*), "takes possession of the mind, and drives forth the thought into exile of utter unbelief."

Stripped of identity, left with an unstable Self, Beckett's collective "I" narrator, having created his "puppets" to keep him company in his anguished solitude, reveals little about himself in any of the three novels that comprise the trilogy. His "aporetics" in part prevent him; so does the "tympanum" he erects between himself and the reader. But he keeps his self-revelatory distance (to equate the narrator[s] with Beckett is a mistake) because his solitude has removed him beyond hearing: What we hear is a faint echo of a person, which has ceased to be personal. As the Unnamable says, *"De nobis ipsis silemus"*—about ourselves we are silent (*U* 375).

Conclusion ∿

Privacy is freedom from social contact and observation when these are not desired;
and *Solitude is the lack of desired contact.*

—Paul Halmos, *Solitude and Privacy* (1952)

Our attitude to solitude . . . is extremely paradoxical. We need it; we suffer
from it; and we flee from it. Potentially positive, solitude is often painful . . .

—Joanne Wieland-Burston,
Contemporary Solitude: The Joy and Pain of Being Alone (1996)

[T]oo much solitude makes of one an animal.

—J. M. Coetzee, *In the Heart of the Country*

[T]he word "I" is as hollow as the word "death."

—Richard Rorty, *Contingency, Irony, Solidarity* (1989)

1

"The essence of solitude . . . is a sense of choice and control. . . .
You choose to leave and return."[1] That is, if you *can* choose,
and involuntary confinement (e.g., prisons) is not the only alternative of choice; nor, as is clear from the previous chapters, is it the only
state of involuntary solitude. As some of the works demonstrate, our inhibitions of choice are many, and are often psychogenically involuntary. At
times, "return" is nearly impossible, and we are irretrievably beyond it, although no external force holds us prisoner.

In one of his gloomiest prose works, *The Lost Ones*,[2] Beckett presents an allegorical tale with echoes from Dante's *Inferno* and Camus's *Myth of Sisyphus,*

except there are no smiling faces here. If the story had illustrations, they might well come from Hieronymus Bosch or Francis Bacon. The narrative takes place in a cylindrical tube with ladders on which mute, naked people try to climb to the top in an ever tantalizing, repetitious but futile attempt to achieve what one must take to be escape: "a way out to earth and sky." No reason for their incarceration in this hellish tube is offered; like a prison, it has its rules, and breaking them elicits what appear to be the only sounds from these occupants: a tumultuous shouting and yelling in protest. Beckett writes, "outside their explosions of violence this sentiment is as foreign to them as to butterflies." To prevent "pandemonium," each body may ascend only "one at a time." Husbands and wives try to make "unmakable love," and their frustration translates itself into repetitious and fruitless attempts. What is so intensely painful is their inability to achieve either solitude or communality; as Freud wrote, "Two people coming together for the purpose of sexual satisfaction, in so far they seek for solitude, are making a demonstration against the herd instinct. . . ."[3] The cylinder has its "vanquished" (mostly women) who no longer attempt ladder-climbs, but become bridging stations for others to negotiate their ascent. Those queuing for an ascent are "immune" from touch; to touch them constitutes the most serious taboo and calls forth the most violent reactions.

The Lost Ones has recently been used by a German philosopher-theologian, Erwin Möde, to support his conclusion that postmodernism has ushered in a new age of anxiety by creating a new sense of solitude. Giving his book the title *The New Solitude of Postmodernity,* Möde argues that the "crisis of the modern has become the 'postmodern condition.'" Whereas the moderns had expressed their Kierkegaardian "fear and trembling" in an anticipatory mode, the postmoderns, unmediated by anticipation, actually experience it. Perhaps another way to put it is that the contingencies of Modernism have become the enabling—even the empowering—mechanisms of postmodernism, which Möde sees as a "nihilistic time" in which "self-annihilation" is an inevitable outcome. In any case, Beckett's tale demonstrates a "'cylindrical tautology' from which the human being cannot free itself. Liberation and deliverance must come from the 'outside.'" Such deliverance being impossible, the "'état final'" of the cylinder is not liberation, but "*exhaustion.*" Möde sees Beckett's cautionary tale as exemplifying the contemporary dilemma: the desire for deliverance and the concurrent awareness that it is impossible.[4]

Certainly solitude, in such circumstances as the "lost ones" find themselves, is no longer an adequate word, whether we call it "new" or not. Isolation in the cylindrical tube is more immolation, and the persons climbing fruitlessly up their ladders neither long for society nor for self-contemplation: Their longing is virtually purely biological—space, air, and copulation. Beckett has moved beyond the stalemate of the trilogy.

In a rather curious book on Gilles Deleuze, James Bruseau attempts to make some distinctions between ordinary solitude or alienation, and "radical alienation." Rousseau's concept of the "savage" and Tournier's Robinson Crusoe "lived on the surface." Their alienation is "shrouded in a community they are being deprived of"—that is, their "difference" (Deleuze's term) is imposed—they have "insufficient community." But Rousseau (and Deleuze) "want to understand an alienation that defines itself, that begins without reference to friends or society. . . . It shoots into solitude. . . . [I]t starts over alone after a major wreck . . . [;] this alienation remains immune to community."[5] Perhaps "radical alienation" is part of the postmodern condition, even though Rousseau (and perhaps Nietzsche) sought it out in the eighteenth and nineteenth centuries respectively. But if the fictions here examined, including those of Beckett, reveal a truth, it is precisely that "radical alienation," in the end, does not exist; however brave the face of solitude, it is never "immune to community." Blanchot, too, attempts to make distinctions between the ordinary solitude "as the world understands it" and a different meaning for the words "*to be alone*"—what he calls the "essential solitude." That solitude he locates in the work of art itself: "The solitude of the work has as its primary framework the absence of any defining criteria. . . . The work is solitary," and the reader affirms that solitude just as the author has risked it. Blanchot argues that this severance from the work discomforts the author, who "increasingly feels the need to maintain a relation to himself." This need tends to urge him toward the journal-form, "a form which at least keeps a semblance of maintaining a relationship with the work of art. The writer "surrender[s] to the risk of time's absence, where eternal starting over reigns. . . . To write is . . . to stay in touch. . . ." In the process of creating, we remain connected, if not to community outside us then to the solitary work of art which, after all, once completed "shoots" not only into solitude, but into the world of community.[6]

2

How did solitude, once the domain of the strong who freely elected it as a balm for the mind and soul (Petrarch, Montaigne and others), devolve to become the condition of the anguished, the forlorn, the misanthropic, the alienated? How did solitude become transformed from a feeling of contentment to an expression of discontent? This study has shown that like all shifts of taste, this one, too, was neither sudden nor followed a straight line. The potential discomfiture of solitude is inherent in the condition itself, and one detects it from the start. Certain outcomes such as melancholia, misanthropy, and arrogance are already latent, and sometimes manifest, in the seventeenth century; by the nineteenth, with the explosive impact of various forms of Romanticism, solitude became equivalent to a conscious attempt to put distance between Self and Other. That effort was animated by a strong, deliberative rebelliousness: Solitude no longer serves as an enclosure that keeps the world at bay, a between-time of rest to seek a palliative in books or Nature. Now solitude encloses the Self hermetically, and books and Nature are replaced by the Self confronting itself, not in peace, but with a shudder.[7] Paul Halmos writes: "Without a balance between individuation and socialisation the predominant one of these two invariably becomes a pathogenic factor."[8] Yet, what remains consistent is the implausibility of life at either extreme. Solitude is not always an experiment (as was, say, was Thoreau's); if it is seriously maintained, all but a select few will yearn for release from solitariness to *some* form of human relationship. At the same time, those for whom the world is too much with them will yearn for release into quietude. Whatever the middle ground may be, we seem unable to attain it, for it should logically embrace elements of each state. But there really is no partial solitude or partial socialization: The so-called compromise that eludes the "pathogenic" can exist only in a perpetual shifting from one state to the other. Such an alternating journey cannot help but bring with it tension and ambiguity as the Self is abruptly positioned from a state of Being to Becoming, from stasis to engagement.

At the end of the nineteenth century, Nietzsche sought to make the confrontational experience heroic and liberating; he did not succeed. What emerged as dominant in his culture was ironically what he most despised: the *maladie de siècle* and the *taedium vitae* of the 1880s and 90s, especially in England and France. Nietzsche's syphilis-induced insanity may have saved him from being fully conscious of these developments, but there are ample signs that he saw them coming. But the full bloom of modern solitude as obsessive self-contemplation appears after the Great War. In the major classic moderns of the four decades when solitude becomes entrenched, almost cultist, and from which the main body of work for this study has been drawn, the overriding tenor of solitude is its anguish and the inability (and unwillingness) of solitaries to overcome it. As the Self seeking identity is itself in danger of dissolution, little remains intact to guide it, and solipsism is close at hand, though ironically the preoccupation with Self also acts as a defense against a confrontation with nothingness.[9] Nevertheless, the aphasic men and women in *To the Lighthouse* anticipate the silences in Beckett.

But Nietzsche's attempt, notwithstanding his fear and premonition of cultural epigoni was significant. Emerging individuality (at least in the West) has been variously dated from the advent of the Renaissance, the counter-Reformation, the Enlightenment, the Romantic era ending with Kierkegaard and Nietzsche, or the modern age of Freud's Ego and Heidegger's Existentialism. It all depends how one approaches the complexities of the developing "I"—the "contingent" "I," as Richard Rorty prefers to call it. Kierkegaard noted a paradox: "The self must be broken in order to become itself. . . ."[10] If one modifies "broken" to reconstituted or reified, then the issues of solitude as exemplified in the works here examined become familiar. From Crusoe to Beckett's "I," the tension between solitude and Society rests on the Self's perception of itself: how much it was willing to sacrifice to accommodate to demands of other or to remain within its "bound"—to use Beckett's word—whatever the loss. Neither solitude nor immersion in the social matrix is without cost; but the Self's reconstitution is a necessary prelude to the Self's confrontation with solitude *or* Society as it moves to and fro between the two and makes its choices. The major triumph, if that is the right word, is the ability *to make* a choice. Nietzsche, according to Rorty, made this his contribution to the dilemma: "He thinks a human life triumphed just insofar as it escapes from inherent descriptions of the contingencies of its existence and finds new descriptions. This is the difference between the will to the truth and the will to self-overcoming."[11]

Zarathustra was, then, the triumph of such overcoming, carving out for himself an individual Self intent on rejecting contingency altogether. But, ironically, such uniqueness of Self led to the precipice of the abyss; even Zarathustra (like his epigone, Hans Castorp) was forced to descend the heights of rarefied isolation. That interval (often too long in duration to be called that) between unmaking and reconstituting the Self is fraught with pitfalls: Whatever freedom may be gained is after all temporary, and soon some form of contingency returns. Overcoming is in danger of being overcome: "The Contingency of Selfhood" is followed by "The Contingency of Community" (Rorty's order of chapters), just as solitude and Society are opposing forces, each attempting to draw the Self into its domain and thereby mobilizing that pervasive tension that the Self either succumbs to or survives.

3

As the twentieth century drew to a close in a period we have for some time called postmodernism, interest in solitude as a desirable state of living, whether temporary or permanent, has been renewed with considerable energy. Much of Beckett's "aporia"—the doubt, the not knowing, the skepticism—has become a permanent feature of the postmodern. But, in spite of continuing tales of Beckett-like human solitude of desperation, a backlash also appears to have surfaced. This reaction is aimed against the negative connotations of solitude; it sometimes offers programmatic steps to revive some of the ideals of solitude. We are encouraged to reject the excessive sociopsychological allegiances to "attachment" and to rediscover solitude's benefits: self-awareness, strength to endure, and the ability to overcome fear and revulsion of Self. In addition, the new communication age has become an overwhelmingly intrusive force assaulting our lives, a force once attributed to industrialized urbanization: The privacy associated with solitude is considered an endangered part of life needful of being protected from impersonalized encroachment.

Books (in English) on this revisionist view of solitude in the last several decades, some very recent, include Thomas Merton's *A Search for Solitude,* Anthony Storr's *Solitude: Return to the Self,* May Sarton's *Journal of a Solitude,* Stephanie Dowrick's *Intimacy and Solitude,* Carol Christ's *Diving Deep and Surfacing,* Joanne Wieland-Burston's *Contemporary Solitude: The Joy and Pain of Being Alone,* Sue Halpern's *Migration to Solitude,* Carolyn Heilbrun's *The Last Gift of Time: Life Beyond Sixty,* and Janna Malamud Smith's *Private Matters: In Defense of the Personal Life.*

All but two of these are written by women; indeed, recent interest in solitude as both beneficial and alienating may be found in the literature by and about women. This comes as no surprise, since women have long been subjected to solitude, cast out by societal conditions in which patriarchy enforces an alienating isolation, or—especially recently—choosing solitude as a step toward independence from such subjugation. (Camus's "The Adulterous Woman" is a poignant case study in which what is alien functions on several parallel levels.) Of course, the isolation of women and its consequences are hardly new themes. Although women were often forced into social functions at the expense of a solitude that might provide time for self-improvement or merely the opportunity to place one's Self at rest in desirable aloneness, the opposite condition also prevailed. In the journals of acolytes and in the fiction (and nonfiction) thereafter, the plight of women subjected to voluntary or involuntary exclusion has been a ripe subject. Some of the most notable examples come from the eighteenth and nineteenth centuries, including many works by male authors: *Clarissa* and *Les Liaisons Dangereuses;* the novels of Stendhal and Balzac; *Madame Bovary, Anna Karenina,* and *Effi Briest;* the novels of Henry James. In America, women's isolation has been explored by men and women writers: Dreiser, Kate Chopin, Charlotte Perkins Gilman, Edith Wharton, Faulkner, just to cite a few. Postmodern fiction comprises too many titles to cite; the tone was set by Canadian Margaret Atwood's *Surfacing* (1972). In her eloquent farewell speech, "The Solitude of Self" (1892), Elizabeth Cady Stanton asked us to imagine a "Robinson Crusoe with her woman, Friday, on a solitary island." Men and women alike, she argued, "come into the world alone . . . leave it alone. . . ." But women's solitude constitutes not merely her equality, but marks her right to independence. Her very nature as defined by men exiles her into "bitter solitude"; but, on the other hand, true "solitude of self" is a leveling condition that she must be granted.[12] Clearly, the problematic history of women and solitude is compelling and in need of a comprehensive study.

In fiction and nonfiction, whether by male or female writers, we see corrective attempts directed at rehabilitating solitude as a rebirth experience, a necessary interlude in the quest to achieve authentic selfhood. Storr's insistence that the real question of one's mental health is *not* whether one indulges solitude to the detriment of the Self's relationship to Society, but whether one is able to sustain solitude as a condition of insight and self-revelation has some convincing resonance. Perhaps, as suggested, we now connect more sympathetically with such sentiments because the communications revolution shows signs of seriously putting in jeopardy our privacy. At the same time, such fear had by no means disappeared, despite Storr's suggestion that the fear of solitude is far more likely to reflect (or to lead to) inner problems than its embrace.

Writing from a Jungian analyst's perspective, Joanne Wieland-Burston sees solitude as an increasing concern, a "motive for desperation," since solitude has become "more threatening than ever before because it is actually more solitary than before." Indeed, she sees "community" and "spirituality" as the only hope for a society that has attached itself to singles' societies, secular retreats, Lilly tanks, and a celebration of independence and "space" from an enduring relationship. In trying to overcompensate against dependency, we have, she suggests, merely created a schizoid condition: "self-sufficiency" ultimately and urgently in search of "symbiotic relationship." Some of her section headings emphasize the dilemma (they read like modernized mid-eighteenth century headings from, say, Zimmermann's *Solitude*): "The Capacity to be Alone," "The Impossibility of Being Alone," "The Threat of Being Alone," "The Bittersweet Reality of Solitude." What has been called throughout this study the "ambiguity" of solitude, she prefers to call its paradox. And even within the most recent reflections on solitude, such a paradox or ambiguity remains intact: As a therapist, Wieland-Burston confronts the serious consequences in patients who embrace a solitude that excludes relationships, whether to another person or to a community.[13] On the other hand, Janna Malamud Smith, while in no way denying the need for relationships, emphasizes the urgency of maintaining solitude to protect our private selves from technological interference.

4

Each of the works examined here makes a unique contribution by articulating the problematic issues of the state of solitude despite the consistency of one pervasive concern: the ambiguity of the solitary state. Such ambiguity centers on the ongoing uncertainty about solitude's beneficial effects when measured against its possibly self-annihilating danger, the loss of identity altogether, as is the case in Beckett. While Crusoe was able to resist the undermining of Self and identity, in the twentieth century that becomes more difficult, if not impossible. Mann's hero is nearly undone by his relentless addiction to solitude; Woolf's characters cling stubbornly to self-perpetuated barriers that preclude the normal flow of language, which creates communication. The antagonists of Sartre and Camus are caught in different forms of inhibiting silences, but their lives are precariously close to becoming merely self-reflexive. And Beckett's "I" is in the ditch—or the bed, the room, the space where he lies "rotting with solitude."

By the early 1960s politics and psychotherapy appeared to shape attitudes about solitude: In political terms, solitude was seen as a selfish abdication of social responsibilities; in psychotherapeutic terms, it became tagged as a symptom of neurosis, a rejection of healthy social intercourse, a characterization challenged by Anthony Storr's provocative book. Political and sociological studies abounded in the late 60s and 70s, both in America and abroad, and many of them attacked solitude and judged its cultivation as an apocalyptic sign of regression and disintegration of the social bond at the expense of conscienceless individualism. One such book, very popular in its day, was Philip Slater's *The Pursuit of Loneliness: American Culture at the Breaking Point* (1970). In condemning the nostalgic revival of the rugged individual ideal by the establishment as well as the rebellious ideal of the Hippie loner, Slater scored some points against a movement no longer confined to America but, since the end of World War II, active in Europe and even beyond. Of course, solitude and loneliness, celebrated in popular culture, especially in popular music, was, as usual, accompanied by the paradoxical search for togetherness. The Hippie or Beat loner seeking freedom on the road took time out to sojourn with the not-so-lonely crowd at Woodstock. Rebellion, an inherent part of solitude, became so pervasive it turned itself into conformity. Experimentation was less existential and more pharmaceutical. This generation refused to be lost: It embarked on a perpetual search to find itself.

A recent *New York Times* article on the alienation of the 1990s asks: "So why is it the more consumers have in common, the more isolated they feel, the more disconnected they feel from the culture and from one another?" The neologism "disconnect," used as a noun, has become common currency. Discussing the paintings of Alex Katz, the author of the article identifies them with the "defining images" of postmodernism: "They are images depicting the height of isolation, figures in close physical proximity but with eyes never meeting." Katz's paintings might illustrate Beckett's *The Lost Ones;* the pictures are described by a book of photographs of Katz's work as "'very dehumanizing in a lot of ways.'" Though Katz had not intended it, his paintings were viewed as a commentary on the "cloistered, unfulfilled empty lives of suburban dwellers" chronicled in the postmodern fiction of John Cheever and others. But, the article concludes, "sometimes it feels that what is driving pop culture today is purely the desperation of people trying to find common ground"—in short, of connecting. And the culture of the Internet faces the paradox of solitude: "The Internet, which was supposed to connect everyone . . . can be so isolating that users meet in cybercafes, to be lone voices on the Internet together."[14] Once again, solitude cannot escape its ambiguities.

By the 1980s and thereafter, some reactions, as we noted, were set in motion against the suspicions that solitude seemed always to arouse; against the judgmental negative connotations associated with withdrawal into oneself. Such solitude, if balanced with social responsibility might, it was argued, restore our Self rather than insulate it. As always, what was wanted was balance. So the debate continues. Whether we locate the heart of this debate in ambiguity or paradox, Auden was on the mark: We seem inevitably to be condemned (to invoke Camus's retelling of the myth) to a Sisyphusian tug-of-war: "in solitude for company."

5

The issues that have always attended the state of solitude have quite naturally been both psychological and ethical, although it is impossible to draw clear boundaries between them, for they often overlap. Our coming to terms with our aloneness; our recognition of both the heady thrill of freedom that solitude bestows, along with its ambushing dangers; the ambiguity that tempts us toward isolation, followed by the inevitable urge to reconnect with human society—these are some of the obvious and predictable elements of the solitary experience. But the ethical dilemmas of solitude are more subtle, more submerged, more insidious. Severance from Society necessarily creates moral crises, especially if such exclusion is voluntary. Whereas Crusoe's inner struggles are centered on his attempts to balance the temptation to savor his freedom with a nagging feeling that somehow it undermines his moral duty to engage in human relations, the voluntary exile of the twentieth-century dramatis personae of the novels here examined engenders a variety of ethical conundrums. For example, the absence from human engagement triggers those feelings of exalted liberation, to be sure; but concomitant with such feelings are what often become Dostoyevskian nightmares of criminality and ethical crises, such as already dominated in *Crime and Punishment* or *Notes from the Underground*. If existence is really that free, if we can push away the "Other" so completely, what pits of nothingness are we staring at? Mann's and Woolf's novels treat the potential of nothingness with subtle, suggestive metaphors; Camus, Sartre, and Beckett pose the question directly, existentially. Contingency always seems ready to be recruited as a bulwark against annihilation; at the same time, the lure of experiment tempts us to the limit.

The retentive dumb show playacting of the Ramsays that undermines communication between them, the seeming impossibility Lily Briscoe must face in linking her painting with either persona or canvas, the subterranean dreams and actions of Hans Castorp, his experiments with skiing in the potential valley of death or his brief participation in the occult: these are probings into the deliciously alluring and devastating possibilities that tempt the solitary. But the rebellious forays of Sartre, Camus, and Beckett are no longer probings: They constitute defiant commitments. No resolution is satisfactory, for it would signal surrender to ignoble forces; but the uncompromising effort to hold on—to go on—exacts its merciless payment. The double bind finally strangles.

Baudelaire observed that hashish "expands time and place," creating what Freud, quoting a friend, called "oceanic feeling." Freud's friend, however, was attempting to define what parallels the religious feeling of losing the Self in some form of universal embrace as the individual Self surrenders. With characteristic skepticism, Freud interpreted this phenomenon more severely. Where Baudelaire conceded that solitude incapacitates, Freud saw something more self-indulgent. The narcotic state (whether induced by drugs or religious feeling) brings on this "oceanic" state that appears, according to Freud's friend, to palliate as well as embolden the individual sense of aloneness, acting as "consolation." Freud, however, interprets such "oceanic feeling" as a self-deceptive "feeling of an indissoluble bond, of being one with the external world as a whole." Indeed, Freud suspects the pathological: the Ego "detaches itself from the external world [and it] . . . separates off an external world from itself." Threatened by forces internal and external, the ego seeks to ameliorate its solitariness by embracing the universe, arrogating to itself friendlier, more protective surroundings. But Freud is convinced that this "derivation of religious needs" is anchored in infantile "helplessness and the longing for the father"; therefore, this need replaces the "limitless narcissism" that the "oceanic feeling" had sought to restore. Refusing to acknowledge the ultimate power of "'oneness with the universe'" to allay the ego's dread of inner and outer danger, Freud leaves us flung back onto ourselves in a solitude from which there is no easy escape.

Both Baudelaire and Freud suggest that a protected solitude is merely a self-indulgent, narcissistic, if not arrogant attempt of the Self to have it both ways: aloneness, with the protection of universal integration. Hashish, writes Baudelaire, "like all solitary pleasures, renders the individual useless to his fellow man, that it and society superfluous to the individual, continually leads him to admire himself and precipitates him day by day toward the luminous abyss in which he admires his Narcissus face[.]"[15] Baudelaire anticipated Freud's suspicion, even conviction, that the Self's indulgence in solitude, with its resulting severance from Society, amounted to a delusional state in which self-love would eventually lead to self-hatred, once the self-deceiver awakens. Such a painful awakening occurs in his prose poem, "The Double Room," the "paradisiacal room" that in the coldness of consciousness again becomes the "hovel" occupied by one "filled with disgust," as he realizes that "[t]ime has returned" and with it, the sufferings of aloneness.

The benign solitude of Petrarch and Montaigne, which required no opiates, is no longer viable. Evolving from the Renaissance, the increasingly complicated development of a noncommunal ego reaches a kind of endgame in the twentieth century. Solitariness is de rigueur, even in the development of film, painting, dance and photography, in all of which the single figure breaks away from its backdrop. But this triumph of individuality also leaves the single solitary figure vulnerable. Standing at the edge of the void, the modern solitary is sometimes drawn within it, as symbolically enacted in Nijinsky's celebrated leap. But as the first chapter of this study established, such a leap has a long history, for if modern solitude has a prophet, it is that seventeenth-century connoisseur of fear, Pascal, who dreaded not only "leaps" into the infinite space of the universe, but also into the horizontal finite space that cuts us apart from one another.

Inevitably, all solitaries are islanders, and solitude is an island-experience. But solitary islanders, especially in modernist fiction, dream of the mainland. Exultant to be free of one bondage, they discover imprisonment in another. Taking the measure of their gain, they also feel the enormity of their loss. So while savoring independence, they fantasize with resentment or sadness (seldom with hope) about lost possibilities of return.

Notes

Preface

1. Maurice Blanchot, *The Space of Literature,* tr. Ann Smock (Lincoln: University of Nebraska Press, 1982), 10.
2. No one will quarrel with the fact that, like "Romanticism," "Modernism" has become a problematic term. Periodization itself is no longer fashionable, and often with good reason, but necessity dictates its continuing utility. Modernism—as used here—generally follows accepted demarcations: Its roots are in Rousseau and grow to full blossom at the turn of the nineteenth century and flourish to the eve of the Great War. Whether the avant-garde is apart from, or a part of, Modernism is beyond our scope. High Modernism or Modernist designate the post–World War I era, the decades dating from the 1920s to the 1950s; Postmodernism is what follows. None of these dates can be precise, but they at least offer a map for discourse. See my "Time and Space and History: Towards the Discrimination of Modernisms," *Modernist Studies,* vol. I (1974), 7–25. Recent works on Modernism are too many to cite, but several are of special interest: Gianni Vattimo, *The End of Modernity: Nihilism and Hermeneutics in Postmodern Culture,* tr. Jon R. Snyder (Baltimore: The Johns Hopkins Press, 1991); Astradur Eysteinsson, *The Concept of Modernism* (Ithaca, NY: Cornell University Press, 1990) and the Introduction to Ann Quéma's *The Agon of Modernism: Wyndham Lewis's Allegories, Aesthetics, and Politics* (Lewisburg: Bucknell University Press, 1999), 11–29.
3. Throughout this study I favor "ambiguous" over "ambivalent" because the latter arrives with too much psychoanalytical baggage, and in most instances carries with it some inappropriate connotations. Of course, "ambivalent" cannot altogether be banished. In a limited way, the ambiguity of solitude is raised by Aleksandra Gruzinska in "From Musset to Cioran: Sampling and Taming Solitude" *Journal of the American Romanian Academy of Arts and Sciences,* no. 20 (1995), 64–75. The article deals mostly with Cioran.
4. Søren Kierkegaard, *The Sickness Unto Death,* tr. Howard V. Hong and Edna H. Hong (Princeton: Princeton University Press, 1980), 64.

Introduction

1. Ursula Lord, *Solitude Versus Solidarity in the Novels of Joseph Conrad: Political and Epistemological Implications of Narrative Innovation* (Montreal: McGill-Queens University Press, 1997), 3.

2. For a mid-century critique of "desocialisation" see Paul Halmos, *Solitude and Privacy: Study of Social Isolation: Its Causes and Therapy* (London: Routledge & Kegan Paul, 1952), chapters II and III.

3. Nietzsche, *The Joyful Wisdom,* in *The Complete Works of Friedrich Nietzsche,* ed. Oscar Levy, VII, Part II tr. Thomas Common (New York: Russell & Russell, 1964), 328.

4. For example, Paul Halmos argues that humans are essentially "gregarious," that modern society frustrates that gregariousness, and that the consequence of such frustration is neurosis: The "culturally induced" sabotaging of "social needs," he contends, "lies at the base of the individual-genetic traumata which the modern schools of psychiatry make responsible for man's neurosis." *Solitude and Privacy* (1952), xvi. Halmos cites Freud (and his successors and rivals) in locating the root cause of our gregariousness in our "psychosexual" needs (16–17). *The Standard Edition of the Complete Psychological Works of Sigmund Freud,* tr. James Strachey in collaboration with Anna Freud (London: Hogarth Press, 1955), vol. 16, 399.

5. Anthony Storr, *Solitude: A Return to the Self* (New York: Free Press, 1988), 11, 13, 21.

6. Storr, *A Return to the Self,* 1.

7. Nietzsche, *The Dawn of Day,* tr. J. M. Kennedy in *Complete Works,* 319.

8. For a brief survey of attitudes toward solitude from the Renaissance to the twentieth century, see Renate Möhrmann, *Der Vereinsamte Mensch: Studien zum Wandel des Einsamkeitsmotivs im Roman von Raabe bis Musil* (Bonn: Bouvier Verlag Herbert Grundmann, 1974), 7–27. As others have done, Möhrmann links modern secular solitude, as in Petrarch, to the awakening of Renaissance individualism and the awakening of the "I-consciousness," 11–12.

9. Frederick Garber, *The Autonomy of the Self from Richardson to Huysmans* (Princeton: Princeton University Press, 1981), ix, xi. The literature on the modern "Self" is vast, and the following is a *very* selective list. Two early collections of interesting essays on the Self are Eugene Goodheart's *The Cult of the Ego: The Self in Modern Literature* (Chicago: University of Chicago Press, 1968) and Wylie Sypher, *The Loss of the Self in Modern Literature and Art* (Westport, CT.: Greenwood Press, 1962). Also, Enrico Garzilli's *Circles Without Center: Paths to the Discovery and Creation of the Modern Self in Modern Literature* (Cambridge: Harvard University Press, 1972) offers a comparative and selective account. *Alternative Identities: The Self in Literature, History, Theory,* ed. Linda Marie Brooks (New York & London: Garland Publishing, 1995) contains a series of essays that focus more on theory than literature. For a "history of ideas" approach, see Gerald N. Izenberg, *Impossible Individuality: Romanticism, Revolution, and the Origins of Modern*

Selfhood, 1787–1802 (Princeton: Princeton University Press), 1992. A more philosophical analysis is Charles Taylor's, *Sources of the Self: The Making of the Modern Identity* (Cambridge: Harvard University Press, 1989). Dennis Brown focuses on the twentieth century in England in *The Modernist Self in Twentieth-Century English Literature* (New York: St. Martin's Press, 1989).

10. This may be an opportune place to say how many writers I obviously had to omit: Proust, Kafka, Hesse, Joyce, Lawrence, Musil, and Gide—just to name novelists—are among the missing. On some of these I have written elsewhere, from a different perspective, but, as much as possible, I wanted to avoid repetition. The main reasons for restricting myself, however, were the limits of space and my wish to choose special examples of solitude in which distinctions of importance transcended similitude.

11. See Lorna Martens, *The Diary Novel* (Cambridge: Cambridge University Press, 1985). Acknowledging the preponderance of twentieth-century "diary novels," Martens's principal objective is to trace the eighteenth-and nine-teenth-century tradition of the genre that led up to that phenomenon in the rich origins and history of first person narratives. Within this tradition *Robinson Crusoe* is, of course, a major player. Martens specifically examines the diary model, such as Crusoe's diary within the "I" narrative of *Robinson Crusoe,* or Werther's diary and the final section of Joyce's *Portrait of the Artist as a Young Man*—all "inserted" diaries within a first person narrative. Her choice of twentieth-century examples is, therefore, somewhat restrictive: Frisch, Butor, and Lessing. For a perceptive analysis of the monologist narrator, including some remarks on Beckett's trilogy, see Dorrit Cohn, *Transparent Minds: Narrative Modes for Presenting Consciousness in Fiction* (Princeton: Princeton University Press, 1978).

12. Nicholas Berdyaev, *Solitude and Society* (London: Geoffrey Bles: The Centenary Press, 69.

13. W. H. Auden, *The Enchafèd Flood* (New York: Vintage Books, 1967), 17.

14. Octavio Paz, "The Dialectic of Solitude," in *The Labyrinth of Solitude,* tr. Lysander Kemp, Yara Milos, and Rachel Phillips Belash (New York: Grove Press, 1985), 195.

15. Theodor W. Adorno, *Notes to Literature,* vol. I, ed. Rolf Tiedemann, tr. Shierry Weber Nicholsen (New York: Columbia University Press, 1991), 275.

16. Jean Paul Sartre, *Nausea,* tr. Robert Baldick (Harmondsworth: Penguin Books, 1965), 222–223.

17. Ernest Gellner, *Language and Solitude: Wittgenstein, Malinowski, and the Habsburg Dilemma* (Cambridge: Cambridge University Press, 1998), 5.

Chapter I

1. Nietzsche, *Human, All-Too Human,* in *The Complete Works,* Part II, tr. Paul V. Cohn, *The Complete Works,* 163; *Ecce Homo,* in *The Complete Works* tr. Anthony M. Ludovici, 105.

2. Søren Kierkegaard, *Either/Or,* vol. I, tr., Howard E. Hong and Edna H. Hong (Princeton: Princeton University Press, 1987), 288. An interesting collection on the issue of solitude and society has recently been published as volume V of the Lynchburg College Symposium Readings, *Classical Selections on Great Issues: Society and Solitude,* ed. Philip Stump (Lanham, MD: University Press of America, 1997). The volume contains readings ranging from Confucius to Marie de France, Chaucer to Spengler, Toynbee to Paz.

3. See Hans Seidel, *Das Erlebnis der Einsamkeit im Alten Testament* (Berlin: Evangelische Verlagsanstalt, 1969), 123–24.

4. Peter France, *Hermits: The Insights of Solitude* (London: Chatto & Windus, 1996), viii-x.

5. Sir Francis Bacon, "Of Friendship," in *Essays, Advancement of Learning, New Atlantis and Other Pieces,* ed. Richard Foster Jones (New York: The Odyssey Press, 1937), 75–76.

6. Daniel Defoe, *Serious Reflections of Robinson Crusoe* (New York: Jenson Society, 1903), 3–18.

7. Henry David Thoreau, *Walden, or Life in the Woods* (New York: Alfred A. Knopf, 1992), 129, 117.

8. Ralph Waldo Emerson, *Society and Solitude: Twelve Chapters* (Boston: Houghton Mifflin, 1870), 13–20. The antithesis between solitude and society much preoccupied nineteenth- and twentieth-century America. See Linda Costanzo Cahir, *Solitude and Society in the Works of Melville and Edith Wharton* (Westport, CT: Greenwood Press, 1999). She begins her Preface by writing: "To an American isolation is simultaneously a dilemma and a desire"—a sort of "*solitude à deux*" (xiii, 50). She is right; but her conclusion applies as well (though in different ways) to Europeans.

9. Marc Froment-Meurice, *Solitudes: From Rimbaud to Heidegger,* tr. Peter Walsh (Albany: State University Press of New York Press, 1995), 100.

10. Octavio Paz, *The Labyrinth of Solitude,* 195–212.

11. See "The Movement of Withdrawal-and-Return," in *A Study of History,* I (Oxford: Oxford University Press, 1947), 217–230.

12. Janette Dillon, *Shakespeare and the Solitary Man* (Totawa, NJ: Rowman and Littlefield, 1981), xiii-xiv. Dillon's account is the clearest and most incisive I have found. Subsequent references to this study will be incorporated in the text in parentheses. An earlier contribution is "Muriel Bradbrook, "Marvell and the Poetry of Rural Solitude," *Review of English Studies* 17 (1941) : 37–46. Joanne Wieland-Burston offers a brief "Historical Overview" of solitude through the nineteenth century, leading to a more detailed account of "Contemporary Solitude" in *Contemporary Solitude: The Joy and Pain of Being Alone* (York Beach, ME: Nicolas Hayes, 1996), 92–130. The book was originally published in German as *Zeiten des Rückzugs—Zeiten der Entwicklung* in 1995.

13. See Linda Georgianna, *The Solitary Self: Individuality in the "Ancrene Wisse"* (Cambridge: Harvard University Press, 1988), 61.

14. Salvatore Quasimodo, *The Poet, and the Politician and Other Essays,* tr. Thomas G. Begin and Sergio Pacific (Carbondale: Southern Illinois University Press, 1964), 65.

15. Douglas Bush, "The Isolation of the Renaissance Hero," in *Reason and Imagination: Studies in the History of Ideas, 1600–1800,* ed. J.A. Mazzeo (New York: Columbia University Press, 1962), 69.

16. Michael O'Loughlin, *The Garlands of Repose: The Literary Celebration of Civic and Retired Leisure: The Traditions of Homer and Vergil, Horace and Montaigne* (Chicago: University of Chicago Press, 1977), 189–200.

17. *Montaigne's Essays and Selected Writings,* ed. and tr. Donald M. Frame (New York: St. Martin's Press, 1963), 93–108. See Hassan Melehy, *Writing Cogito: Montaigne, Descartes, and the Institution of the Modern Subject* (Albany: State University of New York Press, 1997), especially Chapter 3, "Montaigne's "'I,'" 47–69.

18. Pascal's *Pensées,* Introduction, T. S. Eliot (London: J. M. Dent & Sons, 1932), 37–40.

19. Ralph Harper, *The Seventh Solitude: Man's Isolation in Kierkegaard, Dostoyevsky, and Nietzsche* (Baltimore: Johns Hopkins University Press, 1965),25.

20. Victor Brombert, *Romantic Prisons* (Princeton: Princeton University Press, 1978).

21. Renato Poggioli, *The Oaten Flute: Essays on Pastoral Poetry and the Pastoral Ideal* (Cambridge, MA.: Harvard University Press, 1978), 182–193.

22. For the most comprehensive history of solitude in French literature and thought up to the Revolution, see Pierre Naudin, *L'expérience et le sentiment de las solitude dans las littérature française de l'aube des Lumières à la Révolution* (Paris: Klincksieck, 1995). I am grateful to Monroe Hafter for bringing this volume to my attention.

23. W. B. Carnochan, *Confinement and Flight: An Essay on English Literature of the Eighteenth Century* (Berkeley: University of California Press, 1977), 30; 39.

24. John Sitter, *Literary Loneliness in Mid-Eighteenth Century England* (Ithaca: Cornell University Press, 1982), 85; 95.

25. Abraham Cowley, *Essays, Plays, & Sundry Verses in the English Writings of Abraham Cowley,* ed. A. R. Walker (Cambridge: The University Press, 1906), 392–393. For some interesting remarks on Cowley's concept of solitude see Maren-Sofie Røstvig, *The Happy Man: Studies in the Metamorphoses of a Classical Ideal, 1600–1700,* vol. I, 2nd. edition (Oslo: Norwegian University Press, 1962), 48–50.

26. For a psychosocial analysis of this poem see Joanne Wieland-Burston, *Contemporary Solitude,* 39–44.

27. See Ilma Rakusa, *Studien zum Motiv der Einsamkeit in der Russischen Literatur* (Bern: Herbert Lang, 1973). Rakusa's volume does not deal with Zimmermann's impact on Russian literature. It is a systematic discussion of noted Russian authors and their relationship, thematically, to solitude.

28. John George Zimmerman [sic] [Johann Georg Zimmermann], *Solitude or the Effects of Occasional Retirement,* tr. from the German (London, Glasgow, and Dublin: Thomas Tegg, R. Griffin, and Co., and B. Cummings, 1827), 38; 191; 282; 384–385.

29. *Encyclopédie ou Dictionnaire Raisonné des Sciences des Arts et des Métiers,* vol. 15 (Stuttgart-Bad Cannstatt: Friedrich Frommann Verlag [Günther Holzboog], 1967), 324. Translation mine.

30. Zimmermann, 395.

31. Roland Barthes, "The Last Happy Writer," in *Critical Essays,* tr. Richard Howard (Evanston, IL: Northwestern University Press, 1972), 85; 89.

32. In a posthumously published series of essays, Isaiah Berlin rather grudgingly links Rousseau with the Romantics, a relationship he feels has been "exaggerated." He makes a distinction between what Rousseau said and his temperament, "the manner in which he said it": the former is still very much linked to the Encyclopaedists; the latter to the Romantics. Whether temperament alone places Rousseau at the Romantic threshold is certainly debatable, and demonstrably not so with respect to his remarks about solitude. See *The Roots of Romanticism,* ed. Henry Hardy (Princeton: Princeton University Press, 1999), 52ff. As for Rousseau's "legacy" in France, see Dennis Porter, *Rousseau's Legacy: Emergence and Eclipse of the Writer in France* (Oxford: Oxford University Press, 1995). Of special interest is Rousseau's "overcoming of alienation" (58ff).

33. Robert Sayre, *Solitude in Society: A Sociological Study in French Literature* (Cambridge: Harvard University Press, 1978), 54.

34. Garber, *The Autonomy of the Self,* 47–48. See also Thomas McFarland, "Romantic imagination, nature, and the pastoral ideal," in *Coleridge's Imagination: Essays in Memory of Pete Laver* (Cambridge: Cambridge University Press, 1985), 15: "To be sure, the Romantics talked about solitude more frequently than they practiced it. Rousseau's *Hermitage* was actually a cottage for three. . . ."

35. Jean-Jacques Rousseau, *Reveries of the Solitary Walker,* tr. Peter France (New York: Penguin Classics, 1980), 90; 112.

36. Arthur Schopenhauer, *The World as Will and Representation,* tr. E. F. J. Payne, I (New York: Dover Publications, 1966), 203–204, 198.

37. Arthur Schopenhauer, *Essays: From the Parega and Paralipomena,* tr. T. Bailey Saunders (London: George Allen and Unwin, 1951), 22–28. (The selections come from the chapter titled "Our Relation to Ourselves.")

38. *The Living Thought of Schopenhauer,* Presented by Thomas Mann (London: Cassell, 1939), 13.

39. Thomas McFarland, "Romantic imagination, nature, and the pastoral ideal." McFarland refers to Cassirer in quoting this sentence from Diderot's postscript to *Fils Naturel.* He notes Cassirer's disquietude with Rousseau's longing for solitude, which Diderot "'regarded as a singular quirk'" until after his break with Rousseau when he began to see this quest for solitude as "'something uncanny in Rousseau's nature . . . [something] intolerable'" (15). The whole passage by Cassirer may be found in Ernst Cassirer, *The Question of Jean-Jacques Rousseau,* 2nd. edition, ed. and tr. Peter Gay (New Haven: Yale University Press, 1989), 91–92. Nietzsche defends Rousseau with a "transvalued" argument: "'Only the solitary are evil!'—thus spake

Diderot, and Rousseau felt offended. Thus he proved that Diderot was right. . . . The evil man is still more evil in solitude—and consequently . . . he is also more beautiful." In *The Dawn of Day,* tr. J. M. Kennedy in *Complete Works,* 348. For a spirited defense of Rousseau as an integral part of Enlightenment culture, see Mark Hulliung, *The Autocritique of the Enlightenment: Rousseau and the Philosophes* (Cambridge: Harvard University Press, 1994).

40. Berdyaev, *Solitude and Society,* 73–74.

41. Immanuel Kant, from *Critique of Judgment* in Hazard Adams, *Critical Theory Since Plato* (New York: Harcourt Brace Jovanovich), 1971, 393.

42. Frances Ferguson, *Solitude and the Sublime: Romanticism and the Aesthetics of Individuation* (New York: Routledge, 1992), 114.

43. Edmund Burke, *A Philosophical Enquiry Into the Origins of our Ideas of the Sublime and Beautiful,* ed. James T. Boulton (Notre Dame, IN: University of Notre Dame Press, 1968), 43.

44. See Susan Youan, *Retracing A Winter's Journey: Schubert's "Winterreise"* (Ithaca: Cornell University Press, 1991), 216–222.

45. Berdyaev, *Solitude and Society,* 71.

46. Thomas De Quincey, *Confessions of an English Opium Eater and Other Writings,* ed. Aileen Ward (New York: The New American Library, 1966), 140–141.

47. Jacques Blondel, "Wordsworth and Solitude," in *An Infinite Complexity: Essays in Romanticism,* ed. J. R. Watson (Edinburgh: Edinburgh University Press, 1983), 26–45. The specific citation is from page 26. For the most original discussions of the Romantic ambivalence toward "nature," see two works by Geoffrey H. Hartman: *Wordsworth's Poetry, 1787–1814* (New Haven: Yale University Press, 1964) and "Romanticism and 'Anti-Self Consciousness,'" in *Romanticism and Consciousness,* ed. Harold Bloom (New York: W. W. Norton), 46–56. The latter essay deals with the dangers of "self-consciousness" (a form of solitude) that can lead to solipsism and the acute forms of the *néant* that did indeed develop later in the century.

48. McFarland, 17–18. See also Raymond D. Havens, "Solitude, Silence, and Loneliness in the Poetry of Wordsworth," in *Wordsworth and Coleridge: Studies in Honor of George McLean Harper,* ed. Earl Leslie Grisps (New York: Russell & Russell) 1962.

49. Charles Baudelaire, *Intimate Journals,* tr. Christopher Isherwood (London: Methuen, 1949), 26.

50. For an interesting discussion of Romantic solitude through *fin de siècle,* see Walther Rehm, *Der Dichter und die Neue Einsamkeit* (Göttingen: Vandenhoeck & Ruprecht, 1969), 7–33.

51. Rehm sees Friedrich's landscapes filled with "frightful, I-confined solitude . . . ," *Der Dichter und die Neue Einsamkeit,* 13. Translation mine.

52. Ernest Gellner, *Language and Solitude: Wittgenstein, Malinowski, and the Habsburg Empire* (Cambridge: Cambridge University Press, 1998), 46, 5, 12–13, 19, 24–25, 43, 50, 184–185, 189. Gellner's main focus is epistemological,

and the specific details of how we "know" are beyond the issues of this study. However, his work is valuable in distinguishing the two polar opposites of individualism and communality and his critique of both. For a recent discussion of Wittgenstein's solipsism, see Juliet Floyd, "The Uncaptive Eye: Solipsism in Wittgenstein's *Tractatus,*" in *Loneliness,* ed. Leroy S. Rouner (Notre Dame, IN: Notre Dame University Press, 1998), 79–108.

53. Erich Fromm, *Escape From Freedom* (New York: Rinehart, 1941), 20.
54. For *Zarathustra* I have here used the Kaufmann translation since it is less stilted, more direct. The whole text is included in Walter Kaufmann, *The Portable Nietzsche* (New York: Viking Press, 1954). The quotations are from 163–165.
55. Nietzsche, *The Dawn of Day,* tr. J. M. Kennedy in *Complete Works,* 274.
56. By the 1950s the solitary is viewed more as a victim. Cultural historians and psychologists argue that isolation is imposed, and any freedom gained is seriously compromised. The impact of David Riesman's *The Lonely Crowd: A Study in the Changing American Character* (New Haven: Yale University Press, (1950)—one of the first of many subsequent analyses of early postmodern culture—was (and remains) incalculable.
57. Fromm, *Escape From Freedom,* 38.
58. Charles Baudelaire, "Solitude," in *The Parisian Prowler,* tr. Edward K. Kaplan (Athens: The University of Georgia Press, 1997). All quotations from the prose poems are from this translation. Rainer Maria Rilke, *The Notebooks of Malte Laurids Brigge,* tr. M. D. Herter Norton (New York: W. W. Norton, 1992), 160–161.
59. Ben Lazare Mijuskovic, *Loneliness in Philosophy, Psychology and Literature* (The Netherlands: Van Gorum, Assen, 1979), 6.
60. Clark E. Moustakas, *Loneliness* (Englewood Cliffs, NJ: Prentice Hall, 1961), 34.
61. Paul Tillich, "Loneliness and Solitude," in *The Anatomy of Solitude,* ed. Joseph Hartog, J. Ralph Audy, and Yehudi A. Cohen New York: International Universities Press, 1980), 549; 552–553.
62. Ben Lazare Mijuskovic, "Loneliness: An Interdisciplinary Approach," in *The Anatomy of Loneliness,* ed. Joseph Hartog, J. Ralph Audy, and Yehudi A. Cohen (New York: International Universities Press, 1980), 81–82; 67.

Chapter II

1. Virginia Woolf, *The Common Reader,* Second Series (London: Hogarth Press, 1948), 54, 58.
2. Michael Seidel, *Robinson Crusoe: Island Myths and the Novel* (Boston: Twayne Publishers), 1991.
3. Ian Watt, *The Rise of the Novel: Studies in Defoe, Richardson and Fielding* (Berkeley: University of California Press, 1957), 86.
4. Louis James, "Unwrapping Crusoe: Retrospective and Prospective Views," *Robinson Crusoe: Myths and Metamorphoses,* ed. Lieve Spaas and Brian Simpson (New York: Macmillan, 1996), 1.

5. For an extensive bibliography through the nineteenth century, see Hermann Ullrich, *Robinson und Robinsonaden, Literarhistorische Forschungen,* ed. Josef Schick and M. Frh. Waldberg, Heft 7 (Weimar: Emil Felber, 1898). "Adaptations" of Defoe's novel have not ceased to be written. Some recent examples: Michel Tournier's *Friday, or the Other Island,* tr. Norman Denny (London: Collins, 1969); J. M. Coetzee, *Foe* (New York: Viking, 1987) [Crusoe as a woman]; and Thomas Berger, *Robert Crews* (New York: William Morrow, 1994) [Friday as a woman].

6. James Sutherland, *Daniel Defoe: A Critical Study* (Cambridge: Harvard University Press, 1971), 135, 133.

7. Martin Green, *The Robinson Crusoe Story* (University Park: Pennsylvania State University Press, 1990), 1.

8. Seidel, *Robinson Crusoe: Island Myths and the Novel,* 27, 10–11.

9. Ben Mijuskovic, "Loneliness: An Interdisciplinary Approach," 1, 82.

10. Louis James. "Unwrapping Crusoe: Retrospective and Prospective Views," 7.

11. Stephens's comments, and those of the others mentioned here, may be found in the Norton Critical Edition, 2nd. ed of *Robinson Crusoe,* ed. Michael Shinagel (New York: W. W. Norton & Company, 1994), 257–279.

12. Walter de la Mare, *Desert Islands and Robinson Crusoe* (New York: Farrar & Rinehart, 1930), 71, 274–275.

13. Ian Watt, *The Rise of the Novel,* 87.

14. Seidel, *Robinson Crusoe: Island Myths and the Novel,* 55.

15. J. Paul Hunter, *The Reluctant Pilgrim: Defoe's Emblematic Method and Quest for Form in Robinson Crusoe* (Baltimore: Johns Hopkins University Press, 1966.) See n. 34.

16. David Blewett, *Defoe's Art of Fiction* (Toronto: University of Toronto Press, 1979), 47, 31, 39. For an interesting background to eighteenth-century imprisonment and penance, see John Bender, *Imagining the Penitentiary in Eighteenth-Century England* (Chicago: University of Chicago Press, 1987). Bender points to the many occasions when Crusoe speaks of the island as his "prison." In Defoe's work in general, he sees the motif of the "narrative Prison": "Solitude is the occasion, narrative the medium, prison the overarching figure," 52–53, 96–97. For incisive remarks on the significance of the footprint see Michael Seidel, *Daniel Defoe: Island Myths and the Novel,* 62ff.

17. G. A. Starr, *Defoe's Spiritual Autobiography* (Princeton: Princeton University Press, 1965), 116.

18. Michael McKeon, *The Origins of the English Novel, 1600–1740* (Baltimore: Johns Hopkins University Press, 1987), 317, 327, 336.

19. Pat Rogers, *Robinson Crusoe* (London: George Allen & Unwin),(1979), 87, 90.

20. E. M. W. Tillyard, *The Epic Strain in the English Novel* (London: Chattto & Windus, 1967), 33–34, 50. For an excellent discussion of Crusoe's "concealment" from a psychological perspective, see Homer Obed Brown, *Institutions of the Novel: From Defoe to Scott* (Philadelphia: Pennsylvania University Press, 1997), 55ff.

21. Ian Watt, *The Rise of the Novel,* 85–86.

22. Michael Seidel, *Robinson Crusoe: Island Myths and the Novel,* 11.

23. Ian Watt, *Myths of Modern Individualism: Faust, Don Quixote, Don Juan, Robinson Crusoe* (Cambridge: Cambridge University Press, 1996), 167–171.

24. Maximillian E. Novak, *Defoe and the Nature of Man* (Oxford: Oxford University Press, 1963), 23, 25–26.

25. Maximillian E. Novak, *Realism, Myth, and History in Defoe's Fiction* (Lincoln: University of Nebraska Press, 1983), 45, 46, 36, 64.

26. Arthur F. Holmes, "Crusoe, Friday, and God," *Philosophy Forum* 11 (1972): 322–324, 338.

27. Homer Obed Brown, *Institutions of the English Novel: From Defoe to Scott,* 55. Although Brown's study was published in 1997, an earlier version of his remarks on *Crusoe* appeared in an essay, "The Displaced Self in the Novels of Daniel Defoe," *English Literary History,* XXXVIII (1971): 562–590.

28. Leopold Damrosch, Jr., *God's Plots and Man's Stories: Studies in the Fictional Imagination from Milton to Fielding* (Chicago: University of Chicago Press, 1985), 187, 189, 191, 196.

29. Harvey Swados, "Robinson Crusoe—the Man Alone," *Antioch Review* 18 (1958): 25–40.

30. Daniel Defoe, *The Life and Strange Suprizing Adventures of Robinson Crusoe, of York, Mariner,* ed. J. Donald Crowley (London: Oxford University Press, 1972), 142. All references are to this edition and will be incorporated into the text in parentheses. For comments on the Defoe-Joyce connections, see Seidel, *Robinson Crusoe: Island Myths and the Novel,* 10–11, 34.

31. John M. Warner, *Joyce's Grandfathers: Myth and History in Defoe, Smollett, Sterne, and Joyce* (Athens: University of Georgia Press, 1993), 26.

32. James Joyce, "Realism and Idealism in English Literature: Daniel De Foe—William Blake" in *Buffalo Studies,* vol, I, ed. from Italian Manuscripts and tr. Joseph Prescott (December 1964), 14, 25. The editor-translator's comments are to be found on p. 4.

33. Michael Seidel, *Exile and The Narrative Imagination,* 27. Seidel begins his chapter on *Robinson Crusoe* (p. 19) with the Joycean adaptation of the parrot's words.

34. See Dewey Ganzel, "Chronology in *Robinson Crusoe,*" *Philological Quarterly* XL (October 1961): 495–512. Ganzel notes errors of chronology in the text. He believes that the 28-plus year sequence was a mistake in memory, which found its way into the novel "after the completion of the entire island narration . . ." (505). He also points out that the 27-plus year sequence contains the "interprolation" in which Crusoe becomes a converted Christian, noting that this is accompanied by significant changes in attitude toward his solitary state. (507ff). The argument remains speculative.

35. Everett Zimmerman, "Defoe and Crusoe," *ELH* 38 (September 1971), 392.

36. See Seidel, *Exile and the Narrative Imagination,* 35. Seidel distinguishes between "home" on the island and "the exile's traditional *Drang nach Hause,*

his will to return to the original place [i.e., literally Crusoe's English home]." Crusoe's "strength of character" creates a paradox: while it "allows him to re-create a version of home abroad [it] also inhibits and distorts" the will to set out for a return to his ancestral home.

37. Thomas M. Kavanaugh, "Unraveling Robinson: The Divided Self in *Robinson Crusoe," Texas Studies in Literature and Language* 20 (1978): 416–432. For an analysis of *Robinson Crusoe* and Rousseau see G. Pire, *Revue de Littérature Comparée* vol. 30, no. 4 (Octobre-Decembre, 1956): 479–496.

38. Daniel Defoe, "Of Solitude," *Serious Reflections,* vol. III (Cambridge: University Press, John Wilson and Sons, 1903), 4–18. (Specific citations are noted by page number in parentheses.)

39. Frank H. Ellis, Introduction, *Twentieth-Century Views of Robinson Crusoe: A Collection of Critical Essays* (Englewood Cliffs, NJ: Prentice Hall, 1969), 12.

40. Michel Tournier, *Friday or the Other Island* (1967). The novel was first published in 1967 under the title *Vendredi, ou les Limbes du Pacifique.* Page references will be cited in the text in parentheses.

41. "*Vendredi* is essentially a transformation of *Robinson Crusoe* in the light of the new perspectives on Defoe's novel afforded by twentieth-century epistemology—notably the discourses of ethnography, psychoanalysis and philosophy." Martin Roberts, *Michel Tournier; Bricolage and Cultural Mythology* (Stanford: Anma Libri, 1994), 22. Roberts' book leans heavily on these "discourses," pointing to Defoe's omissions in the pre-Freudian age: he considers *Vendredi* a "parody" of *Crusoe,* and while some elements of Tournier's novel are conceivably parodies, parody, I think, was not Tournier's intention. Roberts' reliance on the "discourses" unavailable to Defoe lead him at times to excesses. For example, it is obviously untrue that "Defoe shows little interest in the effects of prolonged solitude on Crusoe's mental stability . . . neither his sanity nor his status as a human being are ever in question" (23). In fact both are "in question," but without benefit of Freud or Lévy-Strauss.

42. In his autobiography, Tournier insists that some of what his critics have made of the novel's philosophy was not calculated, though correct; for example, the parallel of Robinson's developing philosophy to the "three types of knowledge" in Spinoza's *Ethics. The Wind Spirit: An Autobiography,* tr. Arthur Goldhammer (Boston: Beacon Press, 1988), 196. This book was first published in France in 1977 under the title *Le Vent Paraclet.* One critic connects Tournier's novel to Hegel, Marx, Sartre, and Claude Lévi-Strauss: see Susan Petit, *Michael Tournier's Metaphysical Fictions* (Amsterdam/Philadelphia: Johns Benjamins, 1991), 11–12.

43. William Cloonan, *Michel Tournier* (Boston: Twayne Publishers, 1985) calls the island the "limbo" of the French title (33). He offers an insightful comparison between Tournier's novel and Defoe's, 2–24. For a postmodern reading, see David Platten, *Michel Tournier and the Metaphor of Fiction* (New York: St. Martin's Press, 1999), 41–81.

44. For a close analysis of the sexuality in Tournier's treatment of his hero see David Gascoigne, *Michel Tournier* (Oxford: Berg, 1996), 56–68.

45. Michel Tournier, *The Wind Spirit,* 176–197.
46. See Gilles Deleuze, *The Logic of Sense,* ed. Constantin Boundas, tr. Mark Lester (New York: Columbia University Press, 1990), 301–321. Deleuze's analysis of Tournier's novel is based on a Self/Other paradigm that leaves Tournier's hero a modern solitary Self—logically confined to the island, unwilling and incapable of rejoining Society.

Chapter III

1. The critical literature on Virginia Woolf has become voluminous, especially in the last two decades as feminist criticism has embraced her work. In the notes I have made an attempt to cite what I found most relevant and helpful, but I have exercised some restraint. I have consulted many more books and essays than could be cited without cluttering the text or the notes; omissions, therefore, should not be misconstrued.
2. James King, *Virginia Woolf* (New York: W. W. Norton, 1995), 381. Two other biographies have recently been published. Panthea Reid writes of the "formal symmetry" in the novel and calls attention to its structure as a "triptych" that can be perceived "sequentially" as prose and "statically" as a painting. *Art and Affection: A Life of Virginia Woolf* (New York: Oxford University Press, 1996), 295. She stresses Roger Fry's influence. Hermione Lee finds optimism in the fact that the last sentence of the novel, like the first, begins with "Yes": "The ending of the novel is poised between arriving and returning, getting somewhere . . . and being finished." *Virginia Woolf* (London: Chatto & Windus, 1996), 483. For some divergent views see, for example, John Mepham, "Figures of Desire: Narration and Fiction in *To the Lighthouse,*" in *The Modern English Novel: The Reader, the Writer and the Work,* ed. Gabriel Josipovici (New York: Barnes and Noble Books, 1976), 149–185.
3. James Navermore notes that the conquering of space between people is an objective sought in all of Woolf's novels—"to overcome the space between things" in order to attain a perfect "unity." He sees this objective for unity as being "expressed in both physical and spiritual terms" and often with "sexual connotations. . . ." On Lily's painting he comments: "Lily's painting is . . . another example of the intense desire to lose the self through love or union . . . ," another instance of accepting the completeness of 'vision.' *The World Without a Self: Virginia Woolf and the Novel* (New Haven: Yale University Press, 1973), 242; 150. See also Elizabeth Abel, *Virgina Woolf and the Fictions of Psychoanalysis* (Chicago: University of Chicago Press, 1989), 68–83.
4. The *Essays of Virginia Woolf, 1914–1928,* vol. IV, ed. Andrew McNeillie (London: Hogarth Press, 1986), 435. All future references will be inserted in the text in parentheses.
5. Marc Froment-Meurice, *Solitudes: From Rimbaud to Heidegger,* tr. Peter Walsh (Albany: State University of New York Press, 1995), 107.
6. Josephine O'Brien Schaefer, *The Three-Fold Nature of Reality in the Novels of Virginia Woolf* (The Hague: Mouton & Co., 1965), 138. The preoccupation

with silence, though reinvigorated by the Classic Moderns, is by no means new. See Raoul Mortly, *From Word to Silence,* especially vol I, *The Rise and Fall of Logos* ["The Silence Beyond Names"] (Bonn: Hannstein, 1986), 110–124, where he analyzes the "the late Greek pessimism about the efficacy of language."

7. Patricia Ondek Laurence, *The Reading of Silence: Virginia Woolf in the English Tradition* (Stanford: Stanford University Press, 1991), 12. There is a large body of critical work on literature and silence; the bibliography in Laurence's book is extensive. On Woolf and silence, see also Howard Harper, *Between Language and Silence: The Novels of Virginia Woolf* (Baton Rouge: Louisiana State University Press, 1982).

8. Lucio P. Ruotolo, *The Interrupted Moment: A View of Virginia Woolf's Novels* (Stanford: Stanford University Press, 1986).

9. Laurence, 44.

10. R. M. Adams, *Strains of Discord: Studies in Literary Openness* (Ithaca, NY: Cornell University Press, 1958), 194–196.

11. *The Diary of Virginia Woolf,* ed. Anne Olivier Bell, assisted by Andrew McNeillie, vol. IV, 1931–4 (New York: Harcourt Brace Jovanovich, 1982), 253. Subsequent citations will be in the text in parentheses.

12. *The Letters of Virginia Woolf,* III, vol. 1923–28, ed. Nigel Nicolson and Joanne Trautmann (New York: Harcourt Brace Jovanovich, 1977), 208, 211, 214, 218, 227, 235.

13. Leonard Woolf, *Downhill All the Way: An Autobiography of the Years 1919–1939* (New York: Harcourt, Brace & World, 1967), 153.

14. Frank's essay has been revised several times. For the latest version, see Joseph Frank, *The Idea of Spatial Form* (New Brunswick: Rutgers University Press, 1991), 5–66. The volume contains other useful essays on Frank's theory of literary space. For a volume of valuable essays, see *Spatial Form in Narrative,* ed. Jeffrey R. Smitten and Ann Daghistany (Ithaca and London: Cornell University Press, 1981). Surprisingly, most critics on space in fiction do not pay much (if any) attention to Woolf.

15. Dorrit Cohn, *Transparent Minds: Narrative Modes for Presenting Consciousness in Fiction,* 126.

16. There are many editions of *To the Lighthouse.* Aside from the holograph edition, ed. Susan Dick (Toronto: University of Toronto Press, 1982), there are several definitive editions: *The Definitive Collective Edition of the Novels of Virginia Woolf* (London: Hogarth Press, 1990), with variants of the first English and American editions; *To the Lighthouse,* ed. Susan Dick (Oxford: Blackwell Publishers, 1992); *To the Lighthouse,* ed. Sandra Kemp (New York: Routledge, 1994); *To the Lighthouse,* ed. Margaret Drabble (Oxford: Oxford University Press, 1992). I have availed myself of the most readily available edition, the paperback edition of *To the Lighthouse,* first published in 1955 by Harcourt, Brace & World. Nothing vital in my analysis is lost by using this version. The quotation is from p. 24, and all page references henceforth will be included in the text in parentheses.

17. Patricia Ondek Laurence, *The Reading of Silence,* 11.

18. J. Hillis Miller, "The Problematic Ending in Narrative," *Nineteenth-Century Fiction,* A Special Issue on "Narrative Endings," 33, 1 (June 1978): 3. Perhaps the defining book on narrative endings is Frank Kermode's *The Sense of an Ending: Studies in the Theory of Fiction* (New York: Oxford University Press, 1967). Also worthy of mention are Alan Friedman, *The Turn of the Novel* (New York: Oxford University Press, 1966); D. A. Miller, *Narrative and Its Discontents: Problems of Closure in the Traditional Novel* (Princeton: Princeton University Press, 1981); *Reading Narrative: Form, Ethics, Ideology,* ed. James Phelan (Columbus: Ohio State University Press, 1989); Rachel Blau DuPlessis, *Writing Beyond the Ending: Narrative Strategies of Twentieth-Century Women Writers* (Bloomington: Indiana University Press, 1985); David H. Richter, *Fable's End: Completeness and Closure in Rhetorical Fiction* (Chicago: University of Chicago Press, 1974); Marianna Torgovnick, *Closure in the Novel* (Princeton: Princeton University Press, 1981.)

19. Aside from some exceptions mentioned (Auerbach, Adams) most of the earlier critics accepted the "vision" endings on both accounts: the painting Lily completes and the landing at the lighthouse form a unity both within each action and of both. For an early essay, see Morris Beja, "Matches Struck in the Dark: Virginia Woolf's Moments of Vision," in *Virginia Woolf: To the Lighthouse,* ed. Morris Beja (London: Macmillan, 1970), 210–230. The essay was first published in 1964. The collection contains several essays on Woolf's "vision" in *To the Lighthouse.* A number of critics have written perceptively on the artistic dilemmas Lily faces which, in turn, some see reflected in the problems facing Woolf in creating the novel. A *selected* list would include the following: John Hawley Roberts, "Vision and Design in Virginia Woolf," *Publications of the Modern Language Association* LXI (September 1946): 835–847; Keith M. May, "The Symbol of 'Painting' in Virginia Woolf's '*To the Lighthouse,*'" *Review of English Literature* 8 (November–April, 1967): 91–98; Glenn Pederson, "Vision in *To the Lighthouse, PMLA* LXXIII (December, 1958): 585–600; Sharon Wood Proudfit, "Lily Briscoe's Painting: A Key to the Personal Relationships in 'To the Lighthouse,'" *Criticism* 13 (Winter, 1971): 26–38. One of the most insightful revisions of the standard view is Thomas G. Matro, "Only Relations: Vision and Achievement in *To the Lighthouse,*" *PMLA* 99 (March 1984): 212–224. Though he argues that Woolf uses Fry's "postimpressionist aesthetic," he concludes that "[l]ike Lily . . . the novel's readers must relinquish their own propensities for the transcendent insight or illusive moment of perceptual balance . . ." (223). John Mepham offers an original description. He views the endings in Woolf's novels as depicting some sort of "rite"; "*To the Lighthouse* ends with Lily's painting achieving a kind of visual suture, a scar-like line in the centre covering the place where Mrs. Ramsay had been." From "Mourning and Modernism," in *Virginia Woolf: New Critical Essays,* ed. Patricia Clements and Isobel Grundy (London: Vision Press, 1983), 151. The notion of "suture" is close to the rupture, or cancellation, suggested here.

20. I have examined the ending of *Mrs. Dalloway* in *Elegiac Fictions: The Motif of the Unlived Life* (University Park and London: Pennsylvania State University Press, 1989), 202–204.

21. Harper, *The Seventh Solitude,* 13.

22. Du Plessis, 97. See also Susan Stanford Friedman, "Lyric Subversion of Narrative in Women's Writing: Virginia Woolf and the Tyranny of Plot," in *Reading Narrative,* 162–185.

23. Ruotolo, 141. Pamela L. Caughie does not accept the traditional reading of Lily's problems as being solved by "the connection between two things." Rather she argues that this might have been Lily's dilemma in Part I, but by the end of the novel Lily's "problem is solved—or rather, removed—by a change in Lily's concerns: *the distinction to be made is no longer between two things but between different ways of relating things.*" (*Virginia Woolf & Postmodernism: Literature in Quest & Question of Itself* (Urbana: University of Illinois Press, 1991), 33–34. That this may indeed be her problem at the close of the novel is likely; that she has either "solved" or "removed" it is in question.

24. Adams, 204; 203.

25. *Reading Narrative,* 122.

26. George P. Landow, *Images of Crisis: Literary Iconology 1750 to the Present* (Boston: Routledge & Kegan Paul, 1972), 4.

27. Erich Auerbach, *Mimesis: The Representation of Reality in Western Literature,* tr. William Trask (Garden City, NY: Doubleday, 1953), 488; 487. Woolf's ambivalent attitude toward Realism has been much discussed. For a recent study, see Herta Newman, *Virginia Woolf and Mrs. Brown: Toward A Realism of Uncertainty* (New York: Garland Publishing, 1996). For the specific chapter on *To the Lighthouse,* see "'A Portrait of the Artist' in *To the Lighthouse,*" 83–96. See also Patrick J. Whiteley, *Realism and Experimental Knowledge in Conrad, Lawrence, and Woolf* (Baton Rouge: The Louisiana State University Press, 1987). Alice van Buren Kelley argues the issue both ways; see her *The Novels of Virginia Woolf: Fact and Vision* (Chicago: University of Chicago Press, 1973).

28. John Marpham, *Virginia Woolf: A Literary Life* (New York: St. Martin's Press, 1991), 102.

29. Blanchot, *The Space of Literature,* 22.

30. Ruotolo, 118; Blanchot, *The Space of Literature,* 33. On Lily Briscoe's final brushstroke—and its implications for the ending of the novel—see Brandy Brown Walker, "Lily's Last Stroke: Painting in Progress in Virginia Woolf's *To the Lighthouse,*" in *Virginia Woolf and the Arts: Selected Papers From the Sixth Annual Conference on Virginia Woolf,* ed. Diane F. Gillespie and Leslie K. Hankins (Pleasantville, NY: Pace University Press, 1997), 32–38. For Walker, the vision Lily has is of herself: "It is only when Lily announces at the very end that 'I have had my vision,' that she truly has a vision of her own, a vision of herself" (34); "Lily rejects the silence and paralysis that each side [Mr. and Mrs. Ramsay] offers when she makes her final mark, when she

has her own vision" (35). Walker also notes that whether the line Lily draws is vertical (the phallic interpretation that has been favored) or horizontal has been recently recognized as "ambiguous." She argues for the horizontal: "the mark that is the *culmination* of her struggle for artistic expression and subjectivity to date" (36). Her analysis in general is based on Julia Kristeva's theory of the subjective "*procès.*" Walker also cites Elizabeth Abel, *Woolf and the Fictions of Psychoanalysis* (see n. 3) who argues for the "vertical" brushstroke. This disputation between "vertical" and "horizontal" strikes one as somewhat comical, though to be sure the vertical retains the phallic implications that go with the lighthouse, etc. For purposes at hand, it makes absolutely no difference which way the stroke goes, for in either case the "cancellation" of the painting is achieved. However, for what it may be worth, a downward stroke is also consistent with Lily's previous concerns with moving the tree. And in a letter to Roger Fry, disclaiming any particular meaning attached to the lighthouse, Woolf writes: "One has to have a central line *down* the middle of the book to hold the design together" (*Letters, 1923–1928,* vol. III, 385). Italics mine. Avrom Fleishman believes that the final brushstroke is the lighthouse itself, *Virginia Woolf: A Critical Reading* (Baltimore: Johns Hopkins University Press, 1975), 131–134.

31. J. Hillis Miller, "Mr. Carmichael and Lily Briscoe: The Rhythm of Creativity in *To the Lighthouse*" in *Modernism Reconsidered,* ed. Robert Kiely (Cambridge: Harvard University Press, 1983), 173; 169.

32. For an interesting psychoanalytic interpretation of the motif of aloneness in the novel, see Ernest S. Wolf and Ina Wolf, "'We Perished, Each Alone': A Psychoanalytical Commentary on Virginia Woolf's *To the Lighthouse,*" in *Narcissism and the Text: Studies in Literature and the Psychology of Self,* ed. Lynne Layton and Barbara Ann Shapiro (New York: New York University Press, 1986), 255–270. Also of value is Mark Spilka, *Virginia Woolf's Quarrel With Grieving* (Lincoln: University of Nebraska Press, 1980), especially 75–109. The word "alone" occurs 56 times in *To the Lighthouse.*

Chapter IV

1. C. A. M. Noble, *Krankheit, Verbrechen, und künstlerisches Schaffen bei Thomas Mann* (Bern: Verlag Herbert Lang, 1970), 137, 147. Translations mine.

2. Samuel Beckett, *Proust* (New York: Grove Press, 1957), 47.

3. "First discovered as a curse of the *artist's* existence, the isolation motif, the estrangement of man from his world, is nevertheless at bottom a *human* problem—a problem of life, conditioned by modern times yet universal in scope." Fritz Kaufmann, *Thomas Mann: The World as Will and Representation* (New York: Cooper Square Publishers, 1973), 3.

4. For the developing relationship between *Death in Venice* and *The Magic Mountain* see T.J. Reed, *Thomas Mann: The Uses of Tradition,* 2nd. ed.(Oxford: Clarendon Press, 1996), 229ff, and T. E. Apter, *Thomas Mann: The Devil's Advocate* (New York: New York University Press, 1979), 67ff.

6. Kaufmann, *Thomas Mann*, 4.
7. See Harry Slochower, *Thomas Mann's Joseph Story: An Interpretation* (New York: Alfred A. Knopf, 1938), 4.
8. Thomas Mann, *The Magic Mountain*, tr. John E. Woods (New York: Alfred A. Knopf, 1995), 118. All subsequent citations are from this edition and are included in the text in parentheses.
9. It is now difficult to agree with Slochower's optimistic appraisal in a decade when Mann's humanism was seen as a communal socialism: "In Mann's work, the motif of resurrection has been closely tied to the symbol of the pit. . . . Castorp's descent into the war-torn flatland awakens in him a sense of social consciousness for his 'comrades.'" *The Joseph Story*, 11.
9. Nietzsche, *Thus Spoke Zarathustra*, 264.
10. *Essays by Thomas Mann*, tr. H. T. Lowe-Porter (New York: Vintage Books, 1957), 277.
11. Ibid., 273.
12. Hans Mayer, *Thomas Mann* (Frankfurt-am-Main: Suhrkamp Verlag, 1980), 130. (The original reads: "Es gibt Lücken im 'Zauberberg.'")
13. *Thus Spoke Zarathustra*, 265.
14. Nietzsche, *Beyond Good and Evil*, tr. Helen Zimmern in *Complete Works*, 249.
15. See Yeats's "The Statues" and comments in *On the Boiler* and elsewhere; Eliot, *The Waste Land*; Hesse, "Die Brüder Karamasoff, oder der Untergang Europas," *Betrachtungen und Briefe* (Frankfurt-am-Main: Suhkampf, 1957). The fear of the East was widespread among "Western" writers, especially after the Russian Revolution. On March 15, 1922, Eliot wrote Hesse that he would like to have some of his *Blick ins Chaos* translated, as he considered it to have "a seriousness the like of which has not yet occurred in England," and he was "keen to spread the reputation of the book." *The Letters of T. S. Eliot, 1898–1922*, ed. Valerie Eliot, vol. I (London: Faber and Faber, 1988), 508–519. Sidney Schiff, under the pseudonym Stephen Hudson, published translations of two essays in *The Dial* in 1922: "The Brothers Karamazoff—the Downfall of Europe" 62, 6 (June 1922): 607–618, and "Thoughts on the Idiot of Dostoevsky" 63, 2 (June 1922): 199–204. Chris Ackerley has written a brief essay on this matter, "'Who are these Hooded Hordes . . . ': Eliot's *The Waste Land* and Hesse's *Blick in Chaos*," *The Journal of the Australasian Universities Language and Literature Association* 32 (November 1994): 103–106. I am indebted to Haskell M. Block for bringing some of these details to my attention. For an analysis of Western perceptions (and misperceptions) of the East, see Edward Said, *Orientalism* (New York: Pantheon, 1978).
16. Berdyaev, *Solitude and Society*, 70. Freud, *Standard Edition*, vol. 14, 231. On Freud and other psychological observations on time/space perceptions, see Sanford Gifford, "'The Prisoner of Time': Some Developmental Aspects of Time Perception in Infancy, Sensory Isolation, and Old Age," in *The Annual of Psychoanalysis*, vol. 8 (New York: International Universities Press, 1980),

131–154. The quotation from "The Unconscious" is quoted by Gifford (133); in addition, Gifford discusses how certain drugs induce a timeless feeling [139–142] (this section also includes remarks on "Religious Ecstasies"). I am indebted to Dr. Max Day for bringing this essay to my attention.

17. Mann's quotation, and the general effects of opium and hashish, sound as if they come from De Quincey or Baudelaire, who translated De Quincey. I have been unable to find the precise quotation in either, though Mann was familiar with Baudelaire's *Journaux Intimes* and quoted a relevant passage from it (see below). De Quincey lingers on the perception of time and space under the influence of opium. "Space swelled and [was] amplified to . . . unutterable infinity." This disturbed him less, however, than the "vast expansion of time." In addition, De Quincey connected these space/time effects to Asia and the heavy burden of geographical space and temporal history: "Southern Asia . . . is the seat of awful images and associations . . . [To] me the vast age of the race . . . overpowers the sense of youth in the individual" (*Confessions of an English Opium-Eater and Other Writings*, 91, 95). His haunting dreams of the Malay remind one, even if coincidentally, of Peeperkorn's mysterious Malay servant. In *Artificial Paradises*, Baudelaire confirms that drug-induced dreams are distorting: "all notion of time . . . [has] vanished"; a "minute . . . will seem an eternity"; the proportions are distorted. (*Artificial Paradises*, tr. Stacy Diamond. Secaucus, NJ: Carol Publishing Group, 1996, 57, 52). In a letter to Ernst Bertram (1920, four years before the publication of *Der Zauberberg*), Mann wrote, "It is touching to see how the weak-willed, decaying Baudelaire, already succumbing to hashish, attempts to encourage himself to work" (translation mine), and then he quotes a passage toward the end of *Journaux Intimes*, which invokes Baudelaire's self-command to work six hours a day, to seize on an *idée fixe* that will sustain him. *Thomas Mann an Ernst Betram, Briefe aus den Jahren 1910–1955* (Pfullingen: Neske, 1960), 91; for the original, see Baudelaire, *Ouevres Complètes* (Paris: Gallimard, 1975–76), I: 673.

18. Berdyaev, *Solitude and Society,* 68.

19. I have addressed this question elsewhere. See *Elegiac Fictions: The Motif of the Unlived Life,* 173–191.

20. The phrase, of course, is from Stein in Conrad's *Lord Jim:* "The way is to the destructive element submit yourself, and with the exertions of your hands and feet in the water make the deep, deep sea keep you up." Although Hans Castorp and Lord Jim live very different lives, they share a necessity to submit to the "destructive element," not merely to survive, but to face squarely the coexistence of life and death. The whiteness-void is a literary motif especially rich in nineteenth- and twentieth-century European and American literature. A few examples: Mary Shelley's *Frankenstein,* Poe's *Narrative of A. Gordon Pym,* Melville's *Moby-Dick,* Joyce's "The Dead," and Lawrence's *Women in Love.*

21. Berdyaev, *Solitude and Society,* 69.

22. Paz, *The Labyrinth of Solitude,* 195.

23. Thomas Mann, *Joseph and His Brothers,* tr. H. T. Lowe-Porter (New York: Alfred A. Knopf, 1963), 389, 381.
24. Zimmermann, *Solitude,* 4, 195.
25. Taylor, *Sources of the Self,* 480.
26. Nietzsche, *Human-All-Too Human,* tr. Helen Zimmern in *Collected Works,* 5–6.
27. *Thus Spake Zarathustra,* vol. III, 295.
28. Baudelaire, *Intimate Journals,* 48.
29. Thomas Mann, *Doctor Faustus, The Life of the German Composer Adrian Leverkühn as Told by a Friend,* tr. John E. Woods (New York: Alfred A. Knopf, 1997), 8. Woods also chooses to translate *Einsamkeit* (which I have put in brackets) as "loneliness." I have italicized "coldness" since in the original *Kälte* is italicized. Subsequent quotations are from this text and are incorporated in the text in parentheses.
30. Michael Beddow, *Thomas Mann: Doctor Faustus* (Cambridge: Cambridge University Press, 1994), 64.

Chapter V

1. Gordon Baker and Katherine J. Morris, *Descartes' Dualism* (London: Routledge, 1996), 1.
2. For the Cartesian element in *La Nausée,* see Jaques Deguy, *La Nausée de Jean-Paul Sartre* (Paris: Gallimard, 1993), particularly the section entitled "Un Type dans le Genre de Descartes," 44–70.
3. Steven G. Kellman, *La Nausée* in *The Self-Begetting Novel* (New York: Columbia University Press, 1980), 36.
4. I prefer, in this instance, antagonist over antihero. For an elegant discussion of the antihero, see Victor Brombert, *In Praise of Antiheroes: Figures and Themes in Modern European Literature 1830–1980* (Chicago: University of Chicago Press, 1999), 1–9.
5. See especially Terry Keefe, "The Ending of Sartre's *La Nausée,*" in *Critical Essays on Jean Paul Sartre,* ed. Robert Wilcocks (Boston: G. K. Hall, 1988), 182–201. Keefe's notes 1–14 provide a summary of opinions on the novel's ending, both by French and Anglo-American critics. For his own view see, below.
6. Olivier Todd, *Albert Camus: A Life,* tr. Benjamin Ivry (New York: Alfred A. Knopf, 1987), 85. What he objected to, both in the letter and in the review some months later, was the conflation of philosophy and fiction (or, as he called it, "images"). The review was published on October 20, 1938 in *Alger-Républicain,* a new left-leaning daily for which Camus wrote occasional literary reviews under the column title *La Salon de Lecteur.* The review is translated and printed as "On Jean-Paul Sartre's *La Nausée*" in *Lyrical and Critical Essays,* ed. Philip Thody, tr. Ellen Couray Kennedy (New York: Alfred A. Knopf, 1969), 199–202.
7. Camus, *Notebooks, 1915–1942,* tr. Philip Thody (New York: Alfred A. Knopf, 1963), 105. The date is August 21, 1938. The alternative titles are cited in Todd, *Albert Camus,* 101.

8. Camus, *Lyrical and Critical Essays,* 199–202.

9. The ending of *La Nausée* has elicited much attention. The French critic Jacques Deguy speaks of the "enigmatic strategy of the final episode." *La Nausée de Jean-Paul Sartre* (Paris: Gallimard, 1993), 155. Translation mine. And in great detail, Terry Keefe, "The Ending of Sartre's *La Nausée,*" in *Critical Essays on Jean-Paul Sartre,* 182–199. Keefe argues convincingly that Sartre prepares for the ending, that Roquentin, while in search of some stable ethical point that he can stand on, never suggests that he will write a novel since his sentences are merely "conditional." Nor does he see *Nausea* itself as the novel Roquentin wants to write (the "Proustian" explanation). In fact Sartre ends the novel as "inconclusively as he can . . . as messily and indistinguishably as Roquentin sees it doing in life" (193). Perhaps overly influenced by German parallels, Inca Rumold compares Sartre's novel to Rilke's *Malte Laurids Brigge* and finds them both "*Künstlerromane*"; Roquentin, seeing that he cannot live like a work of art, "decides to create one" (translation mine). *Die Verwandlung des Ekels in Rilkes 'Malte Laurids Brigge' und Sartres 'La Nausée'* (Bonn: Bouivier Verlag Herbert Grundmann, 1979).

10. Iris Murdoch, *Sartre: Romantic Rationalist* (New Haven: Yale University Press, 1953), 13.

11. Jean-Paul Sartre, *Nausea,* 181. All subsequent references will be inserted in the text in parentheses. This experience of nausea is "invariably related to the viscous . . . matter which promotes growth . . . the moist, formless consistency of lush typical earth; of mold, moss, and fungus . . . sweat and spermatozoa; of mucous secretions. . . ." Margaret Walker, "The Nausea of Sartre," *Yale Review,* 42, 2 (December 1952): 253. This description of the "nausea" is an echo of Hans Castorp's investigations into the biological sources of life (see the chapter "Research"). Mann's hero and Roquentin are both attracted and repulsed.

12. There are curious echoes in *Nausea* of Henry James's *The Beast in the Jungle,* in which the protagonist is also curiously and obsessively detached, awaiting an "adventure" that passes him by without his noting its passing. The relationship between Sartre's novel and his *Being and Nothingness* (published five years later, in 1943) has been the subject of much discussion. The allusion to the philosophical work here is merely to point out an obvious parallel.

13. See, for example, Sydney Mendell, "From Solitude to Salvation: A Study in Development," *Yale French Studies* 30 (1964): 45–54. Mendell sees Roquentin's journey as a redemptive exploration from the depth of solitude back to "mankind": "*Nausea* is concerned with the descent of the hero into the hell of solitude which paves the way for the recovery of human life" (54). Roquentin may indeed experience the "hell of solitude" (when it is not offered to him on his own terms), but it is not clear that we can speak of "recovery." At best, after his descent—which is willed—he discovers that empirically, isolation is not feasible and determines there must be another way.

14. Claude-Edmonde Magny, "The Duplicity of Being," in *Sartre: A Collection of Critical Essays,* ed. Edith Kearn (Englewood, NJ: Prentuce Hall, 1962), 25–26.

15. Margot Kruse, "Philosophie und Dichtung in Sartres *La Nausée,*" *Romanistisches Jahrbuch* IX (1958): 217, 218, 225. Kruse, as several others, also finds echoes of Rilke's *Malte Laudris Brigge* in Sartre's diary-novel. Translation mine.

16. John Fletcher, "Sartre's *Nausea:* A Modern Classic Revisted," in *Critical Essays on Jean-Paul Sartre,* 174, 178–179.

17. Henri Peyre, *French Novelists of Today* (New York: Oxford University Press, 1967), 260. Leo Pollmann ascribes the title *Mélancolie* to Sartre himself. *Sartre and Camus: Literature of Existence,* tr. Helen Sebba and Gregor Sebba (New York: Ungar Publishing, 1967), 11.

18. Rhiannon Goldthorpe, "The Presentation of Consciousness in Sartre's *La Nausée* and its Theoretical Basis: Reflections and Facticity," *French Studies* XXII, 2 (1968): 120, 131. Much of this essay is expanded and refined in Goldthorpe's *Sartre: Literary Theory* (Cambridge: Cambridge University Press, 1984). See also Fredric Jameson, *Sartre: The Origins of a Style* (New Haven: Yale University Press, 1952): "The 'nausea' . . . is the moment of feeling acutely that we exist. . . ." (33).

19. Victor Brombert, *The Intellectual Hero: Studies in the French Novel, 1880–1955* (Philadelphia: J. P. Lipnicott, 1960), 145, 182, 194–195.

20. Kenneth Douglas, "The Self-Inflicted Wound," in *Sartre: A Collection of Critical Essays,* 41.

21. Keith Gore comments that this passage is a "reflection of [Roquentin's] continued inability to understand the *sense* of his existence. . . ." *Sartre: La Nausée and Les Mouches* (London: Edward Arnold, 1970), 34. Gore's comparison between the pre- and post-war works is to the point: In the novel, Roquentin is fixated on his own existence; in the play, Oreste seeks an "involvement with events" (8). The real point of such a distinction is to minimize—correctly, I believe—the studied "existential" nature of *Nausea* on which a number of critics have insisted.

22. W. Wolfgang Holdheim, "The *Cogito* in Sartre's *La Nausée,*" in *The Comparative Perspective in Literature: An Approach to Theory and Practice,* ed. Clayton Koelb and Susan Noakes (Ithaca: Cornell University Press, 1988), 179–194. See also Jean Boorsh, "Sartre's View of Cartesian Liberty," *Yale French Studies* I, 1 (Spring–Summer, 1948): 90–96.

23. Robert Champigny, *Stages on Sartre's Way* (New York: Kraus Reprint Corporation, 1968), 30, 31, 41–42. Some parts of this essay are derived from an earlier piece, "Sens de *La Nausée,*" *PMLA,* LXX (March 1955): 37–46.

24. Francis Jeanson, "Hell and Bastardy," *Yale French Studies* 30 (1964): 10, 12, 19.

25. Albert Camus, *The Myth of Sisyphus and Other Essays,* tr. Justin O'Brien (New York: Vintage Books, 1955), 10–11. See Theodore Ziolkowski, "The Crisis of the Thirty-Year Old in Modern Fiction: Toward a Phenomenology

of the Novel," in *Comparatists at Work: Studies in Comparative Literature,* ed., Stephen G. Nichols, Jr. and Richard B. Vowles (Waltham, MA: Blaisdall Publishing, 1968). "The typological experience of the thirty-year old begins with a shock of recognition and ends with a conscious decision." In between, the hero lives in a "state of timelessness"; "action is paralyzed"; "analysis is of his own past and his own present moves into the foreground" (153). This description fits Roquentin in almost every respect, and Ziolkowski, of course, counts Sartre's hero among his 30-year olds.

26. Edith Kearn, Introduction, *Sartre: A Collection of Essays,* 2, 11; Terry Keefe, "The Ending of *La Nausée,*" 199.

27. Claude-Edmonde Magny, "The Duplicity of Being," 24.

28. Pollmann, *Sartre and Camus,* 23.

29. W. H. Auden, *The Enchafèd Flood: Three Critical Essays on the Romantic Spirit,* 19.

30. Albert Camus, *The Stranger,* tr. Matthew Ward (New York: Vintage Books, 1989), 34–35. All subsequent page references are to this edition and are incorporated in the text in parentheses.

31. Jean Sarocchi, in his "Afterword" to *A Happy Death* tr. Richard Howard (New York: Vintage Books, 1972), calls the earlier novel a "prefiguration" of *The Stranger,* 167. He has a more elaborate commentary on the two novels in *Camus* (Paris: Presses Universitaires de France, 1968), where he speaks of Mersault as the "major brother of Meursault of *The Stranger,* spawning [*fraie*] his voice" (13).In his foreword to the French edition of *La Mort Heureuse,* he calls that novel the "larve" of *The Stranger* and spends several pages comparing the two novels, concluding with the superior elements of *The Stranger* over the novel Camus left unpublished. *Cahiers Albert Camus I, La Mort Heureuse* (Paris: Gallimard, 1971), 13, 18–19. Roger Quilliot devotes a number of pages comparing the two novels in *The Sea and Prisons: A Commentary on the Life and Thought of Albert Camus,* tr. Emmett Parker (University, AL: University of Alabama Press, 1970), 66–68. The original French version (the English version was extensively revised) was published in 1956.

32. Quilliot, *The Sea and Prisons,* 67.

33. Quilliot, *The Sea and Prisons,* 62–63.

34. Albert Camus, *A Happy Death,* 14. All subsequent citations are from this edition and are incorporated in the text in parentheses (see n. 31). The French *La Mort Heureuse* was published in 1971. 35. Quilliot, paraphrasing Sarocchi, attributes this to both Mersault and Meursault. *The Sea and Prisons,* 66. See Thody's note 1 to "Death of a Soul" in *Lyrical and Critical Essays,* 40.

36. We know how early and often Camus read and discussed Dostoyevsky. See Ray Davison, *Camus: The Challenge of Dostoyevsky* (Exeter: Exeter University Press, 1997).

37. Camus, "Preface to *The Stranger,*" in *Lyrical and Critical Essays,* 335–337.

38. Irving Massey, *The Uncreating Word: Romanticism and the Object* (Bloomington: Indiana University Press, 1970), 42, 21.

39. There is little profit in outlining this impressive and variegated bibliography on *The Stranger.* Our focus remains on the experience of Meursault's solitude. In *Critical Essays on Albert Camus,* ed. Bettina L. Knapp (Boston: G. K. Hall, 1988), Henri Peyre offers an annotated overview of Camus criticism: "Presence of Camus," 15–36. Several critical views since then are cited here where relevant.

40. Roland Barthes, *Writing Degree Zero,* tr. Annette Levers and Colin Smith (New York: Hill and Wang, 1953), 77. There has been a tendency—on the whole misguided—to divide Meursault's "consciousness" too rigidly between Parts One and Two. For example Patrick Henry sees Part One as offering us Meursault the man of "habit" and Part Two the man of "reflection." "Routine and Reflection in *L'Etranger,*" *Essays in Arts and Sciences,* vol. 4 (West Haven, CT, University of New Haven School of Arts and Sciences, 1975), 1–7. William M. Manly offers a subtler account in "Journey to Consciousness: The Symbolic Pattern of Camus's *L'Etranger,*" *PMLA* LXXIX (June 1964): 321–328. But the most provocative essay on this subject is Gilbert D. Chaitin's Lacanian reading, "The Birth of the Subject in Camus' *L'Etranger,*" *Romanic Review,* 84, 2 (1993) 163–180.

41. The editor's comment and the scenario are in an Appendix to *Essays on Camus's Exile and the Kingdom,* ed. Judith D. Suther (University, MS: Romance Monographs, 1981), 307–313.

42. The quotations from "The Artist at Work" are from Albert Camus, *Exile and the Kingdom,* tr. Justin O'Brien (New York: Vintage Books, 1958), 110–158. See also two Catholic critics: Marion Mitchell Stanicoff, "Camus: Solitary or Solidary?," *America: National Catholic Weekly Review* XLVIII, 13 (January 4, 1958): 395–397, and Bernard Murchland, "Between Solitude and Solidarity," *Commonweal* XCII, 1 (October 23, 1970): 91–95. Stanicoff identifies Camus's "poles of . . . feeling," and concludes with a portrait of Camus as neo-Christian humanist in his desire for human connection. Murchland deals mainly with *ThePlague* and *The Fall,* stressing Camus's "ambiguous world in which everything divides by two: exile and the kingdom, life and death, solitude and solidarity . . ." (94). My reading of the ambiguities of *The Fall* appears in *The Unknown Distance: From Consciousness to Conscience, Goethe to Camus* (Cambridge: Harvard University Press, 1972), 320–241. For additional comments on "solitary" and "solidary" see Diana Festa-Mc-Cormick, "Existential Exile and a Glimpse of the Kingdom," in *Critical Essays on Albert Camus,* 114; Gaëtan Picon, "Exile and the Kingdom," in *Camus: A Collection of Critical Essays,* 155–156, and Brian T. Fitch, *The Narcissistic Text: A Reading of Camus' Fiction* (Toronto: University of Toronto Press, 1982), 35, 43–44. For a chapter devoted to this story, see English Showalter, Jr., *Exiles and Strangers: A Reading of Camus's 'Exile and the Kingdom'* (Columbus: Ohio State University Press, 1984), 89–106.

43. Rachel Bespaloff, "The World of the Man Condemned to Die" in *Camus: A Collection of Essays,* 93.

44. Pollmann, *Sartre and Camus,* 139.

45. Albert Camus, *The Myth of Sisyphus and Other Essays,* 9.

46. G. V. Banks, *Camus: L'Etranger* (London: Edward Arnold, 1976), 38. However, Meursault's estrangement, in whatever way interpreted, makes it difficult to indict his insensitivity toward the "Arab," to fault his politics, as several have attempted to do, by attacking Camus's own ambiguity about Algerian politics, which was articulated almost two decades after the creation of Meursault. It is questionable whether Camus's 'colonialism'—as it has been called—is a sustained cast of mind. See, for example, Conor Cruise O'Brien, *Albert Camus of Europe and Africa* (New York: The Viking Press, 1970), chapter on *The Stranger;* and Jan Rigaud, "The Depiction of Arabs in *L'Etranger*"; *Camus's 'L'Etranger': Fifty Years On,* ed. Adele King (New York: St. Martin's Press, 1992),183–192—a much more balanced and incisive analysis of the issue than O'Brien's.

47. Robert J. Champigny, *A Pagan Hero: An Interpretation of Meursault in Camus' 'The Stanger,'* tr. Rowe Portis (Philadelphia: University of Pennsylvania Press, 1969), 19, 87.

48. Maurice Blanchot, *The Space of Literature,* tr. Ann Smock (Lincoln: University of Nebraska Press, 1982), 31 (note), 252. See also Blanchot, *The Gaze of Orpheus and Other Literary Essays,* tr. Lydia Davis (Barrytown, NY: Station Hill Press, 1981), 63–77.

49. Views differ. For example, Frantz Favre quotes a letter from Camus to Ponge, in which the former agrees that he has not lost his "'metaphysical anxiety,'" and that the final "'confrontation without hope is rebellion.'" Favre asks: "Can we pretend that Meursault is deprived of any painful consciousness when he suffers in his solitude so much as to hope for the presence of cries of hate?" While he concedes that there are some doubts about Meursault's "final serenity," he puts these to rest because Meursault's "suffering is not metaphysical." Rather it is to his "anger that Meursault owes the state of being 'purpé, du mal, d'espoir.'" Frantz Favre, "'L'Etranger and Metaphysical Anxiety," in *Camus's 'L'Etranger': Fifty Years On,* 42, 45 n. 24.

50. Albert Camus, "Enigma" in *Lyrical and Critical Essays,* 159–160.

51. David Sprintzen, *Camus: A Critical Examination* (Philadelphia: Temple University Press, 1988), 126–127.

52. Patrick McCarthy, *Albert Camus: 'The Stranger'* (Cambridge: Cambridge University Press, 1988), 61.

53. A reaction set in against Meursault in the 1960s: He was after all a murderer. Perhaps one of the major triggers of this reaction (aside from the moralistic tone of the decade itself) was the publication of Renée Girard's "Camus's Stranger Retried," *PMLA* LXXIX 5 (December, 1964): 519–523. "How can a man commit a murder and not be responsible for it?" Girard asks (521). Nearly 30 years later, Adele King comments that "[r]eaders sympathise with Meursault to such an extent that we almost tend to forget that he is a murderer at all." *Camus's 'L'Etranger': Fifty Years On,* 5. Another critic of the 90s speaks of "Meursault's monstrously criminal nature. . . ." Jack Murray, "Closure and Anticlosure in Camus's 'L'Etranger': Some Ideological Considera-

tions," *Symposium* XLVI (Fall 1992): 231. Murray also points to the anonymity of "the Arab" and concurs with the idea that on this score, Camus was a "racist" (236).

54. Jean-Paul Sartre, "An Explication of *The Stranger*," *Camus: A Collection of Critical Essays*, 111–112. The original may be found in *Situations,* vol. I (Paris: Gallimard, 1947). Its first appearance was in 1943. The original French reads: "Bien que l'absurdité de la condition humaine en soit l'unique sujet, ce n'est pas un roman à thèse . . ." (105); "Ainsi le seul fait de délivrer son message sous forme romanesque . . ." (105). Victor Brombert refers to Sartre's review and the basic distinction between Camus's novel and *The Myth of Sisyphus,* but in the end Brombert feels Camus has failed to make the distinction work. Meursault is a "mouthpiece" for Camus's "ideas" and the result is to make Meursault only passingly interesting and *The Stranger* not "secure" as a work of art. "Camus and the Novel of the 'Absurd'," *Yale French Studies* I (Summer 1948): 119–123.

55. I have rendered Stuart Gilbert's "loneliness" as "solitude," as it appears in the original.

56. Gilbert D. Chaitin sees Meursault's dilemma somewhat differently: "From beginning to end, the narrator is plunged into a present which sweeps him irrevocably onward in the flow of time." "Narrative Desire in *L'Etranger*," in *Camus's 'L'Etranger': Fifty Years On,* 136.

57. Albert Camus, *The Rebel: An Essay on Man in Revolt,* tr. Anthony Bower (New York: Vintage Books, 1956), 280–281. The original was published in 1951 under the title *L'Homme Révolté.* For an imaginative account of Meursault as something less than a rebel against society see Ignace Feuerlicht, "Camus's *L'Etranger* Reconsidered," *PMLA* LXXVIII (December 1963): 606–621.

58. Carl A. Viggiani was among the pioneers who insisted that we look to *The Stranger's* "formal and imaginative aspects rather than its "world view or philosophy": "Camus's *L'Etranger*," *PMLA* LXXI (December 1956): 865. He looked at "myth, names, patterns of character and situation, and symbols . . . for an explanation of the meaning of the novel as a whole" (865). That approach was part of the then waning New Criticism, but Viggiani's essay continues to occupy a respected place in the bibliography on *The Stranger.*

59. Froment-Meurice, *Solitudes: From Rimbaud to Heidegger,* xxi.

60. Maurice Blanchot, *The Space of Literature,* 251.

Chapter VI

1. Thomas Trezise, *Into the Breach: Samuel Beckett and the Ends of Literature* (Princeton: Princeton University Press, 1990), 66.

2. All subsequent quotations from the trilogy are from the Everyman's Edition, Samuel Beckett, *Molloy, Malone Dies, The Unnamable,* with an Introduction by Gabriel Ludovici (New York: Alfred A. Knopf, 1997) and are incorporated into the text in parentheses. The quotation is from *The Unnamable,*

377. Abbreviations are: *M* for *Molloy; MD* for *Malone Dies; U* for *The Un-namable.* Following are dates of publication, the first for the French, the second for the translations into English; the last two are Beckett's own. The English translation dates all apply to the Grove Press editions: *Molloy,* 1950, 1955; *Malone Dies,* 1951, 1956; *The Unnamable,* 1955, 1958.

3. The critical literature on Beckett's fiction has grown to impressive dimensions, and the trilogy is discussed in all such studies as well as in generalized collections on Beckett. However, a fair number of volumes are devoted entirely to the trilogy. Here is a sampling: *Twentieth Century Interpretations of Molloy, Malone Dies, The Unnamable,* ed. J. D. O'Hara (Englewood Cliffs, NJ: Prentice Hall, 1955); Philip Solomon, *The Life After Birth: Imagery in Samuel Beckett's Trilogy* (University, MS: Romance Monographs, 1975); *Samuel Beckett's Molloy, Malone Dies, The Unnamable,* ed. with an Introduction by Harold Bloom (New York: Chelsea House Publishers, 1988); Gönül Pultar, *Techniques and Tradition in Beckett's Trilogy of Novels* (New York: University Press of America, 1996); Thomas J. Cousineau, *After the Final No: Samuel Beckett's Trilogy* (Newark: University of Delaware Press, 1999).

4. This quotation has been much discussed, and Maurice Blanchot's brief essay, "Where Now? Who Now?" (first published in France in 1953) has been often reprinted and referenced. See *The Sirens' Song: Selected Essays by Maurice Blanchot,* ed. Gabriel Josipovici, tr. Sacha Rabinovitch (Bloomington: Indiana University Press, 1982), 192–198. For an excellent discussion of Beckett's use of "aporia," see Leslie Hill, *Beckett's Fiction: In Different Words* (Cambridge: Cambridge University Press, 1990), 63 ff.

5. Charlotte Renner, "The Self-Multiplying Narrators of *Molloy, Malone Dies, and The Unnamable,*" in *Samuel Beckett's Molloy, Malone Dies, The Unnamable,* ed. Bloom, 114; Philip H. Solomon, *The Life After Birth: Imagery in Samuel Beckett's Trilogy,* 145.

6. H. Porter Abbott, "The Harpooned Notebook: *Malone Dies,*" in *Samuel Beckett's Molloy, Malone Dies, The Unnamable,* 129.

7. Among the many books and essays that deal with aspects of Beckett and language, one is especially of interest: P. J. Murphy, *Reconstructing Beckett: Language for Being in Samuel Beckett's Fiction* (Toronto: University of Toronto Press, 1990). See especially the discussion of *The Unnamable,* 28–33.

8. Maire Jaanus Kurrick, *Literature and Negation* (New York: Columbia University Press, 1979), 229, 225.

9. Gabriel Josipovici, "Introduction," Samuel Beckett, *Molloy, Malone Dies, The Unnamable,* xii. For a philosophical interpretation of the trilogy, see Lance St. John Butler, *Samuel Beckett: A Study in Ontological Parable* (New York: St. Martin's Press, 1984). The three major chapters are: "Heidegger's *Being and Time* and Beckett"; "Sartre's *Being and Nothingness* and Beckett"; and Hegel's "*Phenomenology of Mind* and Beckett's *The Unnamable.*"

10. Douglas Dunn, *Two Decades of Irish Writing: A Critical Survey* (Chester Springs, PA: Dufour Editions, 1975), 193.

11. Steven Connor, *Samuel Beckett: Repetition, Theory and Text* (New York: Blackwell, 1988), 75.

12. It is sometimes overlooked that Beckett and Camus were contemporaries who knew and read each other. Camus's *The Fall* was published in 1956, three years after the publication of the French version of *The Unnamable*. Whether Camus had read Beckett's novel is not clear, but there are many aspects of subject and narration techniques that the two authors shared, especially ironic tone and reader/self manipulation.

13. Gabriel Josipovici, Introduction, *Samuel Beckett, Molloy, Malone Dies, The Unnamable*, xi, xii, xvii.

14. Harold Bloom, Introduction, *Samuel Beckett's Molloy, Malone Dies, The Unnamable*, 1. There is ample evidence that Beckett read Schopenhauer.

15. It has been almost universally agreed upon by now that the characters in the trilogy are interrelated (and interlaced), doubles or mirrors of one another. Although there may be room for some further discrimination, throughout this chapter the assumption will be that there is a collective "I" in the three novels. Of course, wherever it seems necessary, the specific character will be named. Some critics go further and see the three novels as repetitions of one another. Daniel Gunn comments that "few readers of Beckett's *Trilogy* will not have felt that *Malone Dies* is a repetition of *Molloy*, and *The Unnamable* of *Malone Dies*." However, he cautions, "Equally few . . . will feel confident to say in what way this is so." *Psychoanalysis and Fiction: An Exploration of Literary and Psychoanalytic Borders* (Cambridge: Cambridge University Press, 1988), 164.

16. Richard Begam, *Samuel Beckett and the End of Modernity* (Stanford: Stanford University Press, 1996). Begam's study leans heavily on Dérrida (and to a lesser degree, Barthes and Foucault); in any case, he views and interprets Beckett as a postmodernist and Dérrida's "*différance*" is a keyword throughout his analysis. Dennis Brown, on the other hand, still incorporates Beckett into Modernism, but regrettably feels hesitant to include Beckett among English writers in his study, *The Modernist Self in Twentieth-Century English Literature: A Study in Self-Fragmentation* (New York: St. Martin's Press, 1989).

17. For some remarks on Beckett and space see Robin Lee, "The Fictional Topography of Samuel Beckett," in *The Modern English Novel: The Reader, the Writer, the Work*, 206–224.

18. Leslie Hill, *Beckett's Fiction: In Different Words* (Cambridge: Cambridge University Press, 1990), 115.

19. H. Porter Abbott, *The Fiction of Samuel Beckett: Form and Effect* (Berkeley: University of California Press, 1973), 123.

20. James Acheson, *Samuel Beckett's Artistic Theory and Practice* (New York: St. Martin's Press, 1997), 140.

21. Wylie Sypher, *The Loss of Self in Modernist Literature and Art* (Westport, CT: 1979), 147, 154–155.

22. Ihab Hassan, *The Literature of Silence: Henry Miller and Samuel Beckett* (New York: Alfred A. Knopf, 1967), 171–172.

23. *The Modernist Self in Twentieth-Century English Literature: A Study in Self-Fragmentation,* (New York: St. Martin's Press, 1989), 177.
24. Alain Robbe-Grillet, *For A New Novel: Essays in Fiction,* tr. Richard Howard (New York: Grove Press, 1965), 112.
25. John Fletcher comments: "For who is Malone, but simultaneously the creator, and avatar, of Murphy, Molloy, Moran, and the others? And what is this book, but the projection and exorcism of private traumas, and their sublimation into art? . . . *Malone Dies* represents a painful—but ultimately successful—'birth into literature' both for its moribund narrator and for its surviving author." "Malone 'Gives Birth to Into Death,'" *Twentieth Century Interpretations of Molloy, Malone Dies, The Unnamabale,* 61.
26. Maurice Blanchot, *The Sirens's Song: Selected Essays by Maurice Blanchot,* 194, 197, 198.
27. For insightful discussions on "repetition" see Rubin Rabinovitz, *Innovation in Samuel Beckett's Fiction* (Urbana: University of Illinois Press, 1992), Chapter Five, "Repetition and Underlying Meanings in Beckett's Trilogy," 65–105. In addition: Steven Connor, *Samuel Beckett: Repetition, Theory and Text* and Magela Moorjani, "A Cryptanalysis of Beckett's *Molloy*" in *The World of Samuel Beckett,* ed. Joseph H. Smith (Baltimore: The Johns Hopkins University Press, 1991), 53–72.
28. A useful essay on postmodernism and Beckett is Nicholas Zurbrugg's "Seven Types of Postmodernity: Several Types of Beckett," in *The World of Samuel Beckett,* 30–52. A recent poststructuralist study of Beckett is Anthony Uhlman, *Beckett and Poststructuralism* (Cambridge: Cambridge University Press, 1999).
29. Maurice Friedman, *To Deny Our Nothingness: Contemporary Images of Man* (New York: Delacorte Press, 1967), 318, 315, 321. See also Hélène L. Baldwin, *Samuel Beckett's Real Silence* (University Park: Pennsylvania State University Press, 1981).
30. Israel Shenker, "An Interview with Beckett" (1956), reprinted in *Samuel Beckett: The Critical Heritage,* ed. Lawrence Graver and Raymond Federman (London: Routledge & Kegan Paul, 1979), 148. Bersani's essay is reprinted in *Samuel Beckett's Molloy, Malone Dies, The Unnamable,* ed. Bloom, 51–70.
31. The concepts of solipsism and nihilism in Beckett have pervaded criticism almost from the beginning and continue to this day, and not without reason. See, for example, Ihab Hassan, *The Literature of Silence: Henry Miller and Samuel Beckett,* especially "The Solipsist Voice," which deals with the trilogy (139–173); and, most recently, Thomas J. Cousineau, *After the Final No: Samuel Beckett's Trilogy,* although as Cousineau's title indicates, there is in his reading of the trilogy something "after" solipsism and nihilism.
32. Chrisopher Ricks, *Beckett's Last Words* (Oxford: Oxford University Press, 1993), 3.
33. See Josephine Jacobsen and William R. Mueller, *The Testament of Samuel Beckett* (London: Faber and Faber, 1966), 78ff.

34. On "couples," and identity see Enrico Garzilli, *Circles Without Center: Paths to the Discovery and Creation of Self in Modern Literature* (Cambridge: Harvard University Press, 1972), especially the chapter titled "The Other and Identity: The Couples of Samuel Beckett," 28–38.
35. "Subjectivity as the Autogenous Cancellation of its Manifestations," in *Samuel Beckett's Molloy, Malone Dies, The Unnamable,* ed. Bloom, 71–72.
36. Among the many references that might be cited, a few will have to suffice. See John Fletcher, "Samuel Beckett and the Philosophers," *Comparative Literature* 17 (Winter 1975): 43–56; Ruby Cohn, "Philosophical Fragments in the Works of Samuel Beckett," *Criticism,* vol. VI, no 1 (Winter 1964): 33–43; Hugh Kenner, *Samuel Beckett: A Critical Study* (New York: Grove Press, 1961), especially the chapter titled "The Cartesian Centaur," reprinted in several collections. Kenner focuses on Beckett's/narrator's obsession with the bicycle as a satirical mechanical symbol for the body/mind split. (A convenient place to find this essay is in *Critical Essays on Samuel Beckett,* ed. Patrick A. McCarthy [Boston: G. K. Hall & Co.], 55–64). Also relevant is Steven G. Kellman's chapter on the trilogy in *The Self-Begetting Novel,* 129–143. The most recent poststructuralist study of Beckett is Daniel Katz' *Saying I No More: Subjectivity and Consciousness in the Prose of Samuel Beckett* (Evanston: Northwestern University Press, 1999). Katz argues that Beckett rejects the Cartesian *cogito.* He also pays close attention to the function of the "I" in the trilogy, particularly in chapters 3 and 4, 71–124.
37. These last words echo the last of Joyce's "The Dead," and if one recalls that Gabriel Conroy, at the moment of his extreme vulnerability, is looking through a windowpane as he sees the snow falling upon "the living and the dead," the echo gains in relevance.
38. Hugh Kenner, *Samuel Beckett: A Critical Study,* 128.
39. A number of critics have commented on aspects of light/dark in the trilogy. See Philip H. Solomon, *The Life After Birth: Imagery in Samuel Beckett's Trilogy,* especially Chapter IV, "Light Falls," 94–113.
40. Ibid., 99.
41. *Samuel Beckett: A Critical Study,* 81.
42. Gabriel Josipovici, Introduction, *Samuel Beckett, Molloy, Malone Dies, The Unnamable,* xviii.
43. Ludovico Janivier, "*Molloy,*" in *Twentieth Century Interpretations of Molloy, Malone Dies, The Unnamable,* 49.
44. Solomon has a chapter titled "A Beckett Bestiary" in his *The Life After Birth: Imagery in Beckett's Trilogy,* 114–143, but he misses an opportunity to explore the important implications of beast imagery in the trilogy.
45. Quoting the sentence "I have lost my stick," Hugh Kenner suggests that what stands behind the collecting and cataloguing in the trilogy are "bundles of romances chronicling the acquisition and dispersal of portable property from *Robinson Crusoe* to *The Spoils of Poynton.*" *Samuel Beckett: A Critical Study,* 63. As one of the first and most incisive critics to emphasize

Beckett's comic side, Kenner is obviously not unaware of the ironic implications of the lost stick in comparison to the earnestness of Defoe and James.

46. Dennis Brown, *The Modernist Self in Twentieth-Century English Literature: A Study in Self-Fragmentation*, 3.

47. Peggy Guggenheim, who had a long relationship with Beckett, referred to him as "Oblomov," in part because of his fondness for the bed. See *Confessions of an Art Addict* (New York: Macmillan, 1960). V. S. Pritchett titled a review of the trilogy "An Irish Oblomov," *New Statesman*, 59 (April 2, 1960), 489.

48. Thomas J. Cousineau, *After the Final No: Samuel Beckett's Trilogy*, 95, 118.

49. Hugh Kenner, "The Trilogy," in *Samuel Beckett's Molloy, Malone Dies, The Unnamable*, ed. Bloom, 48, 47.

50. Gönül Pultar, *Technique and Tradition in Beckett's Trilogy of Novels*, 100. Pultar is one of the few critics who sees Beckett as indebted to Defoe: "The debt of the trilogy to *Robinson Crusoe* and what Beckett made of it have to be kept in mind. . . . [I]t is a double debt unified into one whole: the recounting of an adventurous journey and the fact that this recounting is supposed to constitute spiritual conversion" (101).

51. Gabriel Josopovici, "Introduction," *Molloy, Malone Dies, The Unnamable*, xxi.

Conclusion

1. Janna Malamud Smith, *Private Matters: In Defense of the Personal Life* (Reading, MA: Addison Wesley, 1997), 37.

2. Samuel Beckett, *The Lost Ones* (New York: Grove Press, 1972). It was first published in French as *Le Depopleur* in 1970 and translated by Beckett. Because the work is so slim, I have omitted page numbers.

3. *The Standard Edition of the Complete Psychological Works,* vol. 18, 140.

4. Erwin Möde, *Die Neue Einsamkeit der Postmoderne* (München: Edition Psychosymbolik, 1995), 80, 13, 113. Translations mine. Critical literature on postmodernism shows no signs of abating, as the debate of what—or whether—it continues. On the transition from Modernism to Postmodernism see Gianni Vattimo, *The End of Modernity: Nihilism and Hermeneutics in Postmodern Culture*, tr. Jon R. Snyder (Baltimore: Johns Hopkins Press, 1988); *Modernism/Postmodernism*, ed. Peter Brooker (London: Longman Group UK, 1992); another interesting anthology is *Postmodern Subjects/Postmodern Texts*, ed. Jane Dowson and Steven Earnshaw (Amsterdam-Atlanta: Rodopi, 1995). Vattimo offers "An Apology for Nihilism" (19–30), which is based on Nietzsche and recognizes his impact on postmodern culture.

5. James Brusseau, *Isolated Experiences: Gilles Deleuze and the Solitudes of Reversed Platonism* (Albany: State University of New York Press, 1998), 176–177.

6. Maurice Blanchot, "The Essential Solitude" in *The Space of Literature,* 21–34.
7. The mirror images and the Doppelgänger, staples of the nineteenth century, continue into the twentieth, but in more complex and sophisticated manifestations. See, for example, Max Frisch's *I'm not Stiller* or Philip Roth's Zuckermann novels.
8. Paul Halmos, *Solitude and Privacy,* 19.
9. See Renate Möhrmann, *Der Vereinsamte Mensch,* 19.
10. Søren Kierkegaard, *The Sickness Unto Death,* ed. and tr. Howard V. Hong and Edna H. Hong (Princeton: Princeton University Press, 1980), 65.
11. Richard Rorty, *Contingency, Irony, and Solidarity* (Cambridge: Cambridge University Press, 1989), 29.
12. Elizabeth Cady Stanton, "Solitude of Self" (1892) in *The Search for Self-Sovereignty: The Oratory of Elizabeth Cady Stanton,* ed. Beth M. Waggenspack (New York: Greenwood Press, 1989), 159–167.
13. Joanne Wieland-Burston, *Contemporary Solitude,* 26, 34, 100–102, 172.
14. Amy M. Spindler, "Tracing the Look of Alienation," *New York Times* (March 24, 1998), D28.
15. Freud, *The Standard Edition,* vol. XXI, 64–73. (*Civilization and its Discontents*); Baudelaire. *Artificial Paradises,* 74. For "oceanic feelings," see Sanford Gifford, Chapter IV, note 16.

.

Bibliography

Abbott, H. Porter. *The Fiction of Samuel Beckett: Form and Effect.* Berkeley: University of California Press, 1973.

———."The Harpooned Notebook: *Malone Dies.*" In *Samuel Beckett's Molloy, Malone Dies, and The Unnamable.* Ed. Harold Bloom. New York: Chelsea House Publishers, 1988.

Acheson, James. *Samuel Beckett's Artistic Theory and Practice.*New York: St. Martin's Press, 1997.

Adams, R. M. *Strains of Discord: Studies in Literary Openness.* Ithaca: Cornell University Press, 1958.

Adorno, Theodor W. *Notes to Literature I.* Ed. Rolf Tiedemann. Tr. Shierry Weber Nicholsen. New York: Columbia University Press, 1991.

Auden, W. H. *The Enchafèd Flood: Three Critical Essays on the Romantic Spirit.* New York Vintage Books, 1967.

Auerbach, Erich. *Mimesis: The Representation of Reality in Western Literature.* Tr. William Trask. Garden City, NY: Doubleday, 1953.

Bacon, Sir Francis. "Of Friendship." *Essays, Advancement of Learning, New Atlantis and Other Pieces.* Ed. Richard Foster Jones. New York: The Odyssey Press, 1937.

Baker, Gordon, and Katherine J. Morris. *Descartes' Dualism.* London: Routledge, 1996

Banks, G. V. *Camus: L'Etranger.* London: Edward Arnold, 1976.

Barthes, Roland. "The Last Happy Writer." In *Critical Essays.* Tr. Richard Howard. Evanston:Northwestern University Press, 1972.

———. *Writing Degree Zero.* Tr. Annette Lever and Colin Smith. New York: Hill and Wang, 1953.

Baudelaire, Charles. *Artificial Paradises.* Tr. Stacey Diamond. Secaucus, N.J.: Carol Publishing Group, 1996.

———. *Intimate Journals.* Tr. Christopher Isherwood. London: Methuen & Company, 1949.

———. *The Parisian Prowler.* Tr. Edward K. Kaplan. Athens: The University of Georgia Press 1997.

Beckett, Samuel. *The Lost Ones.* New York: Grove Press, 1972.

———. *Molloy, Malone Dies, The Unnameable.* New York: Alfred A. Knopf, 1997.

———. *Proust.* New York: Grove Press, 1957.

Beddow, Michael. *Thomas Mann: Doctor Faustus.* Cambridge: Cambridge University Press, 1994.

Begam, Richard. *Samuel Beckett and the End of Modernity.* Stanford: Stanford University Press, 1996.

Bender, John. *Imagining the Penitentiary in Eighteenth-Century England.* Chicago: University of Chicago Press, 1987.

Berdyaev, Nicholas. *Solitude and Society.* London: Centenary Press, 1938.

Bespaloff, Rachel. "The World of the Man Condemned to Die." In *Camus: A Collection of Critical Essays.* Ed. Germaine Brée. Englewood Cliffs, NJ: Prentice Hall, 1962.

Blanchot, Maurice. *The Sirens' Song: Selected Essays by Maurice Blanchot.* Ed. Gabriel Josipovici. Tr. Sacha Rabinovitch. Bloomington: Indiana University Press, 1982.

————. *The Space of Literature.* Translated by Ann Smock. Lincoln: University of Nebraska Press, 1982.

Blewett, David. *Defoe's Art of Fiction.* Toronto: University of Toronto Press, 1979.

Blondel, Jacques. "Wordsworth and Solitude." In *An Infinite Complexity: Essays in Romanticism.* Ed. J. R. Watson. Edinburgh: Edinburgh University Press, 1983. 26–45.

Bloom, Harold. "Introduction." *Samuel Beckett's Molloy, Malone Dies, and The Unnamable.* New York: Chelsea House Publishers, 1988.

Brombert, Victor. "Camus and the Novel of the 'Absurd.'" *Yale French Studies* I (1948): 119–123.

————. *The Intellectual Hero: Studies in the French Novel, 1880–1955.* Philadelphia: J. P. Lipnicott, 1960.

————. *Romantic Prisons.* Princeton: Princeton University Press, 1978.

Brown, Dennis. *The Modernist Self in Twentieth-Century English Literature: A Study in Self-Fragmentation.* New York: St.Martin's Press, 1989.

Brown, Homer Obed. *Institutions of the English Novel: From Defoe to Scott.* Philadelphia: Pennsylvania University Press, 1997.

Brusseau, James. *Isolated Experiences: Gilles Deleuze and the Solitudes of Reversed Platonism.* Albany: State University of New York Press, 1998.

Burke, Edmund. *A Philosophical Inquiry into the Origins of Our Ideas of the Sublime and Beautiful.* Ed. James T. Boulton. Notre Dame: University of Notre Dame Press, 1968.

Bush, Douglas. "The Isolation of the Renaissance Hero." In *Reason and Imagination: Studies in the History of Ideas, 1600–1800.* Ed. J. A. Mazzeo. New York: Columbia University Press, 1962.

Cahir, Linda Costanzo. *Solitude and Society in the Works of Melville and Edith Wharton.* Westport, CT: Greenwood Press, 1999.

Camus, Albert. *Exile and the Kingdom.* Tr. Justin O'Brien. New York: Vintage Books, 1958.

————. *A Happy Death.* Tr. Richard Howard. New York: Vintage Books, 1972.

————. *Lyrical and Critical Essays.* Ed. Philip Thody. Tr. Ellen Couray. New York: Alfred A. Knopf, 1969.

————. *The Myth of Sisyphus and Other Essays.* Tr. Justin O'Brien. New York: Vintage Books, 1955.

————. *Notebooks, 1915–1942.* Tr. Philip Thody. New York: Alfred A. Knopf, 1963.

————. *The Rebel: An Essay on Man in Revolt.* Tr. Anthony Bower. New York: Vintage Books, 1956.

————. *The Stranger.* Tr. Matthew Ward. New York: Vintage Books, 1989.

Carnochan, W. B. *Confinement and Flight: An Essay on English Literature of the Eighteenth Century.* Berkeley: The University of California Press, 1977.

Caughie, Pamela L. *Virginia Woolf & Postmodernism: Literature in Quest and Question of Itself.* Urbana: University of Illinois Press, 1991.

Champigny, Robert. *A Pagan's Hero: An Interpretation of Meursault in Camus' 'The Stranger.'* Tr. Rowe Portis. Philadelphia: University of Pennsylvania Press, 1969.

————. *Stages on Sartre's Way.* New York: Kraus Reprint Corp., 1968.

Cloonan, William. *Michel Tournier.* Boston: Twayne Publishers, 1985.

Cohn, Dorrit. *Transparent Minds: Narrative Modes for Presenting Consciousness in Fiction.* Princeton: Princeton University Press, 1978.

Connor, Steven. *Samuel Beckett: Repetition, Theory and Text.* New York: Blackwell, 1988.

Cousineau, Thomas J. *After the Final No: Samuel Beckett's Trilogy.* Newark: University of Delaware Press, 1999.

Cowley, Abraham. *Essays, Plays, and Sundry Verses in the English Writings of Abraham Cowley.* Ed. A.R. Walker. Cambridge: University Press, 1906.

Damrosch, Leopold Jr. *God's Plots and Man's Stories: Studies in the Fictional Imagination from Milton to Fielding.* Chicago: University of Chicago Press, 1985.

Defoe, Daniel. *The Life and Strange Surprizing Adventures of Robinson Crusoe, of York, Mariner.* Ed. J. Donald Crowley. London: Oxford University Press, 1972.

————. *Robinson Crusoe.* Ed. Michael Shinagel. Norton Critical Edition. 2nd edition. New York: W. W. Norton, 1994.

————. *Serious Reflections of Robinson Crusoe.* New York: Jenson Society, 1903.

De La Mare, Walter. *Desert Islands and Robinson Crusoe.* New York: Farrar & Rinehart, 1930.

De Quincey, Thomas. *Confessions of an English Opium Eater and Other Writings.* Ed. Aileen Ward. New York: New American Library, 1966.

Dillon, Janette. *Shakespeare and the Solitary Man.* Totowa, NJ: Rowman and Littlefield, 1981.

Douglas, Kenneth. "The Self-Inflicted Wound." In *Sartre: A Collection of Critical Essays.* Ed. Edith Kearn. Englewood, NJ: Prentice Hall, 1962.

Dunn, Douglas. *Two Decades of Irish Writing: A Critical Survey.* Chester Springs, PA: Dufour Editions, 1975.

DuPlessis, Rachel Blau. *Writing Beyond the Ending: Narrative Strategies of Twentieth-Century Women Writers.* Bloomington: Indiana University Press, 1985.

Ellis, Frank H. "Introduction." *Twentieth-Century Views of Robinson Crusoe: A Collection of Critical Essays.* Ed. Frank H. Ellis. Englewood Cliffs, NJ: Prentice Hall, 1969.

Emerson, Ralph Waldo. *Society and Solitude: Twelve Chapters.* Boston: Houghton, Mifflin and Company, 1870. *Encyclopédie ou Dictionnaire Raisonné des Sciences des Arts et des Métiers* 15. Stuttgart-Bad Cannstatt: Friedrich Frommann Verlag, 1967.

Favre, Frantz. "L'Etranger and Metaphysical Anxiety." In *Camus's 'L'Etranger': Fifty Years On.* Ed. Adele King. New York: St. Martin's Press, 1992.

Ferguson, Frances. *Solitude and the Sublime: Romanticism and the Aesthetics of Individuation.* New York: Routledge, 1992.

Fletcher, John. "Sartre's *Nausea:* A Modern Classic Revisited."In *Critical Essays on Jean-Paul Sartre.* Ed. Robert Wilcocks. Boston: G. K. Hall, 1988.

France, Peter. *Hermits: The Insights of Solitude.* London: Chatto & Windus, 1996.

Frank, Joseph. *The Idea of Spatial Form.* New Brunswick: Rutgers University Press, 1991.

Freud, Sigmund. *The Standard Edition of the Complete Psychological Works of Sigmund Freud.* Tr. James Strachey and Anna Freud. London: The Hogarth Press, 1955.

Friedman, Maurice. *To Deny Our Nothingness: Contemporary Images of Man.* New York: Delacorte Press, 1967.

Fromm, Erich. *Escape from Freedom.* New York: Rinehart & Company, 1941.

Froment-Meurice, Marc. *Solitudes: From Rimbaud to Heidegger.* Tr. Peter Walsh. Albany: State University Press of New York, 1995.

Ganzell, Dewey. "Chronology in *Robinson Crusoe.*" *Philological Quarterly* XL (1961): 495–512.

Garber, Frederick. *The Autonomy of the Self from Richardson to Huysmans.* Princeton: Princeton University Press, 1981.

Gellner, Ernest. *Language and Solitude: Wittgenstein, Malinowski, and the Habsburg Dilemma.* Cambridge: Cambridge University Press, 1998.

Georgianna, Linda. *The Solitary Self: Individuality in the "Ancrene Wisse."* Cambridge: Harvard University Press, 1988.

Gifford, Sanford. "'The Prisoner of Time': Some Developmental Aspects of Time Perception in Infancy, Sensory Isolation, and Old Age." In *The Annual of Psychoanalysis.* Vol. 8. New York: International Universities Press, 1980.

Goldthorpe, Rhiannon. "The Presentation of Consciousness in Sartre's *La Nausée* and its Theoretical Basis: Reflections and Facticity." *French Studies* XXII.2 (1968): 114–32.

Gore, Keith. *Sartre: La Nausée and Les Mouches.* London: Edward Arnold, 1970.

Green, Martin. *The Robinson Crusoe Story.* University Park: Pennsylvania State University Press, 1990.

Halmos, Paul. *Solitude and Privacy: A Study of Social Isolation, Its Causes and Therapy.* London: Routledge & Kegan Paul, 1952.

Harper, Ralph. *The Seventh Solitude: Man's Isolation in Kierkegaard, Dostoyevsky, and Nietzsche.* Baltimore: Johns Hopkins University Press, 1965.

Hassan, Ihab. *The Literature of Silence: Henry Miller and Samuel Beckett.* New York: Alfred A. Knopf, 1967.

Hill, Leslie. *Beckett's Fiction: In Different Words.* Cambridge: Cambridge University Press, 1990.

Holdheim, W. Wolfgang. "The *Cogito* in Sartre's *La Nausée.*" In *The Comparative Perspective in Literature: An Approach to Theory and Practice.* Ed. Clayton Koelb and Susan Noakes. Ithaca: Cornell University Press, 1988.

Holmes, Arthur F. "Crusoe, Friday, and God." *Philosophy Forum* 11 (1972): 319–339.

Hunter, J. Paul. *The Reluctant Pilgrim: Defoe's Emblematic Method and Quest for Form in Robinson Crusoe*. Baltimore: Johns Hopkins University Press, 1966.

Jacobsen, Josephine and William R. Mueller. *The Testament of Samuel Beckett*. London: Faber and Faber, 1966.

James, Louis. "Unwrapping Crusoe: Retrospective and Prospective Views." In *Robinson Crusoe: Myths and Metamorphoses*. Ed. Lieve Spaas and Brian Simpson. New York: Macmillan, 1996.

Janivier, Ludovico. "*Molloy.*" In *Twentieth-Century Interpretations of Molloy, Malone Dies, The Unnamable*. Ed. J. D. O'Hara. Englewood Cliffs, NJ: Prentice Hall, 1955.

Jeanson, Francis. "Hell and Bastardy." *Yale French Studies* 30 (1964): 5–20.

Josipovici, Gabriel. "Introduction." *Molloy, Malone Dies, and The Unnamable* by Samuel Beckett. New York: Alfred A. Knopf, 1997.

Joyce, James, "Realism and Idealism in English Literature: Daniel De Foe—William Blake," *Buffalo Studies* I. (Tr. Joseph Prescott, December 1964).

Kant, Immanuel. "From *Critique of Judgment.*" In *Critical Theory Since Plato*. Ed. Hazard Adams. New York: Harcourt Brace Jovanovich, 1971.

Kaplan, Edward K. *The Parisian Prowler*. Athens: University of Georgia Press, 1997.

Kaufmann, Fritz. *Thomas Mann: The World as Will and Representation*. New York: Cooper Square Publishers, 1973.

Kavanaugh, Thomas M. "Unraveling Robinson: The Divided Self in *Robinson Crusoe.*" *Texas Studies in Literature and Language* 20 (1978): 416–432.

Kearn, Edith. "Introduction." *Sartre: A Collection of Essays*. Ed. Edith Kearn. Englewood, NJ: Prentice Hall, 1962.

Keefe, Terry. "The Ending of Sartre's *La Nausée.*" In *Critical Essays on Jean Paul Sartre*. Ed. Robert Wilcocks. Boston: G. K. Hall, 1988. 182–201.

Kellman, Steven G. *The Self-Begetting Novel*. New York: Columbia University Press, 1980.

Kenner, Hugh. *Samuel Beckett: A Critical Study*. New York: Grove Press, 1961.

———. "The Trilogy." In *Samuel Beckett's Molloy, Malone Dies, The Unnamable*. Ed. Harold Bloom. New York: Chelsea House Publishers, 1988.

Kierkegaard, Søren. *Either/Or*. Tr. Howard V. Hong and Edna H. Hong. Princeton: Princeton University Press, 1987.

———. *The Sickness Unto Death*. Tr. Howard V. Hong and Edna H. Hong. Princeton: Princeton University Press, 1980.

King, James. *Virginia Woolf*. New York: W. W. Norton, 1995.

Kruse, Margot. "Philosophie und Dichtung in Sartres *La Nausée.*" *Romanistisches Jahrbuch* IX (1958): 214–225.

Kurrik, Maire Jaanus. *Literature and Negation*. New York: Columbia University Press, 1979.

Landow, George P. *Images of Crisis: Literary Iconology 1750 to the Present*. Boston: Routledge & Kegan Paul, 1972.

Laurence, Patricia Ondek. *The Reading of Silence: Virginia Woolf in the English Tradition*. Stanford: Stanford University Press, 1991.

Lee, Hermione. *Virginia Woolf*. London: Chatto & Windus, 1996.

Lord, Ursula. *Solitude Versus Solidarity in the Novels of Joseph Conrad: Political and Epistemological Implications of Narrative Innovation.* Montreal: McGill-Queens University Press, 1997.

Magny, Claude-Edmonde. "The Duplicity of Being." In *Sartre: A Collection of Critical Essays.* Ed. Edith Kearn. Englewood, NJ: Prentice Hall, 1962.

Mann, Thomas. *Doctor Faustus: The Life of the German Composer Adrian Leverkühn as Told by a Friend.* Tr. John E. Woods. New York: Alfred A. Knopf, 1997.

———. *Joseph and His Brothers.* Tr. H. T. Lowe-Porter. New York: Alfred A. Knopf, 1963.

———. "Introduction." *The Living Thought of Schopenhauer.* London: Cassell and Company, 1939.

———. The Magic Mountain. Tr. John E. Woods. New York: Alfred A. Knopf, 1995.

Marpham, John. Virginia Woolf: A Literary Life. New York: St. Martin's Press, 1991.

Martens, Lorna. *The Diary Novel.* Cambridge: Cambridge University Press, 1985.

Massey, Irving. *The Uncreating Word: Romanticism and the Object.* Bloomington: Indiana University Press, 1970

McCarthy, Patrick. *Albert Camus: 'The Stranger'.* Cambridge: Cambridge University Press, 1988.

McFarland, Thomas. "Romantic Imagination, Nature, and the Pastoral Ideal." In *Coleridge's Imagination: Essays in Memory of Pete Laver.* Ed. Richard Gravil, Lucy Newlyn, and Nicholas Roe. Cambridge: Cambridge University Press, 1985.

McKeon, Michael. *The Origins of the English Novel, 1600–1740.* Baltimore: Johns Hopkins University Press, 1987.

Mijuskovic, Ben Lazare. "Loneliness: An Interdisciplinary Approach." In *The Anatomy of Loneliness.* Ed. Joseph Hartog, J. Ralph Audy, and Yehudi A. Cohen. New York: International Universities Press, 1980.

———. *Loneliness in Philosophy, Psychology and Literature.* The Netherlands: Van Gorum, Assen, 1979.

Miller, J. Hillis. "Mr. Carmichael and Lily Briscoe: The Rhythm of Creativity in *To the Lighthouse.*" In *Modernism Reconsidered.* Ed. Robert Kiely. Cambridge: Harvard University Press, 1983.

———. "The Problematic Ending in Narrative." *Nineteenth-Century Fiction* 33.1 (1978): 3–7.

Möde, Erwin. *Die Neue Einsamkeit der Postmoderne.* München: Edition Psychosymbolik, 1995.

Möhrmann, Renate. *Der Vereinsamte Mensch: Studien zum Wandel des Einsamkeitsmotivs im Roman von Raabe bis Musil.* Bonn: Bouvier Verlag Herbert Grunchmann, 1974.

Montaigne, Michel de. *Montaigne's Essays and Selected Writings.* Ed. and Tr. Donald M. Frame. New York: St. Martin's Press, 1963.

Moustakas, Clark E. *Loneliness.* Englewood Cliffs, NJ: Prentice Hall, 1961.

Murdoch, Iris. *Sartre: Romantic Rationalist.* New Haven: Yale University Press, 1953.

Navermore, James. *The World Without a Self: Virginia Woolf and the Novel.* New Haven: Yale University Press, 1973.

Nietzsche, Friedrich. *The Complete Works of Friedrich Nietzsche*. Ed. Oscar Levy. New York: Russell & Russell, 1964.

Noble, C. A. M. *Krankheit, Verbrechen, und künstlerisches Schaffen bei Thomas Mann*. Bern: Verlag Herbert Lang, 1970.

Novak, Maximillian E. *Defoe and the Nature of Man*. Oxford: Oxford University Press, 1963.

————. *Realism, Myth, and History in Defoe's Fiction*. Lincoln: University of Nebraska Press, 1983.

O'Loughlin, Michael. *The Garlands of Repose: The Literary Celebration of Civic and Retired Leisure: The Traditions of Homer and Vergil, Horace and Montaigne*. Chicago: University of Chicago Press, 1977.

Pascal, Blaise. *Pensées*. London: J. M. Dent & Sons, 1932.

Paz, Octavio. *The Labyrinth of Solitude*. Tr. Lysander Kemp, Yaro Milos, and Rachel Phillips Belash. New York: Grove Press, 1985.

Petrarch, Francis. *The Life of Solitude by Francis Petrarch*. Tr. Jacob Zeitlin. Urbana: University of Illinois Press, 1924.

Peyre, Henri. *French Novelists of Today*. New York: Oxford University Press, 1967.

Phelan, James, ed. *Reading Narrative: Form, Ethics, Ideology*. Columbus: Ohio State University Press, 1989.

Poggioli, Renato. *The Oaten Flute: Essays on Pastoral Poetry and the Pastoral Ideal*. Cambridge: Harvard University Press, 1978.

Pollmann, Leo. *Sartre and Camus: Literature of Existence*. Tr. Helen Sebba and Gregor Sebba. New York: Ungar, 1970.

Pultar, Gönül. *Technique and Tradition in Beckett's Trilogy of Novels*. New York: University Press of America, 1996.

Quasimodo, Salvatore. *The Poet and The Politician and Other Essays*. Tr. Thomas G. Begin and Sergio Pacific. Carbondale: Southern Illinois University Press, 1964.

Quilliot, Roger. *The Sea and Prisons: A Commentary on the Life and Thought of Albert Camus*. Tr. Emmett Parker. University: University of Alabama Press, 1970.

Rehm, Walter. *Der Dichter und die Neue Einsamkeit*. Göttingen: Vandenhoeck & Ruprecht, 1969.

Reid, Panthea. *Art and Affection: A Life of Virginia Woolf*. New York: Oxford University Press, 1996.

Renner, Charlotte. "The Self-Multiplying Narrators of *Molloy, Malone Dies,* and *The Unnamable*." In *Samuel Beckett's Molloy, Malone Dies, and The Unnamable*. Ed. Harold Bloom. New York: Chelsea House Publishers, 1988.

Ricks, Christopher. *Beckett's Last Words*. Oxford: Oxford University Press, 1993.

Rilke, Rainer Maria. *The Notebooks of Malte Laurids Brigge*. Tr. M. D. Herter Norton. New York: W. W. Norton, 1992.

Robbe-Grillet, Alain. *For a New Novel: Essays in Fiction*. Tr. Richard Howard. New York: Grove Press, 1965.

Roberts, Martin. *Michel Tournier: Bricolage and Cultural Mythology*. Stanford: Anma Libri, 1994.

Rogers, Pat. *Robinson Crusoe*. London: George Allen & Unwin, 1979.

Rorty, Richard. *Contingency, Irony, and Solidarity.* Cambridge: Cambridge University Press, 1989.

Rousseau, Jean-Jacques. *Reveries of the Solitary Walker.* Tr. Peter France. New York: Penguin, 1980.

Ruotolo, Lucio P. *The Interrupted Moment: A View of Virginia Woolf's Novels.* Stanford: Stanford University Press, 1986.

Sarocchi, Jean. *Camus.* Paris: Presses Universitaires de France, 1968.

Sartre, Jean Paul. "An Explication of *The Stranger.*" In *Camus: A Collection of Critical Essays.* Ed. Germaine Brée. Englewood Cliffs, NJ: Prentice Hall, 1962.

———. *Nausea.* Tr. Robert Baldick. Harmondsworth: Penguin Books, 1965.

Sayre, Robert. *Solitude in Society: A Sociological Study in French Literature.* Cambridge: Harvard University Press, 1978.

Schaefer, Josephine O'Brien. *The Three-Fold Nature of Reality in the Novels of Virginia Woolf.* The Hague: Mouton & Co., 1965.

Schopenhauer, Arthur. *Essays: From the Parega and Paralipomena.* Tr. T. Bailey Saunders. London: George Allen and Unwin Ltd., 1951.

———. *The World as Will and Representation.* Tr. E. F. J. Payne. New York: Dover Publications, 1966.

Seidel, Hans. *Das Erlebnis der Einsamkeit im Alten Testament.* Berlin: Evangelische Verlagsanstalt, 1969.

Seidel, Michael. *Exile and the Narrative Imagination.* New Haven: Yale University Press, 1986.

———. *Robinson Crusoe: Island Myths and the Novel.* Boston: Twayne Publishers, 1991.

Shenker, Israel. "An Interview with Beckett." In *Samuel Beckett: The Critical Heritage.* Ed. Lawrence Graver and Raymond Federman. London: Routledge & Kegan Paul, 1979.

Sitter, John. *Literary Loneliness in Mid-Eighteenth Century England.* Ithaca: Cornell University Press, 1982.

Slochower, Harry. *Thomas Mann's Joseph Story: An Interpretation.* New York: Alfred A. Knopf, 1938.

Smith, Janna Malamud. *Private Matters: In Defense of the Personal Life.* Reading, MA: Addison Wesley, 1997.

Solomon, Philip. *The Life After Birth: Imagery in Samuel Beckett's Trilogy.* University, MS: Romance Monographs, 1975.

Spindler, Amy M. "Tracing the Look of Alienation." *New York Times* (March 24, 1998): D28.

Sprintzen, David. *Camus: A Critical Examination.* Philadelphia: Temple University Press, 1988.

Stanton, Elizabeth Cady. "Solitude of Self." In *The Search for Self-Sovereignty: The Oratory of Elizabeth Cady Stanton.* Ed. Beth M. Waggenspack. New York: Greenwood Press, 1989.

Starr, G. A. *Defoe's Spiritual Autobiography.* Princeton: Princeton University Press, 1965.

Storr, Anthony. *Solitude: A Return to the Self.* New York: The Free Press, 1988.

85

Suther, Judith D., ed. *Essays on Camus's Exile and The Kingdom.* University, MS: Romance Monographs, 1981.

Sutherland, James. *Daniel Defoe: A Critical Study.* Cambridge: Harvard University Press, 1971.

Swados, Harvey. "Robinson Crusoe—the Man Alone." *Antioch Review* 18 (1958): 25–40.

Sypher, Wylie. *The Loss of Self in Modernist Literature and Art.* Westport, CT: Greenwood Press, 1979.

Thoreau, Henry David. *Walden, or Life in the Woods.* New York: Alfred A. Knopf, 1992.

Tillich, Paul. "Loneliness and Solitude." In *The Anatomy of Solitude.* Ed. Joseph Hartog, J. Ralph Audy, and Yehudi A. Cohen. New York: International Universities Press, 1980.

Tillyard, E. M. W. *The Epic Strain in the English Novel.* London: Chatto & Windus, 1967.

Todd, Olivier. *Albert Camus: A Life.* Tr. Benjamin Ivry. New York: Alfred A. Knopf, 1987.

Tournier, Michel. *Friday or the Other Island.* Tr. Norman Denny. London: Collins, 1967.

———. *The Wind Spirit: An Autobiography.* Tr. Arthur Goldhammer. Boston: Beacon Press, 1988.

Trezise, Thomas. *Into the Breach: Samuel Beckett and the Ends of Literature.* Princeton: Princeton University Press, 1990.

Viggiani, Carl A. "Camus's *L'Etranger.*" *PMLA* LXXI (1956): 865–887.

Walker, Brandy Brown. "Lily's Last Stroke: Painting in Progress in Virginia Woolf's *To the Lighthouse.*" In *Virginia Woolf and the Arts: Selected Papers from the Sixth Annual Conference on Virginia Woolf.* Ed. Diane F. Gillespie and Leslie K. Hankins. Pleasantville, NY: Pace University Press, 1997. 32–38.

Walker, Margaret. "The Nausea of Sartre." *Yale Review* 42.2 (1952): 251–261.

Warner, John M. *Joyce's Grandfathers: Myth and History in Defoe, Smollett, Sterne, and Joyce.* Athens: University of Georgia Press, 1993.

Watt, Ian. *Myths of Modern Individualism: Faust, Don Quixote, Don Juan, Robinson Crusoe.* Cambridge: Cambridge University Press, 1996.

———. *The Rise of the Novel: Studies in Defoe, Richardson and Fielding.* Berkeley: University of California Press, 1957.

Wiestand-Burston, Joanne. *Contemporary Solitude: The Joy and Pain of Being Alone.* York Beach, ME: Nicolas-Hayes, 1996.

Woolf, Leonard. *Downhill All the Way: An Autobiography of the Years 1919–1939.* New York: Harcourt Brace & World, 1967.

Woolf, Virginia. *The Common Reader.* Second Series. London: The Hogarth Press, 1948.

———. *The Diary of Virginia Woolf, 1931–35.* Vol. IV. Ed. Anne Olivier Bell. New York: Harcourt Brace Jovanovich, 1982.

———. *The Essays of Virginia Woolf, 1914–1928.* Vol. IV. Ed. Andrew McNeillie. London: The Hogarth Press, 1986.

————. *The Letters of Virginia Woolf, 1923–28.* Vol. III. Ed. Nigel Nicholson and Joanne Trautmann. New York: Harcourt Brace Jovanovich, 1977.

————. *To the Lighthouse.* New York: Harcourt, Brace & World, 1955.

Youan, Susan. *Retracing a Winter's Journey: Schubert's "Winterreise."* Ithaca: Cornell University Press, 1991.

Zimmerman, Everett. "Defoe and Crusoe." *English Literary Studies* 38 (1971): 377–96.

Zimmerman, John George. [Johann Georg Zimmermann] *Solitude, or the Effects of Occasional Retirement.* London, Glasgow, and Dublin: Thomas Tegg, R. Griffin and Co., and B. Cummings, 1827.

Index

Adams, R. M., 44, 78, 92
Adorno, Theodor W., 17
Ancrene Wisse, 26
Anna Karenina, 168
Aristotle, 23–24, 26
Arnold, Matthew, 45, 48
Atwood, Margaret, *Surfacing,* 168
Auden, W. H., 21, 171
The Enchafèd Flood, 16, 109, 127
Auerbach, Erich, *Mimesis,* 93

Bacon, Sir Francis, 23, 38
"Of Friendship," 23–25
Bacon, Francis (painter), 40, 164
Bakhtin, Mikhail, 13, 53
Balzac, Honoré de, 168
The Inventor's Suffering, 41
Barthes, Roland, 32, 131
"Bartleby the Scrivener," 134
Baudelaire, Charles, 39, 44, 45, 68,
        103, 114, 122, 125, 136, 149,
        172–74
"Crowds," 68
"The Double Room," 173
"Solitude," 45, 54
Beckett, Samuel, 9, 11, 16, 46, 98,
        135, 141–61, 163–64, 170, 172
and aporia, 142–43, 150, 167
as last modernist, 18, 145
as postmodernist, 18, 148–49, 164
Endgame, 17
The Lost Ones, 15, 19, 163–64, 170
Malone Dies, 76, 141–61
Molloy, 141–61

Trilogy, 1, 13, 15, 17–19, 43,
        141–61, 164, 167
The Unnamable, 15, 18, 46, 76,
        141–61
Waiting for Godot, 146
Bell, Clive, 90
Berdyaev, Nicholas, 16, 35, 37, 103,
        108, 111
Bersani, Leo, "Beckett and the End of
        Literature," 149
Blanchot, Maurice, 1, 93, 135, 139,
        148, 165
Blewett, Daniel, 55
Bloom, Harold, 144
Bosch, Hieronymous, 164
Brombert, Victor, 29, 122–23
Brown, Dennis, 147
Brown, Homer Obed, 58
Browne, Sir Thomas, 111
Bruseau, James, 165
Budgen, Frank, 59
Burke, Edmund, 36
Burton, Robert, 31, 44
Bush, Douglas, 28
Byron, Lord George Gordon Noel, 11,
        38, 148
Cain, 38
Childe Harold's Pilgrimage, 38, 148
Manfred, 38, 39

Camus, Albert, 9, 18, 40, 46, 117–19,
        125–39, 168, 172
Caligula, 137
Exile and the Kingdom, 132–32

The Fall, 13, 40, 44, 52–53, 119,
    132, 134
A Happy Death, 127–29, 131, 136
The Myth of Sisyphus, 125–26, 136,
    138, 163, 171
The Rebel, 136–38
The Stranger, 14, 15, 17, 18, 43, 45,
    118, 126–39, 149, 151, 154
The Wrong Side and the Right Side,
    129
    on *Nausea,* 118–20
Carnochan, W. B., *Confinement and
    Flight: An Essay on English
    Literature of the Eighteenth
    Century,* 30
Cassirer, Ernst, 35
Catherine the Great, 32
Cervantes, Miguel de, 92
Chateaubriand, 38
Chaucer, 26
Cheever, John, 171
Chekhov, Anton, 9, 37, 89
Chopin, Kate, 168
Christ, Carol, *Diving Deep and
    Surfacing,* 168
Clarissa, 168
Cohn, Dorrit, 80
Coleridge, Samuel Taylor, 52
    "Rime of the Ancient Mariner," 37
Conrad, Joseph, 8, 9, 16, 39, 46,
    144–46, 161
    Heart of Darkness, 8, 66, 144
    Lord Jim, 8
    Nostromo, 8, 148, 161
    Victory, 144–46
Constant, Benjamin, 38
Cowley, Abraham, 31
    "Of Solitude," 31
Cowper, William, 32
    "The Castaway," 94–95
    "Retirement," 32

Damrosch, Leopold, 58
    God's Plot and Man's Stories, 58
Dante, *Inferno,* 163

De la Mare, Walter, 53–54
Defoe, Daniel, 12, 14, 23, 24, 25, 39,
    93, 144, 157–58
    Robinson Crusoe, 1, 13, 14, 15, 17,
        24, 25, 30, 42, 48, 49–73, 78,
        92, 142, 157–61, 167, 170–71
        and Other, 64, 68, 73
        and solitude, 24, 50, 52, 53–64,
            68–70
    Serious Reflections of Robinson Crusoe,
        24, 55, 57, 68–70
Deleuze, Gilles, 73, 165
De Quincey, Thomas, 52, 77, 103, 104
    *The Confessions of an English Opium
        Eater,* 37
    Suspiria de Profundis, 37–38
Descartes, René, 117–18, 124, 154,
    159
diary, novel as, 13
Dickens, Charles, 52
Diderot, Denis, 35
Dillon, Janette, 26–28
Don Quixote, 52
Donne, John, 29, 157
Dostoyevsky, Fyodor, 11, 17, 37, 38,
    39, 41, 44, 47, 62, 122, 124,
    133, 138, 139, 147
    The Brothers Karamazov, 38, 103, 106
    Crime and Punishment, 171
    The Double, 42
    Notes from the Underground, 171
Dowrick, Stephanie, *Intimacy and
    Solitude,* 168
Dreiser, Theodore, 168
Du Plessis, Rachel Blau, *Writing Beyond
    the Ending,* 91

Eakins, Thomas, 40
Ecclesiastes, 23
Effi Briest, 168
*Elegiac Fictions: The Motif of the
    Unlived Life,* 2
Eliot, T. S., 46, 89, 103, 147–48
    "The Dry Salvages," 25–26
    The Waste Land, 116

Emerson, Ralph Waldo, 24–25
  "Society and Solitude," 24–25
Erasmus, 28
Existentialism, 119, 122–24, 126, 136,
  138–39

Faulkner, William, 168
France, Peter, 33
Frank, Joseph, "Spatial Form in
  Modern Literature," 80
Frankenstein, 36
Freud, Sigmund, 61, 103, 104, 106,
  164, 166, 172–73
Friedrich, Caspar David, 40
Fromm, Erich, 41, 43, 62
Fry, Roger, 90

Garber, Frederick, *The Autonomy of the
  Self from Richardson to
  Huysmans,* 11–12
Garcia Marquez, Gabriel, *One Hundred
  Years of Solitude,* 41
Gellner, Ernst, 40–41
Gide, André, 9, 27, 124, 147
Gilman, Charlotte Perkins, 168
Goethe, Johann Wolfgang von, 38, 39,
  99, 156
Gogol, Nikolai, 42, 122, 124, 154
Goldmann, Lucien, 124
Gongora, Luis de, *Soledades,* 29
Green, Martin, *The Robinson Crusoe
  Story,* 51

Halmos, Paul, 166
Halpern, Sue, *Migration to Solitude,*
  168
Hassan, Iban, 147
Hazlitt, William, 52
Hegel, Georg Friedrich Wilhelm, 44
Heidegger, Martin, 25, 166
Heilbrun, Carolyn, *The Last Gift of
  Time: Life Beyond Sixty,* 168
Hemingway, Ernest, "A Clean, Well-
  Lighted Place," 129
  A Farewell to Arms, 44–45

"Soldier's Home," 46
Hesse, Hermann, 9, 47, 103
Hobbes, Thomas, 16
Hoffmann, E. T. A., 11, 42, 68
Hölderlin, Friedrich, 144
Holdheim, Wolfgang, 124
Hopper, Edward, 40
Hume, David, 40
Hunter, J. Paul, 55
Husserl, Edmund, 142
Huysmans, Joris Karl, 12, 39

Invasion of the Body Snatchers, The, 121
Iser, Wolfgang, 153
island, 13, 30, 173
  in Beckett, 14, 142
  in Camus, 14
  modern island, 13–14
  in *Robinson Crusoe,* 13, 30, 51, 54–5,
    58, 60–3, 158–9
  in Sartre, 14
  as Self, 14
  in *To the Lighthouse,* 14, 17, 78–9

James, Henry, 92, 132, 168
Jane Eyre, 36
Johnson, Samuel, 31, 52
  The Adventurer, 31
  Dictionary, 31
  The Rambler, 31
Josipovici, Gabriel, 143, 144, 157
Joyce, James, 9, 16, 17, 27, 39, 44, 46,
  57, 76, 92, 147, 157
  "The Dead," 82
  Dubliners, 46
  Portrait of the Artist as a Young Man,
    47
  Ulysses, 47, 59, 60, 104
  on *Robinson Crusoe,* 59–60

Kafka, Franz, 9, 46, 119, 122, 144, 147
  The Metamorphosis, 132, 146
  The Trial, 37, 46, 135
Kant, Immanuel, *The Critique of
  Judgment,* 36

Katz, Alex, 170–71
Kaufmann, Fritz, 99
Kavanaugh, Thomas M., 64–65
Kearn, Edith, 126
Keats, John, 37, 110, 139
  "The Living Hand," 125
Kenner, Hugh, 155, 157, 160
Kermode, Frank, 88
Kierkegaard, Søren, 2, 41, 124, 128,
    138, 143, 166
  Concept of Dread, 119
  Either/Or, 23
  The Sickness Unto Death, 2
Kleist, Heinrich von, 42

La Bruyère, 139
Laurence, Patricia Ondek, 76–77
Lawrence, D. H., 27, 44, 46
Leopardi, Giacomo, *La Vita Solitaria,*
    37
Lermontov, Mikhail, 38
Liaisons Dangereuses, Les, 168

Macaulay, Thomas, 52
Madame Bovary, 168
Mallarmé, Stéphane, 128
Malraux, André, 122
Mann, Thomas, 9, 13, 27, 35, 37, 39,
    44, 46, 97–116, 171
  The Black Swan, 97
  Death in Venice, 97, 98, 115
  Doctor Faustus, 44, 46, 97, 98,
    114–16
  Joseph and His Brothers, 97
  The Magic Mountain, 13–15, 17–18,
    35, 46, 97–116, 147, 167, 170,
    172
    and illness, 18, 98, 101–03,
    106–08
    and love, 115–16
    and time, 103–05, 111–13
Marlowe, Christopher, 99
Marvell, Andrew, "The Garden," 28
Massey, Irving, 130–31
McKeon, Michael, 55–56

Mepham, John, 93
Merton, Thomas, *No Man Is an Island,*
    7
  A Search for Solitude, 168
Miller, J. Hillis, 88, 94
Milton, John, 16, 48
Möde, Erwin, *The New Solitude of
    Postmodernity,* 164
Modernism, 8–9, 11, 16, 40, 103
  see also solitude and Modernism
Montaigne, Michel de, 11, 12, 22, 28,
    33, 68, 165, 173
  "On Solitude," 28
More, Thomas, 27
Müller, Wilhelm, 37
Murdoch, Iris, 120
Nietzsche, Friedrich, 10, 11, 22–3, 25,
    26, 41, 43, 62, 100, 102, 106,
    112, 113, 128, 138, 143, 150,
    165, 166,167
  Beyond Good and Evil, 112
  Thus Spake Zarathustra, 26, 41–42,
    100, 114, 124, 167
Novak, Maximillian, 57–58

Other, 12, 15, 16, 48, 85, 139, 166,
    171

Pascal, Blaise, 29, 173
Paz, Octavio, 16, 23, 25, 43, 111
  The Labyrinth of Solitude, 25
Petrarch, 7, 11, 12, 22, 27, 165, 173
  De Vita Solitaria, 27
Peyre, Henri, 122
Phenomenology, 119–20
Pilgrim's Progress, 52, 161
Pirandello, Luigi, 43
Plato, 26
Poe, Edgar Allen, 11, 38–39, 42, 43,
    52, 68, 124
  "The Fall of the House of Usher," 44
  "The Man of the Crowd," 139
  "The Oval Portrait," 94
Poggioli, Renato, 29
Pollmann, Leo, 126, 134

Pope, Alexander, 30, 52
  "On Solitude," 30
Postmodernism, 18–19, 40, 141–42,
  145, 148–49, 164
Poulet, Georges, 124
Proust, Marcel, 27, 39, 46, 76, 148
Pushkin, Alexander, 38

Quasimodo, Salvatore, 27

Rabinowitz, Peter J., "End Sinister:
  Neat Closure as Disruptive
  Force," 92
Renner, Charlotte, 142–43
Ricks, Christopher, 150
Rilke, Rainer Maria, 9, 45, 47
  Notebooks of Malte Laurids Brigge, 45,
  47
Rimbaud, Arthur, 44, 149
  Season in Hell, 44
Rise of the Novel, The, 51, 57
  see also Watt, Ian
Robbe-Grillet, Alain, 148, 149
Rogers, Pat, 56
Romanticism, 8, 11, 34–41, 44
  see also individual poets
Rorty, Richard, 167
Rousseau, Jean-Jacques, 33–34, 35, 40,
  52, 64, 165
  as inventor of modern solitude, 33
  Reveries of the Solitary Walker, 33–4
Ruotolo, Lucio, 77, 91–92, 94

Sackville-West, Vita, 79
Saint-Amant, Marc Antoine de Gérard,
  33
  Le Contempleur, 29
  La Solitude, 29
Samuel Beckett: The Last Modernist, 18
*Samuel Beckett and the End of
  Modernity,* 18
Sarton, May, *Journal of a Solitude,* 168
Sartre, Jean Paul, 9, 114, 15, 16, 18,
  33, 40, 43, 117–26, 137–39,
  151, 170, 172

Being and Nothingness, 119–20, 123,
  138
Nausea, 14, 15, 17, 18, 40, 43,
  118–26, 138–39, 146, 147, 151,
  154
No Exit, 46
Sayre, Robert, 13, 33
  *Solitude in Society: A Sociological Study
  in French Literature,* 13
Schiller, Friedrich von, 98
Schopenhauer, Arthur, 34, 43, 100
  Parega and Paralipomena, 34
  "Psychological Observations," 32
  The World as Will and Representation,
  35
Schubert, Franz, 37, 113
Seidel, Michael, 50, 54, 57, 60
  Robinson Crusoe: *Island Myths and
  the Novel,* 51
Self, 42–44
  as island, 14
  see also solitude and self
Selkirk, Alexander, 32, 61
Shakespeare, William, 28–29, 92
  The Tempest, 29
Shelley, Percy Bysshe, *Alastor, or the
  Spirit of Solitude,* 36
Shenker, Israel, 149
Sillitoe, Alan, 9
Singer, Isaac Bashevis, 44
Slater, Philip, *The Pursuit of Loneliness:
  American Culture at the Breaking
  Point,* 170
Smith, Joanne Malamud, *Private
  Matters: In Defense of the
  Personal Life,* 168, 169
society, 29–30, 34–35, 37
  See also solitude and society
solitude, definition of, 7, 10, 31
  and alienation, 8–9, 16–17, 22, 30,
  39–40, 44, 165
  and ambiguity, 1–2, 16, 21–22,
  169–70
  in Anglo-Saxon literature, 26
  and Christianity, 23, 26–27

in Eastern philosophy, 23
in the eighteenth century, 29–34
and the Elizabethans, 27–8
and engagement, 29, 171
and Freud, 10, 25
and Modernism, 8–9, 11, 16, 22,
    39–48, 73, 139, 166, 173
as moral aloneness, 41, 43–44
in the nineteenth century, 11, 23,
    34–39, 42, 44, 139, 165–66
and the novel, 1, 12
in the Old Testament, 23
and the pastoral, 29
as pathology, 2–3, 32, 166, 170–72
in the Renaissance, 27–8
and the Romantics, 8, 11, 34–41, 44
and Self, 2, 12, 22, 34–35, 166–67,
    171–72
in the seventeenth century, 26–7
and sexuality, 13–15
in the sixteenth century, 26–7
and Society, 22–25, 31, 32, 33, 41,
    167
and women, 168–69
and youth, 12
versus autonomy, 12
Solitude versus Solidarity in the Novels of
    Joseph Conrad: Political and
    Epistemological Implications of
    Narrative Innovation, 8
Solomon, Philip, 143
Sorel, Georges, 128
Spengler, Oswald, 128
Stanton, Elizabeth Cady, 168
Starr, G. A., *Defoe's Spiritual*
    Autobiography, 55
Stendhal, 29, 92, 168
Stephen, Leslie, 52
Stevens, Wallace, "The Snow Man,"
    110
Stevenson, Robert Louis, 42
Storr, Anthony, *Solitude: A Return to the*
    Self, 10–11, 168, 169, 170
Sutherland, James, 51
Swados, Harvey, 58

Swift, Jonathan, 22, 30
    Gulliver's Travels, 51
Symons, Arthur, 128
Sypher, Wylie, 147

Taylor, Charles, 112–13
Tennyson, Alfred Lord, "The Charge of
    the Light Brigade," 95
Thody, Philip, 129
Thoreau, Henry David, 22–25, 33, 53
    and solitude, 24
    Walden, or Life in the Woods, 24
Tieck, Ludwig, *Der Blonde Eckbert,* 36
Tillich, Paul, 47
Tillyard, E. M. W., 56
'Tis Pity She's a Whore, 77
Thomson, James, "Hymn on Solitude,"
    31
Todd, Olivier, 118
Tournier, Michel, "La Fin de
    Robinson," 73
    Friday, or the Other Island, 70–73
Toynbee, Arnold, 16, 25
Traherne, Thomas, "Solitude," 29
Tristram Shandy, 30
Turgenev, Ivan, 38

Voltaire, 32–33

Warner, John, 59
Watt, Ian, 51, 54, 56, 57
Wharton, Edith, 168
Wieland-Burston, Joanne, *Contemporary*
    Solitude: The Joy and Pain of
    Being Alone, 168, 169
Wild Duck, The, 130, 132
Wilde, Oscar, 39, 42
Wilson, Colin, *The Outsider,* 9
Wittgenstein, Ludwig, *Tractatus Logico-*
    Philosophicus, 40
Woolf, Leonard, 79
    Downhill All the Way, 79
Woolf, Virginia, 9, 11, 13, 15, 17, 44,
    54, 75–95, 159, 170, 171
    "Modern Fiction," 89

"Mr. Bennett and Mrs. Brown," 50
Mrs. Dalloway, 46, 80, 84, 92
on *Robinson Crusoe,* 49–50, 92–3
"The Russian Point of View," 89
To the Lighthouse, 11, 13, 14, 17, 15, 18, 43, 75–95, 166, 172
and Other, 85
and narrative endings, 75–6, 78–80, 88–94
and solitude, 76–77, 80–84, 88, 92–95
and space, 76, 79, 85–7, 94–5
The Voyage Out, 79
The Waves, 76

Wordsworth, William, 38, 52
The Excursion, 38
The Prelude, 38
"Tintern Abbey," 38
Wuthering Heights, 36

Yeats, William Butler, 14, 45, 48, 103, 113
"Sailing to Byzantium," 37
Where There Is Nothing, 14

Zimmermann, Johann Georg, 32, 112, 169
Solitude, 32, 112, 169